Pride Publishing books by KD Ellis

Out in Austin
Teddy's Truth
Shiloh's Secret
Trusting Tennyson

Out in Austin

TRUSTING TENNYSON

KD ELLIS

Trusting Tennyson
ISBN # 978-1-80250-970-0
©Copyright KD Ellis 2022
Cover Art by Erin Dameron-Hill ©Copyright August 2022
Interior text design by Claire Siemaszkiewicz
Pride Publishing

TRUSTING
TENNYSON

Dedication

To the readers who have reached out to me and
urged me to keep writing
and the loved ones who've always been there.
And a special thanks to Raquel Riley for her
enthusiasm.

Chapter One

Then

The boy on the screen was pretty. Blond, with copper-lined blue eyes — cornflower, not steel — and pouty lips made shiny from gloss, he looked like a doll. Men would pay thousands to fuck him and even more to fuck him *up*. It wasn't hard to see why Master was enamored.

Misha hated him. Misha hated everything the boy stood for on the other end of a computer screen, thousands of miles away. He probably lived in some nice suburb with a white picket fence, with parents who paid for braces without complaint, drove him to swim classes and sat down for family dinners consisting of more than just oatmeal and water.

Misha hated his amateur videos that taught boys how to apply makeup, his comparisons of drugstore makeup brands and his mock fashion shows as he strutted around in skirts and heels and lacy blouses.

If the boy weren't so pretty, if his videos hadn't gotten so popular, he could have stayed under the radar and Misha would still be Master's favorite.

The best whore.

The prettiest.

The most obedient.

The good boy.

Instead of sitting there, Master's breath damp on the back of his neck while Misha crept his fingers over the keyboard to lure in his replacement. The pretty boy must get thousands of messages a day. Maybe Misha's wouldn't register, buried beneath the rest. Maybe he'd get it but not reply, and Misha would be safe.

Master's attention, and his hands on Misha's body, might terrify him, but not as much as the idea of losing it.

* * * *

Asher Downs rattled his bedroom doorknob for the third time, just in case it had somehow come unlocked. Then, and *only* then, with his heart pounding in his chest, did he drag out the old Nike shoebox from under his bed, the one that used to hold his soccer cleats. Now, it hid his makeup case.

It was plastic and cheap, much like the makeup inside, odds and ends he'd bought discounted at the drugstore on the corner with change he'd picked up from the sidewalk and pilfered from the ashtray in the Buick, one lonely quarter at a time.

With reverence, he carried the case over to his desk-turned-vanity. The mirror was a cheap thing, bought on sale because it was cracked, the glass spiderwebbed from the top of the frame down one side. When his parents were home, he kept it tucked in the back of the closet, under a ratty baseball jersey he'd outgrown as a preteen.

His phone was already secured in his makeshift tripod — leaning against a book, the bottom half-inch tucked behind a two-pound dumbbell so it wouldn't slide forward. As soon as he laid out his makeup, he could start the video.

His lipstick was barely a nub of pink in the cracked tube, his eyeshadow more dust than pigment. Even his foundation wasn't *quite* right — a bit too dry and a little too light for his sun-kissed, boy-next-door skin, tanned from playing football each summer with the church youth group.

These broken beauties were his prized possessions, worth more to him than the collectible baseball cards in their little plastic sleeves on his bookshelf or the signed poster of Kobe that his dad had been so excited to hang up when Asher had started high school.

Before Asher had gotten caught kissing the captain of the basketball team under the bleachers.

Before the mandatory after-school meetings with Pastor Luke twice a week to 'examine his soul'.

Now, his little brother Ryder wasn't even allowed in the same room with him, his dad could barely look at him without scowling and his mother locked the cabinet doors in the bathroom as if she needed to hide her feminine products from his perverted eyes. She *should* have locked her makeup away instead, back when he'd been a boy and had first discovered the magic it held.

The way a bit of shadow could make his eyes piercing, soften his jaw or sharpen his cheekbones...

How a little color could make him look happy, even when inside he felt like dying.

He'd come a long way since the first time he'd decided to film himself doing this, a silent protest against his parents that he'd devised under the influence of Dad's bitter liquor, pilfered from the expensive stash he kept on top of the fridge. He hadn't expected the video to go viral.

Now, he filmed sober, but nerves still birthed butterflies in his stomach. The fear of getting caught, which had him rattling his doorknob again, mingled with the excitement of watching his view counter tick steadily upward. He had almost a hundred thousand subscribers now, enough to put a little money into the secret bank account he'd opened as soon as he'd turned eighteen.

He *could* use it for better makeup or a ring light, but he was saving it to escape, maybe move out West, somewhere he wouldn't have to hide anymore. He'd dipped into it once already for a better laptop after his old one had crapped out. He was going to need to upgrade his phone soon, too—an expense he couldn't avoid but was delaying as long as he was able. His subscribers were already starting to comment on the graininess of the videos, and those wouldn't take long to become complaints.

Mom promised he could stay with them until he graduated, but that was it, leaving him with just over a month to get a plan in place. College was out of the question. Unlike his younger brother Ryder, he wasn't a computer genius who already had a dozen scholarships to choose from, and unlike they would for Ryder, Mom and Dad would never cover his expenses.

If he wanted out, he was going to have to do it on his own, a thought that finally motivated him to draw in a breath, plaster on a smile and push the red circle to start filming.

"Everything sucks and we're all dying, but I'm going to look pretty doing it. Who's ready to play with the pretty paint and give themselves a plus ten to their charisma check?" Asher jumped in with his quirky and somewhat nerdy greeting, smothering his real-world concerns beneath the joy that he got from doing makeup.

It wouldn't last long — only until the video ended — but for now, for these handful of minutes, he was going to enjoy it.

* * * *

Asher closed the live stream with his highest view count to date, and even when the camera stopped rolling, the little red number on his notification tab kept growing. He itched to tap it, to start scrolling through the comments and likes and shares. Knowing many of them would be haters — homophobic assholes who couldn't live-and-let-live — didn't stop the curiosity.

He couldn't yet, though — not like this. While his parents, who were off at their Bible study at Mrs. Worther's house, should be gone until evening, he couldn't risk it. If Mom got one of her migraines, if Dad got into another argument with Mel Geist or if Karen forgot the cookies again, they could be home early, and he would be fucked.

He wiped his face half-raw with the cheap makeup remover wipes, until it was greasy and red but makeup free, before he risked, even in an empty house, crossing their hallway to the bathroom so he could wash it.

The house was still empty when he was finished, but he locked his bedroom door again, anyway. It was against the house rules, but he'd rather get grounded for that than the alternative. He dropped back into his chair and opened his laptop, pulling up the desktop version of his channel. Finally, he opened his notifications.

Half of them he could delete immediately. The slurs and insults, the propositions and dick picks, the crazy right-winged conservatives with their MAGA hats and conspiracy theories. He wasn't into politics to begin with, but if he *were*, he didn't think some guy from a reality show should be able to nuke anything that didn't come out of a microwave.

After his routine cleaning, he was still left with dozens of messages to sort through. It was probably his favorite part of making content, if he were honest with himself — even when the message was more of a critique on his blending technique, like this one. Maybe he'd take the advice *@gayboy93$* gave him and try it out in a later video, just to see. If it worked, he'd learned something, and if it didn't, he'd get a good laugh.

Just as he was about to log off, his computer pinged again.

@BoyInADress13 sent you a message.

Curious, Asher clicked the box.

@BoyInADress13: I know u probably get a bunch of messages, but I wanted to tell you that your videos literally saved my life.

Asher flushed at the thought that his videos would mean that much to anyone, especially a stranger. He clicked on the username to visit the user's profile, but it was pretty bare. All it said was that he was nineteen, and he was from Texas. The thumbnail image by the username was just a pair of shiny pink lips, clearly male but otherwise unidentifiable.

He went back to his messages, hovering his fingers over the keyboard for a long moment before he finally replied.

@ThemBoyFemBoy: I don't know what to say to that, except I'm glad they helped. R u okay?

@BoyInADress13: no but your videos help, so thank u. I wish I was as brave as u

@ThemBoyFemBoy: Not brave. Just dumb and drunk and got lucky. My parents don't know I'm doing this.

Asher knew he shouldn't admit that, knew that talking to strangers on the Internet was dumb. Every single 'stranger danger' lecture talked about it, about how the person on the other end of the computer screen was never a teenage girl but some old, creepy pervert trying to lure someone into his trap, but it wasn't like Asher was going to tell him where he lived or anything.

@BoyInADress13: Still brave. My dad would kill *me. He says it's wrong. But I just want to be pretty.*

Asher was going to reply, but before he could, another message pinged through.

@BoyInADress13: Sorry, TMI. U probably have better things to do than listen to me. Sorry… I'll go now.

@ThemBoyFemBoy: no, ur fine! I like talking to u. It's nice to talk to someone who gets it. My parents will be home soon, but we can talk until then, K?

@BoyInADress13: really?

@ThemBoyFemBoy: Yeah. what's ur name?

@BoyInADress13: Devon

They kept chatting about everything and nothing. Somehow, they went from discussing makeup to Asher trying to explain the new MMORPG video game he'd started playing a few weeks before—an open-world fantasy game called EverQuiet that he was becoming obsessed with. They even made plans to play together after school the next day, if Devon could convince his dad to buy it for him.

He said he thought his dad would go for it, since video games were things teenage boys were *supposed* to be obsessed with. Devon said they'd probably be ecstatic that he was taking an interest in it in the first place.

Asher hoped he was right. Playing online was fun, but it was better when there was someone to play with. Besides, if Devon's dad *did* get it for him, they could talk on the headset and he'd know for sure that the other guy *wasn't* a creepy pervert.

The front door slammed, and Asher jumped, glancing at the clock in surprise. He felt like he'd only been talking to Devon for a few minutes, but it was already almost nine at night. He hastily typed out a goodnight to his new friend and shut off his laptop, unlocking his door only seconds before his dad stomped up the stairs.

He flung himself on the mattress with his chemistry book just in time for the door to swing open. Dad loomed in the open space, a dark silhouette backlit by the hall lights.

"It's almost bedtime. Shouldn't you be getting ready?" Dad barked, his arms crossed.

Heart thumping at the close call, Asher waved his chemistry book in excuse as he answered. "I have a test tomorrow and lost track of time, I guess. How was Bible study?"

Dad harrumphed. "That idiot Mel wouldn't know how to interpret a verse if the Lord himself stood in front of him with a dictionary. Poor man."

"It's a good thing you and Mom are there to guide him, then." Asher tried to sound earnest instead of sarcastic, and he must have succeeded because Dad just nodded, thumping his fist lightly on the doorframe.

"That's true. Well, get to bed, son." He left, and Asher tried not to flinch. Dad rarely called him 'son' anymore. Rarely called him anything, to be honest. It was like, in moments like these, he could forget for a minute that Asher was a sinner. Tomorrow he would be back to ignoring him, unable to look Asher in the eye.

Asher tossed his chemistry book toward his backpack then rolled out of bed to shut his door again and flip off the light. He stripped down to his briefs and crawled under his comforter. It was only spring in Delaware, still chilly out, but Mom already had the air cranked up high enough to freeze his balls off. He used to argue that her hot flashes shouldn't leave him with frostbite, and she used to laugh. Since getting outed, though, he didn't dare.

Instead, he curled into a ball under the thick comforter and closed his eyes, his thoughts drifting back to his conversation with Devon.

Chapter Two

Now

Liam Tennyson didn't miss his fancy Manhattan apartment. He only lived in it for a few weeks out of each year, and he could barely map the floor plan out in his mind, let alone picture the art on the walls. They were little more than blank, hundred-thousand-dollar canvases to his memory.

And while it would be nice to have his Ferrari to cruise around town in on his off nights, his Ducati Diavel with its twin-spark engine was keeping his inner daredevil satisfied. He had signed a dozen waivers back at the Bureau to authorize the use of his personal vehicle. Only the argument that it suited his image — muscle from out of town with too much money and not enough sense — had finally swayed his superiors.

He *did* miss the bespoke suits that his tailor delivered personally every six months like clockwork, and he regretted leaving behind his Armani briefs most of all.

According to the fake backstory the Bureau had cooked up, his name was Andrew Tennet—close enough to his real name for the nickname 'Ten' to make sense. They'd laid a trail of red flags going back twenty years—a dishonorable discharge from the Army at twenty-two, followed by a spotty job history, covering anything from security to chauffeuring to bouncing bars, with rumors of bribery and some misdemeanor possession charges thrown in just for fun. And, topping it all off, a suspiciously full bank account with no tangible explanation. If that didn't scream that he had his fingers in something illegal, he didn't know what would.

He even had a half-dozen gangbangers in Los Angeles who could identify Andrew Tennet by photo if the *La Familia* cartel *really* wanted to dig around, since his cover was one that they'd carried over from an undercover op he'd done half a decade earlier.

It was, quite possibly, one of the *best* covers he'd ever been given.

Which was why he found himself missing, not his apartment or his art or his car, but an explanation as to how this whole op was quickly falling to shit before his very eyes.

The *La Familia* cartel wasn't particularly well run, nor to the FBI's knowledge had it established especially strong ties in Austin. They knew the names and addresses of half-a-dozen or more mid-level operatives and the identities of at least three cops on the cartel's payroll.

So, there was no reason they were always two steps behind and falling further.

And yet here he was, sitting on an overly springy mattress in a pay-by-the-hour hotel, waiting to hear from literally anyone in the cartel about what the fuck was going on. After months of working his way into Julian DeAza's inner circle as a bodyguard, the ringleader was dead.

Shot by one of his own men in a warehouse downtown while Tennyson was off threatening a heroin dealer with sticky fingers.

And except for a single text message from an unknown number telling him to *"Sit tight,"* he hadn't heard shit—not until this morning, anyway—and that had been just a time and an address.

Tennyson figured this was going to go one of two ways. Either he was going to meet the new man in charge or his cover was blown and he was walking into a trap.

As annoying as *that* would be, at least then they could finally make some arrests and he could move on to the next assignment—after, of course, a Bureau-mandated mental health evaluation and a brief vacation to his apartment. Several months on the job meant he'd had only clandestine blow jobs in club bathrooms and a single overnight with a hooker to take care of his needs. A few weeks back in his apartment with a twink or two would slough the tension right off his shoulders.

Liam let his fantasy play out in his head as he left the motel and straddled his bike to head to the provided address. It was a short drive that traffic made longer. His fantasy twink was in the middle of an expert imaginary blow job when he parked the bike outside what turned out to be a café and turned off the ignition, shoving the keys into his pocket.

"You in place?" Ian Romero's voice in his Bluetooth earpiece dragged his mind out of the gutter. His handler was one step up from a probie compared to Tennyson but had an impressive track record behind him.

"About to head in. Doesn't look like anyone is here yet," Tennyson replied quietly, scanning the few people he could see through the café's windows. A mother with a small child in a car seat, a college student tapping away on a laptop and a homeless man sleeping in the corner. Not exactly a bustling crowd.

"I'll stay on standby, but try to give me a heads-up before moving to a second location." Romero sounded stressed, not that Tennyson blamed him. The man had only been in the FBI for a handful years, and this was his first time on the other side of the wire without a trainer. He'd been an excellent field agent from all reports, but Ian Romero's desire to bring down the *La Familia* cartel had been too strong. Since they couldn't put him undercover in his hometown, he'd been transitioned to being a handler instead.

"You got it, Probie." Tennyson hung up before Romero could reply, trusting the listening device in his pocket to do its job. The pen was unobtrusive. It wrote in plain black ink if it needed to and could be shut off with a simple click if someone tried to scan him for bugs.

He left his bike on the curb and headed inside the coffee shop, ordering an Americano with an extra shot. He took it with him to a small, two-person table near the window to wait. Then, he started scrolling through his phone, angling it just enough that it *looked* like he was watching the screen, while he was actually monitoring the sidewalk outside instead.

Eighteen minutes later, his gaze landed on a white man in a business suit—a Brioni, unless he was mistaken, which he rarely was. *Too upscale for this neighborhood.* Even the man's bodyguard—or so Liam assumed, based on the shoulder holster and earwig— wore Hugo Boss.

Tennyson fixed the first man's image in his mind. He was in his upper forties—or a well-preserved fifty— with hair grayer than black and sharp brown eyes. He wasn't conventionally handsome, but the tailored suit and expensive haircut gave the illusion of attractiveness, as money was wont to do.

"Incoming," Tennyson muttered before the bodyguard, a white man with a crew cut and a scattering of freckles, could open the door for his boss. Then, he went back to staring at his phone.

The older man sat smoothly in the chair across from Liam, leaving his bodyguard to take a seat at the next table over, facing the door. Tennyson tucked his phone away and took a casual sip of his drink. "Afternoon, sir."

"Please, call me Henry." One of the baristas hustled over with a cup of black coffee and set it in front of the older man, along with a napkin, a bright smile on her face. Tennyson filed the information away that Henry had been here before, often enough that the barista knew his order without asking.

"Henry, then." Tennyson tipped his head, acknowledging the request. "I was starting to wonder if I was going to have to look for other work."

"We've been cleaning house. Changing management, you know how it goes. I hear you went through a similar situation back in LA." Henry's voice was calm, but it was clearly a pointed notice that he'd done his research.

"Different circumstances, but yes," Tennyson acknowledged, lifting his cup in agreement.

"Not like a few weeks of vacation will strain a wallet like yours, am I right?" Henry said, smirking as he gestured out of the window to the Diavel on the curb. "I was a bit surprised to hear a man with your means wanted in as muscle. I'm used to men like you being more interested in the 'demand' side of things."

A smirk and a casual shrug by Tennyson had Henry laughing. Tennyson clarified, "I'm a bit of a daredevil. Gotta get my kicks somewhere. Besides, the quickest way to lose money is to start dipping your fingers into the products, yeah?"

"Or your dick," Henry added with a leer, and Liam leaned in at the first bit of concrete evidence proving that the cartel was involved with human trafficking. Everyone *suspected*, but the two sides of the business — drugs and people — had been kept firmly separate under DeAza.

"Now *that* I have a bit of a weakness for," Tennyson sighed, forcing his shoulders to relax. He shook his head, feigning disappointment in himself.

Henry looked pleased with the reply. "Tell you what... I have a few openings on my staff to fill, and I'd prefer to hire someone with...fewer ties to previous management. Come work for me and I'll make sure we throw in some perks along the way."

Chapter Three

Then

Misha's hands shook as he picked up the gray and green controller with the complicated buttons and little joysticks he didn't know how to use. He'd had to reimburse Master for the controller — and the game and the Xbox — with his mouth, even though it was Master who wanted him to get to know Asher, the boy from the videos — not that Master would care if Misha claimed it was unfair.

Now that he had all the equipment, though, he didn't know what to do with it. He barely remembered the last time he had been able to watch TV, let alone anything so radical as play a video game, not when Master thought he'd use it to call for help. Who would he even call? The only family he had was the man who'd gotten him into this situation in the first place. What was he going to do, call his Uncle Urvan and beg him to take him back? He had nothing to offer—

nothing except his body, which hadn't been his since he'd been a child.

Master lost patience with his stupidity quickly, ripping the controller from his hands with a curse. Misha watched as he moved his thumbs over the buttons to get the console set up to the large television, then downloaded the strange game that the boy — Asher — had said he liked to play. Master even set up his login before he chucked the controller at Misha. It struck his chest hard enough to bruise and landed in his lap, but he knew better than to flinch.

"Thank you, Master," he said instead, offering a small smile he thought Master would like.

Master just threw a headset with a mic at him. "Get set up." He grabbed Misha's blond hair and yanked, tilting his face harshly up until their eyes met. Master's were dark and cold, narrowed in threat. "And don't forget. My men are listening to every word out of your cock-sucking little mouth. Go off script and I'll slit your throat. Give myself a new hole to fuck. Got it?"

"Yes, Master," Misha gasped, crying out in pain as Master gave his hair another harsh tug. "I'll be good. I promise." He was stuck, and he arched his back severely to lessen the painful pressure on his neck, until Master grunted and released him.

"You can play with your new friend until dinner. I expect to hear you've made progress." Master spun on his heel, his shiny black shoes squeaking on the wood floor, and left.

Misha gripped the controller tight, his hands shaking as he plugged the auxiliary cord of his headset into the little headphone jack. He pulled the heavy headphones over his ears and almost immediately got nauseous, fear swelling at the way it muffled the room around him.

He wouldn't be able to hear Master if he walked up behind him right now to shove him forward or tighten a hand around his throat or…or anything he wanted to do while Misha was distracted.

It left him feeling weak and vulnerable, more so than he always did.

A loud *ping* filled his ears before he could dwell on the discomfort as he received a friend request from *ThemBoyFemBoy*, which he quickly fumbled to accept. A few seconds later, a box popped up on the screen, asking to voice chat, which he accepted as well.

The voice that filled his ears was familiar from the videos, yet at the same time different. Asher sounded less scripted, more real.

"Devon?"

"Hey," Misha replied to the name Master had given him to use, his own voice shaking with nerves. Except for Master, his friends and the few guards that patrolled Master's compound, he hadn't talked to anyone since his uncle had sold him. "Um. I'm really excited to play with you, but I don't know what I'm doing."

"No worries. I can talk you through it. The game's pretty simple, not so much a fighting game as an exploring one. Have you used an Xbox before — or are you more of a PlayStation guy?"

"Neither," Misha replied with an awkward laugh. "I think board games are more up my alley?" Not that he'd played any of those lately, either, but he used to love Candyland.

"A gaming virgin, then." Asher sounded darkly amused, and Misha could imagine him rubbing his hands together. He didn't have the heart to say he hadn't been a virgin, in any sense of the word, in years. "Don't worry. I'll be gentle with you. Okay, so you see the joysticks? The left moves the camera, the right moves your character. See?" Slowly, with Asher's help, Misha got the hang of the controls, and within a half hour, their two characters were strolling side by side through a glade, searching for some treasure called the 'Chest of Knowing'.

He didn't understand the point of the game, but playing was secondary to talking to Asher anyway. The only reason Master had got him the Xbox was to get closer to the boy, and he needed to remember that.

Needed to remind himself not to get attached.

They weren't friends — *couldn't* be friends. Best-case scenario for Misha, Asher bought the lies he told him — that his parents were divorced and his dad was a dick and all he wanted to do was go to college to be a fashion designer but his dad wanted him to be a lawyer like him — all things Master had coached him to say to be more relatable and to engender sympathy in a boy like Asher.

Best-case scenario for Asher, though, he saw through the lies to the truth. Better if he found Misha boring or stupid, not worth wasting his time on. Better if he logged off and never logged back on.

Misha would be punished for not holding his attention, for not reeling him in like a fish on a line, but Asher would be safe to follow his dreams. Misha would remain here until he got too old or too ugly to keep Master's attention, then he would be cast aside, sold to one of the cartel's brothels until he was used up.

It was just a matter of time.

* * * *

Asher stood on the sidewalk, clutching his diploma and a backpack in his shaking hand. His life stretched before him like bare skin ready to be painted, to go from plain to airbrushed perfection. He had just enough money in the bank for a bus ticket to anywhere and a month's rent, just enough clothing to last for a week until laundry and just enough hope to ignore the pain of leaving the relative safety of his parents' house.

And just enough phone battery to last him until he got where he was going. It was reckless to leave like this, on a whim, to meet a boy he only knew from the Internet, but he felt like he knew Devon better than himself. Not a single day had passed in the last month without them talking, either online, on the Xbox or, more recently, on the phone.

Devon's voice was always soft and slightly anxious, an endearing murmur that made Asher want to just squeeze him tight. They'd even Skyped once, for a few minutes, and he'd been surprised by how cute the other boy was. His hair was even lighter than Asher's, though less curly, his skin so pale it looked like polished ivory.

Asher didn't really have a type. He was equally attracted to both burly men with strong shoulders and to slender waifs like himself. Devon was even smaller than he was.

He'd taken quite a lot of pleasure in telling the other boy how cute he was, watching his skin turn from cream to blushed pink to scarlet. They hadn't been able to talk long. Devon's dad, a big man with silver-streaked hair and a scowl, had invaded the screen to say it was time to do his chores, but Asher still cherished the memory.

It was proof that Devon was *real*, not some creepy old man planning to lock him in his basement.

Asher took one last look at the house he grew up in, with its blue siding, black shutters and white picket fence, then left it behind him. He'd left a short note for his little brother to say goodbye, but he didn't say where he was going. He probably wouldn't get it anyway, if Mom or Dad found it first. They hadn't let him talk to Ryder in forever, afraid he was going to corrupt him or, worse, that being gay made him some sort of sick pervert.

He'd get settled in Texas then email him. Maybe they could talk on social media sometime, keep in touch.

It was going take him almost two days and three line transfers to get where he was going, but Devon had promised he'd be there to meet him.

He boarded the Greyhound from Wilmington to Richmond, sending a quick text to Devon before he shoved his phone into his pocket so he could store his backpack in the overhead compartment.

It closed with an audible click. Asher dropped down into the off-gray seat by the window, trying to ignore the mystery stain just off-center. It was no larger or less suspicious than the one on the aisle seat, and he'd worn his oldest jeans, the ones just a bit too baggy in the ass, for a reason.

The bus quickly filled up. He'd shown up early to get a good seat, one not too close to the bathrooms but not too far away, either, by the window if he could manage it. By the time the bus rumbled into motion, a young woman was sitting nervously beside him, clutching a handbag on her lap like it was a grenade.

"First time?" Asher asked. He'd intended on keeping himself *to* himself for the trip, staying quiet and playing on his phone maybe, but she looked terrified, her eyes skipping from one passenger to the next, like any one of them was going to shank her while her back was turned.

She flinched before eying him up and down. She relaxed a bit, probably because his glitter-crusted pink shirt with a unicorn on the front was about as threatening as a bag of cotton candy. "That obvious?"

Asher shrugged. "Just a guess. It's my first time, too."

"I shouldn't be nervous. I'm only riding to Richmond. It will barely even be dark when I get there, and my boyfriend's going to pick me up. God, I'm so dumb." She loosened her grip on the handbag for the first time since sitting down.

"It's not dumb to be scared of something new," Asher said. "I'm fucki— Sorry. I'm terrified right now. I'm going to see my...my boyfriend, too. Um, in Austin."

"I've never been, but I've heard it's a really um...accepting city." The woman's smile was shaky.

Asher's phone buzzed in his pocket, cutting off the somewhat nice but a little awkward conversation. He dragged it out and grinned at the message from Devon waiting for him on the screen.

Can't wait to see you

Thank goodness the Greyhound had charging ports, because his battery was flashing red. He pulled his charger out of his other pocket and plugged it into the wall. Then, he leaned back in his seat to text his boyfriend. They had a lot of plans to make and a lot of dreams to wish for.

* * * *

At nineteen minutes after nine in the evening, the bus grumbled to a stop outside the Greyhound terminal in Richmond. Asher had a three-hour layover before he could get back on, so he wasn't in a huge hurry to disembark. He let most of the other passengers make their way off before he grabbed his backpack from the overhead compartment and swung it over his shoulder.

Stepping out onto the sidewalk had Asher gripping the straps of his backpack a little tighter. The sky was that hazy not-quite-black, not-quite-purple that all cities seemed to have, light pollution from the streetlamps dimming the stars. In the almost-dark, the lights from the stadium across the boulevard were blinding. Rather than comfort him, though, it only made the trash on the curb more noticeable.

A man in a threadbare black coat lay across a bench by the nearest trash can. A lady in a daringly short skirt was leaning against the defunct, graffiti-covered newspaper dispenser.

She looked him over with a leer. "Hey, cutie, feeling lonely?"

"Um..." Asher's face felt like it was on fire as he stumbled over his words, "No, thanks. I um...have to..." He waved toward the pair of doors leading inside.

Her leer softened slightly. "You be careful in there, honey."

"I will, definitely. Um...have a good night..." Asher hurried inside, nearly tripping over a wet floor sign in his rush, almost bumping into a lady with a bright pink suitcase to avoid it. He mumbled an apology before skirting toward the wall to get his bearings. Several rows of uncomfortable-looking chairs took up most of the left side of the floor, while a crowd control belt barrier weaved across the right half up to the ticket booth. Above, several screens flipped through arrival and departure times.

Reluctantly, he bypassed the vending machines to head to the men's room instead. His stomach grumbled in protest, but he couldn't afford to waste money on junk food. The little bit that he had he needed to get him through the rest of the trip. From what he'd read online, there was a restaurant here. Not a good one but it was cheap, and if he was going to buy something, he was buying it from there.

But first, he had to pee.

Of course, when he went into the bathroom, he immediately wanted to *nope* the fuck back out.

Not only did it *reek* of stale shit and marijuana, the first thing he saw on entry was the black-and-red graffiti spray painted over the once-white-tiled walls. It had clearly been tagged more than once because he couldn't read it, and he could almost smell the bitter ozone of fresh paint. The second thing he saw was the half-dozen used condoms littering the floor by the sinks.

If that wasn't enough to make his pee crawl back up into his body, the woman panting under the baritone of a grunting man from the stall had him backing back into the hallway and closing the door carefully.

Maybe after he got something to eat.

Or, *maybe*, there'd be a giant dumpster fire that needed putting out, and he could piss on that instead. It would probably be more sanitary.

Instead, he waited for ten minutes in line for fries, which were over-full but undercooked, then carried them back to find a seat by the arrivals board. When he glanced up fifteen minutes before he was slated to get back on the bus, however, he groaned. The estimated arrival time had switched from twelve forty-nine a.m. until almost three.

"Shit." Asher dropped his head back against the edge of the chair and sucked in a deep breath before standing to go track down the information desk.

* * * *

"I really don't know what to tell you, sir," the lady said for the fourth time since he'd come up to the desk, *again*. For some reason, he thought she sounded highly sarcastic when she called him 'sir'. "There was an accident on the freeway and the bus got delayed. I promise it will be here as soon as it can."

"That's what you said an hour ago, but it's almost five, and I'm exhausted. I can't exactly leave, though, if you won't tell me when the bus will be back," Asher tried to reason with her, even though it wasn't like he could leave anyway. There was no way he was dropping cash on a motel, but he *was* thinking of taking a nap on one of the benches, and he couldn't set his alarm without a time to set it for—not if he didn't want to be setting it for every ten minutes.

"I understand you're frustrated sir, but you'll need to take a seat like everyone else. I promise we'll have an announcement with any further updates." She pursed her lips into a tight smile until he rolled his eyes and walked—okay, stomped—back to his bench.

Which, of course, was now claimed by another passenger, his leg cocked up to take up the whole seat, a phone glued to his ear. Asher kept walking, past the only other empty bench with a suspect wet puddle, to drop down against the wall instead, using his backpack like a pillow. He was just going to close his eyes for a few minutes.

* * * *

"I thought you said there was going to be an announcement?" Asher huffed, barely restraining himself from slamming his hand onto the desk.

"There *was* an announcement, sir."

"What did you do, whisper into the intercom? The only announcement I heard was about finding someone's lost phone in the toilets." Which, to his disgust, he'd broken down and used over an hour before after his bladder had started screaming at him.

"I don't know what to tell you, sir. As you can see, all the *other* passengers made it to the bus on time." She waved pointedly around at the slightly less crowded depot. To be fair, she wasn't entirely inaccurate, but he *did* know at least one other person who had missed the transfer as well, since the man had huffed and muttered something about going back to his hotel to catch the next one.

Asher, unfortunately, didn't *have* a hotel.

"Can't you have it turn around? It's only been gone for *two* minutes." Maybe, if he pled hard enough, she'd take pity on him.

Instead, she shook her head. "That would put us behind schedule, and it would hardly be fair to all the other passengers who *did* make it on time."

"Behind schedule? You're five hours behind schedule already!" Asher couldn't help that his voice was creeping up an octave. He really couldn't.

"Please lower your voice, sir. You're scaring the other passengers."

Asher looked around, from the man chewing gum loudly at the ticket station, to the woman tapping on her cell phone, to the old man picking his nose on the bench. "Sure." He sucked in a breath, then let it out slowly. "Please, can you call the bus back?"

"The next bus to Dallas will be boarding *promptly* at eleven p.m."

* * * *

"You've got to be fucking kidding me," Asher screamed at the dingy bricks as he kicked them, still staring at the back of the masked man hightailing it away from him.

Hightailing it away from him with Asher's wallet, backpack and cell phone.

Pretty much everything he owned, except for the clothes on his back, the ticket stub in his pocket and the rolled up hundred-dollar bill he'd slipped into his sock back at home, on the advice of a travel advisor he'd followed, just for shits and giggles.

Because he wasn't going to get mugged... That happened to other people, in places like Detroit or New York or shit, not to him in fucking *Virginia* — except that he'd just fucking gotten mugged by a guy in a ski mask barely more than a block away from the bus depot, fifteen minutes from the time he was scheduled to board the bus to Dallas, of course, so he couldn't even stop to file a police report, unless he wanted to miss the bus and be stranded here...*again*.

He fucking hated Virginia.

At least it would be better in Austin.

Chapter Four

Now

Tennyson could tell when his probationary period working for Henry—last name Barnes, age fifty-two, VP of Lidman Oil and Gas and no criminal history to speak of—ended. Instead of waiting in the car, as he'd done for the past three weeks, Barnes waved him out to follow him inside.

"Ten, Knowles, you two with me. The rest of you wait by the car," Barnes snapped, heading up the sidewalk toward the seedy club his meeting was being held in. It wouldn't open for several more hours, not until after dark at the earliest, so the lot held only a handful of vehicles except theirs, and the normally bright neon sign was dull.

Despite being closed, the main entrance was unlocked, allowing Barnes to push his way through the door without issues. To Ten, it seemed reckless. What was the point of having bodyguards if you didn't have them scout the place first? But wealthy men were arrogant and criminals over-bold, and Ten wasn't a real bodyguard, anyway. It wasn't an issue he cared to push if it meant stirring up trouble.

The inside of the club was, paradoxically, overly bright for being closed. With all the overhead lights on, it was hard to miss the sticky, grimy floor or the condoms still littering the usually dark corners. Tennyson had only ever seen it at night, with the strobing lights and pounding bass to distract him.

Barnes moved easily through the main floor and into a hallway tucked behind the bar. Clearly, he'd been here often enough to know where he was going.

Ten stayed quiet in his shadow, prepared to be bored and learn nothing of interest. Barnes had invested heavily in half-a-dozen nightclubs, bars and retail businesses in this neighborhood, all above board, so he expected the meeting to be either long or boring or both.

It was neither.

Ten could barely hold himself back from dialing his superiors before the meeting was even over. It had lasted five minutes.

Five minutes — and he now had the date and location of what Barnes claimed would be the biggest slave auction of the year. Not only that, but Barnes had promised his unnamed conspirator that there'd be plenty of 'candy', 'jellies' and 'ice' to go around.

If they set the sting up right, they could round up several major drug runners at the same time they busted a human trafficking ring. Hopefully, if they grabbed enough mid-level operatives, someone — or multiple someones — would flip and they could take the whole thing down. Or at least the Austin branch.

In the end, it took him until nearly midnight to extricate himself from Barnes and back to his hotel room, and it was nearly dawn when he was finally able to collapse on his cheap mattress, exhausted but with a plan in place.

Fingers crossed, he'd be back in his Manhattan apartment in less than a month, a twink in his bed and at least a few weeks of freedom to look forward to.

Chapter Five

Then

"Make it pretty for him. We want him to feel welcomed, don't we?" Master, like always, spoke to Misha as if he were a child, with that high-pitched voice some people used for babies, going so far as to pet his hair.

"Yes, Master," Misha answered obediently.

Master left him with a bucket of pink paint, a paint roller and unspoken instructions not to mess it up.

As he dipped the roller into the tray, watching streams of liquid bubblegum trail off, he worried.

Worried about messing up the currently gray walls with their white trim, worried about spilling the gallon of paint on the cold hardwood floor, worried about whether Master would like it...

Worried more about what would happen if he did than if he didn't. He could take a punishment in stoic silence, but he didn't know how to be replaced—

shuffled aside for a newer model, abandoned like a broken toy.

Already, the boy—Ash, Misha forced himself to remember—was the first thing Master spoke of in the morning, while his penis was still buried in Misha's throat.

And already, Asher had privileges Misha had spent years earning, like a bed instead of a ratty blanket on the floor, clothing to cover his nudity, a mirror. Misha couldn't even remember what he looked like now. The only time he was allowed to see his reflection was when he caught it by accident in the corner of a windowpane or cast against Master's glasses before he removed them. The longest he'd seen his own face was in the small thumbnail in the corner of the screen when he'd Skyped with Asher.

It wasn't hard for him to realize he was jealous and only a little harder to acknowledge how silly that was. How could he be *jealous* of the innocent boy who he was helping lure into this...this...God, he didn't even know what to call it.

Торговля людьми, a small voice whispered in the back of his mind. He could pretend all he wanted, lie to himself that Master cared for him, but deep down he knew it was sex trafficking—that Master had been gifted him by his Uncle Urvan, a *vor* in the *mafiya*, in hopes of establishing ties between the bratva and the *La Familia* cartel.

Maybe it had worked, and maybe it hadn't. He'd never found out. He barely remembered the meeting, hadn't realized what was going on. Hadn't known when the gruff uncle he'd barely met had shoved Misha toward the stranger that it was going to be a watershed moment, flipping his life on its axis.

Ten years old and still reeling from the death of his parents, he'd barely spoken English, let alone Spanish, and the two men had conversed so quickly. He'd mistakenly thought he was going to the zoo when he'd been bustled into the backseat of a black sedan. He'd waved and yelled through the window, "*Poka, djadja!*"

And his uncle had turned, not even acknowledging him, and he'd had a moment...just a moment...of doubt.

Nine years later and the doubt had left, replaced with a certainty. There'd been cages when he'd arrived, but no zoo. The only animals in the compound were the guard dogs, pit bulls trained to bite and maul.

He'd felt their teeth only once, when he'd tried to run the first time Master had shared him with his friends. He still had the scar on his calf, several silvery crescents to remind him of his folly.

A drop of paint slid down the handle of the roller to stain his fingers, sticky on his skin. It distracted him from his memories, the way it gleamed against his sun-starved flesh. For a moment, it left him off kilter. It was pink instead of red, cold instead of blood-warm.

"Oh, Misha." Master's disappointed voice chilled the air from behind him and he froze, scanning the single wall he'd painted so far. It looked...

Messy. It looked messy, pink staining the formerly white trim and dotting the floor in splatters. His chest tightened, smothering the breath in his lungs.

"What am I going to do with you, *conejito?*" Misha hated being Master's little bunny, but he forced himself to stand strong, to hold the roller over the tray to contain the drips, to look loving instead of scared. "Let's hope your new brother finds your carelessness endearing."

"I tried my best, Master. I wanted you to be proud of me." Misha couldn't help the way his lip pouted out. He didn't know how much of the move came from himself and how much of it was him trying to please the older man, but out it popped. Master's gaze heated, his mouth parting in an expression Misha knew well.

Then Master shoved him back until he hit the wall, paint smearing on contact. It stuck to his spine and shoulder blades, along with the curve of his hip where it dug into the drywall.

Master's mouth hit his with the force of a hurricane, forcing Misha's lips open and his head back. His tongue was fat and slimy as it invaded the hollow of his mouth, demanding submission. Misha used to gag, revolted by the feel, but he'd learned to comply — to accept Master's tongue on his tastebuds and his fingers in his hole.

They speared into him with only paint for lube and he hissed at the burn, though he knew better than to flinch. Master's probing seemed more exploratory than leading, a way of reminding Misha that he was just a toy to play with than anything more, so he stayed relaxed, pliant as putty in his hands.

When Master's fingers slid free of his ass, Misha knew he'd read him correctly. "Go ahead and finish up, *conejito*. Maybe you'll do better with the rest." Master smiled and it was devious. "When you're done, I have some friends here to meet you."

* * * *

With the bitter taste of semen on his lips, Misha knelt by Master's chair at the conference table. If he were lucky, the other men speaking with Master in rapid-fire Spanish would be satisfied with his earlier performance and he would only have to please Master when the meeting finally ended.

He'd picked up just enough Spanish since being transported to Austin to know that they were talking about a product transfer. The details were fuzzy, and he caught just enough to know he knew nothing. The man Master called 'DeAza' kept bringing up a new formula he wanted to try.

At some point Misha stopped trying to listen, staring instead at the stitching on the toes of Master's leather shoes, the subtle way the laces were tucked in at his thick ankles. They looked so normal resting on the pale blue carpet, a businessman's shoes at a meeting of associates...like they'd never stepped on Misha's fingers and pressed them into the wood until he screamed or dug into his side below his ribs.

He yelped as his hair was gripped by a heavy hand, his head yanked up with a forceful tug. "Boy, pay attention," Master snapped, and his expression was a minefield.

Misha thought quickly, knowing he needed to step carefully. "I'm sorry, Master. I just didn't want to distract you..." His eyes watered from the pain in his scalp.

Master softened his gaze, letting go of Misha's hair to brush his large hand over Misha's cheek. "Aw, were we boring you, baby? Were you feeling ignored?" Master glanced over Misha's shoulder, nodding to someone he couldn't see. "You can go keep my *amigo*'s cock warm in your pretty little mouth."

Misha turned to see one of the men pulling his penis out of his pants, already hard and leaking. It was the one Misha was most afraid of, the white-haired man who liked to smile at him while he choked him, the one who wore a priest's collar and made Misha pray for forgiveness for 'tempting' him, all with a dirty leer on his technically handsome face.

Misha obediently crawled under the table and took the penis into his mouth as he'd been ordered, wishing he'd paid more attention earlier to avoid this. He knew it wouldn't have mattered — likely he'd have ended up like this again today, anyway — but telling himself that didn't make him feel better.

The meeting continued, except now the men passed Misha's mouth back and forth between them at some signal Misha couldn't catch, until his jaw ached and he felt himself drifting, slipping into the safe place in his mind — the place where his parents hadn't died in a car crash coming home from a movie and he'd grown up safe, just another kid in Brooklyn.

The place where his mother still made him *zefir* on Sundays and put *zelyonka* on his scraped knees. The place where his dad and his friends played *durak* every Wednesday after work. The place where the only penis he'd ever touched was his own.

* * * *

Asher stepped off the Greyhound bus in Austin a hot mess — emphasis on both hot *and* mess. Despite being nearly dusk, it was eighty-six degrees and climbing, and even Asher's sweat was sweating, pouring down his spine like a slip-and-slide. Of course, he didn't have deodorant, either, which explained the nice bubble of empty space quickly forming around him.

But while it felt like he was standing in a swimming pool inside an industrial oven, he was ecstatic. He was finally in Austin, hopefully minutes away from seeing Devon.

He scanned the crowd for the familiar blond hair, waving wildly when he finally spotted it. Devon stood awkwardly near a large black SUV, his right hand gripping his left forearm. Asher couldn't see it, but he imagined Devon's thumb was tapping nervously over his pulse.

Asher hoped Devon was as excited to see him as he was to be here.

He wanted to skip as he made his way over but restrained himself to a fast walk. He couldn't keep the smile from breaking across his face. Devon seemed to grow paler the closer he got, but he supposed it was okay to be nervous, since Devon probably had the same fears he did.

He was almost in touching distance when the driver's door opened and a large, vaguely familiar man stepped out. His hair was slate-silver, flecked with pepper, and he wore a suit that looked expensive, a gaudy silver watch glinting on his wrist as he closed the door.

Asher slowed to a stop, frowning while he placed him as the man from the Skype call, *Devon's dad* – who Asher *thought* didn't know he was coming, since Devon had said he wasn't accepting.

"Devon?" Asher didn't really know what he was asking but Devon answered only with lowered eyes.

Instead, Devon's dad smiled like a chainsaw – all threat and teeth – and Asher almost stepped back. "You must be Devon's friend," the man said, dropping a large hand on Devon's shoulder. "Do we need to grab your bags, or..." He trailed off in question, looking at Asher's empty hands, and Asher flushed.

"I got mugged at the bus station. Um…I've got this though." He crouched quickly and fished the sweaty, rolled up hundred-dollar bill from his sock and held it out. Immediately, embarrassment flooded him, and he yanked it back, drying it off on his shirt before extending it again. "Sorry…"

The man waved him off. "Keep it, *michi.*"

"Um, it's Asher, actually," he corrected hesitantly.

Devon's dad laughed. "Sorry, Asher. It means 'kitten'. Your hair right now. It's just…" The man made a gesture by his skull, quirking his lips up.

Asher swiped a hand through his hair, feeling the way it stuck up every which way, then blushed, heat burning in his face. What an impression to make on a man predisposed to dislike him.

"Go ahead and take the front seat, Asher. Devon will be fine in the back. Won't you, boy?" Devon's dad said.

"Yes, M…Sir," Devon stuttered, giving Asher an inscrutable look before climbing into the backseat. Then, his dad held open the door for Asher with a bland smile. *And shark eyes*, Asher thought, but after only a moment's hesitation, he climbed in.

He knew he was judging the man only because of things he'd inferred from his conversations with Devon, but maybe things had changed. They must have, if his dad had driven him here to pick up Asher.

Asher sat in awkward silence as Devon's dad navigated the large SUV onto the street and started driving, presumably toward the apartment Devon had already rented for them. All Asher knew was that it was within walking distance of a coffee shop and a grocery store…and not too far from a bus stop, which was great, because first thing tomorrow, he was going to have to find his way to a bank, cancel his debit card and *hopefully* convince them to refund any fraudulent charges as well.

And he had to get a cheap cell phone at some point and probably a change of underwear or two.

But those were all tomorrow's problems. Today, he was just going to be excited to be here.

He spun in his seat to look back at Devon, who looked even smaller in the large bucket seats than he had on the computer screen. He was staring out of the side window, his brows lowered over distant eyes.

"So, Devon," Asher said, feeling guilty for a second when the other boy startled, "you gotta tell me all the cool places to visit. I want to experience *everything*."

Devon smiled, but it looked more queasy than excited. "Um... I don't even know where to start. There's the, um..." He shifted his gaze to the side, toward the rearview mirror, and his dad cut in.

"Devon's kind of a homebody, but don't worry. We'll make sure you have *lots* of new experiences now that you're here. We're so happy to have you." Asher couldn't help but think that there was something a bit *off* about the way the man phrased it, but he shook it away. It was obvious from the hint of an accent he had that English wasn't the man's first language, if the Spanish he'd slipped in earlier hadn't given it away.

Which was funny, too, since Devon didn't look like he had a hint of Hispanic in him, not with his pale skin and hair.

It was weird how genetics worked sometimes.

Asher turned back to watch the road, staring at the hundreds of new things to see. It was so different from Wilmington—everything brighter, both in terms of actual sunlight and color. He didn't know where to look.

He was expecting them to pull up to an apartment complex — probably somewhere a bit rundown, a place cheap enough they could afford it if they lived on a diet of ramen and fruit snacks. Instead, they seemed to be driving to the outskirts of Austin, where the houses grew larger and the lawns lusher — and the fences no longer chain link but ornate wrought-iron.

Devon's dad must have noticed the confusion on Asher's face because he slowed slightly and gave him a quick smile before returning his eyes to the road. "I know you and Devon were planning on getting your own place, but I talked him into staying at home for a few more months. That way you can save up some money. Besides, we have a cook, so I'll know he's getting enough protein."

Asher glanced at the waif-boy in the backseat, with his cheekbones like cut glass and wrists like crystal stemware — poised to shatter.

He turned back to Devon's dad. "You're sure you don't mind, sir?"

"You can call me 'Dad' or 'Mr. B'. And no, I don't mind at all. The more the merrier."

* * * *

Devon's home — and his for now — turned out to be a sprawling, double-gated compound on at least five acres that Asher could see. Beyond the large villa, he could see a cabana by a pool, what looked like a tennis court and a putting green.

Asher had guessed from the expensive suit and watch that the man had money, but he hadn't realized he was *rich*. Mr. B pulled the SUV to the side of the circle drive by the main door and cut the engine. "I know it's overwhelming at first, *michi*. Don't worry. We'll give you a tour later, won't we, Devon?"

"Yes, Sir." Devon twisted his hands in his lap, so Asher shot him quick, reassuring smile. Probably the boy was worried that he would be angry about the change of plans, but come *on*. There was a pool. Who could be angry about that?

"Come on, boys. Let's show Asher his room and get him all settled." Devon's dad clapped Asher on the shoulder, his hand lingering a second too long before he started guiding him up the stairs and inside. "I'm sure you'll want to take a shower after that long on the bus. Right, *michi*?"

Asher nodded but bit his tongue on correcting the nickname again. It seemed a bit...*odd* to call your son's boyfriend 'kitten,' but it wasn't like his parents were a functional example to go off of.

"Should I take my shoes off?" Asher asked as they stepped onto the white marble floors just inside the entryway.

"Go ahead. Leave them by the door and one of the girls will have them cleaned for you."

Asher toed off his sneakers and nudged them neatly against the wall where, hopefully, they would be out of the way, then followed the older man through the lower level and up the winding staircase that led upstairs, Devon a silent shadow behind him. Asher tried not to stare but it was hard, with the large paintings on every wall and thick rugs and weird little sculptures.

"Everything's so *nice*," Asher said, mostly to himself.

"What can I say? When I want something, I get it." Devon's dad laughed and slowed a bit so Asher could stare. "Isn't that right, *conejito?*"

Behind him, Devon said quietly, "Yes, Sir."

"Come on up here, boy. Stop being so shy." When Devon stepped up beside his dad, rather reluctantly by the expression on his face, the older man dropped an arm around his shoulders. "Let's keep moving." Still clutching Devon, he started walking and Asher followed, trailing only slightly behind. They stopped outside a thick wood door a few hallways away from the top of the stairs. Asher was worried he was going to need a map to find his way out again.

"This is your room here. Devon painted it for you, so it's a bit of a mess, but hopefully it'll do for now." Mr. B laughed again like he hadn't just insulted his son, who turned slightly pink and dropped his eyes.

"I can't wait to see it." Asher plastered on a bright smile, excited to see where he'd be staying but not expecting much more than a bed and a dresser.

Devon's dad slid a silver key into the lock and twisted it until a click sounded, then pushed open the door, waving Asher in.

The walls were Pepto-Bismol pink and so was part of the floor he could see, and in place of a light was a delicate crystal chandelier. Even the coverlet on the queen-size bed was pink, except for the white lace trim. The mattress overflowed with pillows—some white, some pink, some gray with little sparkly bedazzles.

To be honest, it was a bit more girly than he'd expected, but he couldn't say he hated it, so he turned away from the room to give Devon a brilliant smile. "I love it. You didn't have to go to so much effort. I'd have slept on the couch, you know." He winked to make sure Devon knew he was joking.

Despite that, Devon looked queasy, his gaze locked on the floor. "It's fine," Devon mumbled. "I wanted you to like it here."

Asher looked between the two, sensing an undercurrent of *something* he couldn't pinpoint. Before he could, Devon's dad backed out of the room and gave a sharp smile. "You have a private bathroom. Go ahead and put your clothes in the laundry chute to be washed. I left a few outfits in your closet you can wear until we get you some more. We'll let you get settled in."

Devon followed his dad out, giving Asher one last inscrutable glance before he shut the door. Asher waved right before it closed, then grinned as he turned away. After seeing this room, which looked like it belonged in a palace, he couldn't wait to see the bathroom.

Chapter Six

Then

Master locked Asher's bedroom door as soon as they heard the shower kick on, then grabbed Misha's hair in a tight fist, dragging him down the hallway toward the bedroom. Not *his* bedroom, because Misha didn't have one of those. He had *a* bedroom that he was allowed to sleep in when Master was gone on business or sampling a new whore from the Rose, but only if he'd been good. Otherwise, he had a kennel in the back of Master's closet or a cement floor in a room in the basement.

Master shoved him to his knees at the foot of the bed, already fishing his penis from his pants with the hand not tangled in Misha's hair. He pressed the blunt head to Misha's lips until they opened, shoving in, careless of his comfort, before he started speaking.

"Did you see him? So fucking pretty. He's older than I thought I wanted but — goddamn, your mouth, whore, so good — how could I resist? Got a matching set now—relax your throat—yes, just like that. Can't wait to see him fuck you," Master grunted his pleasure as his hips pumped roughly, burying his penis in Misha's throat over and over, ignorant and uncaring of the tears burning Misha's eyes. "Wanna see him make you his bitch. I know you want him. I saw this little dick"—Master pressed his leather shoes painfully against the crotch of Misha's too-tight jeans, the ones that felt foreign on his normally nude skin—"plump up for him. You want him to kiss it, *conejito*?" Master backed up a half-step, letting Misha gasp in a breath. "Yeah, I knew you did, stupid little slut."

Misha didn't want that, didn't want to have sex with the boy locked in the other room—not now, not here, not like *this*. He had never looked at another person and thought, *I want him.* He couldn't say what *want* felt like...or need. His penis got hard from physical stimulation but even that left him feeling sick.

But maybe Master saw something on his face, something he couldn't see for himself, because if he *did* want to have sex with anyone, it would be a boy like Asher—a boy with laughter in his eyes and soft lips and hands more used to holding a makeup brush than a whip.

How long until that laughter faded and died?

How long until the lips split and bled?

How long until the hands pinched and prodded?

Master slapped him, the *crack* of flesh hitting flesh sounding before the pain could register and Misha cried out, clutching at his throbbing cheek. "Pay attention, slut. Pull your pants down and bend over the bed."

* * * *

Master unlocked the door to Asher's bedroom while the shower was still running, then squeezed Misha's bicep in a final warning. He was to make Asher feel *comfortable* and *flirt* and, under no circumstances, was he allowed to leave the room without fooling around on the bed at least a little bit. And of course, he had to make it look good for the cameras hidden around the room.

Misha knew how to flirt, in theory, but he only had practice on old men who'd already paid to fuck him, so it wasn't real.

Arranging himself in a subtly erotic way on the pink covers felt weird. He started by reclining against the pillows, but he felt that he must look like a limp fish, so he rolled on his stomach instead, his head facing the edge of the mattress and, therefore, the bathroom door.

He propped his head up on his palm and kicked his feet in a way he hoped looked cute, his heart pounding in his chest as he heard the shower kick off. Barely a minute later, the bathroom door opened, and Asher stepped out, his blond hair dripping water. It ran from his golden chest to his abs, all the way down to the small white towel barely swaddled around his hips.

Asher stopped as soon as their eyes locked, his cheeks turning pink. "Oh, um...hey, Devon."

Misha bit his lip before sucking in a breath, taking a risk to say, "Can...can you call me Misha?" He didn't want to be Devon, the normal boy with the normal life and the normal problems.

Asher's brows lowered for a moment. "Misha?"

"Devon is my American name, but I was born Dimitri," he explained. "Misha is my nickname."

"Okay." Asher gave him a bright smile like it was a gift. "Misha it is." His focus skirted to the door, then back to Misha, lingering on his cheek where Master had slapped him, the skin still flushed and warm. "Is um…your dad okay with you being in here? I mean, you just said he was not very accepting, so I don't want you to get in trouble."

Misha couldn't hold Asher's gaze while he lied, so he dropped it to the coverlet, picking at an imaginary thread. "We talked, and he's okay. I guess it's different when it's your kid or something…"

"Good, that's good." His voice sounded strained, and when Misha looked up, Asher was clutching the corner of his towel like a lifeline, an obvious erection tenting the front. He was pink from his cheeks to his nipples. "I…I should get dressed…"

Misha licked his lips as he gathered his nerves. "You don't have to…"

"I've never… I mean." Asher cleared his throat. "I've *thought* about it, but I haven't… Have you?"

Misha closed his eyes in near-pain. Asher was a *virgin*. He hated that the other boy's first time was going to be here, at the hands of his master.

"I, um… Yeah, I have, but it never *meant* anything." Misha stumbled his way through an answer, unwilling to lie but reluctant to speak the truth, either. "But it *would*, now," he hastily added, then felt his cheeks turn to flame. "I mean, if we did, which we don't have to, because I'm sure you don't want…" Misha forced himself to shut up, dropping his face into his hands with a groan. "I'm just going to die now."

The bed dipped then slender fingers carded through his hair. Asher sounded amused when he said, "Oh, I definitely *want*."

Misha looked through his fingers to see Asher sitting beside him, his right foot tucked under his left thigh, the other dangling off the bed, only the towel and a prayer keeping him modest. Except the expression on his face wasn't modest at all, and it was the one Misha was afraid of.

Except...

Except on Asher, it didn't seem so scary.

"Can I kiss you?" Asher asked, and his voice was airy, like the wind in a dream.

Misha's voice cracked as he answered, "Yes."

He held his breath as Asher leaned in, afraid that he was going to hate it but even *more* afraid that he wouldn't, and the fear mingled with the guilt in his stomach. They were putting on a play, but only one of them knew they were acting.

Under the fear and guilt, a spark of pleasure kindled in his chest, synchronizing with the fluttering of his heart at the gentle press of Asher's mouth, so different from what he was used to. There was no demand, no dominance, just a sweet insistence of soft lips on his.

It was by far the least sexual kiss he'd ever been given—and the most perfect. They separated on a sigh. Misha kept his eyes closed for a moment, storing the memory of this one, perfect kiss away somewhere safe.

Then, he looked up at Asher through his lashes, a coy look he'd learned through trial and error. Done right, he'd end up on his knees or back, but done wrong and he'd end up bleeding. "You can kiss me again, if you want."

And he did.

And it wasn't horrible.

* * * *

Asher watched Misha slip from his room in the middle of the night, then collapsed, breathless, against the fluffy pillows. He thought he'd been kissed before, but now? Now he knew that the others had been nothing, just practice for this moment. Misha was *perfect*.

His skin was as soft as it looked and as delicate, pink bruises blooming from the gentlest suction. And though he said he'd been with others, he'd seemed surprised at each moment of pleasure Asher had wrung from his body, the sweetest moans and gasps spilling from his lips like candy.

And he hadn't even gotten the boy naked, just stroked him through his jeans. It wasn't that he didn't *want* to go further, but he knew if he got Misha naked, he wouldn't be able to resist. Not only did they not have any supplies for that, but he had an inkling, from the blush Misha wore so well, that he wasn't ready for it, not yet.

If he were honest, Asher wasn't sure he was ready yet, either. He knew the theory of sex, had given and received decent enough head, but he wanted his first time to be special. That meant that Misha had to want it as bad as he did, so he could wait as long as was needed.

Kissing had been nice, though.

He definitely wanted to do more kissing.

* * * *

Asher woke to a knock on his door, confused for a second about the lack of alarm before he remembered his phone had been stolen and he hadn't been able to replace it yet.

"Asher?" Misha sounded nervous, and it was so cute. Not even the fact that he was exhausted could keep him in bed.

He rolled off the mattress and bounced over to the door, tugging it open to beam at the other boy. "Good morning, Misha."

Misha looked startled, but whether it was at his exuberance or the door being opened so suddenly was a mystery Asher wasn't worried about unraveling. "Um…there's breakfast waiting downstairs."

"Can't wait. I'm *starving*." Asher glanced down at his bare chest. "Just…give me a second." Leaving the door open, he bounced back to the white dresser and dug out a shirt to pull on. It was just a bit too small, but if the way Misha was looking at him was any indication, that wasn't a bad thing. "Okay, I'm ready. Lead the way."

Asher followed Misha downstairs. He couldn't help but notice, now that he wasn't as starstruck by the expensive art and fixtures, several dozen armed men loitering in the hallways.

Part of him wasn't surprised, once the initial shock wore off. A man who could afford a house like this *had* to have security, except…they didn't look like any security firm he'd ever seen before, which he supposed wasn't saying much, all things considered. It wasn't like he ran in these kinds of circles back home. The fanciest place he'd ever gone was the big church on Christmas morning, in place of their usual chapel down the road.

Maybe it was because the guards weren't in uniform and their guns looked more like something a militia would carry — big and scary looking, like they could punch a hole through a wall *and* the person standing on the other side. A *big* hole.

Asher was happy with having only the number of holes he was born with, so he resolved to give them a wide birth, side-stepping a bit closer to Misha.

Misha gave him a weak smile. "Don't worry. They don't bother us unless we stick our noses into their business."

"Business? Are they like...special security or something?" Asher was confused, because he didn't really think guards had *'business'*.

"Kind of, but not exactly. They work with M—my dad." Misha stuttered a bit, dropping his eyes to the floor as they passed the nearest guard. Asher didn't like the way the man, bald and heavily muscled with a snake tattoo on his neck, leered at Misha.

"Does he *always* look at you like that?" Asher asked quietly after they were passed.

Misha turned pink and ducked his head further. "It's not a big deal."

"Kinda looks like it could be."

"Just...leave it alone, okay?" Misha looked at him pleadingly. "He won't do anything."

"Better not," Asher growled, even though he kind of sounded more like a puppy than a wolf.

Misha seemed to think the same thing because he smirked, looking at Asher through his lashes. "What will you do if he does? Will you defend my honor?"

Asher glanced around as they turned the corner, making sure they were out of sight of the faux guards, then backed Misha up against the wall, caging him in with his arms but not touching. "Can I kiss you?"

Misha nodded, tongue wetting his lips. "Yes, please."

Asher wanted to ravish him, pin him to the wall and steal every breath from his mouth, so he did. And when Misha gasped, Asher slipped his tongue inside, tasting the other boy's spearmint-fresh heat. One hand curled lightly around the arch of Misha's neck to feel the vibration of his moans.

Asher was hard under his basketball shorts — but so was Misha. He felt the erection jutting into his upper thigh with every roll of his hips. He wanted to slip his hands inside and stroke until he whined, but just when he was thinking of doing it, a throat cleared and they sprang apart.

Misha's dad had a smirk on his lips as he stared at them. "Having fun, boys?"

"Oh, um…we were just…" Asher waved down the hall, "Breakfast?"

"Well, you were certainly eating *something.*" The older man winked. "Run along and grab some food, then meet me by the front door. I have a *surprise* for you."

* * * *

Breakfast tasted like sawdust in Misha's mouth as he went over and over in his head what Master's surprise could be. After years of a diet consisting primarily of oatmeal, bread and water, except for treats, the blueberry pancakes should have been heaven. Why was he surprised Master had found a way to ruin them?

Asher didn't seem worried, but why would he be? Master was putting on a play, with himself in the starring role and Misha as his supporting character. They were a happy, normal family, who did happy, normal things. Unlike Misha, Asher didn't know the script had an end date—as soon as Master was certain Asher's family wasn't looking for him, as soon as he knew the police had given up searching for a runaway adult...

Misha gripped his fork tightly and glanced at Asher discreetly. Could he help him escape? He hadn't been able to get himself out but maybe... Asher had no reason to be suspicious, so maybe Master would be less on guard?

Could he create a distraction and somehow convince Asher to run?

Could he survive the consequences if he were successful?

Could he live with himself if he didn't try?

"Everything okay, Misha? You're not eating much," Asher said, interrupting his thoughts.

"Yeah, sure. Just excited to see the surprise, I guess," Misha replied, forcing himself to swallow a large bite of the pancake. It went down like a rock, but Asher looked appeased.

"Me, too. What do you think it will be?" Asher pushed his plate away and rubbed his belly.

"Not sure. Shopping, maybe?" Misha had absolutely no idea. What kinds of things did fathers do with their kids, anyway?

"Hmm-m." Asher frowned at that and looked down. "I hope not. I can't afford to buy anything. I do need to get a phone, though, at some point."

"I wouldn't worry. M-my dad will take care of that if he's taking us somewhere," Misha said. He stood up and reached for Asher's plate, carrying it with his into the kitchen and loading them into the dishwasher. When he turned around, Asher was leaning against the doorframe.

Misha couldn't keep himself from staring. With his black basketball shorts slung low around his hips and a too-small tank top riding up his stomach, revealing a happy trail Misha just wanted to run his fingers through, Asher looked like an all-American frat boy — except for the lip gloss, which Misha could still taste on his own mouth.

"Do you think he'd let us stop somewhere after? Maybe I could put in a few job applications," Asher asked, not seeming to notice Misha's perusal. Instead, he looked excited at the thought of getting a job, unaware that it would never happen.

Master would never let him out of his sight or out from under his thumb. "I don't know," Misha lied, his eyes straying to the empty knife block, the locked cupboard…the lack of anything that could be used as a weapon — all the clues that Asher wasn't noticing but Misha couldn't help but catalog.

"We should probably get going." Misha fiddled with the buttons on the dishwasher until he figured out how to start it before fleeing the kitchen.

Master was waiting with one of his guards, a big bald man with a disarmingly kind smile but mean hands by the front door. He was on his phone, but he hung up as soon as he and Asher approached. "Ready to go, boys?"

Master grinned wickedly when they agreed, then unlocked the front door with the silver key he kept on his body at all times. He led them out to the waiting limo. Misha climbed in first with Asher behind him, sharing the far bench and leaving Master the other, facing them.

Asher kept running his hands over the supple leather seats and craning his neck to stare through the tinted windows, clearly impressed.

"Ever ridden in one before?" Master asked suddenly, making Misha jump before he caught himself.

Asher laughed. "No, never. We were supposed to get one for prom, but my dad backed out when he found out I was planning on going stag. It's really nice."

"Wait until you see the best part." Master smirked and leaned over to pop open the mini fridge, pulling out a bottle of chilled champagne. "Now I know you're not twenty-one yet, but it seems like such an arbitrary law, doesn't it?" Master said as he opened the bottle, splitting the bubbly liquid between three glasses before setting it aside. "At eighteen, you can go to war, get married...have sex." He winked at Asher, who blushed under his gaze. "A little alcohol won't harm you. Am I right?"

Master passed them both their glasses, fixing Misha with a pointed look, a silent order to drink it without protest or tears. Misha knew what the bottle was laced with — a bit of ecstasy to lower their inhibitions if he was lucky, GHB if he wasn't. Master forced him to drink it sometimes, probably because he knew how much Misha hated the loss of awareness — hated knowing Master could do anything to him and he wouldn't remember.

The only time Master let him watch TV was after one of those parties, when he wanted Misha to see himself be used and degraded.

Asher swallowed the champagne down without question or hesitation, setting his empty glass in the cup holder beside him, while Misha sipped at his with more reluctance. He did finish it, however, knowing better than to risk Master's anger.

Misha sat quietly next to Asher, who bounced in his seat, turning his head from one window to the next, even standing up to stare out of the moon roof for a few seconds before the drugs hit him and he seemed to get dizzy, tumbling back to the seat with a loud laugh. *Ecstasy, then,* Misha decided, feeling his own body grow warmer, his heart thumping faster. Soon, he would be loose-limbed and pliant, although the drug no longer left him blissed out.

By the time the limo pulled up to the edge of a sidewalk, Misha was jittery, invisible ants crawling up and down his spine as he fought to sit still. His heart drummed a dance-club beat in his chest from the drugs.

Beside him, Asher was flushed pink, his pupils blown. But unlike Misha, he was grinning, his straight white teeth on display like piano keys. He hummed off key as he stumbled out of the limo after Master. Misha moved slower, placing each foot as carefully as he could so as not to stumble.

He wished they could run.

The limo was parked less than a dozen feet from the door, but that still gave him almost twelve steps to try. Like he did for every one of these events, he imagined himself doing it—running and not looking back, heading for the street, any street, any car, any possibility of help.

But like he did every time, he just ducked his head and shuffled inside. Now more than ever, he couldn't risk it, not with Asher too drugged to run and too naïve to even know he should. Misha couldn't leave him behind.

"What is this place?" Asher asked, his voice loud enough to jolt Misha from his thoughts and make him look up.

The locations of the parties changed each time. Sometimes they were held in warehouses or factories closed for just this purpose. Others were held in the back rooms of one of the cartel's clubs. Rarely, like tonight, they were held in the private home of one of the sponsors. Misha had been here before. He recognized the rug in the entryway, remembered being shoved to his knees on it, a party favor to share upon entry.

Master clapped a heavy hand on Misha's shoulder, doing the same to Asher on his other side, and steered them farther into the house. "Come on, boys, before the party starts without us."

Chapter Seven

Now

Ryder read computer code like children's books.

On nights like this, when he was supposed to be screen free, it was the only way he could sneak in a few more moments of searching in the scant handful of minutes between watching cartoons in his blankie on the living room floor and bubble-bath time, while Daddy was busy gathering his toys and jam-jams for bed.

It was against the rules to be 'big' during 'little' time, but he *needed* it. No matter how many times Daddy reminded him that it wasn't his fault, the guilt kept creeping up. If he had just ignored his parents and talked to his brother after they'd seen him kissing that boy, maybe Asher wouldn't have run away. If he'd found a way to sneak him notes, or...or hacked his Xbox to use the chat feature from his phone, or...or something... He should have tried harder.

It was why he made sure to squeeze in every second of searching he could, even though disappointing his partner left a sour taste in his mouth and a stone in his belly. He'd never cared about disobeying his bio-dad. He'd known since he was small that his overly conservative parents didn't really care about *him*. They cared about how his behavior had reflected on them. Even when he'd lived at home with them, he'd called his dad 'Father', not 'Daddy'.

'Daddy' was a title he'd reserved for someone special. That someone had turned out to be Mason. The older man was everything he'd dreamed of, and it sucked knowing he was going to disappoint him.

Ryder just needed two minutes. Two minutes to scour the dark web and run facial scans on Facebook, just in case. Two minutes could never make up for the two weeks he'd wasted.

Two weeks.

Two weeks his brother had been missing before his parents had even bothered to tell him that Asher wasn't at a sleepover. Two weeks he could have been searching... Two weeks he could have been using his computer skills to find him instead of playing video games and studying the stupid *Bible*.

He could be 'big' for two minutes to find his older brother. He'd been missing for five years, since Ryder had been fourteen. Five years of being alone, wherever he was. He'd be twenty-three now. Ryder wondered if he still had the dorky cowlick Asher used to think made him look like that guy from *Fullmetal Alchemist*.

"Ryder Immanuel Lockhart, that doesn't look like cleaning up your toys," Daddy scolded from the doorway of Ryder's home office.

The booming voice made Ryder, still *partially* in 'little' space, jump violently in his chair, his fingers banging on the keys and wrecking his code. "I...I was just *looking*, Daddy," Ryder whined, pouting at the disappointment he heard in every word.

"You know you can't use screens after eight on the weekend."

"I could turn the monitor off?" Ryder hopefully suggested, sending Daddy the wide-eyed look that normally got him extra fries at Mickey D's.

"All the way off, boy."

Ryder slumped with a pout but obediently backed out of his code and switched off the computer. He stood and shuffled his bare feet along the carpet until he stopped in front of Mason.

"Sorry, Daddy," He mumbled around his jutting lip.

Daddy's big fingers ruffled his curls. "I know, buddy. Come here. Let's talk for a second."

Ryder's chin wobbled. He didn't want to *talk* about it. Daddy would tell him why he was disappointed, and Ryder would feel even more bad than he did. Daddy had saved his life...*literally.*

As soon as Ryder had turned sixteen, he'd dropped out of high school and gotten his GED instead. He'd used the money his parents had given him for college to buy a big ugly van and a top-of-the-line laptop and gone in search of his brother.

He'd known something was wrong.

Nobody just disappeared. Not in this day and age, with the Internet tracking every login and purchase and every street corner littered with cameras. He should have been able to find Asher easily, even if he for some reason forwent all social media to live in a cave or something, which was nothing like the boy he remembered.

But there'd been nothing, absolutely nothing. It was like his brother had gotten on a bus and just…vanished.

Wherever he was, Ryder knew it wasn't good — not that anyone would believe him, not his parents, not the police. So he'd decided if no one else was going to look, he'd do it himself.

A few days after his eighteenth birthday, he'd ended up in Dallas, after a newer facial recognition software found an old partial match at a bus station. The angle was bad, but the blond hair looked just how Ryder remembered it. It might not have been him, but it *could* have been, so Ryder had driven overnight and through the whole next day to get there.

Where he'd promptly been mugged and left in an alley for dead. Mason had found him by chance and nursed him to health. Ryder'd followed him back to Seattle, and six months later, they'd tied the knot at the courthouse.

When people online said kinky relationships grew serious quickly, they weren't lying.

He couldn't imagine living without Mason now — or the small team of bodyguards his husband employed who had quickly become family, which was why disappointing Mason felt just that much worse.

Ryder followed Mason to the large rocking chair in the nursery and obediently climbed into his lap. Daddy just held him at first, running his big hands over Ryder's much smaller back. He'd always been tiny and frail. He knew that was why his real father didn't like him, even if his mother denied it. He'd wanted tough sons, the kind who played sports and kissed girls.

He'd failed with both his kids.

Ryder couldn't help smiling at the thought that his father would hate everything he'd become since leaving that sham of the American dream house.

A submissive 'little' with literal Daddy issues, who wore skirts and makeup and sometimes played with dolls.

"What am I going to do with you, buddy?" Mason sighed, his chest moving Ryder's head up and down with each breath.

"Love me?" Ryder pleaded, looking up at him with watery eyes.

"Always, baby. Always."

Chapter Eight

Then

Asher wanted to move, or dance or...or jump, *anything* to get rid of the restless energy filling his limbs from the inside out like static. His mind buzzed with a million thoughts but still somehow seemed to be moving too slowly for him to follow.

He'd never felt this alive before, even if it was a strange sort of feeling. Not quite natural, though maybe it was just the excitement of going to a party with Misha and Mr. B. He'd never been to a party before, not a real one—just the silly kids' parties the church hosted for holidays. His parents hadn't even celebrated birthdays once they hit double digits.

Misha's dad's hand on his shoulder was hot and a bit uncomfortable, but since Asher was feeling a bit off balance, he didn't try to shrug it off. He just let the older man guide him through the fancy house.

As they walked, he couldn't help noticing that a lot of the other party guests were...older, well-dressed like

Misha's dad, and most of them were staring. The few people close to Asher's age seemed quiet and withdrawn, hovering in the shadows. They were dressed funny, too, in shorts that fit like skin and leather harnesses with large padlocks and little else.

What kind of party is this?

Before he could wonder more, he was steered into a fancy living room with dim lights and the sweet stench of cigars. "We're going to have so much fun, aren't we, Misha? Tell *michi* how much you enjoy these little parties."

Between the music playing through stereo system and the strange energy coursing through him, it was hard for Asher to concentrate, but he still caught Misha's small nod.

"Here... Sit down, and relax a bit," Misha's dad said, and though it sounded like a suggestion, the way his hand gripped Asher almost painfully made it clear it wasn't.

Asher sank down onto the couch, his brain sluggish. Misha dropped beside him a second later, close enough that they touched from shoulder to knee. It was a pleasant distraction, his skin on Misha's, even if Misha felt like he was vibrating, and he found himself zoning out, swaying to the music and just...being.

Until he opened his eyes again and found himself staring at a boy on his knees in front of the other sofa, between an older man's thighs. His face burned as he realized what was happening and he looked away quickly, back to Misha with a question in his eyes. It was hard to think with the buzz in his head, but he *did* notice that Misha's expression looked strained.

"Everything okay?" Asher asked, bumping his knee into Misha's as he briefly forgot about the scene on the other side of the room.

"Yeah, sure. Of course," Misha said, but his voice didn't sound confident.

"So, this looks like an…interesting party?" Asher's voice rose at the end as he glanced around, trying not to stare but unable to keep himself from notice the subtle—and not so subtle—making out of the other guests.

Misha bit his lip, teeth digging into the fleshy pout. "Yeah. Um, Asher, there's something—"

"You boys don't look like you're having fun," Misha's dad's voice boomed from behind them before he could finish his sentence.

Misha flinched, skin paling slightly, and Asher grabbed his hand to squeeze it. He didn't understand why Misha always seemed to go quiet when his dad entered the room, because to Asher, the man was always pleasant, if a bit heavy-handed.

"Sorry, Mr. B." Asher grinned at the older man. "I've just never been to a party like this before."

"Don't worry. You'll get to come to plenty more. Misha, stand up and show your friend how to have a good time. Why don't you dance for him?" Mr. B dropped onto the couch on the other side of Asher, draping his arm over the back of the couch, his fingers tickling his shoulder. "Show him how you move those sexy hips."

Such an odd thing to say about your son, Asher mused through the fuzziness of his brain.

Misha stood up slowly, moving in front of Asher. He looked hot in his tank top and tight black shorts, his skin glistening under the dim lights. The beat of the music was thumping and fast, but Misha moved slow, swaying his hips in a seductive tease, dipping his fingers into the band of his shorts before lifting the hem of his tank top to give a glimpse of his taut abs. His face was strangely blank, like a porcelain doll instead of a real boy.

Asher couldn't look away, his breath catching in his chest at the sight.

Then Misha moved closer until he stood between Asher's knees.

He got lost in Misha's seafoam eyes and soft skin, in his slender fingers and pouty lips. Lost in the way his breath caught in his chest at the brush of a finger, then Mr. B said something he didn't catch, and Misha was in his lap, grinding against his throbbing dick.

Asher skin went hot, and he found himself torn between arousal and embarrassment. Mr. B was still beside him, his hairy thigh against Asher's bare knee, caressing Asher's shoulder with his fingers.

"Look at my sexy boys." Mr. B's voice was throaty, and it made Asher uncomfortable. It wasn't something a father should say about his son and his son's boyfriend. But then, this wasn't the kind of party he thought a parent should bring their child to, either.

Before he could puzzle his way through it, Mr. B was speaking again. "Hold him for me, Misha," and Asher was being shifted on the couch, his arms gripped tightly behind his back by a pale Misha.

"I'm sorry. I'm so sorry," Misha kept muttering, distraught. Asher didn't understand. He didn't...until he did. With his arms held, he couldn't resist when Mr. B unbuckled his belt and grabbed Asher's hair, tugging him into his lap. No amount of struggling freed him, and no amount of apologies from Misha made any of this okay.

* * * *

"Is he even your dad? Why did you reach out to me in the first place? Was everything a lie?"

The questions Asher had asked him two nights ago, ground out through clenched teeth on their way home, cycled through Misha's head over and over again. The words had hit him harder than Master's fists ever had, turning themselves over and over through his head as Asher had been locked in his room to sleep off the drugs.

Misha had gotten no such luxury. He'd been shoved to his knees again in the hallway, until his attention drifted too much, and Master got angry. For once, he was grateful for the beating. It felt like a fitting punishment for the suffering Asher had to go through because of him, because he'd not been strong enough to stand up to Master or smart enough to warn Asher in advance.

So here he was, lying on the floor of what amounted to his bedroom in the basement, only a thin blanket between him and the cement. Maybe, if he was particularly well behaved, he would earn his lumpy pillow back.

He didn't have his hopes up.

Carefully, his body aching, he rolled onto his other side to stare at the slit of sky visible through his tiny window. It was still dark out, but for the fuzzy orange just starting to creep upward. Misha's stomach had stopped aching at some point during his fitful sleep, the gnawing hunger turning his stomach to a stone. Now, it was the cold that bit at him instead.

As much as he didn't want to, he couldn't stop his mind from going to Asher, tucked into his pretty bedroom upstairs, warm under his frilly pink covers. Master had even given him a shower.

All Misha had was a toilet.

He wasn't jealous, he *wasn't,* even if it wasn't fair, even if he'd always done everything Master asked and even if he didn't think he deserved to be punished.

But Master knew what he deserved better than he did and wondering why he wasn't worth more would get him nothing but a headache.

Two days.

What was Asher doing now? Was he with Master, learning to be the kind of toy Master wanted? Learning to take Misha's—admittedly unwanted—place? Was Master already planning how to get rid of him?

Misha shuddered at the thought. A new home was one of his biggest fears. No matter how bad things got here, no matter how hungry or sore he was, at least he knew the rules. Master didn't like marking up his toys, so while his beatings hurt, they didn't leave the gruesome scars some boys carried at the parties.

A spark of anger flickered in his chest. Asher had been upset over something as small as a relatively gentle blow job and a light spanking, treatment Misha would have killed to receive most days. He had no right to yell at Misha like a scorned lover when he'd gotten off so easy.

The sound of the lock tumbling was his only warning before his bedroom door was thrown open, a dark silhouette standing backlit in the frame until it moved, revealing the familiar features.

"Up you get, lazy bones," Master snapped, and Misha hurried to scramble to his feet.

"Yes, sir," he answered and moved quickly to stand in front of the older man, waiting for instructions. He kept his hands folded politely behind his back.

"I'm having some friends over tonight." Master grabbed a fistful of Misha's hair and yanked, tipping his head back. "I want you and Asher to clean the playroom."

Misha shivered, holding back his wince when it tugged on several strands of hair. He hated the playroom and everything it entailed—the toys that would be used on him, the whips and crops and bindings. And Asher... Misha's anger flickered out. Asher would hate it, too, but he didn't have the same defenses Misha did.

He wouldn't know how to sink into that place in his head where he'd be safe. Didn't know which men to avoid if he could, or how to smile when inside he wanted to die. Guilt swarmed Misha like biting flies, nipping at his skin.

* * * *

Asher glared at the boy currently wiping down the leather seat of some weird bench thing in the so-called playroom. "Is your name even Misha?" he finally snapped, unable to keep quiet now that Mr. B had left them alone, locking them inside. Hearing the lock tumble hadn't stopped Asher from yanking at the door anyway.

Misha—or whatever his name was—flinched, dropping his wad of paper towels onto the marble tiles. "It is."

"You're probably lying anyway." Asher stubbornly turned away, clenching his jaw to stop himself from apologizing at the struck look on Misha's face.

After a few seconds, he heard the sound of scrubbing start again, so he stomped to the other side of the room to glare at the weird wooden cross contraption. It had cuffs dangling off it, leather and metal things stained with something dark near the edges. He grabbed it to study, then let it fall with a clank of chain as he moved on.

He kicked the leg of another bench. "What even is all this shit?"

He didn't expect an answer but quietly, Misha said, "That's a spanking bench."

Asher shuddered and took a half-step back. "What the fuck kind of place is this? I should have known you were a pervert. Everyone's a pervert on the Internet." That was probably what made this the worst... He'd known better, everyone talked about Internet safety and stranger danger, and he'd just thought he was *so* much smarter than that. Yet here he was, just another idiot duped by a creep.

Misha didn't answer, though the sound of him cleaning slowed for a second before picking back up. For some reason, that made him even more angry. How could he just...keep cleaning, like this was normal? Like there was nothing wrong with them being locked in a...in a fucking dungeon full of sex equipment...by his *dad*.

Except...he didn't think Mr. B was actually Misha's dad. They didn't look at all alike, to begin with. He remembered thinking that when he had climbed off the bus and seen them waiting. He was such an *idiot*.

Asher spun back around, planting his fists on his hips, the suddenness of the movement making Misha flinch. Not that he *cared,* he reminded himself. "He's not your dad, is he." This time, it wasn't a question, which was great, since Misha didn't answer. He just tucked his head and kept scrubbing at the leather.

Asher saw red. He stomped over until his shadow fell on the smaller boy, who finally stilled, even if he didn't look up. "Do you think this is a game? Do you find it funny? God, why won't you just...fucking...look at me already?" He didn't mean to, but he was so angry that he saw red and the next thing he knew, he was shoving Misha back—not to hurt him, not really. He was just swarming with pent-up anger, and he needed to release it, needed...*something,* and Misha was right there.

A convenient target, as the reason he was here in the first place.

Misha stumbled, falling back onto his ass, lifting his arm immediately to block his face like he thought Asher was going to hit him. To be fair, Asher *wanted* to, but seeing Misha cower away from it made him hesitate.

Instead, he stepped back. "I can't believe you made me think I loved you. Such a fucking *joke.*"

He didn't know what came over him. Later, he might be able to analyze the thoughts that led to him grabbing the industrial size gallon of what he thought was sanitizer and popping the lid off. He could tell himself he didn't think it was a big deal...that it would clean up easily...that Misha *deserved* it... But in the moment, it was like someone else took control of his limbs.

So he twisted off the lid and watched himself pour the clear, viscous liquid over the entire surface of the bench, watched the sticky fluid seep into the stitching and run down onto the floor to puddle around Misha's knees. He dropped the empty bottle. It landed with a soft *plop* in the puddle.

It wasn't sanitizer, he noticed absently. Sanitizer smelled too strong, and this was odorless, but it was also thicker than it should be, stringy and sticky. *Lube,* he realized, his stomach sinking slightly.

Before he could even consider trying to clean it, the door behind Misha opened, Mr. B strolling in, only to pause at the sight.

He knew how it looked...Misha on his knees, the jug on the floor just beside him, lube spilling everywhere and Asher standing over it all.

Mr. B looked at both of them, his eyes narrowing, looking angry for the first time. Asher cringed, taking a half-step away before the man thundered, "Stop!" He froze where he stood. "Who is responsible for this?"

Asher glanced toward Misha. The other boy was shaking, his skin nearly white, eyes wide.

"I see," Mr. B said, his voice icy. "The strap, Misha."

Misha, despite the tears spilling down his face, didn't hesitate. He pushed himself up and moved to a chest of drawers against the wall, pulling out a vicious-looking braided leather...thing. It was too wide and short for a whip, too rope-like for a crop but like no strap Asher had ever seen before. Misha carried it back and held it out with shaking hands.

Asher wished he could say he didn't understand...that he didn't realize Mr. B had taken his silence and his glance toward Misha as an answer, but he did. He knew what Mr. B was thinking but he let him continue, unwilling to risk the punishment. He might have poured the jug, but *wasn't* it Misha's fault? If Misha hadn't roped him in, hadn't talked him into 'running away to be with him forever', *none* of this mess would have happened.

Why should he be punished for being angry over something he had *every* right to be pissed about?

But then Mr. B took the strap with his right hand and grabbed Misha by the throat with his left, and Asher's convictions wavered. Mr. B shoved Misha over the sticky bench hard enough that only the fact that it was screwed down kept it from sliding. Then, he gripped the waistband of Misha's shorts and dragged them down, revealing a slew of purplish bruises already marring the pale skin.

Asher couldn't go through with it. He stepped forward and blurted, "It was my fault. I did it. I poured it out because I was angry."

Rather than cooling him down, though, Asher's admission seemed to make Mr. B even more angry. He shoved Misha's face into the leather bench and growled for him to stay put, then straightened up. He grabbed a fistful of Asher's T-shirt and yanked him close.

"I can't abide a boy who lies," Mr. B said, releasing his shirt to grab Asher's chin in a tight grip instead.

"I never lied," Asher protested immediately, against his smarter judgment. Misha hissed an unspoken warning that Asher should have listened to. Instead, Asher doubled down. "I didn't. I didn't say *anything.*"

A vicious glint lit Mr. B's eyes, and Asher barely saw his hand tighten on the strap before it was moving, striking him across the shoulders with a stinging *crack.* Once, twice then Mr. B slapped his palm across Asher's face. His head jerked to the side before the pain even registered. He cowered, waiting for another hit that didn't come.

Instead, Mr. B yanked him back to his feet and shoved the strap into his hand, spinning him toward Misha. "Hit him."

Asher flinched, the only thing keeping him from dropping the strap the fear of what Mr. B would do if he did. "I...I can't!"

"You give him ten stripes or I give him twenty," Mr. B threatened.

"It's not his fault," Asher whined, his hand shaking. He couldn't *hit* Misha, no matter how mad he was.

Mr. B struck him again and he felt his lip split where his tooth caught it, the taste of copper staining his tongue. The man yanked the strap from his loose fingers and, with a vicious twist of his wrist, brought the braided leather down onto Misha's ass.

Asher flinched harder at the sound of the crack than Misha did, despite the fiery red welt that immediately raised. Mr. B lifted his arm to swing again, but Asher leaped forward. "I'll do it." Surely, ten hits from him would be better than twenty from Mr. B, especially if Mr. B was going to do it so hard.

The strap was pressed into Asher's hand, but while he noticed its heavy weight, he was otherwise numb to the texture. He couldn't feel anything...not the stinging pain across his chest he knew was there or the slice in his lip or swollen cheek...just the panic swelling in his chest holding down his lungs.

He couldn't hit Misha, but he didn't have a choice.

He wished someone would take over his body now, lay the stripes for him so he didn't have to. Instead, it was all him who raised his arm and let the first strike land, harder than he'd meant to. A second welt crossed the first. It wasn't as red or angry but more painful in his mind for him being the one who laid it.

"Nine more," Mr. B ordered, giving him no time to stall.

By the time he let the last fall against Misha's skin, the boy was sobbing silently, his shoulders shaking, the knuckles of his right hand shoved into his mouth to smother the sound.

Asher was just glad it was over, his own hands shaking as he dropped them to his sides, the strap dangling.

Except it wasn't over, not even close, because Mr. B just reached down to open the zipper of his pants, and Asher realized it was just the beginning.

* * * *

Master painfully pulled out of Misha's abused ass and let him slide off the bench to the floor. Misha watched his black leather shoes move away with only a parting, "Clean this shit up," before the door slammed shut. He barely had the energy to flinch at the noise.

He wanted to close his eyes and sink back into his safe place for a second, but he couldn't, not until he'd finished the job Master had given him. So, he pushed himself up to his hands and knees, his body screaming. His ears were ringing, until his breathing evened out and he realized it wasn't his ears but Asher speaking.

" —so sorry. I didn't want to do it. You gotta wake up. Talk to me, Misha. Come on," Asher was rambling, and it didn't make sense, because Misha wasn't sleeping. He *was* awake—until he realized that while he'd shifted to his hands and knees, he was still on the floor. With a groan, he sucked in a breath and shoved himself up to his knees.

"Shit, you're bleeding. Come on. Let's get you up." Hands — *Asher's hands, soft, gentle* — picked him up off the floor. He'd been good, staying silent through the lashing, through Master's brutal assault but now, with Asher, he cried out, the pained sound echoing off the walls.

Asher shushed him, but not in a way that seemed mean. It reminded him of being a child, of getting soothed from a nightmare by his mother. He couldn't help leaning into Asher's hands, even though he knew the other boy would want nothing to do with him.

He should be lucky that Asher was even touching him now, that he wasn't bringing him more pain, more punishment. He deserved it. He knew he did.

But instead of pain, instead of leaving him to pick himself up, Asher helped him onto a clean bench, laying him on his side to avoid the worst of the damage. He stayed crouched in front of Misha once he was settled, his lips pulled down in a frown, though his eyes were wide and wet. *Not anger, then, but something like sadness or pity*. He couldn't tell.

Regardless, Asher sighed. "I want to hate you for dragging me into this, but it's hard. I don't know what you got me into, but I have to wonder if you even did it on purpose."

Misha clenched his eyes shut but shook his head, swallowing the sob that grew like a parasite in his throat, smothering his breath. Fingers carded through his hair, and he struggled not to flinch from the soothing gesture. "Just rest here. I'll clean everything up."

"Not...not for too long, though, I just...need a sec. Party tonight," Misha mumbled through stubborn lips. "Just need a second..."

Asher replied, but Misha was already drifting.

* * * *

Misha jerked upright, pain screaming through his body at the sudden movement. He was still on the laminate. It was chilly against his skin. He traced the seams between the slats with a fingertip and breathed through the ache. It was a familiar thing, this feeling upon waking.

What wasn't usual was the warm presence at his side.

Asher knelt beside him, not touching, but his hand stretched out like he'd thought about it. Had he planned on helping Misha up or pushing him back down? To soothe the pain or add to it?

He wouldn't know for sure, might never know, but history told him the latter. Nobody ever touched him without bringing pain, ever only to add injury. So, while he might imagine a helping hand, it was only that...a dream.

With a groan, Misha pushed himself to his feet. He didn't remember pulling his shorts up but they were back in place, the waistband digging into the lash marks on his hips. The first thing he looked to was the bench, thankfully clean of lube. Or at least, as clean as it typically was, since the dark leather always glistened just a bit too much.

"How long...?" Misha asked, trailing off as he debated what to call it. It wasn't sleeping, but not quite passed out.

"A little over an hour, I think," Asher answered. "I think everything's clean, though who the fuck knows what that bastard expects it to look like."

Misha grimaced as he slowly walked around the room, inspecting the work Asher had already done. It was as good as it was going to get, but Master would find something to complain about, anyway. He liked to punish Misha for any imagined slight. Asher might be a shiny new toy, but he doubted Master was going to change his ways.

"I tried the door, but it's still locked," Asher continued, not moving from where he was sitting by the spanking bench.

"He'll let us out when he wants us out." Misha settled carefully on the thinly padded seat of a centurion horse, his ass smarting at the pressure. "*If* he lets us out." With a party that night, he might not. Master found it funny sometimes, drawing out the apprehension.

"He said...there was a party?" Asher said it quietly, a bit lost. "Will it be like last time?"

"Probably not," Misha answered, watching Asher relax immediately and feeling guilty enough to add, "Master was on his best behavior then. He plays...different...in public." Or anywhere he wasn't in complete control.

Asher's shoulders slumped slowly, his confidence crumbling like a rockslide. "So it'll be worse, then?"

Misha shrugged, staring down at his bare feet. The pink nail polish was starting to chip. "It'll be different. He'll have guests, so he likely won't play as hard, but he likes to put on a show." Misha shifted his weight, wincing when the corner of the horse dug into a particularly tender bruise.

"How did you end up here? Since he's not really your dad, I mean?" Asher asked after a long stretch of silence.

Misha shrugged. "My parents brought me over from Russia. My dad had a work visa, and he got to bring me and Mom. They'd just gotten full citizenship when they died in a car crash. I was ten. It's funny what you remember." Misha rubbed the back of his neck, hunching down at the memories. "I don't remember what my mom looked like, just…just the shape of her face. And I remember my dad's voice was always loud, but not what it sounded like. But I remember the lady who came to tell me that they were never coming home clear as day. She had this ugly green sweater with brass buttons, and she wanted to send me back to the motherland to stay with…some cousin I'd never met. I thought I was so lucky when my dad's brother stepped forward to take me." Misha hadn't even known the man was in the US, as his dad had barely ever talked about him. He'd known his name was Urvan, like his grandfather.

"What happened?" Asher asked.

"I thought I was going to the zoo, but my uncle gave me to Master, and I've been here ever since." Misha condensed the sordid story down to a single sentence.

"Some uncle," Asher grumbled. Misha looked up just to see Asher glare at the floor.

"Yeah." He didn't know what else to say.

Asher apparently didn't, either. But though he stayed silent, he moved over to the centurion horse and sat beside Misha. When he grasped his hand, Misha didn't pull away.

Chapter Nine

Now

As a Penetration Tester for the National Security Agency, Ryder got to do the thing he was good at — hacking — without finding himself locked up in a maximum-security prison somewhere. It was a win-win, especially since he only *got* the job in the first place because the other option was prison.

Apparently, the NSA didn't particularly like being hacked, especially by dumb seventeen-year-old kids. But he could still remember the look on the agents faces who had shown up at his hotel room to arrest him and found him sitting on his couch in footie pajamas eating Cheetos and watching *Paw Patrol* to de-stress.

So instead of Juvie, he had gotten a conditional job offer the day he'd become a legal adult. The best part was that most days, he could work from home. It was the only reason he hadn't gotten fired less than six months after receiving his first paycheck, when he'd packed up everything and moved to Texas to chase a lead, then packed up again to follow Mason to Seattle when that lead had fallen through.

Unfortunately, he couldn't work from home all the time. Occasionally, there were days like today, when mandatory meetings dragged him to the cryptologic center in Colorado to do things he couldn't talk about to anybody. It was kind of fun, like being a spy, and if it didn't mean putting the search for his brother on hold while he was gone, he'd enjoy it, especially since Mason never made him take the trips alone.

He couldn't wait to get home.

This trip had been harder than normal because it involved assisting the FBI in hacking into the online presence of a cartel down in Texas that was suspected of both drug and sex trafficking. Cases like that always drained him, since he couldn't' help but think of his brother being caught up in one. He was just grateful that he'd heard they were getting close to making some arrests.

"Can we have 'little' time?" Ryder asked Mason as he pulled onto their street and their house came into view, a lovely suburban number that looked like it came out of a catalog. Mason had bought it for them the week they'd gotten married, upgrading from his bachelor pad in the city.

"Of course. I've got nuggies for you in the freezer," Daddy said agreeably. He never minded when Ryder needed 'little' time unexpectedly, not the way he did when Ryder went 'big' too early — probably because he knew Ryder needed this time to de-stress. He was always looking out for Ryder.

"Thank you, Daddy."

"You never have to thank me, buddy." Mason parked the car in the garage and climbed out. Ryder waited patiently in his seat for Daddy to round the front and come to his side to unbuckle him and help him out.

Ryder gripped his hand and let Daddy help him up the few stairs into the house, standing still while Daddy tugged off his shoes. "Go wash your hands, buddy. I'll get your nuggies and tots into the oven."

Mason watched Ryder skip back to the bathroom, finally free of the heaviness that had seemed to drag down his shoulders to a slump the whole plane ride back to Seattle. His husband might be young in body, but he bore the weight of years of worry.

The dinosaur-shaped nuggets and smiley fries went into the oven and chocolate milk into a sparkly pink sippy cup that he carried into the living room — not the one they used for guests, with its leather armchairs and carefully fluffed pillows, but the smaller one off the dining room.

Mason set the sippy cup on the *Paw Patrol* activity table, straightening up the scattered coloring books while he was there. Ryder came in when he was dragging over a bright blue bean bag chair.

"Hey, buddy. Why don't you color me a picture while I go check on dinner?"

"Okay, Daddy." Ryder plopped down on the squishy chair with a giggle, and Mason couldn't help smiling. 'Little' Ryder was so different from his focused, determined husband that sometimes he felt like a different person. Mason counted his blessings every morning he woke up with the boy in his arms that he'd taken a wrong turn that day in Dallas on the way to a new client meeting.

He couldn't imagine his life without Ryder.

He'd never expected his soulmate would be a man twenty years his junior. He'd known he was a Daddy, though, since he'd been eighteen himself, and it wasn't like he was a stranger to age-gap relationships. His mother was twenty-two years older than his dad. Mom always called him her miracle baby. Mason knew he was a happy accident.

Mason put the nuggets and fries on a plate, adding a few carrots he knew Ryder would whine about and a liberal squirt of ranch, then carried it back out to his husband. Ryder's tongue stuck out from between his lips as he concentrated on staying between the lines.

"What do we want to watch today, buddy?"

"Princess," Ryder corrected without looking up.

"Sorry, Princess. What do you want to watch?"

"Wanna watch water movie."

"*The Little Mermaid*?" Mason suggested, crouching by the table.

"No! Water movie with ocean and chicken." Ryder slammed his crayon on the table and pouted.

"*Moana*?" Mason switched gears easily, knowing that mood swings were common when Ryder was 'little', as he let go of the control he kept so tightly the rest of the time.

"Yep." Ryder smiled brightly and went back to coloring, so Mason got the movie all set up.

"Okay, Princess. Eat your dinner, then I want you to lie down and watch the movie, okay?"

"Don't wanna lie down." Ryder jutted his lip out again.

"If you don't lie down during the movie, you'll have to lie down without one afterward."

"Not fair." Ryder shoved the last nugget in his mouth and lifted the plate to lick up the last of the ranch. Mason, who couldn't stand the stuff, grimaced but didn't argue. He had to pick his battles, and salad dressing wasn't worth it.

"Them's the rules, Princess." Mason ruffled Ryder's long hair, now free from its bun. The curly locks fell to his shoulders in a tangled mess. "Want Daddy to brush your hair before you lie down?"

Ryder thought about it for several seconds before he finally nodded. Mason went into the bathroom and grabbed the pink princess brush from the drawer and some strawberry scented detangler.

"Remember, Princess. You have to sit still so I don't pull it."

"Yes, Daddy. I be good boy." Ryder made a show of sitting super still.

He must have been even more stressed than Mason realized to regress this far. Mason changed his plans for the next few days to compensate, since likely it would take his boy a bit longer to come out of it than usual. Instead of the steak he'd planned for tomorrow, he would make spaghetti carbonara instead. It was enough like 'little' food that it wouldn't be too jarring.

Mason settled behind Ryder and began brushing his hair, humming along to the familiar songs while he worked the tangles free.

Chapter Ten

Now

Asher glared at his shattered reflection in the mirror. Applying eyeliner through half-a-dozen spiderwebbed cracks wasn't easy — or quick, or particularly neat. "Here... You do it," Asher finally snapped, holding the black pencil out to Misha.

"Are you sure that's a good idea?" Misha hesitantly took it from him, his fingers still slightly swollen from the loss of circulation. Twelve hours left dangling by his wrists would do that to a person.

"Can't do worse than I'm doing." Asher closed his eyes and tipped his face up for Misha. A few minutes of hesitation, then he felt the liner press against the corner of his eye and start working a line along his eyelid.

In the years since Asher had become a prisoner in this mansion, Misha had helped him with his makeup more times than he could count, and every time it felt just as intimate. Misha finished one eye and moved to the other, but when he was finished, he didn't pull away, his hand lingering on Asher's cheek.

Asher couldn't resist turning his face and pressing his lips to Misha's palm for the barest of seconds. He knew better to enjoy the forbidden touch for long. Master's house, Master's rules. The two of them could only play together under Master's orders, only touch when Master allowed it.

Only love when Master wasn't looking.

It was true what he'd always heard—hate and love were two sides of the same coin, and he couldn't have told anyone when it had flipped for him—when he'd gone from loathing the sight of the other boy to not wanting to let him out of it.

It hadn't taken long.

A few months, half a year.

"We have to go." Misha voice was quieter than ever, barely more than a whisper. Asher dreaded the day it went away completely, crushed by the terrible weight pressing down on their shoulders, threatening to swallow them.

They were two mice in an endless maze, two flies in a web—two wheels on a stationary bike, endlessly spinning but going nowhere.

"I know."

A door slammed somewhere downstairs, and they both flinched. The eyeliner fell to the floor with a quiet clatter as they both twisted to stare at the door, Asher's heart thudding as he watched the knob. When it didn't turn, he loosed a sigh of relief that was echoed by Misha's.

"Come on." Asher straightened. And, though he wanted to take Misha's hand, he slipped past him carefully without touching. He'd risked a beating for both of them already with the brush of his lips on Misha's palm, if Master chose to peruse the cameras.

Misha trailed him out into the hall like a shadow. One of Master's bodyguards — or prison wardens, as Asher liked to think of them — leaned against the wall opposite their door, scrolling through his cell phone. Briefly, Asher imagined snatching the phone from his hands and calling the police, pictured the dramatic, cinema-worthy rescue of SWAT storming the estate, but it was just that — fiction.

After all, the bodyguard would evade him easily and all he'd end up with was few bruises or broken bones. And, even if he did manage to get the phone *and* call the police *and* they managed to triangulate his location since he didn't know the address, he couldn't trust the cops anyway. He knew of at least one, some ruddy-faced man with a bloated belly, who liked to show up to Master's parties in full uniform and thought it was hot to make the pair of them suck him off while staring at his badge.

He could recite the shield number by memory.

If one cop was dirty, they all could be, so he turned his back on the guard and headed downstairs, Misha pressed so tight to his back that he could feel the other boy breathing.

In and out, fast and shallow.

He wished he could grab Misha's hand.

The party went as it usually did. He and Misha put on a show for Master's friends, where he struggled to ignore the catcalls and hooting. At least a lot had been in Spanish lately, so even though he got the gist of what they said, the words slipped by. Ever since Master had hosted a rare, closed-door meeting without Misha and him to please his guests, there'd been more strangers than usual—men who spoke rapid Spanish and wore heavy chains and bandanas.

If Asher had to stereotype, which he supposed he didn't but couldn't resist, he'd guess they were in some kind of gang. All that mattered was Master seemed concerned with their satisfaction—and what Master wanted, Master got.

After their usual performance, which hit with its typical aplomb, since the creepy men who attended Master's parties loved to watch a pair of nearly identical boys get it on for their amusement, they circled the area, giving blow jobs and more to whoever asked while Master held congress in another room. There was going to be an auction later, Asher learned, where men bored of their current slaves could sell them off or trade them away.

Part of him feared that Master had brought them along to do the same. The older man had seemed distant and cold, more so than usual, his fuckings more perfunctory and his beatings impersonal. As much as Asher wanted out, a new owner wouldn't fix anything, especially not if he and Misha ended up separated.

He forced himself to bury the thought and the fear. He couldn't change it, and a bad performance here would only help make up Master's mind if he was still on the fence.

Master returned later in the evening with a stranger at his side, a tall man with the body of a runner—sleek and lithe, like he should be wearing a suit in place of the faded jeans and leather jacket. He'd never been to one of these parties before. Asher would have remembered. He had dark, brooding eyes and a sharply trimmed beard that only emphasized his strong jaw.

In other circumstances, he'd have found him attractive. Now, he saw the breadth of his shoulders and weight of his hand as only a warning. He could break Asher's arm in a too-tight grip.

"Boys." Master snapped his fingers, gesturing to the floor in front of his feet. Asher scrambled off the lap he was sitting on, holding back the pained wince as the man slipped out of his body too quickly in Asher's haste to obey Master. He slammed to his knees at Master's feet, ducking his face obediently to wait for orders. Misha dropped beside him a half-second after, his chest heaving. "This is my new friend, Mr. Ten. You can call him 'Sir'. He's going to call you bitch, or slut, or whatever he wants. Make him feel good."

Asher looked up just enough to see Master give the man a friendly slap on the shoulder. "Can I take them somewhere a bit more private? I prefer to play with my toys without an audience." Ten leered down at them. "I want to give them a test drive before I drop any cash. I have...specific tastes."

Master laughed. "Sure. There's a room set aside for private play. Misha here" — Master reached down and yanked on Misha's hair — "will show you."

Asher fought his immediate desire to yank Misha away from both men and shield him with his own body. Misha, always obedient Misha, just stood, smiled and led the man out of the room. Asher must have moved too slowly for Master's taste, because the bastard kicked him, the toe of his shoe digging sharply into Asher's side. "Stupid boy, go with them."

Asher scrambled to his feet and followed Misha down the hall to the room set aside for just this purpose. It wasn't truly private. Master had cameras everywhere.

He was slower to kneel than Misha, clumsier in his presentation. Any punishments Ten wanted to dole out, he would accept if it kept Misha from feeling his fists.

But no blows landed, and the man didn't reach for his belt and zipper. Instead, he crouched in front of them. "Can you tell me your names?"

"Whatever you want them to be," Misha answered immediately.

"No, your *real* names," Ten said, his voice surprisingly kind.

Tension split the silence before Asher finally spoke up. "I'm Asher, and he's Misha."

"Nice to meet you both. I don't want you to be scared. I'm not going to hurt you. We just need to kill enough time to make this believable." Ten smiled, not moving to grab or pinch or prod. Asher's mind raced as he tried to come up with an explanation, but nothing made sense. Thank goodness the man spoke quietly enough that Asher doubted the mics, if there were any, would pick it up, because the last thing he needed was Master thinking he was in some way conspiring with whoever this man really was.

"There are cameras," Asher said without thinking, hoping he wasn't making things worse for either of them. "I don't know if there are mics, too, but he's probably already watching."

Ten's eyes narrowed, darting from one corner of the ceiling to the lamp on the nightstand by the bed, probably looking for them. Asher glanced toward the mirror, then toward the picture frame over the mattress, where he knew at least two were hidden.

The man lowered his voice further. "Then I guess we'll have to put on a show. But I'm going to make you a promise. I will not hurt you and there will be no penetration—just an act for the camera. Can you both play along?"

Asher glanced to Misha, who gave a small nod. Asher wasn't so quick to agree. "Why? What's in it for you?" He was no longer a naïve eighteen-year-old trusting strangers on the Internet.

"I can't tell you, but I need you to trust that I won't hurt you." Ten looked toward Misha and added, "Either of you."

Unfortunately, Asher wasn't big on trust anymore. He'd go along with it because Master had told him to obey, but he wasn't getting brought down with this man if something went wrong. He'd keep his cards close to the chest and his options open, on guard for both him and Misha.

Chapter Eleven

The two boys might have a similar appearance, but Tennyson could see already that their personalities were nothing alike. Misha, the smaller of the pair, was as submissive as they came. If he had to guess, he'd say the boy had been there the longest, long enough to have the fight beaten out of him — probably literally.

He knew that what he was about to do would likely traumatize them even further, but he didn't have a choice, not if there really were cameras in the room, which he didn't doubt. He had to make this believable — not just for the case, but to make sure that all three of them made it out alive and in one piece.

He'd barely managed to talk his superiors into holding off on raiding the party as it was, after he'd learned of a brothel offsite with even more victims. If they stormed the premises now, they might never find that location. They were too close to the finish line to risk everything out of good intentions.

Still, knowing why he was doing it didn't make the simulated sex feel any less *dirty* — not when he saw the way Misha's eyes glazed over just going through the motions, a clear sign of dissociation, nor when he felt the way Asher's muscles tensed like steel cords under his skin as Tennyson pinned him down.

He forced himself to spend over an hour with them, doing whatever he could to make it look realistic. He was never more grateful when knuckles wrapped on the door and he was able to drag his jeans over his hips, leaving them unzipped as he crossed the room to yank it open.

Henry Barnes stood in the doorway, leering at the disheveled boys Tennyson had left on the mattress. "Up to your standards?"

He plastered on a leer. "Not bad at all. Not sure they warrant the money you're asking for, but if you're willing to negotiate?" A real buyer would haggle and bargain, so that's what he did, though he'd happily have paid twice what they'd agreed on, of his own money instead of the Bureau's, if it meant getting the broken boys free from the bastard's clutches.

"I'm willing. I've got a newer model coming in on a ship from...well, somewhere. All those little countries sound the same. It'd be nice to have an empty house when he arrives." Barnes didn't seem to notice the small whimper from the bed, but Tennyson did. He had to force himself to ignore it.

They agreed on a number with less haggling than Tennyson expected, and he made arrangements for the money to be sent over the following day to an overseas account. As soon as he came back for the boys and got them safely off the property, the FBI would have enough evidence to take Barnes down and, hopefully, the trafficking ring with him. It wasn't the drug charges they were expecting, but where there was smoke, there was fire. With the evidence they had, a warrant to search the premise would be easy to get.

Maybe their luck had finally broken.

As much as it killed him to leave the boys in the 'tender' care of Barnes, he didn't have a choice. Pushing to take them now would mean using his personal accounts. If he was confident the FBI would still be able to trace the funds, he'd do it in a heartbeat, but he couldn't risk putting the case in jeopardy just to cut a few hours off the timeline. He'd just have to trust that Barnes wouldn't hurt the boys too much on their final night together.

Out of sight of the estate, he broke down and dialed his handler. Romero answered on the third ring. Tennyson didn't even let him get out a greeting. "I need a hundred and fifty grand transferred to this account by tomorrow morning." He rattled off the account number and the rest of the details, then added, "I'll also need a safe house set up for the boys. Until the case is settled, we can't risk anything happening to them."

"You got it, boss. I'll make sure it's all taken care of. You have no idea how happy I'll be to have this all behind us."

* * * *

Tennyson arrived five minutes early in his motorcycle boots, even if he was driving an Escalade, with an audio transmitter tucked into his pocket and a rock in his stomach. It wasn't the first time he'd traded cash for goods to break a case, but he didn't think he'd ever get used to handing over payment for real, living persons. He wondered if this was what the agent who had rescued his dad had felt like, back when Tennyson had still been a kid and his dad had been held for ransom. That agent was the reason Liam had gotten his degrees in psychology and finance, and why he'd worked so hard to learn Spanish.

Taking a deep breath, he reminded himself of all the other stings he'd completed, the successes and failures. He wound the memories of all the people he'd saved — the ones he knew and the ones he didn't — with the years of trainings. Then, as calm as he could get, he knocked on the estate door and allowed himself to be led inside to a sitting room.

He memorized the floor plan so he could make a quick getaway if needed. His phone was on vibrate in his pocket, with plans in place for Romero — who was listening in a van a block away to not only the audio transmitter but to the half-dozen bugs Tennyson had managed to plant the night before at the party — to call only if there was an emergency. He was as ready as he was going to get.

Which was not ready enough. When Barnes came into the room, the fear on the two boys' faces as they followed struck him like a hammer. It was nearly impossible to stay impassive when all he could see was the red-rimmed eyes and tear stains.

Instead, he had to paste on a leer and look to Barnes. "While I don't get why you'd give up such a pretty matching set, your loss is my gain. I can't wait to get them home."

"Then I shouldn't keep you." Barnes laughed and reached out for a handshake, which Tennyson was happy to oblige, if only because it got him out of there sooner. "Tell you what. Take the week off, yeah? Break 'em in, and show them who the boss is. Maybe send a few pics if you're feeling particularly satisfied."

Barnes reached over to the smaller boy and pinched his cheek hard enough that the skin blossomed red. "Look at you boys, all grown up and ready to leave the coop." The boisterous laugh made Tennyson want to clench his fists, but he managed to restrain himself, if barely.

Every second of idle chat felt like torture, but finally, Barnes glanced at his watch and announced he had a meeting starting soon. Tennyson knew Romero was listening in the surveillance van a block over. If Barnes left the estate before SWAT was called in, Romero would make sure he was tailed to the next location. All Tennyson had to worry about was getting the two boys out safely.

He regretted that he couldn't give them any reassurances, not even a smile, to avoid tipping Barnes off that something wasn't right. Instead, he grabbed each boy by the collar with a grip that looked harsher than it was and half-dragged them out to the Escalade, securing them in the backseat.

The child locks were activated, so he wasn't worried that either of them would take a leap into traffic if he slowed at a light, but he wasn't thrilled at having them at his back while he was driving. He had to trust that their sense of self-preservation outweighed their fear of the unknown long enough for him to explain.

He climbed into the front seat and started the car, backing carefully through the open gate and onto the road. He'd planned on driving straight to the safe house, a pay-by-the-hour motel near the airport, but soft sobbing from the rear had him hesitating. In the end, he kept going, ignoring his desire to pull over and offer comfort in favor of safety.

He couldn't spot any tails but that didn't mean there wasn't one, and until he was able to call Romero, he had no way of knowing how the arrests had gone. Barnes could be safely in custody or on the streets seeking revenge.

Asher sat frozen against the door as Misha cried. Everything inside him screamed at him to gather Misha up and wipe away his tears, but he couldn't bring himself to move. Their new Master had seemed kind at the party, at least in his willingness to only pantomime sex, but Asher knew better than anyone that appearances could be misleading. There were a million reasons why the man could have only *pretended* to fuck him, the vast majority of them easily explained away by shyness or performance anxiety.

When they got wherever they were going, there was no doubt in Asher's mind that it wouldn't end well for either of them. There was nothing he could say to reassure Misha, and he was afraid of touching him without permission, without knowing the rules or the consequences for breaking them. He felt...paralyzed. He might as well have been in cuffs and spreader bars for all the control he had over his body

But when Misha's chest started heaving and he was literally shaking, gasping out air faster than he can bring it in, Asher knew he didn't have a choice. Whatever the consequences, he'd have to accept them. With fear dusting over his skin and standing his hair on end, he made himself move.

Scooting over to the middle, he laid his hand on Misha's wrist, circling his thumb over his pulse. It was a familiar motion, one they did often when they weren't allowed to talk but needed to provide reassurance.

Misha's shaking slowed...but not enough. Keeping an eye on their new Master, whose eyes intensely scanned the road, Asher slid even closer. He switched Misha's wrist to his left hand and lifted his right to the base of Misha's neck, stroking over it. Misha slumped almost immediately against him, digging his head into Asher's shoulder.

Quietly, Asher started humming the melody to Misha's favorite song, a lullaby from his childhood that Asher had never heard until Misha had sung it for him once. He knew he wasn't getting it completely right, but it must have been close enough, because Misha's breathing finally slowed.

He wasn't surprised that Misha was freaking out. Except for trips with Master, Misha hadn't left the property since he'd been a child. As terrified as Asher was, Misha'd had it so much worse. Even a certainty of pain was less scary than an uncertain future.

He should have been paying attention to the drive, and a small part of him knew it was careless not to. When they pulled into the lot of a motel, he couldn't have said the first thing about where they were or how they'd gotten there.

Now Asher found himself shaking as well. A motel meant a few things, none of them good. Was Ten not from Austin? Asher had been here three or four years — he'd lost track of the days early on — but some tiny part of him still clutched to a bit of hope that *someone, somehow* was going to find him. His brother, maybe, since he doubted his parents cared to look for him. If they left Austin, that last connection he had to his home would disappear.

Who would find him then?

When Ten opened the back door, he wasn't alone. The man with him was a bit younger — no steel in his hair — a bit rounder and a *lot* redder. From the stubble on his scalp to his sunburned cheeks, everything was red.

"These are the witnesses?"

"Yeah. We need to get them inside," the man called Ten replied, his voice gruff.

Sucking in a breath and holding it helped slow the shaking but did nothing to lessen the fear of what was about to happen. At least with Master he knew, to some extent, what the limits were.

Now, with this man, everything was changing — the rules, the expectations. He wanted to take Misha's hand and run...away from these men and this hotel. They could find an alley to camp in for a day or two — or a bridge. It wouldn't be the worst place they'd slept, not even the most dangerous. And unlike back in Delaware, even in winter the nights here never got *too* cold.

They were survivors, and they could make it. Scrounging food from dumpsters would keep them fed, well enough anyway. It couldn't be worse than the fetid oatmeal they lived on most days now. He could blow a few men for enough cash to get a pair of bus tickets.

He didn't stop to think further. When their new master and his friend stepped back, feigning kindness in their voices as they asked them to get out of the car, Asher obeyed, but he gripped Misha's hand tight and squeezed.

As soon as they were both on the sidewalk, he took off, dragging Misha along with him. The two men shouted, and their steps pounded the pavement behind him, but he knew better than to look.

He'd run track in middle school, but it was little help to him now. Pure adrenaline kept them moving.

He didn't know where they were, and the stores were mostly chain things, except for some discount tire store up ahead. He yanked on Misha's hand, tugging him across the busy street, ignoring the horn from an SUV that narrowly avoided them.

On the other side, he risked a glance behind him, hope blaring when he couldn't see the two men anymore. They'd made it.

Or so he thought, until he went to turn around and slammed face first into a stone-like chest, hands clamping tight down on his arms.

Chapter Twelve

The city was so big, so *much* bigger than Misha could ever have imagined. Nothing like the bits and pieces he remembered of his hometown back in Russia or the small suburb of the large city his parents had moved him to when they'd immigrated. In the car with Master, he rarely got to look out of the windows. Sometimes he could steal a glance or two while the older man was busy on a call or something.

Only Asher's hand in his kept him moving, though they'd barely crossed the street and his lungs were already heaving, filled with a burning fire. He couldn't keep enough breath to ask where they were going, but the fear of the punishment for running kept him moving forward, even when he knew that if he let go — let *Asher* go — the other boy might make it out.

It was selfish of him.

He'd almost talked himself into uncurling his fingers and stepping back into the crowd, letting himself get left behind, when Asher slammed to a stop in front of him, tearing his hand free by accident. Misha stumbled, falling to his knees on the rough sidewalk. He smothered a cry as he felt his skin tear open, red seeping from the scrapes.

Slowly, his heart thrumming like a bass string in his chest, he looked up. Then up and up, cringing when he saw Asher in their new Master's clutches, fear plain on Asher's pale face. Despite that, he was struggling to pull away.

"Run, Misha!" Asher cried to him, but Misha couldn't. He couldn't leave the other boy behind to save himself.

Misha wished he were brave.

If it were Misha in the man's clutches and Asher free, *he* wouldn't be cowering on the sidewalk like a child, sniveling over scraped knees and frozen with fear. He'd...he'd kick Ten in the balls or scratch at his face or...or *something*.

But it was too late for Misha to try, because the red-faced man was looming over him now, looking down on him with a frown. "Well, boys, I hope you know how much I hate running. You're lucky you didn't get run over."

Misha wished he could melt into a puddle on the sidewalk at the disappointed tone, but then flinched as the man reached out, waiting for the smack that never came. Instead, the man's hand just...stayed there, open. Like he was waiting for something, and it took Misha too long to realize the guy was waiting for him to grab it.

Slowly, waiting for the trick, he grasped it and the man tugged him to his feet. He and Asher were marched back across the street—this time using a crosswalk. The man gripping Misha's wrist unlocked one of the doors on the first floor of the motel then they were brought inside.

As soon as the red-faced man released him, Misha's training kicked in. He dropped to his knees at the foot of the bed, crossed his wrists behind his back and tipped his face to the floor.

The room stayed silent for several moments, then their new Master crouched in front of him. He used a finger to tip Misha's face up.

"Don't touch him!" Asher hollered from the door, where he struggled now in the red-faced man's grip. Misha forced himself to keep his gaze fixed on their new Master and not on the struggle, knowing he could only help Asher by keeping Master's attention on him.

"You don't need to be afraid anymore. You're safe now," Master said gently, ignoring Asher's shout, even though he *did* take his fingers from Misha's skin.

Misha shuddered. Safe? He didn't even know what 'safe' was.

"That's Officer Newman. He works for the Austin police department. My name is Special Agent Liam Tennyson. I work for the FBI," Master said, and immediately Asher went silent and still, though Misha didn't know why. He didn't know what that meant, and perhaps the man could tell. "It means I work for the government to get criminals, like Barnes, off the streets."

Misha bit his lip until he tasted copper. He didn't believe him. *Couldn't* believe him, because then when it turned out to be a lie, the disappointment would wreck him.

Asher clearly believed him, though, because his face split in a wide, almost manic, grin and the other man finally let him go. "Did you guys arrest that fucker?"

Misha sucked in a breath at the thought. He hated Master, hated what the man had done to him, but for the past decade, Master had been the only thing standing between him and death. Every drop of water, every ounce of food had all come from his hand.

A belt tightened around Misha's throat, smothering his breath, and sweat beaded on his brow. "But...if he's gone, who will take care of us?" The words came out like broken glass.

Master — *was* he still their Master, if he was here just to get criminals off the street? Or did he think Misha and Asher were criminals, too? — frowned. "He never took care of you, Misha. He used you and he broke you, and for that he's going to spend a long, *long* time in prison — *if* he doesn't get the chair. You and Asher are going to be just fine. I promise."

Misha's muscles went weak, and he fell back on his butt, tugging his scraped knees to his chest as he shook his head. He wasn't going to be just fine. What was he supposed to do?

Living with Master was painful and terrifying, but it meant a roof over his head and food — even if it wasn't the best — in his belly. He'd lived with Master longer than his parents.

What was he supposed to do *now*? Asher could go home. He had parents out there, a family who probably missed him — a brother somewhere, a college fund in trust. Asher would leave him.

What was Misha supposed to do *then*?

Rather than reassure, Tennyson's words seemed to send the boy spiraling even further. Liam shot Officer Newman a harried look for help, but the man just shrugged, tugging his phone out and staring pointedly at the screen. But the other boy, Asher, approached slowly, cautiously—looking at every moment like he was waiting for Tennyson to hit him. He squatted beside Misha and, draping his arm over the smaller boy's shoulders, hummed something under his breath.

"Are you guys hungry?" Liam finally asked, unsure what else to do. He couldn't force the boys to believe him and only time would convince them that he was safe. But maybe, food would help.

He'd rescued a stray mutt once, as a child, coaxing it closer with purloined bits of bacon and pilfered lunchmeat, until it had finally allowed him to pet his ratty fur. He hadn't been allowed to keep the animal, since his mother was allergic, but they'd found it a nice home with an older couple down the street.

The younger boy, Misha, didn't answer, but Asher, after several seconds of glaring, finally gave a jerky nod.

"What kind of food do you like? We can get just about anything delivered. Italian, Chinese... You can even get breakfast for dinner if you—" Liam said, but then Misha interrupted.

"No oatmeal!" the boy cried, then flinched like he expected to get struck.

"Okay, okay," Liam hurried to reassure him, mentally marking that for the future. He didn't know what the reason was for the violent reaction, but it was clearly traumatic. "How about spaghetti? Do you like spaghetti?"

Misha shrugged, then nodded.

Maybe it was just the situation, but something about the young man awakened instincts in Liam that he'd let lie dormant for years. He hadn't felt the need to find a submissive for years, not since his previous long-term relationship during the last decade. It had ended poorly, with Greg accusing him of hovering too much but also, at the same time, somehow not being strict enough to be a '*real*' Daddy.

"What about you?" Liam turned to the taller boy. "How do you feel about spaghetti?"

"What do I have to do for it?" Asher countered, his sharp edges showing through the words. "I'm not going to blow you."

Liam bit down his instinctive response, the one that demanded he take the challenge the boy so obviously laid. "The only thing you have to do is tell me what food you'd like. If you don't want spaghetti, we can order in burgers or sushi or something else. I don't expect you to do anything to earn it."

"I don't believe you," Asher said immediately, and his words were blunt with honesty, even if his skin paled with fear.

"That's okay." Liam knew he couldn't expect trust from them, not now — maybe not ever — with everything they'd gone through. But it was important that he try, because he knew they'd eventually need someone in their corner.

It was likely they were going to have to testify.

Against Barnes, specifically, unless by some miracle he accepted a plea deal the state was unlikely to offer, but against the other cartel members as well, once the FBI had gotten their statements. Romero had reported their location to the Bureau when he'd arranged for the safehouse, and Liam was expecting a whole host of agents to descend on the place over the next week, from Victims' Advocacy Specialists to their contacts in the DEA. Soon, the boys would be overwhelmed with questions while they tried to put the final touches on the case they'd been building for years, to get it as airtight as possible.

Then, after all that, they also had to track down the two men's families—if they had them—arrange for mental health support so they could recover from their trauma, figure out if it was safe for them to return home or if they needed to get WITSEC involved for witness protection.

He'd be as involved as the agency let him, but they'd only let him if he could prove it was in the young men's best interests.

It felt like a win when Asher finally answered. "Spaghetti is fine."

* * * *

Officer Newman left at ten that night, his replacement a rookie who spent more time twitching the curtains and fiddling with his plain shirt than watching the sidewalks. Liam wasn't too worried, though. He'd finally heard from Romero, who'd assured him that Barnes and several other key players had been taken in without issue and nobody seemed to suspect that Andrew Tennet was really undercover Special Agent Liam Tennyson.

Which meant, in theory, that nobody was looking for their witnesses quite yet.

Liam looked up from his magazine, unable to stop himself from searching them out. They'd fallen asleep shortly after the food had come. They'd scarfed the spaghetti down like it was their last meal. Or, more likely, as if they didn't know when they would get another one. Then, they'd practically passed out on the double bed near the bathroom, wrapped around each other so tightly that it was hard to tell whose limbs belonged to whom.

He knew it wasn't right, but he couldn't help finding it cute the way Misha's head slotted into the space between Asher's neck and shoulder, or the way Asher's fingers, just the tips, stayed tucked into the waistband of Misha's overly large sweats. Liam had given a pair to each of the boys, making note to get better fitting clothes for them sometime in the next few days.

Sometime after midnight, Liam lay down on top of the comforter on the other bed to get some shuteye, leaving the rookie in charge of keeping watch. As always while on the job, he dropped quickly into sleep.

Later, he couldn't say which sound woke him, if it was the door opening or an engine outside the motel as a car pealed out, but he woke with a start in the hazy light of pre-dawn, his heart thudding.

He stayed still, listening, until he heard the sole of a boot click on the linoleum entryway. He jumped up, rolling free of the mattress, yanking his gun from the holster on his hip with the ease of years of practice.

The long barrel of a silenced gun entered the room first and Liam didn't hesitate, didn't waste time announcing himself or giving up his presence. As soon as the man stepped into the darkened room, his body a silhouette in the doorway, backlit by the streetlamps, Liam fired center mass.

He heard the boys scream at the loud gunshot but didn't have time to reassure them, because the sound of multiple men cursing came from outside. The shooter wasn't alone. From the red bandana tied around the dying man's face, Ten recognized that he was with the cartel.

Tennyson kept his gun aimed on the doorway as he backed toward the mattress, his focus skirting the room. The rookie officer was gone, and Liam cursed.

He should have known better than to trust the Austin PD, but he'd thought they'd been vetted. Neither Newman nor the rookie had any known ties. It should have been safe.

The two boys had scrambled off the mattress and were huddled by the wall, their eyes wide with fear. "Into the bathroom," Tennyson ordered, his voice low. They half-crawled, half-ran to obey, and he followed on their heels, firing off shots at the entryway to stop the others from coming in.

He slammed the bathroom door closed and threw the clumsy sliding latch into the hole in the wall. It wouldn't do much to hamper anyone's entry, but he had nothing else to secure it with. At least he'd already scoped out the room and the motel's surroundings.

"We have to go through the window," Tennyson said, sliding it up as quietly as he could. His army knife made quick work of slicing out the screen before he stepped away. "Asher first. I'll give you a boost. Once you're on the sidewalk, I'll lower Misha down to you. If you see anyone coming around the building, you *run,* okay? You don't wait."

"Run where?" Asher yelped as Tennyson helped boost him through the small window. The boys were tiny enough that it was an easy fit, but it would be a tight squeeze for Tennyson.

He didn't have time to answer, because he could hear the men in the other room already. It wasn't like there was anywhere else for them to go. The only upside was at least they seemed to think the three of them had nowhere to run, because they were yelling mocking insults outside the door instead of busting it down.

Tennyson held onto Asher's wrists as he lowered him down to the sidewalk, then turned to Misha, lifting him through the window feet first and helping him down as well, watching Asher grab the smaller boy by the hips to assist.

Squeezing into the window himself was a feat of flexibility Liam didn't know he had in him, and it was a far from graceful tumble to the ground, but he ignored the gravel that bit into his skin to roll to his feet.

"This way," he quietly urged them farther into the alley. There was no way the parking lot to the motel wasn't being watched, but he hoped they hadn't bothered to put people in the lot of the bar next door.

The first two cars he tried were locked, but the third, a VW Passat in maroon with rust dotting the wheel wells, opened. By now, he knew they'd have found the bathroom empty and would be searching outside. He hurried the boys into the backseat. "Stay down as low as you can. *Don't* look out of the windows. Don't give them anything to shoot at."

He had to ignore the fear on their faces as he slammed the door shut and climbed into the driver's seat to hotwire it.

It rumbled to a stuttering start just as several men in scarlet balaclavas ran into the lot, their guns firing. Bullets sprayed the car, one shattering the passenger side window and narrowly missing him.

They were out of time.

Liam threw the car into drive and jumped the curb to pull into the street, the struts grinding in protest. They couldn't keep this car long. If the gangbangers didn't pick them up, the police would, and, clearly, he couldn't trust them.

He drove it as far as he could, abandoning it in the parking lot of a Walmart off the highway. The boys were silent as corpses in the backseat as he ushered them out, pale and shaking, into a boring black SUV. It was a testament to their trauma that neither of them asked questions.

Chapter Thirteen

Now

"Mason!" Ryder fell off his spinny chair in his hurry to leave the office, but he just pushed back onto his feet and ran to find his husband. "Mason, I found him!"

He hadn't expected it. It was the seventh or eighth time he'd hacked the FBI in the past five years, each time coming up blank, so he hadn't thought it would be different this time. He'd looked more out of boredom and lack of other options than anything, so when Asher's name popped up in a case file, he'd screamed.

Well, not his *full* name, but…it had to be him. How many Asher's in that age range would be in Texas and show up connected to a trafficking ring? It wasn't exactly a common name.

He found Mason in the kitchen just in time to see him drop the gallon of milk he was taking out of the fridge. "You found him? Your brother?" Mason looked shocked.

"In Austin!" Ryder leaped at his husband, who grabbed him from the air and spun him around.

"Oh my God, Ryder, that's amazing! You didn't book a flight or anything yet, did you?"

"Not yet, I just...I can't believe it! I haven't even finished reading the file yet. I saw his name and a description and just...I had to tell you. Will you read it with me?" Now that the initial excitement was dwindling, the situation hit him fully.

They'd found him in a *trafficking* ring, which meant...which meant he'd been somebody's prisoner for the past *five* years, doing...doing.... He couldn't even think of it. Was he forced to run drugs? Beat people up? Or... Or was he one of those people trafficked for *other* things?

He couldn't read it alone.

"Let's go find him, baby."

* * * *

Ryder was certain that, probably, Austin was a lovely city, full of culture and life and all sorts of pretty things, but he couldn't see any of it. Instead, he saw its dark shadows as they disembarked the plane and squeezed into a taxi—he and Mason and enough luggage for an extended stay.

He couldn't believe that he'd found his brother only to immediately lose him again.

The file from the FBI was a mess—or the situation was. It seemed like they'd sent an agent undercover to break up a drug-running ring and uncovered a human trafficking one instead. Somehow, the agent had rescued his brother with some other guy, but then all three of the men—the agent and the two victims—had disappeared. The motel room was empty, a window busted out and bullet holes in the walls the only signs of an altercation.

The police officer, some first-year cop named Finnegan, was claiming that the undercover agent had opened fire on him out of nowhere and he'd had to flee the premises to wait for backup.

Since all the bullets found seemed to match the type of gun standardly issued to agents of the FBI, it was plausible. The cop was thankfully unhurt, but Ryder couldn't care about that when it meant his brother was missing…again.

Thank God Mason owned his own business, since it meant they could pack up and leave for Texas with no warning. And because the business Mason owned was a security firm, they had access to the private jet, the ability to pack as many weapons as his husband thought they'd need in an emergency, along with top-of-the-line surveillance gear. Plus, one of Mason's bodyguards was currently stationed in Austin, protecting the heir to Beckett Industries, so they had a place to stay when they landed.

Ryder had met Shiloh and Gage several months before, shortly after he'd married Mason, in fact. They hadn't been able to meet in person much since, except for the weekend they'd flown down to see Shiloh dance for his opening performance with one of the premier dance companies in the state. Not seeing him in person didn't stop them from texting back and forth quite often, and Shiloh was one of the first people Ryder had texted after he'd figured out what was going on.

And Shiloh hadn't hesitated to offer to let him and Mason camp in their spare room for as long as it took.

They unloaded all their gear into the garage, then Shiloh gave him and Mason a tour of the large house. Ryder tried to pay attention, but he couldn't help thinking of his brother, out in this very city somewhere, with a corrupt FBI agent and no one to save him.

Shiloh must have noticed his distraction, because the next place he led them was a room that was set up as an office. "You can use this while you're here. I bought it to keep up with my college classes, but I ended up hunkered down with a laptop in the den, anyway. I cleared off the desk for you."

Ryder moved silently toward it, unpacking his laptop, his mind racing ahead to what he needed to do next.

"Say 'thank you' to Shiloh, Ryder," Mason said from the doorway, but Ryder wasn't listening. He needed to scour all the dark web chatrooms. An FBI agent didn't snap overnight. If he was dirty, there'd be a trail, and by God, Ryder was going to find it.

"Ryder!" Mason snapped, using his Daddy voice to full effect.

Ryder flinched. "Sorry, Daddy! Thank you for letting me use your office, Shiloh," Ryder hurried to add, knowing that his friend had gone above and beyond and that he should be grateful, even if all he wanted to do was get to work.

"No worries. Um…I have to get going, but Gage and I should be back for dinner. We'll handle cooking."

Mason and Shiloh talked for a few minutes, but Ryder tuned them out, dropping down in front of his freshly reset computer to start his search. At some point, he realized Shiloh had left, but he couldn't have been gone long because Ryder heard him come in what seemed like a few minutes later, saying something about spaghetti that Ryder waved off. He had loads of time until dinner, he was sure of it, and he didn't really care what he ate.

Not until Daddy walked up beside him. "That's enough for the night, buddy."

"No!" Ryder snapped, refusing to look away from the screen. There was nothing, absolutely *nothing* about the agent, Liam Tennyson. As far as Ryder could tell, the man had never been on the dark web, never done anything that hinted he was dirty. The closest thing to a crime he'd ever done—outside of his undercover work, which seemed to have all been approved and within the limits of the law — was a few speeding tickets as a teenager.

"Ryder," Daddy snapped, laying his hand on Ryder's shoulder in warning. "That's enough. You can't work yourself into the grave. It's nearly midnight. I let you work through dinner, but it's time to put the computer away. You can try again tomorrow."

"But..." Ryder's anger leeched out of him, his tears spilling instead. He hadn't been on the computer *that* long, had he? "I didn't find *anything*, Daddy. He's *gone* again. What if I lose him?"

"Then you'll find him again, won't you." It wasn't a question. Mason said it with such surety that Ryder knew his husband believed it. "But you won't if you make silly mistakes because you're tired or if you put yourself in the hospital with dehydration again. That's why we have these rules."

"I know," Ryder answered miserably, finally conceding and shutting the computer down. They had sat down and set up the rules together—no screentime on weekends, not skipping meals, keeping a bottle of water with him all day—after the last time he'd gotten lost in his work and made himself sick.

Not sick, he corrected, forcing himself to acknowledge the seriousness of what had happened, like Daddy always reminded him to. He'd nearly died. Daddy had been on a two-week trip to some conference down in New Mexico, and Ryder had put himself in the hospital with dehydration.

"I, um…I know I missed dinner, but can I have a snack instead?" Ryder asked quietly, guilt swishing around his chest like muddy slush in winter. Shiloh and Gage had been so kind to let them stay, and he'd basically ignored them, locking himself in their office.

"We saved you a plate. Come on. Shiloh stayed up to wait for you."

Ryder took Mason's offered hand and followed him to the kitchen where, true to his word, Shiloh was waiting, leaning against the kitchen counter with a mug in his hand.

"I'm sorry," Ryder apologized again. He had a feeling he was going to be doing that a lot, unless Daddy helped him.

"Don't be. I get it. I don't have any siblings, but if anything happened to one of my friends, I'd tear the world apart looking for them," Shiloh said, looking for a moment like a man who was fully capable of doing so.

"I've just never been this close before. I'm afraid if I stop, even for a second, he'll slip through my fingers," Ryder admitted.

Mason warmed up the plate and set it down at the little table by the large glass windows. "Come eat, Ry."

In the end, he felt like he pushed more food around the plate than he ate, but his stomach felt tiny — like the stress of the day had squeezed it into a little ball.

Chapter Fourteen

"Okay, so, full disclosure, the apartment isn't very nice," Ian said, his voice tinny as it came through the phone on speaker. "But it was the only thing I could find at short notice without getting the Bureau involved."

A stone settled in Liam's stomach. "Don't tell me they're dirty, too."

"I don't know, but something's up. I contacted Deputy Director Knowles, and she seemed...too concerned about your location and whether you were armed. I asked around and Austin PD is claiming you opened fire on their officer for no reason and ran. There are at least four officers backing up that rookie. And since the only bullets at the scene are yours..." Ian Romero trailed off pointedly.

Tennyson cursed. "And she believes them?"

"I'm not sure *what* she believes, but I doubt she's going to take any chances. If even a rumor hits the streets that the agent involved in this bust could possibly be dirty, she'd sacrifice you in a heartbeat. You know she's running for congress next year, so she won't risk taking the hit to her name."

"And officer killed in the line of duty sounds better than a shady bust." Liam hated politics. He cursed again. "Shit. So this apartment is off the books?"

"The rest of this *op* is off the books. I'll fish around, see what I can find, but honestly, I doubt they'll loop me in anymore—not until after this mess is cleared up. I paid for the apartment for a week. I'd suggest you use that time to get out as much cash as you can, change up your appearance and make other arrangements, unless you want to drive the witnesses up to the Bureau and hope for the best, but honestly? I wouldn't be surprised if the FBI is compromised as well."

* * * *

The underbelly of the camper was more rust than metal, the windows nicotine-stained yellow, but the engine turned over beautifully, and the tires were new. Liam handed over the eight hundred dollars and hurried the boys into the back with their new supplies.

He'd spent the last week in the apartment Ian had rented for them burning his undercover identity—and doing his best to bury his real one. He'd risked going into the bank to pull out just under ten grand in cash and made one final call to his handler, Romero, before he'd dumped his phone into the bed of a truck with Alabama plates. With any luck, anyone tracking it would think he'd fled the state.

He might be paranoid, but it was more than just his life at stake. The only person he was absolutely positive would *never* be involved was Romero. Ian Romero's boyfriend, Teddy, had been under the cartel's thumb for years and had nearly died the previous year. There was no way the man would be passing them information.

The best place to hide was right under their noses. Nobody would expect him to linger in Austin, and maybe that was because it was a dumb decision. He had to hope it would pay off.

But, while he was taking the risk of staying in the city, that didn't mean he needed to be stupid about it. Even paying cash to motels would leave a paper trail. Instead, he drove to Raymond's Lay Up. The RV park was sprawled across a lumpy, bumpy dirt patch with sparse patches of grass growing sporadically along some sites. The fire pits were rusty metal barrels half-buried into the ground.

Raymond was really Larry. He had a seventies porn 'stache, an oily beer gut peering out from under his tank top and a surprisingly nice smile.

"Well, I'd love to have y'all stay, but we're mostly full up. Got some year rounders, and just had a bunch drop in for some concert in the city later. I can squeeze you into the back, by the dump station. Give you a nice discount?"

While Liam wasn't pleased about the nearness to the sewage dumps, the back of the RV park meant less visibility and also, likely, a back drive he could take in an emergency. So he handed over enough cash for a month. They probably wouldn't stay the whole time, but this way, by the time the man came looking at him for more cash, they'd be long gone.

And if anyone else came looking, Larry wouldn't know when they'd left. And that was if he connected the descriptions to them anyway, since Liam was letting his stubble grow longer than ever and the two witnesses were no longer nearly identical blonds. Asher was now a brunet and Misha a redhead, courtesy of some cheap box dye, and a pair of costume glasses made Asher look older.

* * * *

Two weeks later, Liam was beginning to regret his cavalier attitude about their camp spot. He'd reassured both boys that it would be fine, not that either of them had seemed concerned. He'd said something to Asher about the smell, and the boy had just rolled his eyes, saying, "*Trust me. Neither of us are going to complain about a bit of shit.*"

It made him wonder what they'd been through and whether running with them was the best choice. Should he have risked staying, let them start seeing their therapists and hoped Ian's gut instinct was wrong? He shoved the thoughts down, knowing better than to let himself go down the path of 'what ifs'.

And true to their words, neither of the boys so much as reacted to the odor.

A breeze kicked up shortly after breakfast, carrying with it another cloying blast of sickeningly sweet stench, and he slapped his crossword down on the picnic table.

"Oh, come on! There are codes for this shit, you know?" He hollered toward the dingy check-in station.

"I don't think he can hear you from here," Asher said, from his perch on the fold-out steps by the camper door. Misha was napping between his knees, his head balanced on the other boy's thigh.

"Should I yell louder?" Liam lifted a brow and smirked.

"You'll lose your voice before he hears you." Asher shrugged, but Liam saw the way his lips quirked up. It was almost a smile, one of only a handful Liam had seen so far. "How long are we staying?"

"A few more days," Liam guessed. "Why? You going to miss this place?"

"The smell is growing on me," Asher dryly answered, pulling at the collar of his T-shirt and wrinkling his nose. "Literally."

"I can take you and Misha down to the showers after dinner, if you want?" Liam offered, picking his crossword back up so he didn't have to watch the boy's face—the way it brightened at the simple suggestion of a shower or the way it fell as he wondered what the catch was.

Over the past two weeks, he'd learned their expressions well. The way Misha was tentative and too-trusting, obedient to the point of naivety, Tennyson had a feeling if he told Misha to stick his hand in an open flame, he would do it without question. Asher though? Asher still feared every too-sudden motion, every extension of kindness Tennyson offered, like a beaten dog.

Two ends of the same spectrum.

"That would be okay," Asher finally said, breaking the stretching silence.

"Okay."

* * * *

The shower stalls were barely big enough for both of them to squeeze in. The water pressure was nonexistent—the water just this side of tepid—and

Liam refused to let them step inside without the cheap foam flip flops.

It was *amazing.*

Even if every time Asher pulled the thin blue plastic curtain closed, he wondered if this was the day Liam was going to yank it back open.

Even if he wondered whether today was the day that the larger man was going to expect them to repay him for the cheap, cherry-scented bodywash and two-in-one shampoo and conditioner.

Which was why Asher nudged Misha in first, made sure he was tucked closest to the showerhead, farthest from the curtain. Misha hummed as he lathered the soap through his long, now-red, hair. The color was growing on him.

As much as Asher loved it on Misha, he wanted to take a kitchen knife to his own, saw the long strands into something that didn't have quite so many bad memories attached to it. He didn't dare.

"Let me get your back?" Asher asked. Misha nodded, so Asher poured a dollop of the pink soap into the palm of his hand and started working it down the bumps of Misha's spine, over the curling ribs that, thankfully, grew less prominent each day.

It was a novelty and a blessing, this freedom to touch. He wanted... He wanted to sew himself to Misha's skin so they never had to stop. And Misha... He softened under each brush of Asher's fingers like a cat, practically purring.

"You can fuck me," Misha said, no shame in his voice as he arched his back, pressing his ass against Asher's hips. He probably felt the slight hardening of Asher's length, more a reaction to the closeness than a true desire for sex.

"Do you want me to?" he asked, willing to if that's what Misha needed, even if he was not necessarily enthused.

Misha stayed quiet, which to Asher was answer enough. Instead, Asher brushed a dozen kisses over Misha's shoulder and down his spine, one on his hip, another on his knee. He didn't think Misha really wanted sex—not now, anyway. He suspected that he wanted *touch*, like Asher did. So, Asher gave it to him, washing him gently from the soles of his feet up to his neck.

Misha stretched up on his toes to press the tip of his nose to Asher's. "Love you."

"Love you."

"My turn." Misha smiled and grabbed the soap.

Chapter Fifteen

Misha watched the little boy at the next campsite. He was chubby and blond, and his cheeks were red from the sun, but he was laughing. And his mom was watching him play while she read a paperback book with a shirtless man on the cover. His dad held a beer in one hand and a stick in the other that he was using to shift logs in the firepit, sending bright little embers fluttering into the air with each poke.

"What are you doing?" Asher asked, dropping down beside him. Misha turned away from the other campsite and settled against his side.

"Nothing, just...watching."

Asher looked over, his gaze piercing as it moved from the kid to the adults, then back to Misha. "Do they remind you of your parents?"

Misha had told him bits and pieces about them, in stolen moments between nightmares. "Not really," he admitted.

And it was true. Misha's dad drank, but it was vodka and dill. Misha's mom only read those magazines about fancy people's houses. "I don't remember ever being that happy, though."

His childhood was a series of snapshots — being cold and hungry in the motherland, the lonely feeling of being an outsider in Brighton Beach, his mother's worries and his dad's fatigue.

"Me neither," Asher admitted, and they sat together in silence for a long while, watching the kid scoop dirt into a chipped plastic pail, until the mother hollered him over for bed.

"I always wondered if it was my fault," Misha finally admitted when the little family next door abandoned their fire to the mosquitos.

"Hm-m? Of course, it wasn't." Asher grabbed his hand and squeezed it tight. "Your uncle was an asshole and Barnes a pervert. None of that is your fault."

"I guess. But...I always figured if I'd been smarter, or better behaved, maybe my uncle would have kept me, and we really would have gone to the zoo. But..."

Asher glanced toward the ratty camper next door. "If they sold that boy, like your uncle sold you, would that be his fault? Would he deserve it because he threw a tantrum? Or...or failed a spelling test?"

"Of course not!" Misha protested the thought immediately, disgusted by the insinuation.

"Then why would it be yours?" Asher asked, and Misha opened his mouth to answer before he realized that...he couldn't. Because...it *wasn't* his fault. Asher let him think for a second before bumping their shoulders together. "Anyway, I bet you were *perfect*."

"I bet *you* were perfect," Misha corrected, grinning at the thought of little Asher. "I bet you played peewee and soccer and baseball. I bet you even had a little *girlfriend*."

"Okay, but that's not fair! I didn't want to kiss her. I just wanted to wear her pretty hair bows," Asher said, pouting.

"Don't care." Misha laughed and plugged his ears, until Asher yanked one of his fingers out to blow a raspberry into it instead. Even Mr. Liam couldn't hold in a snort from where he sat at the picnic table. Misha was coming to think of it as *his* spot, the one that gave him a really good view of the rest of the campground.

"Mr. Liam?" Misha said, feeling his voice shake slightly. "Do you have a girlfriend?"

Mr. Liam gave him a smile he was used to seeing only on Asher's face. "Have you ever tried putting a jigsaw together? And you have those two pieces that look like they should fit together, but no matter how you try, they just don't? Yeah, that's how I feel about women."

"So...no?" Asher said at the same time Misha went, "What's a jigsaw?"

Mr. Liam pressed his lips together and let out a slow breath, like he was trying not to laugh. "Yeah, exactly..."

Asher snorted and looked at Misha. "No. He doesn't have a girlfriend. And if that's how he tries to answer questions, he probably doesn't have a boyfriend, either."

Misha snickered.

* * * *

Misha couldn't sleep.

Asher had fallen into sleep ages ago, his mouth parted in little snuffling snores, the afghan shoved to his knees. Misha watched him for a while, his fingers curled tight in his tank top to avoid touching the little tuft of yellow hair on Asher's underarm or tracing the constellation of freckles along his collarbone.

Then it got hard to resist, so he had to stop watching, rolling onto his back and staring at the yellow-stained ceiling instead. Misha loved the camper. Everything he needed was right there, in sight and easy access. He couldn't be locked out of the kitchen when it didn't have a door. And it smelled delightfully musty, so different from Master's house.

Mr. Liam was sleeping on the floor in a black sleeping bag, his head pillowed on his forearm. Or at least, Misha thought he was sleeping, but when he shifted and the pull-out bed creaked under him, Mr. Liam looked over with sharp eyes. Not angry, but watchful. Aware.

Definitely not sleeping.

"Everything okay?" Mr. Liam said softly, rolling onto his side.

"Can't sleep," Misha whispered.

"Not tired? Or something else?"

"Not tired," Misha said, but a wide yawn made him feel like a liar. "I mean, I *feel* tired, but my eyes don't?"

"Ah. One of *those* nights." Mr. Liam nodded sagely and sat up. He stretched out a hand. "Come on. I'll make you a hot chocolate and we'll go look at the moon. That always helps me."

"Okay."

The moon was just a sliver in the sky, a French-tip fingernail in a bed of black. "There's no stars," Misha said, a bit disappointed. In his dreams, there were always stars.

"They're still there, but you just can't see them. Austin gives off too much light." Mr. Liam pointed to a bright light in the distance. "See that? It's one of the last of the moonlight towers."

"Why?"

"People kept falling off them."

"No, I mean...wouldn't they rather see the stars?"

Mr. Liam shook his head. "Back when they built them, they were the tallest things in the city. They thought it would stop crime and make the city safer."

"Did it?"

"Not really. Pretty, though." Mr. Liam smiled.

"I guess."

Mr. Liam leaned back on his hands, staring at the moon again. "We don't see the stars in New York City much, either, now that you mention it. I hadn't really noticed."

"Why not?"

Mr. Liam shrugged. "Always too busy, I guess. When I'm back home, there's too much to do and not enough time to do it in. The city that never sleeps really does never sleep."

"Sounds lonely," Misha decided. "Always being busy, I mean."

"Maybe. I guess it is, a bit. I talk to my sister a lot, though, when I can, when I'm not undercover."

"It's so confusing."

"Hmm?" Mr. Liam shifted to glance at him.

"This 'being undercover' thing, I mean. So you work for the government, and they tell you to go do bad things, so you can convince other people that you are also a bad person, just so you can stop *them* from doing bad things. But...you have to do bad things, too, so they believe you. But *you're* not a bad person." Misha frowned, trying to make it make sense, but it didn't.

Asher had tried to explain what it meant, but maybe it was something Misha would never grasp.

"Most of the time, when we're undercover, we don't *actually* do bad things. It's all made up. Like…my boss makes up a name and gives that fake name a false backstory. All I have to do is pretend that I *have* done those things," Mr. Liam tried to explain.

"It must get confusing though, right? Always pretending to be other people?" Misha sat up, crossing his legs and tucking his hands together. "Don't you miss getting to be yourself?"

"I get time off, but you're right. It does get hard sometimes."

"So who are you right now? Are you *yourself*? Or are you someone else?" It was important for Misha to know the difference, though he couldn't quite say why.

"This is me, I promise. I will always be *myself* with you and Asher."

"Pinky promise?" Impulsively, Misha stuck his pinky out, smiling when Mr. Liam curled his much longer one around it to shake.

"Pinky promise."

* * * *

"Well, there's not much left, but I think I can scrounge together some pancakes. As long as you don't mind boring ones." Liam grinned over his shoulder at Asher and Misha.

Asher shrugged. "I like pancakes." Anything was better than oatmeal and dry bread. He wasn't going to complain that they didn't have any chocolate chips in them this time.

"Misha, want to help me mix the batter?"

Misha bounced off the couch to wash his hands.

I'm not jealous, Asher thought to himself later, watching Liam help Misha scoop out a ladleful of batter and pour it carefully onto the pan on the stove. What did he have to be jealous of? Liam, for being able to make Misha smile like that? He should just be happy that Misha was happy. But a small part of him realized that he was also, confusingly, a bit jealous of *Misha.*

Misha, who Liam kept giving secret little talks to outside at night when he thought Asher was asleep. It wasn't like Asher didn't *know* that Misha was the sweet one, with his big eyes and sensitive heart. Asher was thorny as a cactus. Of course Liam would never ask *him* to help with the pancakes — not when he had Misha there, looking at him with stars in his eyes.

"I'm going to the bathroom." Asher stood abruptly and darted out of the door, ignoring Liam's startled question. It cut off abruptly anyway when Asher let the door slam behind him.

He didn't run, because even angry he knew it was better not to draw attention to himself, just in *case* — but he wanted to. He settled for a fast walk, his hands shoved into his sweater pockets. It was hot out, sweat slipping down his spine, but he wasn't going to take it off and risk Liam taking it away.

"Asher!" The older man's voice filtered to him, growing louder. Asher walked faster, until a firm grip on his arm yanked him to a halt and he was spun around.

Liam was pale, and it was his hand still gripping Asher's arm. Misha stood a few feet behind him, his eyes down. His arms were curled protectively across his chest.

Immediately, Asher felt guilty for worrying him. He drew in a breath, trying to shove his feelings back down into their safe place in his chest, but they seemed too big now—like they were a helium balloon, dragging themselves up through his sternum to his throat and getting stuck.

"Asher, you can't just leave like that. It's not safe for you to be out here on your own. You have to wait for me."

"You were busy, and I had to piss," Asher said, stubbornly crossing his own arms now, an angry copy of Misha. "Didn't realize I was *your* prisoner now."

Liam looked like he'd been struck. "You're not, Asher. I promise. I didn't realize you felt that way. It's just not safe out here, but I would *never* keep you from going to the bathroom—"

Asher's anger flickered away and he sighed. "I *know*. I'm just being cranky, I guess." He refused to admit that he was jealous of the easy way the other two were beginning to act around each other, like Asher wasn't needed anymore. "I shouldn't have said that."

"No, you should be able to say whatever you're feeling. I'll try to be better about giving you more space, if that's what you need—"

"No!" Asher yelped at the thought of feeling even more left out. "I don't. I'm just tired. I didn't mean it."

"If you're sure…"

"I'm sure."

They walked in silence to the bathrooms, where Asher forced himself to pee, even though he didn't have to. He kept his head down afterward, trailing behind Liam back to the camper. Misha stuck close to his side.

The pancakes were burned.

Asher picked at the charred, black skin of the rubberlike pancake, guilt crawling under his skin like ants. Misha had been so excited to cook, and his little temper tantrum had ruined it.

Why couldn't he just be happy? Be grateful that they'd been rescued, and that Liam liked *Misha*, at least, even if that meant Asher got left out? Maybe Barnes had been right, and Asher really was a greedy boy.

Then Misha elbowed him. "Look!" Misha had carefully peeled off the slightly less charred exterior of his in places so now his lumpy pancake looked like it was smiling. He was happily chewing on the black strips he'd removed as if it *didn't* taste like ash, syrup beading on his lip until he licked it away.

"It's a happy pancake," Misha giggled, then squeezed another large dollop of syrup on the eyes. "I'm going to eat its face right off."

For some reason, that strangely sadistic comment out of Misha's typically sweet mouth made Asher laugh, and he felt a bit better.

* * * *

"Fuck!" Liam cursed at the cheap silicone piece of shit. He'd dropped almost ten dollars in quarters into the stupid vending machine outside the bodega and ended up with six keychains, four stickers and a weird rubber alien thing just to get two matching watches. And apparently, he needed tiny raccoon fingers just to program the stupid little alarm.

That was what he got for buying watches from a vending machine.

Maybe they would think it was stupid.

He just would never be able to get Asher's panicked face out of his memory, or Misha's soft whisper, asking how they would know when he would be back. He needed to get them food for another few weeks. The cupboard in the camper was downright bare, and he'd pushed it off too long already.

And as much as it worried him to leave the boys alone, one man would attract less attention than three, especially since both Misha's and Asher's roots were starting to show. He'd grabbed a few more boxes of dye, as well.

Getting them watches was such a small thing, but if it helped…

God, he hoped it helped.

Chapter Sixteen

It took Asher three hours and seventeen minutes to realize that Liam had given him a watch and he hadn't immediately asked what he had to do to keep it.

It was a cheap thing, flimsy blue silicone and plastic — the kind that came from a vending machine for a paltry cost of a pair of quarters. Liam had given Misha a watch, too, a green one. Both had quiet little alarms that beeped over and over, until they pressed the tiny button by the face.

Liam told them it was so they could keep track of when to take their new chewy vitamins.

Asher liked his new vitamins and his new watch — and he liked the smile that Misha wore when he saw it.

Mostly, he liked that even though he hadn't asked what he had to do for it, Liam had given it to him and asked for nothing.

Asher watched Misha putter around the little camper kitchen. He wasn't doing anything, really — just opening the cupboard doors, one by one, to stare at the boxes of cereal and loaves of bread and jars of peanut butter and jelly. "Look, Asher. There's so much of it! What's this one like?" Misha held up a bright orange box of mac and cheese.

"It's pasta with cheese on it." Asher walked over and stared at the picture, filled with a sense of nostalgia. It had been *ages* since he'd had any. Mom had stopped making it for him when he was in middle school.

"Cheesy Pasta?" Misha's face lit up.

A heavy fist landed on the window. "You boys hungry?"

Asher jumped and Misha dropped the box, both reaching for each other instinctively. A strange man stared at them through the blinds, grinning and waving. "My wife and I got some extra dogs if ya want to come next door!"

"Dogs?" Misha yelped, twisting in Asher's arms to look up at him in horror. Before Asher could explain that the overly tanned man likely meant hot dogs, Liam came up to the stranger from behind, his hand tucked under the flannel shirt, likely gripping the hilt of his gun.

"Everything all right here?" Liam asked, his gaze moving from them to the squat man.

"Heya, neighbor! Was just inviting your sons here to pop over for a bite. We got plenty of food. We're tripping across the whole state for the summer, coming up from San Antonio. What about you boys? Enjoying your summer vacation? I bet you're not looking forward to that school year starting, am I right?"

Neither Asher nor Misha spoke until Liam cleared his throat. "Come on out, boys. Let's be neighborly."

Slowly, Asher disentangled himself from Misha, but he couldn't force himself to drop his hand. He clutched it like a lifeline as they slipped out of the door and over to Liam. Misha gripped him so tight that it was painful, but the ache grounded him.

"Got a pair of well-turned-out kids here, Mister," the man said. "My name's James Johnson Jr., but you can call me Jimmy. Or Junior, I guess, though Senior kicked the bucket 'bout ten years ago, God rest his soul." Jimmy kissed his fingertips and pointed them at the sky.

"Well, it's certainly a pleasure," Liam said, his voice slowing to a drawl, so unlike the fast New York accent Asher had grown used to in the past few weeks. "I'm Lee. These here are my boys, Ace and Micky. Their poor ma passed this last winter, and it shook 'em something awful."

Asher flinched when Liam reached over and ruffled his hair, out of surprise more than fear. Liam leaned into the other man with a smile that looked *almost* right. It was just too big for Liam's normally sober face. "She'd been fighting that cancer all year, poor thing."

"I thought they looked lower than a gopher hole. Well, better bring them 'round. The wife'll sandpaper me if she knows these poor boys are over here all motherless."

Jimmy ambled away and Liam sobered immediately, turning sharp eyes on both him and Misha. "I don't like it, but we'd best play the friendly neighbors tonight and skip out early in the morning. I don't want our faces to stick in his mind as anything but the family next door."

"Why can't we just leave now?" Asher asked, hunching his shoulders.

"What's more likely to stick in his mind if people start asking around?" Liam again lifted his hand to Asher's head, but this time he just rested it there, fingers curling around the nape of Asher's neck. "Three solitary men in an RV who left immediately, acting all aloof? Or a grieving widower and his two sons? People are less likely to think poorly of someone they were friendly with. We'll be just another family they met on the road."

* * * *

Asher glared at Liam when Jimmy's wife scooted even closer on the picnic bench. If she got any closer, she'd be in the man's lap.

"So, Ace, where y'all from?" The teenage girl sitting in the folding chair next to Asher said, blinking wide blue eyes at him like she had something stuck in them. It was *probably* crusty flakes of mascara, guessing by the heavy-handed application.

Asher shrugged, looking back toward Liam with another glare. "We moved around a lot," he lied. It'd be easier to say they were just from Texas, but four years in the south under Barnes's thumb had done little to budge his yank accent. Misha, though, had almost no trace left, and Liam faked it like a native.

"That's just so *romantic,* isn't it? Getting to see so many new places? Meet new people? I bet you have *lots* of friends. You're so nice," Sophie—Sarah?—sighed dreamily and scooted her chair even closer in an imitation of her mother.

"Not really," Asher answered curtly.

"But you must have a girlfriend?" she asked.

Finally, Asher turned his gaze back to her, incredulous. He glanced down at his bright pink sweater and tight shorts. What on earth would give her the impression he liked *girls?* "I'm gay."

She stared at him for a second before her big eyes widened even further. "Oh! That's... Well, now I feel silly. You know what we should do tomorrow? We could go shopping and look at boys! This campground is filled with old people. It's so boring!"

Since Asher was one of those old people at twenty-two, even if he looked younger, he really had no desire to go shopping with a teenage kid. "No thanks. I don't have any money, anyway."

"Did your dad take your allowance away? Mine does that sometime. It's so not fair."

"He's not my dad!" Asher finally snapped after listening to her ramble on for several minutes, louder than he'd meant to, and the whole campsite went quiet, except for Misha's small gasp from where he was sitting by the fire. Asher cringed when he realized he'd just let his short temper blow Liam's whole cover story.

"Boy!" Liam snapped, frowning just like, Asher had to admit, a disappointed father. "Come over here right this second, you hear me?"

Asher, heart careening in his chest, scrambled off his chair and over to Liam, wringing his hands. "I'm sorry, Sir," he said plaintively, but Liam just pointed to the ground between his knees. Asher dropped immediately.

Liam, rather than strike him, just ran his hands through his hair again. "Their dad left when they were barely ten. Went out for smokes and never came back," Liam said to the Johnsons, voice quiet like he was sharing a secret. "They'd just barely started accepting me around when their mother got sick, poor thing."

"Oh, that's so *sad*. Poor boys, losing both of their parents like that," Mrs. Johnson tittered and slid even closer. Asher glared at her leg when it touched Liam's.

"But bless your heart, taking them in like that. Aren't you just an *angel?*"

Asher was going to gag.

* * * *

"Come on, boy. Up you get. Time to go home."

The words were muffled, since Asher's ear was bent rather painfully against the hard, warm pillow under his head. He blinked open fuzzy eyes and realized he was still slouched between Liam's knees. His skull felt like it was stuffed full of cotton balls.

"Is it bedtime?" Asher asked, not fully awake and unwilling to move. He felt strangely safe there, tucked between the sturdy thighs. He blinked sand from his eyes and glanced around. Mrs. Johnson was missing, as was her daughter, and Jimmy was smothering the fire in the burn barrel. Misha had, at some point, moved his chair closer to the picnic table and he had his feet hooked around the legs and his head tilted all the way back, staring at the sky.

Liam pat Asher's shoulder. "Definitely, for you at least. Come on. Up you get."

"Don't wanna." Asher shifted his head to uncrimp his ear then froze when he felt the back of his head rub right up against the zipper of Liam's jeans and, beneath that, a distinctly hard length.

Either Liam didn't notice or he had more self-control than Asher had because he didn't comment, nor did his hips thrust against the pressure. Instead, he just tugged on the ends of Asher's hair. "You might be able to sleep outside, boy, but my back would yell at me in the morning."

Something in the way Liam said *boy* this time had Asher capitalizing it in his head and he found he didn't hate it. He lingered a second longer but finally sighed and stood up, his knees wobbly. Thankfully, a moment later, Liam stood and took his elbow for support.

"Tell Mr. Johnson 'thank you' for having us," Liam said, the same drawl from earlier coloring his voice.

"Thank you, Mr. Johnson," Misha and Asher said together.

Jimmy laughed. "Call me Jimmy. I ain't no 'mister'."

"Yes, Mr. Jimmy," Misha chirped back, giggling when Jimmy just waved them away.

Asher's legs felt sturdier after a few steps, but he continued leaning on Liam anyway. For the first time in a long time, he didn't hate the feel of a hand on his skin. He still didn't want to fuck him, but...the gentle guidance felt nice, like Liam cared if he made it safely back to the camper or not.

He was more tired than he realized, though, because back inside—after Liam double-checked that all the blinds were completely closed this time—Misha had to help Asher with the button of his shorts when his fingers kept fumbling.

He was asleep before he pulled the cover all the way up.

Chapter Seventeen

Liam packed them up before dawn the next morning and drove them to a new park across the city.

It was just as crowded, but instead of being stuck by the dump, now they were stuck by the pool. Which was, of course, closed for maintenance and smelled vaguely of algae. Asher refused to look at it after he saw the first snake crawl out of the water.

The first night, he had a nightmare that one slithered into the camper and onto the pull-out bed he shared with Misha, which meant he spent the rest of the night with his legs and arms buried under the musty orange and brown afghan, despite the sweltering heat that made the tin can feel like an oven, even at nighttime.

Then he saw a scorpion and realized snakes were the least of his problems.

"You can't live on the counter," Liam said, and Asher tracked the smirk tipping up the corner of his lips.

"Don't laugh at me," Asher said. He wasn't crazy. He could still see the gross smear left on the linoleum from where Liam had stomped it with his heavy boot.

"I'm not laughing, I promise, but it's dead."

"Could have a friend."

"Scorpions don't have friends."

"Could have a boyfriend."

"Certainly don't have boyfriends."

"Could have a *mom.*"

"At some point, you have to go to the bathroom," Liam pointed out.

Now Asher had to pee. "Asshole."

Asher perched on top of the picnic table and glared at the dirt Misha was currently sprawled across. Not because he was angry at Misha. He was wondering what kind of creepy-crawlies were about to be disturbed.

"Here you go." Liam held a hot dog over Asher's shoulder and waved the bun around a bit until he grabbed it. "You can go back to bug patrol after you eat."

Misha scrambled up to sit on the bench beside Asher to get his own dinner. "Did you see the lizard?"

Asher shuddered. Who could have fucking missed it? "Yeah, it was...nice."

"Maybe someday we can have a pet—" Misha started to say, until Asher interrupted.

"With fur. Lots of fur."

"Ooh, we can get a cat!"

"With fur," Asher said again, because he'd seen those weird furless rat-cats that looked like naked babies and left ass prints all over glass tables. He was sure someone thought they were cute, but he was not that someone.

"And a dog!" Asher *didn't* feel it necessary to specify with fur this time, because he'd never heard of a naked dog. But, if there was one, he could put it in funny sweaters.

"And a bird!"

"The cat would eat it," Liam pointed out as he sat down with his own pair of hot dogs.

* * * *

Asher was snoring.

Misha didn't mind. The sound was gentle, like he imagined the ocean would be. It was just a background lullaby, not quite strong enough to put him to sleep. It was quiet enough that Misha could hear Asher's steady heartbeat in the slender chest he was using like a pillow.

It was nice, being able to snuggle tight together on the fold-out couch, even nicer since he knew it wasn't to share body heat. Even at night, it was boiling hot in there. The skin under Misha's cheek was sticky with sweat, and he could feel the small rivulets running down his own sides and back. Asher cuddled with him anyway.

Misha smiled and scooted in even closer, drawing in a deep breath. He didn't care that Asher smelled a bit like salt and vinegar under his normal aroma. It was Asher, so it was perfect.

Faintly, he noticed a strange tingling near his hips. He didn't recognize it at first, but a glance down had him gasping at the sight of his cock swelling. It was smaller than Asher's, just big enough to fill his hand when he reached down to test its weight.

He...he was *hard*.

He giggled, then smacked his other hand over his mouth to smother the sound, holding his breath. Nobody moved, so he slowly released it, then lowered his hand to his throat instead.

Back with Master— *No*, he corrected himself. Back with *Barnes*, erections were a rare occurrence. Mas— *Barnes* usually resorted to drugging him with molly or Vicodin if he wanted Misha erect—which, to be fair, wasn't often.

Since escaping, he found himself regretting this inability, *especially* when Asher was touching him like when Asher would wash his back so gently in the shower or hold him under his arm on the camper steps.

He wanted to be closer to Asher, as close as they could be, but he knew Asher wouldn't fuck him if he was soft. Asher wouldn't believe that Misha wanted it—in his head, at least—even if his body wasn't on board yet.

Misha nudged him softly. "Ash," he whispered, nudging him again when Asher just groaned but didn't wake. The second nudge had his eyes fluttering open, then Asher's whole body tensed.

"What's wrong?" he blurted, flitting his gaze around the camper.

"Sh-h!" Misha hushed him with a grin, "Nothing! Look!" He rolled onto his back and took his hand off his cock, albeit reluctantly.

Asher glanced down, his eyes widening. His lips parted, then he slipped his tongue out to wet them. He looked back up at Misha, his gaze searing over every inch of skin his thin PJs exposed. "You... Do you...you want..."

Misha nodded his head quickly. "Yes." He wanted Asher. But more than that, he trusted Asher to never take him further than he could handle.

Asher rolled onto his side, making sure Misha could see every motion of his hands. He reached down and curled his fingers around Misha's throbbing length. "You'll have to be quiet, or we'll wake Liam."

"I can be quiet," Misha whined, his hips jerking up at the nice, firm pressure. It felt like...like his first time eating chocolate, but better — better by a thousand. Asher had him shaking in minutes, playing him like the violin Misha vaguely remembered owning at one point.

It didn't take him long to cry out, coming in spurts over Asher's hand and hip. But, even though his cock was wilting, falling sated against his thigh, the *need* was still there, dancing in his chest.

"Thank you, Ash... Can I play with you now? Please?"

Liam clenched his jaw, hard, to keep in the groan growing in his throat. It had been difficult enough staying still and quiet, feigning unconsciousness in his sleeping bag on the floor when he'd first heard Misha's small gasp and realized what was happening. He'd thought the boy was hurt at first and went to get up. He'd barely turned his head when he saw the boy with his cock in his hand and a small, surprised smile on his face.

It broke his heart a little more. He couldn't imagine being in their shoes, taken from their homes and abused when they should have been learning about their bodies on their own. It was no wonder Misha looked so surprised. Liam wondered if he'd ever gotten hard on his own before.

And immediately kicked himself for the inappropriate musing. He shouldn't be thinking of them like *that*, not while they were vulnerable and under his protection.

He'd forced himself not to watch as Asher took Misha to the edge and over, but he heard every sound, every broken moan and gasp and whine. His own dick was a steel rod in his briefs, and he couldn't even adjust it. He didn't want the sound to stem their exploration. They would freeze up if they thought he was awake, and they deserved these moments together in privacy — or at least, this illusion of privacy that was all he could give them.

So he bit his cheek hard enough to taste copper and closed his eyes, trying to ignore the pretty sounds floating down from the pull-out couch.

It didn't work.

* * * *

Asher's midnight tryst with Misha left him tired the next morning but in a better mood than ever. Misha was beautiful when he came. He'd known it before but had buried the thought, fearing what kind of person that made him.

"Here... Eat some more." Asher grabbed the box and dumped another handful or so of cereal into Misha's rainbow milk when he saw it was mostly empty.

"Thank you, Ash," Misha answered sweetly and immediately started digging out the marshmallows with his spoon to eat. Asher flushed scarlet as it dragged his thoughts right back into last night's bed.

He cleared his throat and looked away, only to see Liam blushing red as well, staring hard at the toast on his own plate.

Asher frowned, wondering why — until he realized that the only reason he'd have to blush was if his mind *also* had gone right back into last night, when Misha had said those exact same words, and he'd been less asleep than Asher had realized.

Asher sucked his lower lip into his mouth and looked down, pondering the strange way that made him feel. It *should* make him feel angry, right? Or...or violated? Or something other than this odd, not-quite-pleasure? He found he didn't mind the thought of Liam listening.

Somehow, he'd come to know that Tennyson wouldn't take anything they weren't willing to give. If he'd heard them last night and said nothing, *did* nothing, maybe...maybe they really could trust him.

Possibly it was mean, but Asher couldn't help himself. He grinned and looked up, meeting Liam's gaze. "Did you sleep okay? We didn't wake you up, did we?"

Liam, for just a moment, looked startled, before he smirked. "Don't worry. I didn't hear anything I found alarming."

"Good," Asher said, then took a big bite of his toast.

"Good," Misha echoed, still fishing out marshmallows. "I didn't hear anything, either, except that weird bug thing that sings all night."

Asher and Liam both laughed, since clearly Misha had no clue they were talking about the *other* nocturnal singing from the night before.

"What?" Misha finally looked up, glancing between them, confusion plain on his face. "Why are you laughing? Did I miss something?"

Asher couldn't resist. He leaned over and planted a chaste kiss on his lips, not even bothered by the overly sweet flavor of sugary cereal he was left with. "No, I was just teasing Liam."

"Oh." Misha paused for a second, then shrugged and went back to eating.

Asher watched Liam stretch across the table to ruffle his hair. Before Asher could get jealous, Liam reached over to Asher's and tugged on his. "You keep pushing this out of your face. Want me to trim it up for you?"

His stomach got jittery at the thought. "Really? You'd let me cut it?"

"It's your hair. You don't need my permission." Liam said it like it was obvious, and maybe to him, it was.

"I don't think I want it *all* gone. But maybe a little?" Every time it tickled his shoulder or the top of his back, it felt like creeping fingers, dredging up memories he finally felt ready to start leaving behind.

"To here?" Liam brushed his fingers along Asher's scalp, just over the crest of his ear.

"Yeah, if...you think it'll look okay?" His voice rose near the end as self-doubt took over.

"Yeah." Liam cleared his throat. "Yeah, I think it'll be perfect."

There wasn't much room to work with. Liam puttered around for several minutes, getting a comb and scissors and the electric shaver the three of them shared and lining them up on the kitchen counter, between the sink and the toaster — unplugged, now, so they could plug in the shaver. Then, he dragged over the folding step stool and set it up as close to the center of the floor as he could.

Once Asher perched on top of it, the safety bar digging into his spine, the kitchen seemed doubly small. Liam slid in behind him, and for just a second, Asher tensed. Surprisingly, he wasn't afraid.

Instead, he found himself anxiously waiting for Liam's touch.

It came slower than he expected, after Asher heard the sink turn on then off again. Liam's fingers were damp, carding through the strands until water dripped down the side of Asher's neck. He shivered when Liam chased it with his fingertips.

"Okay?" Liam asked, his hand stilling until Asher nodded. "Tip your head a bit," Liam said, waiting until Asher did to start taking the scissors to the strands, snipping off a few inches at a time. The curls fluttered to the ground, each one bearing the weight of memories.

By the time he ruffled the much shorter hair and told Asher he was finished, Asher felt calm and slightly floaty.

"Misha, grab me a towel?" Liam asked. Misha brought one over and Liam draped it over Asher's head. Asher closed his eyes and just *felt* as Liam painstakingly dried each lock of hair, even going so far as to run the towel along the base of his neck to mop up the little rivulets afterward.

"You've got some hair here." Asher shivered as Liam ran his fingers inside the collar of his T-shirt, barely skimming his skin. "We can run down to the showers if you want, or I can clean it up for you."

"Will you?" Asher asked, reluctant to move away from Liam's hands.

"Can I take this off?" Liam touched his shirt, not moving until Asher nodded. Then, he gripped the bottom and carefully pulled it up and off, dropping it somewhere behind him.

Asher shivered again, though it was hot in the camper and he felt like he was burning from the inside out. But he was naked from the waist up, his skin bare to Liam's touch, Liam's eyes...and Misha's, who sat on the pull-out bed with a coloring book. He would scribble his crayons for a few seconds, then look up at Asher and Liam and smile.

Now, with Asher's chest bare, when Misha looked up, he didn't look back down. He dropped his crayon on the mattress and stared as Liam picked the towel back up and started slowly swiping it across Asher's shoulders and down his spine. Then, Liam circled around to give Asher a critical look from the front.

"I think I got it all," Liam finally said, clearing his throat and tearing his gaze off Asher's chest to meet his eyes. "Just let me know if you get itchy and decide you need a shower after all."

Asher's voice broke and he had to swallow around it to say, "Okay."

"I need a shower," Misha piped up from the bed. From his pink cheeks and the way he was shifting his hips on the mattress, Asher thought the shower might just be a euphemism for something else.

"Yes. Shower, please," Asher agreed.

* * * *

The water was lukewarm and the pressure almost nonexistent, but Misha didn't care. They'd barely stepped under the stream before he pounced on Asher, pressing his throbbing cock against the other boy's thigh.

"Someone's feeling needy, I see," Asher purred, shoving him back—not hard, Asher would never hurt him—against the sweaty tiles. "Do you like my haircut that much, baby?"

"I liked watching him touch you," Misha answered, his voice thready. More than liked, he realized. Watching Mr. Liam run his big fingers through Asher's hair so gently, like Asher was a skittish cat in need of petting.

"Yeah? We're you imagining it was you?" Asher's lightly furred thigh moved between Misha's, back and forth, rubbing against his balls and shaft like a naughty carousel horse. Misha's moan echoed around the stall. The pleasure was almost too much, a string tightening in his chest.

"Sometimes," Misha admitted. "I wanted to be touching you, too, but I wanted *him* to be touching *me* at the same time." He stilled as he felt his cheeks heat. "But only in my imagination. I...I don't think I'm ready for that for *real*. But it's okay to pretend, right?"

"Yeah, baby. You can pretend." Asher gripped his hips and started rocking against him again, his own cock bumping Misha's hip bone. "Tell me what you imagined, baby. I want to hear it."

"Oh God, I can't," Misha whined, gripping Asher's shoulders like a lifeline. His skin was damp and slippery.

"But you can, baby. Tell me. Was he standing behind you? Or was he just like this?" Asher shifted impossibly closer, sliding his hands up Misha's chest to pluck at his hard nipples like a violin *pizzicato*.

"Behind me," Misha admitted, bowing his back into the touch. "You were in front."

Asher hummed agreeably and dropped his mouth to Misha's ear, dipping his tongue inside for a second before he murmured, "Were his hands here?" Asher dropped them back to Misha's hips, sliding his fingers along his hipbones.

Misha shook his head. "Uh-uh."

"Higher?" Asher pressed, dragging them up over his abs.

Misha shook his head. "No! Please, Asher. I need…"

"I know what you need." Asher promised, then he was on his knees on the shower tiles and his warm mouth closed around Misha's cock.

Asher didn't love the taste of Misha—it stirred up too many memories—but he loved the way Misha *sounded,* the broken gasps and little mews, the way his breath caught behind his pretty pink lips. And he loved how Misha *looked,* with his half-lidded eyes and pleasure-strung body.

Mostly, he loved Misha.

"Coming," Misha warned, and Asher let him slide from his mouth, gripping him instead in his palm and stroking him to climax, angling the tip toward the shower drain. He watched Misha's pearly fluid mingle with the lukewarm water until it ran clear, and Misha squirmed under his hands, oversensitive. Asher pressed a kiss to the softening cock before standing.

"My turn." Misha sank to his knees with more grace, his eyes locked on Asher's throbbing dick.

"Only if you want… I can finish myself." Asher's words bit off into a groan when Misha swallowed him down. Misha worked him slower to climax but when

Asher spilled, Misha caught it in his palm, rubbing the sticky fluid over his chest like lotion, only to rinse it off under the showerhead when he stood.

"I want to smell like you," Misha said, earnest as could be. "That's okay, right?"

"Perfect," Asher agreed.

Chapter Eighteen

Liam wasn't sure how to look the two boys in the eye after the steamy shower session he'd had no choice but to listen to. It was hard enough keeping his thoughts pure around them to begin with, without knowing that they were fantasizing about *him* joining in.

It didn't take much for him to see the fantasy clearly — standing under the water, Misha sandwiched between him and Asher, Asher on his knees, this time for Liam, or better, Liam on his knees for both of them, playing with their cocks until they were begging to cream.

He needed to call his handler before he did anything reckless.

As much as he wished they could, the three of them couldn't live in the bubble they'd created here in the camper forever. Eventually, he had to get them back into the real world, reach out to the FBI, get them started in therapy and moving on with their lives.

Their lives without him.

And the way that thought physically hurt, leaving a pang in his chest, was a sign that he was already too invested. But even knowing that, he couldn't force himself to step back. He wanted to stay in this bubble as long as they could, enjoy it until it popped and the *real* world invaded.

They moved parks again, and maybe it was true what they said, that the third time was the charm, because they managed to get a fairly decent lot for the first time. It was nothing too special, but far enough away from the dumping station to not smell it and no pool to draw in snakes.

Not that there were *no* snakes, but Asher's shrieking tended to be a fairly good warning that one was nearby.

Liam was getting better at not laughing.

"They're playing a movie tonight," Asher said, for all the world sounding like it didn't matter, but Liam could see the question in his eyes when they darted to Liam's and back down.

"Yeah? Anything good?" Liam dropped the newspaper he wasn't really reading anyway back on the table to give the boy his full attention.

Asher shrugged. "Just *Star Wars*."

"Episode IV?" Liam clarified, already running through the security risks if they went. It wasn't any more dangerous then chilling out at a picnic table, he supposed. "Do you wanna go watch it?"

Asher shrugged. "We don't have any chairs."

"We can bring a blanket, sit on the grass," Liam suggested. "Have a picnic."

"Misha's never seen it. Do you think he'd like it?" The boy shifted on the other side of the bench, teeth digging into his bottom lip.

"Maybe. What kind of movies does he like?"

"He didn't get to watch them," Asher answered, scratching his nails over the wood grain. "So I don't know."

"Well, that settles it. Now we *have* to watch it, don't we?" Liam grinned and slapped the table playfully. "Everyone should know what movies they like."

"Can we bring popcorn?"

"Of course. It's not a movie night without it."

* * * *

The park had set up a portable screen and projector along the edge of the parking lot, large box speakers loudly broadcasting the sound through the park. Most of the residents had claimed patches of grass with their camping chairs or blankets already when Liam, Misha and Asher headed over. They spread the afghan out on an empty patch near the edge. The angle was a bit awkward, but they had more room to sit than they would have had elsewhere.

If Misha minded seeing the movie at a slant, he hid it well. His eyes were wide as saucers as he stared, his mouth parted slightly in apparent wonder. He was so into the movie that he ignored the popcorn, a telling sign from a boy who normally ate all food put in front of him like he'd never get more.

Asher watched the movie with only slightly less fixation. Liam was glad that in the end they'd decided to go. It was worth it to see the happiness on their faces, and he resolved that the next time he left for supplies, he'd look for a portable DVD player and some videos for them to watch.

The sky darkened steadily as the movie continued. Misha didn't seem to care, but Asher shuddered, the spell of the movie finally leaving him as he sat up, wrapping his arms around his knees and looking around like, at any moment, someone was going to leap out and grab him.

Liam shifted the bowl of popcorn and quietly said, "Come here, Asher."

Asher hesitated but only until a noise from another campsite sounded and he shuddered, moving quickly to Liam's side, huddling under his arm. "I'm, um… It's cold?" Asher whispered, and though it was pointedly untrue, Liam didn't point out the mid-seventy-degree weather.

"Do you want to go back?" Liam asked.

Asher immediately shook his head, looking over at Misha. "I think he likes the movie. He needs to see the ending."

"Mm-m. Okay, but we're leaving as soon as the credits roll."

And they did, Misha chattering the whole way to the camper about the scenes he loved and the scenes he only liked and peppering them with questions about how they made the spaceships fly.

Most of the questions were ones that Liam couldn't answer since, while he loved films, he knew next to nothing about how they were made, but he answered the ones he could. Misha was still happily chatting when he pulled on his PJs and dropped onto the bed next to the much-quieter Asher.

"What was your favorite part, Asher?" Liam asked when Misha yawned, hoping to draw Asher out of his head a bit.

"When they blow up the Death Star," Asher answered immediately, which sent Misha off on another tangent. This time, Asher participated, finally seeming to leave behind the funk from outside, at least enough to engage. There was still a worrisome shadow in his eyes, though.

Liam's suspicion that Asher hadn't left the fright outside completely behind him were confirmed later, after Misha fell asleep and Liam crawled into his sleeping bag on the floor.

He heard Asher tossing and turning for nearly an hour, and argued with himself and his instincts, which were to call the boy down, wrap him in his arms and promise that everything was going to be okay.

He was nearly ready to cave when Asher spoke up, voice quiet and shaky. "Liam?"

"Hm-m?"

"Can I...can I sleep down there with you? Just for tonight?" Asher asked. Liam must have taken too long to answer, worried about the appropriateness of doing so, because Asher's voice was small when he said, "Never mind. It was a dumb idea."

"No," Liam interrupted, "I mean, yes, you can sleep down here tonight. No, it wasn't a dumb idea. I'm sorry. I didn't mean to make you think you couldn't."

"Are you sure it's okay?"

"As long as you don't mind that the floor is hard, I'm okay with it." Liam shifted, holding the sleeping bag open so Asher, after he carefully disentangled himself from Misha, could crawl in.

"Thank you," Asher whispered, after several long minutes.

"Get some sleep," Liam softly replied, barely resisting the urge to smooth a kiss over the boy's forehead.

Chapter Nineteen

Mason was worried about Ryder. His boy was sulky and withdrawn, and getting him to play with his toys, take his bath or even eat his snacks was becoming a daily chore. Getting him to do anything that meant his boy had to shut off his laptop was like pulling teeth.

It was rare that he didn't know what to do and, not for the first time since they'd decided to make their stay in Austin more permanent, he was grateful that the house he'd bought was only two down from the one Gage and his boyfriend lived in.

Currently, Mason was on their back patio, a coffee in his hand, wishing it was beer. "I just don't know what to do, Gage. This isn't like him."

"Are you sure? Don't take this the wrong way, man, but you haven't known him very long." Gage shot him an apologetic glance from where he stood by the grill, flipping burgers. "Don't glare at me, Mason. You know it's true. You've known Ryder for, what? A year? Year and a half? And he's never been good at taking care of himself. That's why he *needs* a Daddy."

"You think I'm taking it too easy on him?" Mason pondered that for a bit, rolling the past few months in his head. He was reluctant to push, not with his boy already in such a fragile state.

"You'll have to answer that for yourself. Shiloh and I aren't lifestyle like you two. We only play when he needs it. All I *will* say is that your boy loves you, and he's going through a rough time. I can't imagine being in his shoes — getting this close and then…nothing." Gage's expression twisted in empathy. Gage certainly knew something about partners going through a rough time. He'd met Shiloh when he'd only been his bodyguard, just as the boy's life was falling apart.

"It's killing me, too. I want him to find his brother — don't get me wrong — but a part of me…a *small* part, mind you, hopes he finds out *anything*, even if it's bad news. Just so he can move forward, you know? Then I kick myself for thinking it, because of *course* I don't want it to go that way. It's like a vicious cycle."

"It's a hard position to be in," Gage sympathized. "I know you'll do what's best for Ryder in the end."

Mason made it three more days. He reached the last straw when he came home from meeting a new client at nearly nightfall and found Ryder, still in his pajamas from the night before, glued to his computer screen with a barely touched waffle abandoned on the desk beside him.

Clearly, he hadn't eaten anything all day or gotten up to do much of anything. He hadn't even used the bathroom. Mason could see one of the rarely used diapers peeking out from the waistband of his pants.

"Ryder Immanuel Lockhart, you best explain yourself real quick before my hand gets reacquainted with your backside!"

Ryder jumped, knocking the paper plate off the desk to the floor and spinning around. "Daddy! You're home early…"

"Actually, I'm almost an hour late, which you'd know if you bothered to look at your phone," Mason replied, anger swimming in his chest. He knew better than to deal with the many infractions Ryder had accumulated today while upset, but that didn't mean he wouldn't make damn sure his boy knew *exactly* how disappointed he was.

Ryder's cheeks turned pink, and he dropped his eyes, clearly realizing he'd screwed up, but Mason couldn't just sweep it under the rug — not again, not this time. If he let his boy keep breaking the rules just because of the situation, Ryder was going to put himself in the hospital again…or worse. He had no way of knowing how long it would be, if ever, until they found Asher. It could be months or years. *Or never,* the thought crossed his mind before he buried it.

His boy needed a Daddy. Needed *him* to be his Daddy, like he'd promised in their wedding vows, even when it was hard. They had a contract, after all, unless or until Ryder safeworded.

"Did I give you permission to put on a diaper?" Mason asked after several deep breaths brought him back off the precipice.

"No, Daddy," Ryder whispered, wringing his hands pitifully in his lap.

"Do those belong to you?"

Ryder shook his head, shoulder's slumping. His voice broke in a sob as he answered again, "No, Daddy. I'm sorry."

"Oh, baby." Mason shook his head. "Not yet, but you will be." He reached out a hand. "Laptop and phone."

Ryder's head jerked up, mouth gaping in horror. "No, Daddy, you can't! I need them!"

"It's Friday. I know you're off work until Monday. You can have them back then." He refused to back down. Ryder might not realize how obsessive his search had become, how *unhealthy*, but Mason did, and as Ryder's Daddy, it was his duty to step in.

"Asher needs me! I have to find him, Daddy. You can't take it away, you *can't*. I need it, I have to find him!" Ryder grew more panicked with each word.

Mason crossed the floor and dropped to his knees in front of his boy, looking up at him with a broken heart. "Baby, Asher needs you to be *healthy*. You can't find him and bring him home if you're not here for him to come home to. You trusted me to be your Daddy before. Has that changed?"

Ryder sucked in a breath and shook his head. "No, Daddy! I trust you. I do!"

"Then trust me to do what's best for you."

Both of their faces were wet with tears when Ryder finally placed his laptop and phone in Mason's hands.

"You'll get them back on Monday," Mason promised, slipping them into the drawer of Ryder's desk and locking it, adding the key to the house ones in his pocket. Then, he gathered Ryder in his arms and picked him up, carrying him out of the home office and to the stairs. A decade ago, he might have been able to carry the boy up them, but he no longer trusted himself not to drop him, so he lowered Ryder to his feet on the first step.

"To the bathroom, boy."

"Yes, Daddy," Ryder answered miserably, gripping the railing with white knuckles as he slowly trudged his way upstairs and into the en suite. He waited by the bath with a lowered head.

Mason stripped him carefully, making sure to fold each article of clothing nicely as he removed it, proof to Ryder that even though he was disappointed, he would still treat him with the care he deserved. He left the swollen diaper for last.

Rather than remove it, he ran his finger over the duckies on the front. "Who does this belong to, baby?"

"You, Daddy."

"That's right," Mason agreed. "If you want to play with Daddy's toys, you are supposed to ask first. Care to tell me why you put one of Daddy's toys on without him?"

Ryder shrugged, averting his eyes.

"Was it just that you didn't want to have to get up from the computer?" Mason pressed, relieved when Ryder shook his head. "Were you maybe feeling a bit overwhelmed?"

Finally, Ryder nodded, tears welling over his eyelids and down his cheeks.

"I'm sorry. Daddy should have noticed that you needed this. I should have pushed you, shouldn't I? Did you maybe push back so hard on Daddy's rules because you wanted me to take over a bit more?" Mason had been so worried about what he thought Ryder *wanted* — more grown-up time to find his brother — that he'd completely missed what his boy *needed*. He needed his Daddy to tell him it was okay to stop, to put himself first for a little bit.

To be 'little' if he wanted, even if it meant he had to leave his computer and his research until the next day.

KD Ellis

"Don't worry. Daddy won't mess up like that again," Mason promised, finally opening the tabs on the diaper and removing it with ease, discarding it into the diaper genie by the toilet. "You'll be 'little' all weekend. We'll take a bath tonight, get a fresh new diaper and have some 'pa-sghetti' for dinner. How does that sound?"

Ryder nodded, his thumb creeping to his mouth

Hopefully, a weekend de-stressing would give him back the kind, happy boy he knew and loved, but even if it didn't, he now knew exactly what Ryder needed from him.

Chapter Twenty

Asher watched Liam through the window. The cracked vinyl under his elbow stuck to his skin and the curtain kept falling from where he'd tucked it aside, but Asher barely noticed.

"Is he still talking?" Misha asked. He was lying on his back, his head in Asher's lap, feet dangling over the armrest.

"No, now he's just sitting at the picnic table."

"Does he look angry?"

"Not really."

"Sad?"

"No. I think he looks frustrated," Asher decided.

"What do you think that means? Does it mean we have to leave? Or that we get to stay? I want to stay."

Asher looked down at him, tweaking the pouting lip with his finger. "Yeah. Me, too." The camper might be small and smelly, and the showers never got truly hot or truly cold, and maybe it would be nice to have more than a microwave and toaster, but everything felt...calm.

He was afraid that when it was finally safe to leave, it was all going to change. He would fight tooth and nail to stay with Misha, but would they let him? Without documentation, would they make Misha go back to Russia? How would he survive there, in a country he couldn't remember with family he didn't know? Or worse, would they send him back to his uncle, who'd sold him in the first place?

And what about Asher's family?

Did they even know he was safe?

Had they known he wasn't safe in the first place?

His parents might have, but he doubted they cared. Maybe Ryder would, if the kid even remembered him. Asher could still see him in his memories, if he closed his eyes and thought really hard. He'd been blond, like Asher, but he wore glasses — the thick-rimmed kind that got him picked on when Asher wasn't there to defend him.

Would Ryder even remember him?

Did he think Asher had just left, never cared enough to call?

He couldn't explain why he did it, except that Ryder thinking he had abandoned him felt like a dagger to his heart, but after lunch, while Liam was washing the dishes in the little sink, Asher quietly reached into Liam's bag and pulled out his phone, the one he said was for emergencies only.

The one that Liam only took out once a week to call his friend from the FBI.

Then he talked Liam into taking him and Misha to the showers.

With Tennyson standing guard by the door and Misha staring at him with a hand over his mouth — and the sound of the running water for cover — Asher dredged up the memory of a phone number he hadn't dialed in years.

"Mom?"

* * * *

"What do you mean, you told him not to call you again?" Ryder shrieked into the handset, already racing toward his office. The call had happened supposedly within the hour. As long as they hadn't moved, he could trace them. Finally, he could *find* him.

"I don't need him and his deviant ways rubbing off on your sister, Ryder dear. He can't disappear for years then expect me to welcome him back like nothing happened," Mom rationalized.

"He was *abducted,* you bitch! And I'm gay, too! Are you going to keep me away from Sarah?" Ryder dropped into his chair and powered up the computer.

"That's different, dear. You know Sarah loves when you visit."

"She's barely a year old. She doesn't know me from the mailman. And it's *not* different. You just need to justify your decision to kick a teenage kid out onto the street without a backward glance."

Mom huffed in his ear. "You were too young to see anything but the good days, Ryder. You don't remember—"

"So what? He wore makeup? I wear frilly panties and like to call my husband Daddy!" Ryder snapped, not caring anymore that she might judge him, that it was a secret he'd kept from his homophobic family for ages.

He knew that what he shared with his husband wasn't perverted or wrong. Neither one of them would ever hurt a child. Being a 'little' was about...about feeling cared for and protected. And Daddy liked to take care of him. That was all.

But Mom gasped in his ear like he'd just admitted he liked to kill kittens.

Before she could spout off whatever vile thing was running through her head, Ryder interrupted. "Don't call me again. If Asher isn't your son anymore, then neither am I." He hung up without listening for a response, already digging through the call logs to find the phone number, the only one with a five-one-two area code. Slowly, painfully slowly, he ran the trace.

"Gotcha." He grinned, nearly manic, as it pinged a location—the *Are We There Yet RV Park.*

He took a moment to print off a picture of Asher and another of the FBI agent who'd taken him. Hopefully, one of the other residents would have seen them and be able to point him to their lot.

"Daddy!" Ryder grabbed the pictures and sprinted out of the room, "Daddy, I found them!"

But he was answered with only silence, and he cursed. He'd forgotten. Mason had told him this morning before he'd left that he was going with Gage to look at an office building coming up for sale. He was home alone.

He yanked his phone back out of his pocket and dialed his husband. It rang straight to voicemail, and he cursed again.

He couldn't wait for them to get back. What if they left before he could get there and his *one* chance to find his brother vanished? He'd just have to go alone.

It didn't take him long.

He knew the combination to open Mason's gun case.

He knew how to pop the magazine in, rack the slide and attach the holster.

Everything after that was easy.

Grab the keys to the rental that Mason left with him, 'just in case' he needed to go to the store.

Leave Mason a note on the coffee table.

Drive.

Chapter Twenty-One

Asher felt guilty.

He shouldn't have used the phone. He knew that. He *definitely* should tell Liam he'd used it...right?

But every time he opened his mouth to admit it, he froze — not even because he was scared of Tennyson, because he wasn't. He trusted him completely. And that was the problem... It wasn't Liam who wasn't trustworthy, it was *him...Asher.* Liam was going to be so disappointed in him, and Misha...

Misha was going to be upset that they had to move already. And what if Tennyson decided that thanks to his slip up, to his *stupid* decision to call his parents, that they were too much trouble to bother protecting and just...took them back?

And it *had been* a stupid decision.

His mother hadn't been happy to hear from him. She'd yelled and told him not to talk to them again, and when he'd tried to ask about Ryder, she'd said... She'd said that they'd all moved on with their lives, that no one missed him and he should just stay wherever he was—that they didn't need his perversions around their new child.

It had hurt.

He'd expected it, but it still *hurt*.

So he'd betrayed Liam's trust for *nothing*.

"You look sad," Misha whispered, again staring up at him from his lap. His hair, still slightly damp, was a nice coolness against Asher's thigh.

Asher glanced out of the window, watching Liam. He was sitting at the picnic table, again doing a crossword. Asher lowered his voice. "I did something stupid."

"I'm sure you had a good reason," Misha immediately replied, grabbing his hand to set it on his chest, over his heart. "You wouldn't have done it otherwise."

"When I...I called my parents." Asher dropped his head back to stare at the ceiling, unwilling to see the disappointment he knew would be crossing Misha's face.

"I'm sorry it didn't go well." Misha said, leaping up at him to wrap his arms tight around Asher's chest and squeeze. "I'm sorry."

"I should have known. Now I have to tell Liam that I broke the rules for...for *nothing*."

"He won't punish you," Misha said, voice muffled. "You know that, right? I trust him. He might be disappointed, but he won't hurt you. He *won't*." To Asher, it sounded like he was trying to convince himself too.

"I know. But *disappointed* is worse, isn't it?" Asher finally looked down, meeting Misha's blue eyes with his. "Is it weird that I don't want to disappoint him?"

Misha shook his head. "I like him, too. It's okay to like him, you know."

Asher felt his face flush. "I didn't say I *liked* him."

"You don't have to. I can see it on your face when you look at him. You think he's *hot*."

"I think *you're* hot," Asher said, embarrassed that Misha read him so easily.

"You can think he's hot, too, you know. I won't be jealous. I think he's hot, too." Misha gave him a cheeky grin and peered over his shoulder. "I mean...look at his butt."

"It's a nice butt," Asher agreed.

"You didn't even look," Misha teased. "So how would you know? Unless you've been looking at it. Have you been looking at his butt, Ash?"

"I plead the fifth," Asher said.

"What's that mean?" Misha sat back, getting more serious for a second.

As he usually did, Asher explained the idiom.

Something was up with Asher.

Liam had noticed it after they got back from the showers but hoped giving him time would help him open up. Instead, Asher clammed up further. He kept opening his mouth like he was going to speak before snapping it shut again, and he wouldn't meet Liam's eyes.

If Liam didn't know better, he'd say the boy felt guilty. But...over what? The overheard rendezvous from before? If that was it, it was certainly a delayed reaction. Liam just wished he knew whether it would be better to confront Asher and get it out in the open or let it simmer until he was ready to speak on his own.

He wasn't a therapist.

He'd come out and sat at the picnic table with a newspaper pilfered from one of the neighbors' trash cans to pretend to do a crossword, just to get away from the strained tension inside the camper.

He'd given up expecting Asher to talk when he heard the squeak of the screen door opening and looked back. The young man lingered on the step for a long stretch of silence, biting his lip and staring at the dirt, sky and street—anything but Liam.

Tennyson sucked in a breath to speak just as Asher cleared his throat. Finally, Asher came over to the picnic table, sinking slowly down onto the bench beside him. He kept his gaze down, his fingers picking at the splintered wood.

"Can I tell you something?" Asher mumbled.

Liam immediately folded the paper and set it aside. "Of course."

"And you won't get mad?" Asher added, glancing up quickly before looking back down.

"I think you'd better tell me either way, Ash. I can't help you if I don't know what's wrong." Liam knew better than to make promises he wasn't sure he could keep, but even if he was mad, he wouldn't abandon the boy or raise his voice more than he could help.

Asher dug his teeth even harder in his lip and Liam winced, wanting nothing more than to reach over and free it from the abuse. "I...I did something bad."

Liam stayed quiet, just listening. There were so many varying degrees of bad. For all he knew the young man had burned a slice of toast in the cheap, dollar store appliance and felt guilty.

"Maybe we can fix it."

"I...took your phone out of your bag. I just wanted to call my mom." Asher dropped his face into his hands and curled in on himself, his shoulders shaking. Despite the sobs, he was silent, achingly so. Liam hated to think what the boy had gone through over the past half a decade to learn to smother the cries so well.

It wasn't *optimal,* and on the scale of 'bad things,' it definitely could have been better, but it wasn't unfixable. They'd have to dump the phone and possibly the camper, but it was about time for that, regardless. In his calls with Ian Romero, the other agent had suggested they consider it soon, anyway.

Liam scooched along the bench, very slowly lifting his hands to place them on the smaller man's shoulders, pausing when Asher flinched at the touch. But Asher didn't pull away, so after a moment, Liam gathered him in.

"It's okay to want to talk to your mom. I'm not angry. We'll just get rid of the phone and head out. It's okay."

"She told me not to call again. She...she called me a pervert and...and said she didn't want me to infect their new kid. I have...I have a little sister, and I'll never get to see her." Asher collapsed against Liam's chest like a ragdoll.

Liam closed his eyes against the pain in the younger man's voice. "I'm sorry. I wish I could make it not hurt."

"They didn't even look for me." The words were muffled, spilling into the fabric of Liam's tee with his tears. "Am I that worthless?"

"No," Liam growled out, tightening his grip on the boy. "You're *not* worthless. They should have looked for you. *I* would look for you."

Asher sniffed, his breath ragged, and the sound broke Liam's heart further. "You would?"

"I would. And I wouldn't stop until I found you, I promise. You're *not* worthless, Asher." Liam shifted him back a bit, gently tipping Asher's face up. With his thumbs, he softly wiped away the tears dampening the pink cheeks. "I don't speak of it much, but my family is *very* wealthy. Trust me when I say I know when something is worthless and when it is worth more than all the treasures in the world. You and Misha? The both of you are *priceless.*"

Maybe it was too much, too revealing, but it was important to him that Asher believed him. That he knew, to Tennyson at least, that he meant something…was slowly growing to mean *everything.* He'd grown bored of this assignment those last few weeks before everything had gone to shit, wanting nothing more than to retreat to his New York apartment. Now, he feared it ending, that the Bureau would uncover the mole, collect their witnesses and send him back home like nothing had happened.

This shitty, cramped camper felt more like home than his penthouse ever had.

Asher's skin blushed hot and he ducked his face. Liam let him hide behind the soft curtain of his newly shorn hair. He curled his fingers over the young man's slender shoulder, tracing the edge of his shirt collar with his thumb. "Asher—"

"Get your hands off him!" A man's voice interrupted, a high-pitched shriek that had Tennyson flinching hard, lurching to put his body between Asher and the interloper.

At the same time he moved, he dropped his hand to his hip, his palm barely grasping the grip of his gun when his eyes landed on the barrel of the one pointed at him.

The world went silent, drowned out by the rushing of blood in his ears. *A Glock,* his mind noted absently, taking in as many details of the man as it could in a split second — young, blond, vaguely familiar in a passing manner, shaking hand and wide eyes.

Liam gripped Asher's shoulder tight and shoved him off the bench, into the dirt between his back and the camper. "Go inside," he started to say, wanting him out of danger, but the motion startled the gunman.

His torso jerked from the impact, searing pain tearing through his body before his ears even heard the gun fire.

Chapter Twenty-Two

Ryder dropped the Glock.

He stared, horrified, as the dirty cop turned gray and red, his hand moving like molasses up to his shoulder to cover the growing bloodstain.

He hadn't meant to squeeze the trigger.

It was just supposed to be a threat.

He hadn't meant to shoot him.

He'd recognized his older brother immediately, even with the dyed hair and baggy sweater. Seeing him crying, with that man's hand on him, it had just *happened*.

"Oh my God," he moaned, covering his mouth at the sight of blood. "I didn't mean…"

Nobody was listening to him. Asher was crying and the cop, despite the gunshot, darted forward, snatching the fallen Glock from the ground and deftly removing the magazine and emptying the slide.

The door to the camper banged open and a second boy, one who looked remarkably like Ryder's brother, stumbled pale and shaking down the steps, his eyes skipping across the three of them in panic.

"I didn't mean..." Ryder stuttered, taking a step back.

"Don't move," the agent ordered, his voice dripping with authority as he pulled his own gun and aimed it directly at Ryder. "Misha, go inside and grab our bags. Asher, go grab his keys."

Ryder flinched when Asher nodded quickly, his eyes wide and obedient. Clearly, he'd been brainwashed.

Asher was only a few steps away from Ryder when he glanced up and met his gaze, stumbling to a stop. "R-Ryder?"

Ryder didn't care about the gun aimed in his direction—or the dirty cop, or the neighbors who'd surely already called the police about the gunshot. He folded in half, his hand clapped over his mouth to smother his sobs. Asher *recognized* him.

"Oh my God, *Ryder!*" Then Ryder stumbled back as Asher practically tackled him, flinging his arms around his neck and gripping tight. "How did you find me? Mom said you didn't remember me. I can't believe you're here! What are you *doing* here?"

"Asher!" Tennyson snapped. Ryder felt his older brother flinch in his arms. "We have to go before the police show up here. Get his keys. I'll need you to drive. We have to go."

"Sorry," Asher said softly but pulled the keys to Ryder's SUV from his front pocket. "He can come with us, right, Liam? We can't leave him here. It's not safe. He's my brother. *Please,* Liam?"

Ryder darted his gaze between the two men. Asher wasn't treating the cop like an enemy, and the way he spoke... Had Ryder gotten it wrong?

He opened his mouth to demand an answer just as the other boy—Misha?—scrambled back out of the camper, a black gym bag hanging over one shoulder and two book bags gripped tight in one of his hands. The other clutched a ratty brown knit blanket.

Tennyson didn't look happy about it but he agreed, hurrying the three of them toward Ryder's SUV as sirens sounded in the distance. Curtains fluttered in several campers as they ran past. Ryder scrambled into the passenger seat beside Asher, who fumbled getting the key in the ignition but started it on the second try. The cop, who was maybe not as dirty as the file made him seem, climbed into the back with the other boy.

Asher drove slowly but Ryder saw his knuckles turn white on the leather steering wheel, and the way his brother's eyes kept looking up at the rearview mirror. At first, Ryder thought he was looking for police, even though the sirens had ended up being a firetruck careening past the RV Park, but then Ryder realized he was looking into the backseat, where Agent Tennyson was quietly talking the other young man through tending his wound.

Ryder only tried to look once before the sight of the blood made him queasy, but from the little he saw, it looked less bad than he'd feared, just a deep slice across the top of his shoulder, like the bullet had skimmed it in passing.

They drove randomly for several moments until Asher finally cleared his throat. "Where are we going?"

No one answered for several seconds before Tennyson sighed and sat forward, glaring at Ryder from the gap between the seats. "So, trigger finger, you're Asher's brother?"

Ryder swallowed and gave a short nod.

"Don't suppose you have a hotel we can crash at?"

"I… No, not a hotel, but…" A quick glance at Asher made Ryder hurry to add, unwilling to watch his brother's face fall any further, "You can come back with me to my house. Daddy won't mind. He owns a security firm, so maybe…you can talk to him? I mean, there must be a reason you took Asher and ran, right? Unless you really *are* dirty, and…"

"Dirty? No, but someone in the Bureau is." Tennyson's whole face grew stormy.

"That's why you ran away from the safe house?" Ryder pressed for information, hoping to get an explanation before he had to give out his address.

It was Asher who answered, taking his eyes off the road just for a second to look over at him. "A bunch of people broke in. They were yelling and shooting and threatening. Liam kept us safe."

Ryder relaxed slightly in his seat. None of his research into the agent's background had even hinted at malfeasance. If he really had taken Asher and the other young man just to protect them…? Well, it meant that he wasn't bringing home a dangerous double-operative to his husband and friends, but also that he had not only shot someone…but someone innocent.

Quietly, guilt swimming in his stomach, he relayed directions to his brother.

Daddy was going to kill him when he got home.

* * * *

Mason heard the front door open and immediately, the heavy weight on his shoulders lifted slightly. He'd been borderline panicking ever since he'd gotten home from his meeting with the real estate agent a quarter-hour earlier to find his husband missing and nothing but a note to tell him why.

What the hell was he supposed to do with a '*Got a lead. Call you soon*' scrawled on a napkin? How the hell was he supposed to help if something went wrong? If it was a trap meant to lure his husband in so they could dismember him into a thousand tiny pieces, never to be recovered?

He'd put a call in to their tech guy, Sin, to track the LoJack on the rental and the GPS on Ryder's phone, but he hadn't heard anything back yet. Ryder knew how to bypass those if he wanted, which he might have if he'd wanted to make sure he wasn't followed.

Sin was good, but Ryder was better.

"Ryder Immanuel Lockhart, you are *so* grounded," Mason called out as he rounded the corner into the hallway at a spring, freezing when he noticed that his husband wasn't alone.

Years of military service let him take the situation in quickly—two young men, a few years older than his husband, hovered by the wall, leaning on each other in a fragile way, a taller, dark-haired man closer to Mason's own age with his back against the door, gun in plain sight on his hip. Mason kept a wary eye on the weapon just in case he needed to draw his own. He doubted it, with the amount of blood weeping through the man's dark tee.

"Ryder...explain," Mason snapped, then winced as his husband flinched at his tone.

Before he could apologize, Ryder burst into tears, rambling on about finding a lead and tracing calls and not wanting to wait then accidentally shooting the agent who, apparently, was keeping his brother and the other young man safe from a bunch of dirty cops and loose cartel members. Only a year of experience decoding Ryder's breakdowns let him follow the stumbling, stuttered flow of words.

"Ryder. Hey, *Baby*," Mason finally couldn't take it any longer and stepped forward, enfolding his husband in a hug he desperately appeared to need. "Baby, calm down. Breathe in with me, okay? On the count of three, come on. You can do it, One, two… Good boy, that's it. Now another." Ryder sucked in first a gasp, then a shaky breath before he finally appeared soothed.

Mason brushed his hand over the back of his boy's head, threading his fingers through the messy hair. He looked over him to the three men still standing awkwardly in the entry way. "How about we all go into the living room and sit down? I've got a first-aid kit. We can take a look at that shoulder."

Reluctantly, Liam allowed the man to stitch up the deep slice in his shoulder. He learned the man's name was Mason Lockhart, that he was the husband — much *older* husband, Liam noticed — of Asher's younger brother and that he'd brought with him enough tech and weapons to arm a small militia.

After the larger man threw a bandage over the stitches, Liam gratefully pulled on the shirt Mason had lent him. Liam wasn't exactly a *small* man, but he was still swimming in the fabric. Liam managed to talk

Mason out of a burner phone as well, so he could contact Romero.

In the end, it was easy.

Too easy, for as much trouble as it had given the Bureau.

Asher's brother, a hacker at the NSA, managed to find a series of dark web conversations between a mid-level FBI technician and a cartel moneyman. The tech, a fifty-year-old white male by the name of Jeffrey Harper, who had been working for the Bureau for just under two years, wasn't directly involved in the case, but, as a computer guy, he had access to most of the files.

Once they knew the identity of the mole, all it took was a few hints dropped to their superiors at the Bureau by Romero. A few wire taps on his office and home phone, and the Bureau was able to round up another half-dozen previously undiscovered cartel members.

A bit of pressure from the federal government and two of them flipped, giving up the names of several dirty cops in the Austin PD, including Officer Newman and the rookie from the motel.

Not that Liam got to see any of the action in person. He stayed with Asher and Misha, tucked safely into the well-furnished living room of a two-story house in the suburbs while it all went down.

Twelve hours after his first call to the Bureau, the case was wrapped up in a pretty bow for the agency and half-a-dozen agents swarmed the house. They divested Liam of his gun and took his statement separately from the boys'. All he wanted was to rush back into the living room and shield the two young men from the probing questions and demands.

They were probably terrified…uncertain.

He'd seen the way they had folded in on themselves like crumpled origami when the Bureau had taken over the house.

It's for the best, he told himself. They had a victims' advocate in there with them right now and a therapist on the way. And Asher had his brother, a young man who, despite their mother's claim, had never forgotten him for a moment—a young man whose husband had already reassured Tennyson that the two young men would have a place with them for as long as they wanted one.

They didn't need him anymore.

With the evidence Ryder had uncovered on Harper's computer and the confessions from the cartel members and dirty cops, it was likely they'd not even need to testify.

And like Tennyson's supervisor had said, her voice sharp in his ear, "*The best thing you can do for those poor boys is go home and let them move on.*"

So he would.

It took every iota of strength he had to scrawl his cell number down for them and leave with only a "*call me if you need anything.*" He wanted to say so much more. *Needed* to make sure they knew how much they meant to him, but he didn't. What they needed was more important, and they needed to move on.

Chapter Twenty-Three

Misha looked around his brand-new bedroom, wishing he felt anything but numb. His first bedroom all to himself in years, something he'd dreamed of having but never thought he'd actually get, and all he felt was lonely.

Asher was in a bedroom just across the hall, on the advice of some lady claiming to be a therapist. Misha didn't really remember much of the conversations everyone had been having around him. There were too many people and yet, not the one he wanted.

Liam was gone, and Misha was just waiting for Asher to leave as well.

Asher had his brother now. Misha didn't know how long it would take him to realize he also didn't need Misha.

He'd thought about going first, before he had to hear Asher say it. But how? He didn't even understand how money worked. Was three dollars for a gallon of milk good or was he getting ripped off? He could barely figure out how to work the cell phone Asher's brother had bought him, so how was he going to figure out how to pay rent?

And even with two locks on his door, he still panicked when he heard Mason tread too loudly on the stairs, so how could he live with strangers?

So he crawled under the ratty brown afghan and curled up in the center of the bed to wait for sleep.

It was the biggest, softest bed he had ever been in.

It was warm, but not *too* warm.

Misha still couldn't sleep.

Twice, he got up, making it all the way to the door, even going so far as to unlock it, before he second-guessed his decision to seek out Asher and climbed back into bed.

He tugged the afghan over his head and curled back into a ball. He didn't remember falling asleep, but he woke up tired.

* * * *

Asher loved living with his brother, seeing the man that the kid he remembered had turned into, but something was missing.

Misha was quiet. Too quiet, skirting in and out of rooms like a ghost on silent feet. Asher tried to give him space, knowing that as hard as it was for *him* to reacclimate to real life, Misha barely remembered living a normal life at all. At least in the camper they'd had Liam there to lean on. Asher refused to admit how much it hurt that the man had just…gone. Gave them a napkin with his number and told them to call *"if they needed anything."*

They needed *him*, damn it.

Finally, after a week of watching Misha get smaller and paler, the bags under his eyes growing like lavender fields, Asher decided that enough was enough.

He waited until Ryder and his husband went to bed and the house was quiet before he tugged on a pair of pajama pants and slipped out of bed, crossing the hall to Misha's room.

Their therapist, a young woman with smile lines around her eyes, suggested they keep their own rooms for a while. She said it would help them 'assert their individuality' and 'learn to be their own persons' and not 'be so codependent'. Asher hated it. He didn't want to 'be his own person' if it meant losing Misha.

He didn't bother knocking.

The door was thankfully unlocked when he twisted the knob, and he slipped inside the dark room.

He didn't see Misha, just a small lump under the brown afghan they'd stolen from the camper.

Asher closed the door. The click was quiet, but he still saw the lump flinch.

"It's me," Asher whispered. The thick carpet was soft under his bare feet as he crossed it to climb on the mattress. He didn't unbury Misha from his blanket cocoon. Instead, he curled around the lump like an elbow macaroni.

They just lay together in silence until Misha finally squirmed around, peeking his head out from the top of the blanket. His eyes were red-rimmed and his lip swollen from biting, but he didn't roll away.

"Hey," Asher whispered, leaning forward to touch their noses together.

"I miss him," Misha blurted.

"Liam?" Asher asked, doubting he was talking about Master.

Misha nodded. "It's stupid. I know he wasn't really *with* us, you know? But…he made me feel safe."

"Me too." Asher didn't say anything else. He just scooted a bit closer to Misha and kissed his forehead, silently riding out the night together.

* * * *

Liam sat at his desk at the New York Field Office. His monitor was buzzing but he hadn't looked at it since he'd gotten back from lunch. His office phone was ringing but he ignored it, glaring instead at his silent cell. It had been a month since he'd left Texas, and he felt like an addict for his next fix.

It was rare, but *sometimes*, Misha texted him. He'd gotten the last one early yesterday morning.

I'm learning about climates today.

He wanted to praise him, ask him dozens of questions about his schoolwork and his new room and the new cartoon he found on television. But his supervisor's words circled his head, stilling his thumbs, so all he'd replied was "*Good job.*"

Maybe it was him, not the boys, who needed to see a therapist. He'd never had a case affect him like this. His supervisor, Deputy Director Heather Knowles, had even commented on his distraction at their last meeting.

Which, he mused, was why he was still riding a desk instead of out in the field. It was the only way he could keep her from putting him on paid leave to deal with his shit.

He knew at least part of the problem.

While the corruption hadn't reached as far as he'd feared, seeing even one dirty agent made him wonder how many others there were. He'd always held the

Bureau to such high standards, always been so *proud* to be one of their agents. Now…

Now he'd seen the rot beneath the shiny surface. He'd based so many of his decisions in his life on that *one* moment. That *one* agent who had brought his family home.

He'd let himself put the agency on a pedestal, and now it had crashed around his ears and he couldn't pick up the pieces fast enough.

Maybe it was time to retire.

* * * *

His last day at the Bureau, Tennyson cleared out his desk. The cardboard box had looked small in the passenger seat of his Lexus, but it was only half full—a picture of his sister and her son—the nephew he saw twice a year at best—a photo of his parents on vacation somewhere in Africa, or…maybe that was Asia, a few odds and ends, spare pens and half-used notebooks.

Nothing that mattered as much to him as the frayed string bracelet Asher had braided for him one night in the camper when it had been raining too hard to sit outside or the crinkled napkin with the blotchy spaghetti stain on the corner that Misha had doodled a stick figure comic on.

He'd eaten a piece of the too sugary, lopsided cake in the Bureau breakroom, drunk a mug of the bitter Bureau coffee, then left.

At his penthouse, he walked the rooms aimlessly, staring at the many expensive *things* he'd accumulated over the years—meaningless pieces of art he didn't really like, electronics he'd rarely turned on, photos he never looked at.

He wasn't really living here, he was just...inhabiting space between jobs. Now, he had no more assignments, just an endless stretch of empty days ahead.

Liam stopped beside the steel-and-glass end table in the corner, glaring at the Tiffany lamp atop it. How had he never realized how ugly it was? A waste of space, just like his whole apartment. Maybe he should put it on the market, downgrade to a smaller place — somewhere less clinical, less clean. When he brushed his teeth before bed, all he could see was the single sink set into the white marble countertop. Asher and Misha would knock elbows if they tried to share it. *Not,* he reminded himself, *that they will ever see it.*

He didn't need to make room in the cabinet for their toiletries or in his walk-in closet for their clothes.

When he made his coffee the next morning, he couldn't help but stare at the island. It was too small to fit two stools. If Misha and Asher were here, they would have to stand or go to the dining room. Liam wandered over, mug in hand. What would they think of it? The windows were large, giving a nice view of Central Park, but they were covered in the thick black curtains his decorator had insisted were all the rage. He bet they'd think it too stodgy, too fancy. He could almost see them, skirting the edge of the room, hesitant to touch anything. Liam abandoned his mug on the table with a curse. It didn't matter that they would hate it, because they would never see it. He was torturing himself with 'what if's' that would never happen.

He wondered if the exposed brick mantelpiece would increase the market value. His sister would know. She'd been hounding him to come visit ever since he got back to the city.

Which was how he ended up a few hours later sitting awkwardly on the lumpy couch in his sister's living room, trying to ignore the spring digging into his backside.

Everything in her quaint suburban house was like that. Even though, like him, she could have furnished it ten times over with the most expensive *things,* she always ended up with a table she found on sale at IKEA or discount lamps from Art Van — things with character that never quite matched but made the house feel more like a home than a showpiece.

Lynette was currently in the kitchen, making coffee since she still refused to trust him with her appliances after the *last* time. Liam was watching her three-year-old son, Nolan, sprint from wall to wall with a Matchbox ambulance in his hand, screeching a high-pitched siren.

Lynette came out with a pair of mugs and an apologetic smile. "I'd offer you earplugs, but he ate the last pair."

Liam waved her off but accepted the coffee. "Let him wear himself out. He'll sleep better for you later."

"Ha." She snorted and rolled her eyes. "Sleep? What's this mysterious word you speak of?"

"It's like dying...but shorter."

"You're hilarious. A real comedian. So, brother mine, tell your older sister what's troubling you," Lynette said, dropping onto the couch beside him and taking a sip of her coffee.

"Ten months does not a guru make," Liam pointed out dryly, but she just laughed, staring until he gave in. "I quit my job."

Lynette choked on her coffee. Coughing, she set it down and wiped her mouth on the collar of her blouse. "You? Left the agency?" she said when she finally got her breath back. "Who are you and what have you done with my workaholic brother? Are you sick? Dying? You're dying, aren't you?"

"No," Liam interrupted. "Everything's fine. My last case just… Well, it made me readjust my priorities. Opened my eyes on some things, that's all."

Lynette waited like she expected him to explain further but when he didn't, she narrowed her eyes. "That's all I get? Come on, spill Li-Li."

"There's nothing *to* spill, Netty."

"Don't sell me that snake oil. Just because I only see you twice a year doesn't mean I don't know you better than that."

Liam huffed and dropped back against the couch. "Fine. I met someone — *two* someones — while I was undercover. And coming back to the city made me realize how empty everything here seems."

"You miss them."

"Yeah."

"So go back." Lynette said it like it was the easiest thing in the world — just pack up and move halfway across the country. For her, maybe it was. She was a real estate agent at one of the most senior brokerages in the state.

"I can't."

"Why not?"

Why not? He opened his mouth to hotly defend all the reasons it wasn't that easy before he stopped and took a breath. "I'm not sure that's what's best for them."

"Is that their choice, or are you making it for them?"

She was always the smart one. He didn't have to barge back into their lives and take over. Even if they didn't want to date him, which was a good possibility, considering their pasts, he could be friends. He wasn't tied to a desk in the city anymore. He could lease out his penthouse and take an extended vacation to Austin, if he wanted — check in on them, make sure they were doing okay.

And if he got bored, well…Mason Lockhart had not-so-subtly hinted that his security firm was hiring more bodyguards, now that they were planning to stay in Texas indefinitely.

"Be honest. You're just already bored seeing my face," Liam halfheartedly teased, mind already racing ahead, planning his move.

"I can't help that it's so ugly. You know Mama cried when she saw it."

"Brat."

"Ferbie."

The familiar sibling ribbing made him laugh, and for the first time in a very long while, his heart felt light.

Chapter Twenty-Four

"I'd like you to try," Ms. Allard, Misha's therapist, said calmly from her seat in the wingback chair.

Misha shook his head, shoving his hands farther under his armpits.

"Just to the end of the driveway and back."

"I don't want to."

"It's important that you push yourself out of your comfort zone, just a little bit. I'll be right here."

Misha was literally shaking in his seat. The thought of stepping out of the front door alone turned his breath to ice in his chest. He wasn't allowed outside of the house by himself. That had been one of Master's earliest, strictest rules.

Master might be in jail, but the fear was still here, clinging to Misha like a shadow.

"I'll walk with you to the door, and I'll wait right there for you. I promise that you will be completely safe, and no one will be angry at you."

Reluctantly, Misha stood and followed in her footsteps to the door. She unlocked it and held it open, but he couldn't convince himself to take the first step, to cross the threshold onto the front porch.

"I can't," he finally cried, sinking down and yanking his knees to his chest, pressing his forehead against them.

After a second, he heard the latch as the door closed again. A shadow fell over him as Ms. Allard crouched beside him.

"That's okay. We made it to the door this time, and that's still progress. We can try again tomorrow."

The next day, Misha made it onto the porch.

The next week, he made it to the mailbox.

The week after, he almost made it into the back of Mr. Lockhart's car to go visit Asher at his new job.

Mr. Lockhart told him they'd try again the next day.

* * * *

Asher liked his job.

Well, that wasn't true.

Asher *wanted* to like his job.

He was surrounded by makeup palettes and lipstick and shadows and powders. Working at Sephora was literally a job he would have killed for—five years before.

Now he saw the giggling teens and wondered how many of them were going to be broken in half a decade.

Saw the parents and wondered how many would look for the beaming kid trailing behind them if they went missing. Saw the men shopping alone and wished for his pepper spray that was tucked in his bag in his locker backstage.

The bell over the door dinged and he looked up with a wide, fake smile. It turned real when he spotted

Misha. His arms were wrapped around his chest like he was making himself smaller, his eyes darting from one display to the next, but he was *here*.

"Welcome to Sephora," Asher bounced over immediately, waving away the other cast member, a woman a few years his senior, who had already started over. She lifted a brow but backed away. "How may I assist you?"

Misha, now that Asher was in front of him, seemed to brighten. "I just wanted to cheer you on at work, but your brother demanded I spend at least fifty dollars before he'll let me back in the car. That...seems like a lot, right?"

Asher laughed and grabbed his hand, dragging him over to the foundations. "Not in here, it's not. Let's see what we can do."

It took only a few minutes to have Misha loaded up, but Asher drew it out longer, flirting and teasing, drawing blushes out like cotton candy, just as sweet. He wanted him to stay all day, but a gaggle of teenage girls tripped over each other as they spilled in, scaring Misha back out to the car where Ryder waited, hopefully patiently.

"I didn't know you had a *boyfriend*." Minnie leaned on the counter, twirling a tube of lip gloss against the glass, after the girls left emptyhanded. "He's adorable."

"I um...I don't know if he's my boyfriend? He's my..." *Everything,* Asher wanted to say. Boyfriend wasn't right. It seemed too playful, too transitory, for what they were. "He's my partner," he settled on.

"You guys are so cute together," Minnie said, and the way she was looking at him made his skin heat. "So." She leaned in, forgetting the lip gloss she was supposed to be stocking completely. "Which one of you...you know?"

"Hm-m?" Asher shifted his weight, uncertain what she meant.

"*You* know." Minnie wagged her eyebrows.

"No?"

"Which one of you is the girl?" she asked, just as their director walked in from backstage.

"Minnie! Are you a few pickles short of a barrel or what?" Champagne pursed their red lips. They did drag nights every Thursday and Friday night at a club and hosted Drag Queen Story Hour every Tuesday morning at the public library, and their makeup was always perfectly applied.

Minnie's foundation was so heavily caked on that Misha couldn't tell if she blushed, but she definitely dropped her eyes as she stammered an apology and scurried to the other side of the store.

"That girl," Champagne tittered. "Dumb as a box of hair, but her heart's in the right place."

Asher felt hot, like he was standing under a spotlight, and his words lodged in his throat.

Champagne just gave him a sympathetic smile. "Your shift's almost over anyway, sweetie. Why don't you head on out? Give that boy of yours some extra attention."

Asher probably should have protested but he didn't have the energy to fake it anymore. "Thank you. He'll be really happy to see me early."

Asher was right. He called his brother to come get him, and when he walked into the house, Misha sprang off the couch like a jack-in-a-box. "You're home! Guess what, Asher? Ryder got me a new game. Will you play with me?"

"Sure, just let me wash my face."

Ten minutes later, he was sitting beside Misha on the couch playing Mario Kart.

* * * *

Ryder loved having his brother and Misha living with him. After years of searching, having Asher right under foot was the only thing that let him fall back asleep after waking up in the middle of the night in a panic, fearing he'd gone missing again.

Unfortunately, having his brother and Misha *right under foot* did make it difficult for Mason and him to engage in some of their...extracurricular bedtime activities.

Namely, Ryder had been 'big' for almost a month, and he was really starting to notice it. So, after he dropped Asher off at work, while Misha was in his room studying for his GED, Ryder searched out Mason.

He was in his office, tapping away on his laptop. Ryder barely made it through the door before he dropped to his knees, choking on a "Daddy? I need you."

"Then come here." Daddy pushed his chair back from the desk and pointed to the carpet, between his knees. Quickly, Ryder obeyed, crawling over to rest where directed. Daddy cupped his cheek, tipping his head until it rested on his thigh. "Stay."

Ryder stayed, watching Daddy slowly unzip his trousers and pull out his cock with his other hand. "You've been such a good boy for me the past few weeks. You've had to do so much adulting, haven't you? You deserve a treat." Daddy stroked Ryder's cheek with his thumb. "Open that pretty mouth, baby."

Ryder did, and Daddy rewarded him by sliding the tip of his dick, leaking pre-cum, over his tongue. Daddy knew he loved this — the slightly messy, possibly demeaning but not to *him*, precursor to the actual act.

Daddy painted his lips like gloss, then dragged the pre-cum up his cheek in a parody of a smile. He waited until Ryder was whining, straining his neck to get closer, before he put it in his mouth for real. "Go ahead and suck me, baby. But Daddy has got to work, so you have to be quiet. Be my good little cock warmer."

Ryder already felt himself sinking into subspace, the weight of the cock on his tongue and slipping into his throat like a security blanket. He knew Daddy didn't want to come right now, so he just used him like a pacifier, leaving aside his typical tongue acrobatics.

Eyes closed, the warm shaft in his mouth, he finally felt calm, like he was floating in a placid pool of water.

Perfect.

* * * *

Misha finally gave up and dropped his pen to the spiral-bound notebook. He didn't understand the equation to calculate the volume of the cylinder. He'd followed all the steps in the book, but he was still getting it wrong.

Mr. Lockhart had told him the last time he had trouble — figuring out the difference between sexual and asexual reproduction in science the past week — that he could come to him for help anytime. Misha didn't want to bother the nice man while he was at work, but he'd tried everything he could think of.

So, reluctantly, he grabbed his math book and carried it downstairs. Mr. Lockhart's office door was closed, but it normally was, so he didn't think anything of it. He knocked lightly on the door and thought he heard a muffled reply, so he twisted the knob and pushed.

For a second, it was a frozen tableau, one his body registered before his mind. Mr. Lockhart in his office chair, his head thrown back, his face warped in a snarl. Ryder was on his knees, his fingers twisted in the dark fabric of a pair of trousers. Mr. Lockhart was yanking on the long blond strands of Ryder's hair.

And he was stuck in his past again, on his knees for Master, tears burning his cheeks as his throat convulsed. Part of him knew it wasn't real. The part of him that went to therapy told him to breathe. The smaller, animal piece of his mind urged him to either run, before Mr. Lockhart could grab him, or drop to his knees and wait his turn.

The disjointed thoughts had him stumbling as he tried to move back and drop down at the same time. He smacked his elbow into the corner of a bookshelf, sending a picture frame tumbling to the carpet, and the noise was enough to startle Mr. Lockhart, who released Ryder with a curse.

Ryder spun on his heels, his face red and messy, eyes wide. "Misha!"

"I... S-sorry...I sh-sh..." He stumbled through an apology but couldn't move.

"Sit down, here. Come on," Ryder urged him into the decorative armchair in the corner of the room, not-so-subtly swiping his shirt over the mess on his face. "I'm really sorry. I should have locked the door."

"I..." Misha dragged in a breath and clenched his eyes shut, counting backward like his therapist had told him to before he slowly reopened them. Looking quickly over Ryder's shoulder, he saw Mr. Lockhart's back. He was standing in front of one of the bookshelves, his left arm planted on the side, the right one picking at his hair in what seemed a nervous manner.

Misha lowered his voice to a bare whisper. "I'm sorry he does that to you. Are you okay? Can I help?"

Ryder looked confused for a second before his expression curdled to horror. He crouched in front of him, so they were face to face. "Oh, no, Misha, it's not like that—not at *all*, I..." His cheeks turned pink with embarrassment. "I *ask* him to do that. I *like* it when he... Um, so there's this thing called a power exchange relationship. It's where two people agree, *consensually*, to... It's not playing, but, kind of. I let Dadd— Mason tell me what to do because sometimes I don't want to make decisions, and sometimes I forget to do things like eat or go to bed on time. And sometimes I like it when Da—Mason—is a bit forceful with me."

"Why?" Misha didn't understand.

Ryder turned even redder. "I have a really stressful job, and with Asher missing, I was even more worried about him. So when I'd come home, a lot of times I wanted to be able to just...shut my brain off and—"

Misha shook his head and interrupted, "No, that makes sense. I don't want to think either, sometimes. It's hard remembering to go and eat, and I don't like sleeping, and Asher helps me, too. But why do you like it when Ma—Mr. Lockhart"—he still couldn't call him by his first name, it felt *wrong* in his mouth—"is forceful? Doesn't it hurt?"

"It makes me feel like all I have to do is listen to him and do what he says. If Daddy makes me do it, then I know *he* wants me to, and I won't do it wrong. It makes

KD Ellis

me feel safe to do the things that I want without feeling like he'll judge me for it afterward." Ryder smiled gently at him. "But don't worry. Everyone is different and likes different things. I just want you to know that everything you saw in here was completely my choice, and Daddy would have stopped if I'd wanted him to. He would never hurt me for real."

It seemed like something Misha would have to talk to his therapist about the next day, just to make sure he understood, so he just nodded and said instead, "And you call him Daddy?"

"It's not an incest thing," Ryder immediately reassured him. "I don't pretend he is, or want him to be, my *real* dad or anything. It's just a...well, term of respect, for people in lifestyles like ours."

"There are more people like you? Who...who do things like this?" Misha felt his eyes widen at the thought. If it were *common*, then maybe it would be okay for him to talk to Asher. He definitely didn't want a new Master, but he liked the thought of someone helping him get better about taking care of himself, and Asher always seemed so worried about him.

Maybe Asher would be his Daddy.

* * * *

Something was up with Misha.

Ryder seemed abnormally quiet when he picked Asher up from work but, assuming he was just preoccupied with his work, Asher let it go. But then he went inside, Misha bounced over with a bright smile and squished him with a tight hug. "Asher, guess what? Did you know there are relationships with Daddies and boys?"

Asher choked and looked down at Misha, guessing from the way his eyes felt that they were bugging out at the rather abrupt comment. "Have you been online again?"

"No! I walked in on Ryder and Mr. Lockhart in their study, and he explained it all to me."

Now it was Ryder choking. Asher couldn't look his brother in the eye, so he stared over his head instead, trying not to smile.

"I'm going to…go…somewhere else…" Ryder said, then scurried out of the room, leaving the two of them alone.

"Let's go sit down. I feel like this will take a second." Asher led Misha into the living room and sat down on the couch beside him, tangling their fingers together. "Let's start at the beginning."

"I was having trouble with math so I went to ask Mr. Lockhart if he could help." Misha bit his lip and tipped his head down, looking up at Asher through his lashes for a second. It was a coy, shy glance that Asher knew Misha didn't do on purpose. "He told me I could ask him. I wasn't trying to bother him or anything."

"I know you weren't," Asher reassured, squeezing Misha's hand. "Keep going."

"Well, I knocked, and I thought he said come in. I really did. I promise. And when I went in, Ryder was… He was…" Misha lowered his voice and whispered, "Sucking him off. Like Master used to have us…"

Asher swallowed at the mention of Master — *Barnes,* he corrected himself, *that fucker* — but waved for Misha to keep going.

"I told Ryder I was sorry because I thought it was the same, just like with us — that he didn't want to, you know? But he said he did! That he liked it, that Mason was his *Daddy* and that Mason helps him remember to eat and go to bed on time and sometimes even lets him watch cartoons or play with crayons and Play-Doh — and doesn't that sound nice, Asher?"

To Asher, it made perfect sense that Misha, who hadn't gotten a childhood — or much of one, anyway — would be so enamored with the lifestyle. It was just unfortunate that Asher would never be a good Daddy. He felt his heart turn to lead but forced a smile anyway. "That does sound really nice for you, Misha."

Misha smiled, but it slowly died. "Just…for me?"

"I can't be your Daddy." He could barely take care of himself. How was he supposed to take care of Misha?

* * * *

Misha was silent at dinner, picking at his spaghetti with his fork. He hadn't cried when Asher had told him no, but his eyes had burned like he'd wanted to. Asher had been really nice when he'd said it, and Misha could see that it hurt him, but he didn't know where that left them.

Would Asher be mad at him for asking? Misha didn't care that it couldn't happen. He knew he needed to be able to do these things on his own, but would Asher know that it was okay?

Asher seemed so weird around him now, staring at him when he thought Misha couldn't see him but looking away as soon as Misha stared back, stammering when he told Misha dinner was ready, like somehow Misha was going to expect him to feed him now.

That wasn't what he wanted, anyway. Asher already did everything Misha needed by telling him it was okay to go eat.

Did Asher know that?

Misha peeked over at him.

Asher was frowning at his plate, twirling and untwirling the same noodles.

Across the table, Mr. Lockhart and Ryder were also quieter than usual.

"This is really awkward," Misha finally said, sitting back in his chair, gripping the seat with his fingers. "I think I'm going to go to bed," He scooted away from the table and grabbed his plate.

"No. Stay, please?" Asher immediately said, standing as well, his expression pleading. "You need to eat something."

"I'm not hungry."

"You only ate a few bites of bread. You'll be hungry later." Asher picked at the napkin crumpled in his hand.

Misha shrugged. "None of you are eating with me out here."

"It's not you," Mason said, at the same Ryder snickered and said, "You two are too much fun to watch, that's all. It's like watching a first date."

Misha sank back down but didn't pick up his fork. Asher dropped more roughly into his chair, saying, "I don't want you to hate me or to not be enough for you. But I can't give you up, so you can get what you need, either. It's not fair."

"I would *never* hate you." Misha scooted his chair closer, ignoring the screeching noise the legs made against the floor, and he grabbed Asher's hand.

Asher closed his eyes for a brief second, and when he opened them, they were swimming. He leaned forward and pressed his forehead against Misha's. "You deserve to have absolutely everything you want."

"I want *you*," Misha whispered.

He'd forgotten about their audience until Mr. Lockhart broke the silence that followed to say, "So Liam is moving to Austin. He wants to see you when he gets here."

Misha's heart skipped in his chest, and he pulled away from Asher to look at Mr. Lockhart. "Liam is coming back?"

"Why?" Asher asked at almost the same time, and when Misha turned back to him, it was to see the suspicion on his face that barely covered the hope. Misha knew that he'd been just as hurt as him when Liam had disappeared with barely a goodbye.

"He didn't say much, but I get the impression that *something* here made him rearrange his priorities."

"He missed you," Ryder clarified for his husband, a big grin on his face. "Both of you, from what it sounds like."

"We were just a job to him," Asher stubbornly insisted, crossing his arms.

"Trust me. If you were just a job to that man, then he takes his work *way* too seriously."

Misha fingered the silicone watch he only took off to shower. Would he have given the watches to them if he was only doing his job? Or handed them each a napkin with a cell phone number on it, telling them to call if they needed anything?

Not, of course, that Misha had dared. He'd sent him a few carefully written texts, mostly just 'Good *morning*'s', or a picture of his room or an update about

his schoolwork. Liam's replies were always short—
never rude but never longer than a 'Good job', either.

He'd saved every text.

Was he just doing his job each time he'd answered?
Misha's heart fell at the thought and he hunched his
shoulders. But if it was just a job, why *was* he coming
back?

Chapter Twenty-Five

Austin was as hot as Liam remembered, but he wouldn't trade it for the chill of the city. With help from his sister, he'd sold his penthouse outright for a cool eight-digit payout. He'd grown to hate every wall in the place. If he ever decided to go back, then he'd start over fresh.

Thanks to advice from Lynette, who had reassured him that property was never a bad investment—no matter what 2007 had said—he'd bought a four-bedroom ranch-style home in the Cherrywood neighborhood of East Austin. She'd assured him that it was one of the most sought-after areas, and that while it was quiet, there was plenty to do. And if he decided to leave, it was located so close to the University of Texas that he'd have no problem leasing it out to students or professors.

He'd spent a week crashing in Lynette's guest room while they waited for the movers to ship the furniture he was bringing cross country. There wasn't much, mostly just his bedroom set and his grandmother's kitchen table that he'd finally gotten out of storage.

He was going to furnish the rest himself.

The pictures didn't do it justice. The limestone exterior and big windows already made the house look more like a home than his old place had. And as he walked through the rooms, he could see himself living here with his two boys.

He could see them sitting in the large living room on the family couch, playing video games or watching a movie, see them sitting beside each other at the bar in the kitchen, their bare feet swinging as he made breakfast, see them splashing in the pool in the small backyard or roasting s'mores over the firepit.

He gave himself one week to get the bones of the furnishings in place. It was only a skeleton of the finished home, but he didn't want to decorate it until he had his boys there—if, of course, he managed to convince them to forgive him for leaving.

Even if they were only friends... Hell, even if they only saw him as the person who had helped them through a rough time, he would force himself to accept that and move on.

He needed to start living, not flitting from assignment to assignment, always being someone else.

It was time for a fresh start.

Liam picked up his phone and hesitated. In the end, he called Mason.

"Liam, good to hear from you," the man said, smile coming through in his voice. "Settled in okay?"

"Yeah, it's all good. Finally got food in the fridge and sheets on the mattress."

"Doing better than we did. Took me longer than that to figure out where the packers stuck our toothbrushes. I'd already broken down and bought new ones."

They chatted for a bit, Liam getting details about when Mason wanted him to start working. He was only committing to one-off protection details, working security for events or filling in on days off. He wanted to have time to repair his relationships with Asher and Misha, not get roped into a twenty-four seven job again.

But finally, he couldn't stall any longer. "How are they doing?"

"They're improving. I doubt they will ever be *better*, but they're getting there. They miss you, though I doubt Asher would admit that. I probably shouldn't tell you this, but they had a bit of a tiff last week."

"Oh?"

"Misha walked in on Ryder and me while we were...well, being intimate. He had some questions."

"I bet." Liam grimaced in sympathy, even though he knew Mason wouldn't see him. It hadn't taken him long to spot the special nature of their relationship, even with the bullet wound and all the shit wrapping up with the cartel. Misha, with his history...

"How'd he take it?" Liam asked.

"Hard, at first, until Ryder explained that it was consensual. But then he realized he might like it, but Asher didn't, and...it spiraled from there."

"You saying Misha wants a Daddy? And Asher doesn't?" Liam rubbed his chest, saddened at the realization that to be with them, he might have to lose that element of his personality. He would do it. He'd had vanilla relationships before, but something about the two boys called to that part of him strongly.

"No, I'm saying Misha wanted *Asher* to be his Daddy, and if I'm honest? I think Asher would rather have one, too. It was almost heartbreaking, watching them. They normally stick to each other like glue, so seeing them tiptoeing around each other felt wrong. So, I *may* have warned them you were moving back to Austin." Mason paused a second. "Sorry...not sorry."

"They were going to find out eventually," Liam said, perking up at the explanation. "Better it not come out of the blue anyway. Will you ask them if they want to meet with me? For breakfast, at Stars tomorrow?" He threw out the name of one of the restaurants in the neighborhood he'd driven by but hadn't stopped at yet.

"I'll ask. What time are you thinking?"

"Nine?"

"I'll get back to you."

Liam waited patiently by his phone. If by patiently, he meant that he picked it up and stared at it religiously every ten minutes and triple checked his volume was up, just to make sure he didn't miss any messages.

And when the time finally came in, he *definitely* didn't spend far too many hours in front of his closet picking out his outfit.

And he only showed up to the café an hour early, so he *wasn't* desperate to see his boys, not at all. It was a perfectly normal thing to do.

Liam stood with his back to the door, staring at one of the paintings on the café wall. It was a painting of the café he was standing in, a quite good one, really. He wasn't really looking anymore. He felt...nervous, which made no sense. He could stare down the barrel of a loaded gun, talk down a suicide bomber and ingest suspiciously laced cocaine undercover without hesitation.

But seeing Asher and Misha? *That* frightened him?

Maybe it was that this was the first time they'd be meeting him completely as himself, not the leather-jacket-wearing criminal or the plain-clothed agent trying to stay under the radar.

He'd finally decided to wear his black-calf-and-red-suede Bemer's over his Waddington socks, to match his bespoke Brioni suit. He'd shaved, losing the scruff he'd worn in the camper out of necessity, and his haircut was an eight-hundred-dollar Julien Farel. His hair had gone gray early, before he'd left his twenties behind. Normally, it didn't bother him, giving him an older, distinguished appearance that helped sell his cover stories, but now he wondered if Misha and Liam would think him too old at nearly forty.

The only thing he'd kept was his vertical labret piercing, though he'd swapped the cheap silver bar for black rhodium.

He'd almost dressed down, had pulled half a dozen outfits out and discarded them, but at the last minute he'd changed his mind. This was who he was — a flashy gay man with expensive taste and enough money to fund it. He needed to know if they'd accept him like this, because just like he couldn't expect them to be someone else for him, he knew he had to hold himself to those same expectations.

The most important part of a relationship was honesty. He needed to be upfront about exactly who he was.

"He's not here." Misha's disappointed voice echoed through the café and Liam turned.

"Hello, Misha, Asher." Liam swallowed at the sight of their faces for the first time in months, then glanced over their shoulder to Mason. "Thanks for bringing them."

"Of course." Mason grinned, then crossed his arms. His biceps stretched the sleeves of his shirt. "But don't think that just because I like you that I won't find a place to bury your body parts if you hurt them."

"I'll even dig the hole," Liam assured.

"Yes, you damn well will. Be good, boys." Mason patted each of them on the shoulder then whistled as he left.

Misha gave him a brilliant smile, practically bouncing, but Asher stood a half-step behind, his hands shoved the pockets of his over-sized fuchsia sweater. His mulish expression made Liam want to smile.

As soon as they sat down, Misha gave him the biggest, widest puppy-dog eyes and asked, "Can I have hot chocolate? And Ryder says they have French toast. Can I have that? With Nutella? Ryder said it's the best."

"You can have whatever you want. What about you, Asher?"

Asher glared at his menu, then slapped it down on the table. "If I get an omelet, do I have to blow you after?"

"Ash!" Misha whined, tugging at his sweater.

"Well, he's been gone for so long. He must want something if he's back now. Right?" Asher turned his glare on Liam. He probably meant to look angry, but all Liam could see was the pain lurking underneath the stubborn words.

"How about you get your omelet, and the only thing I want from you is for you to accept my apology. I thought I was doing what was best for you—for *both* of you—when I left. I thought that sticking around would just be a painful reminder. It was wrong of me to make that decision for you two without asking." Liam closed his own menu, not really caring what he ended up eating as long as he could convince Asher and Misha that he was serious.

Asher picked up his silverware, fiddling with the spoon before starting to tear the edge of the napkin. "Whatever. But I want fries with my omelet—and a hot chocolate...and nachos."

He looked at Liam like he expected him to say no and was preparing to argue, but Liam shrugged, relaying the orders to the waitress, just asking for whatever their special was for himself.

Then, they sat there in an awkward silence for several seconds. Misha broke it before it stretched too long. "Did you see the picture of my new room? Ryder let me put up a poster."

"Of BTS." Asher smirked. "He doesn't even know any of their songs."

"They're pretty, though. I like them."

"You don't like their music, though."

Misha pouted. "Does that matter?"

"No," Liam interrupted. "You can put a poster up of whatever you want. You don't have to have any other reason than you like them."

"Well, *I* put up a poster of Tom Daley," Asher bragged, meeting Liam's eyes in what could have been a dare.

"Well, *you* don't even know how to swim," Misha teased back.

"You don't have to know how to swim to admit that man looks *fine* all covered in water."

"I used to have a Bowie poster," Liam said, shifting his silverware over so the waitress could start distributing their plates, waiting until she left again to continue speaking. "I've always had more of a thing for stylish blonds." He hadn't minded the red and brown, had grown used to it in the months in the camper, but he was glad they'd let it go back to natural. It reminded him that they were safe now.

Asher turned pink and Misha giggled, and Liam felt like, maybe, the conversation could be considered a success. "Eat your food."

"Yes, sir," Misha happily agreed, taking a large drink of his hot chocolate, wincing slightly at the heat. Asher was slower to stab a forkful of egg.

"You can call me Liam, you know," Liam said, even if he did like the way the word rolled off the boy's tongue. He just didn't think Misha knew what that word meant to him.

Misha turned scarlet and leaned into Asher, whispering something in his ear. Asher listened, then relayed to Liam, "He says it feels too weird. He likes you too much, and it seems disrespectful."

"I suppose if you feel more comfortable, you can keep calling me 'sir'. But I don't want you to feel obligated to, either of you. And you need to know, Misha"—Liam turned his attention on the slighter of the two boys—"that it means something more to me than it likely does to you. As long as you are okay with that, I won't say anything else."

Misha whispered in Asher's ear again, the two of them conferring for what felt like ages, before Asher finally turned to Liam again. "He says he knows what it means, and that's why he wants to use it." Asher's skin pinkened again as he added, "He also says not to worry, that he's been researching power exchange online and that Ryder made sure it wasn't just porn. He says he wants you to be his Daddy someday, but for now, he'll settle for you being his 'Sir' instead."

"Misha." Liam leaned in a bit and lowered his voice, keeping it gentle as he corrected him. "If you don't feel like you can speak to me about this directly, then I'm worried it's something you're not truly ready for."

Misha cringed like he'd been slapped. "I'm sorry. I'll do better. I promise."

He couldn't watch him be upset and not do anything, so he reached across the table and gathered the boy's hand in his, thrumming his thumb over the pulse in his wrist. "I'm not angry, and you don't have to apologize. We can take everything slow, as slow as the *both* of you need. I'm not going anywhere this time, not unless you tell me to. I'm willing to consider being your 'Sir' when you are able to ask me yourself. Until then, you can call me 'sir' if you wish, but it will only be a term of respect, not a title."

"Okay," Misha agreed, biting his lip and staring at his French toast with watery eyes.

"Please don't cry. It's not a bad thing or a punishment. I need you to know how honored I am that you want that from me, and that someday, when the *both* of you are ready, we can talk about it again, okay?"

Misha nodded.

Asher reached across Misha's plate to grab the Nutella, setting it by Misha's knife. "Try this on your toast."

Obediently, Misha scraped it out without question and spread it over the already too-sweet bread. Liam, inwardly cringing, could see he was going to have his hands full with the pair, especially since he had a hard time telling them no.

They were going to be the most spoiled boys in existence.

They deserved it.

* * * *

Misha applied a thin layer of clear gloss to his lips and rubbed them together, then pouted at Asher. "Should I go with pink instead?"

"If you want to, but I think that one looks okay," Asher said. "Besides, you don't want anything too sticky, anyway."

"True," Misha agreed and tucked his makeup away.

They were standing shoulder to shoulder in the hall bathroom, each touching up their makeup to get ready for their date. Asher was still hesitant, Misha could tell, but he *had* agreed to go. Misha thought that was a good sign.

Asher was pretending to be angry, but Misha knew better. He knew that really, he was hurt. For the weeks — months — that they had spent in the camper, just the three of them, they'd let their guard down. Liam — even in his head, it felt weird to use his first name — had been the only person they'd had to rely on, and he'd taken such good care of them. Misha knew now, thanks to his therapist, how easy it would have been for someone to have taken advantage of either of them.

Liam hadn't. He'd done everything he could to make sure they knew they were safe. Then suddenly, he'd been gone. It was like their foundation had been ripped out from under them. And it wasn't like Misha was handling it better than Asher was. It was just...different.

Some part of him had always expected Liam to leave, and Asher, too. Thankfully, he'd been wrong about Asher.

"Do my eyes?" Asher asked, handing Misha a black liner and hopping onto the counter, leaning forward so Misha could reach. The familiar position soothed the edges of Misha's frayed nerves, and he methodically ran the pencil along Asher's waterline. When he was finished, Asher jumped down.

"Your turn, now."

Misha preferred to stand, so he leaned against the counter and closed his eyes. He enjoyed the way Asher's fingers felt on his cheek and over his eyes, the gentle pressure as he stretched the skin to apply the makeup better. The gentleness had always felt like a promise.

A promise that he would never hurt him, unless he *had* to, unless Master made him. Even then, only to save him more pain at Master's hand. These few stolen moments helping each other with makeup had always been his favorite part of the day. They didn't need to gather those seconds like spare change and hoard them anymore, but Misha didn't think he'd ever feel different about them.

They'd always be precious.

Even if he didn't wear as much makeup, now that he wasn't beaten if he didn't apply it correctly.

But he wanted to look nice for Liam.

They left the bathroom, Misha barely restraining himself from skipping toward the door, Asher more restrained as he followed. He couldn't wait for Asher, who had passed his driver's test the past week, to drive them across town to the ice cream parlor.

He could tell Asher was nervous. He checked the mirrors three times in the used Ford Focus Ryder had gifted them and reached over twice to double-check Misha's seatbelt, before he pulled out onto the street.

Misha didn't care that they were driving slowly and the other motorists were honking as they zipped by. Unlike when he rode with others, he didn't have that small voice in the back of his head with Asher, the one that told him he was being dropped off somewhere bad because he was too much work. Instead, he got to press his nose to the glass and stare out at the brightly colored shops and pedestrians.

The ice cream parlor was white brick, but the letters on the sign were neon rainbows, like sprinkles on vanilla, and the best part was, he could see Liam waiting for them just inside the door.

Misha snickered. "He's going to drip on his suit." He was surprised he liked them on Liam as much as he did. Usually, the fitted business wear reminded him of Master and his friends, but none of *them* had ever filled theirs out like Liam did, like it was a part of his skin begging for touch. Misha bet the fabric was soft.

"I doubt it," Asher teased, "since *some* of us can eat our food like a grown up."

Misha stuck out his tongue and leaped from the car. "Race you!"

Asher ran after Misha, cursing under his breath when the other boy barely looked before darting into the street. Traffic was slow, but not slow enough for *that*. Even Liam looked alarmed, pushing the door to the parlor open and stepping halfway out before they even made it to the sidewalk.

"Dimitri!" Liam snapped, his skin gray. "Are you *insane?*"

Misha stumbled to a stop and Asher nearly smacked into him from behind, skidding to a halt himself. "I... Are you angry? I just wanted to see you..." He stepped back into Asher, who could feel him start to shake.

He wrapped his arms around Misha's waist from behind and pulled him tight to his chest. At the same time Liam's face softened. "I'm sorry. I didn't mean to yell. You just scared me, running across the street like that. You could have been hit."

Misha wiggled in Asher's arms, turning until he could bury his face in Asher's neck. They were nearly the same height, but like this, Misha felt dainty and fragile. "I'm *sorry,*" Misha whispered.

Asher glared at Liam over Misha's head. He'd been scared, too, but that didn't give him the right to yell...especially not at Misha.

"Maybe we should go home," Asher suggested.

Misha shook his head, hair tickling Asher's neck. "No. I want ice cream. You *promised.*"

"Misha, we can—" Liam stretched out his hand to touch his shoulder.

Asher jerked back, tugging Misha with him. "Don't touch him. You yelled at him. You don't get to touch him after that."

"I'm sorry," Liam said again, and Asher wavered. He really *did* look apologetic. "I shouldn't have yelled. I won't do it again."

"You better not. And because you did, you owe him at *least* two scoops...with sprinkles." To make sure Liam knew he was serious, Asher glared extra hard as he slipped past him to lead Misha inside.

"And gummy bears?" Misha added quietly, finally pulling away slightly. He didn't make Asher let him go, but now it looked more like an awkward hug than clinging for dear life, at least.

"And gummy bears," Asher relayed to Liam, who turned slightly green at the suggestion but nodded.

"Two scoops with sprinkles and gummy bears, coming right up. Should I get you the same?"

Asher grimaced. "*Blek*. No, I want chocolate…with chocolate chips and syrup."

"Find us a seat, and I'll bring it right back."

A smidge out of spite, Asher chose a small table in the back, the ones clearly made for children. It was a bit of a squeeze for Misha and Asher to fit in, but it would be hilarious watching Liam try to fit his muscular ass onto the third.

Even Misha giggled, covering his mouth to smother it.

Especially when Liam turned to find them and he looked so fricking confused, glancing between them and the empty seat. "It's *pink*," Misha whispered.

Unfortunately, when Liam came over with their ice cream, they didn't get to see him try to sit in it. Instead, he dragged over a regular chair from the empty table beside them and spun it around, straddling it and resting his arms on the back. Instead of ice cream, he had a shake.

Asher only pouted a *little* before the ice cream called his name and he had to try it. It was like a chocolate orgasm in his mouth, and he moaned, barely noticing the strange expression that crossed Liam's face. He *did* notice the way he shifted in his seat, which made Asher flush and look away.

Misha was quieter as he ate his, and surprisingly neat, taking little candy-loaded bites and savoring each one, like he'd never had ice cream before — which, come to think of it, could be true.

"What do you think?" he asked, nudging Misha with his elbow.

"It's cold. I like the sprinkles."

"Of course you do, they're all sugar. What about the gummy bears?"

"I like how they look but they're really chewy." Misha's face scrunched up when he said it, a tell-tale sign that they weren't living up to the fantasy he'd created for them in his head.

Asher hated them, but he knew Misha was going to force himself to eat them, so he held out his hand. "Want me to help?"

"Really?" Misha brightened and dug out five of the six bears, dropping them in Asher's palm. They were just as gross as he remembered, even with the sticky vanilla cream, but Asher diligently swallowed each one, drowning the taste with a big heap of his own ice cream after.

Misha happily finished his bowl.

* * * *

Liam dressed down for their third...could he call it a date yet? That's what they were, to him at least. Instead of his best suit, he wore a pair of dark trousers and a black Henley, about as casual as it got for him. This time, Asher was planning their excursion and all he'd told Liam was an address and to *"wear something he didn't mind getting dirty."*

Unfortunately, there wasn't much in his closet that fit that description. He'd settled only on the Henley because it was a size too big, and he hadn't bothered taking it to the tailor yet.

He wouldn't be devastated if it got a little mud on it or something.

Or, as it turned out, paint.

Liam tried to hide his grimace as he took a small gulp of the boxed wine that came with the Wine and Paint party passes. It was cheap, which he supposed he should expect as part of a ten-dollar ticket, and far too dry for his taste, but Asher and Misha both seemed to like it. They were a glass-and-a-half in each and already giggling.

Of the three of them, only Misha had a recognizable flower on his canvas. Sure, the petals were lopsided, but Asher's looked more like a deformed Barney, and Liam's? Well, saying it was abstract would be putting it mildly.

The cuffs of his Henley were damp from where he'd accidentally dunked his forearm in the paint water, and his collar was speckled with blue and purple after he'd dropped his brush a time or three, but he found he didn't care *nearly* as much as he should.

"You got a bit of... Here, let me." Asher gave up trying to direct him to the paint and reached up with his napkin, dabbing gently along the curve of Liam's jaw. It was a surprisingly tender moment Liam hated to break, but eventually Asher swallowed and lowered his hand. "There. Better."

He swallowed. "Thank you."

"Well," Asher huffed, skin turning pink as he averted his eyes. "Can't have you walking around like that, can I?"

Liam didn't plan on doing much walking, not until the erection in his pants subsided, at least. Thankfully, by the time the class was finished and they were carrying out their mostly dry canvases to the Uber, it had.

At Asher's urging, the paintings got shotgun and the three of them crammed into the backseat. Thanks to his inability to say no, Liam was smooshed in the middle seat, an elbow digging in his ribs on one side, a knee pressed against his thigh on the other.

"Where to?" The balding man in the driver's seat sounded bored as he waited for directions.

"Can we go see your new house?" Misha chirped up from Liam's right.

"Is that okay with you, Asher?" Liam asked, not wanting to push if he wasn't ready. But Asher just shrugged, so Liam gave his address to the driver.

As the car dropped them off on the sidewalk, Liam fiddled with the edge of his canvas, overcome with a strange feeling of embarrassment as he stared at the exterior of his house. "It's nothing fancy..."

"It's huge." Asher gave him a strange look before shoving his hands in the pocket of his sweater.

"Can we go in?" Misha asked, curling his arm around the crook of Asher's elbow with a brilliant smile. Despite it, Liam could tell he was nervous. It was easy to read in the way he kept dropping his eyes but then forcing them back up, and in how he was biting into his lower lip.

"Of course. After you?" Liam opened the door but stepped back to let them in. Misha went in first, Asher after a long hesitation.

"Don't lock it?" Asher blurted as Liam stepped in and closed the door behind him.

"I won't. And here, why don't you hold onto these for me?" Liam handed over his keys, knowing it would help the skittish young man feel more comfortable to keep them in his possession. He wouldn't need them, anyway.

Asher's hands shook as he took them, but Liam didn't comment. A couple months of therapy could never eradicate five years of trauma, and the young man had all the reason in the world to be nervous.

"Thank you," Asher said, and his voice was quiet but strong. He shoved the keys into his pocket, then folded his arms, fiddling with the fabric of his shirt with his fingers.

"Would you like to explore on your own, or do you want the guided tour?" Liam was fine with either. He wouldn't mind having a few moments to go to the kitchen and get snacks ready.

"Explore on our own for now," Asher said.

"Guided tour later," Misha added, almost at the same time. Almost like they really *were* brothers, finishing each other's sentences. Back to blond now, they both looked like they could be.

Liam shook the thought off. "I'll go grab us some drinks. Take your time."

In the kitchen, Liam took his time putting on a pot of coffee. While it brewed, he poured out cocoa, butter and a little dash of milk, mixing them in a bowl then setting the paste aside. He pulled out an aluminum saucepan and poured in more milk, whistling while he whisked it until it steamed. Then, he scraped in the chocolate mixture.

He continued stirring until it was thick and hot, then carefully poured the hot chocolate into a pair of mugs, adding a few drops of vanilla and cinnamon, then topped it with whipped cream. He was just replacing the canister into the fridge when Misha appeared in the doorway, Asher his shadow.

"It smells good." Misha came closer.

"Good, because it's for you." Liam slid one of the mugs along the counter to Misha, then held the other out for Asher to grab.

"Thank you," Asher muttered as he gripped the handle, his cheeks pink. Liam was glad when the young man took a drink without hesitation. Despite his prickly attitude lately, it seemed he still trusted Liam enough to accept food from him.

"Are you hungry?" The question was for both of them, but Misha perked up immediately.

"Do you have snacks?"

Snacks turned out to be a bowl of popcorn each that they munched on from their position on the couch. Misha sat cross-legged on the center cushion, while Asher lounged next to him against the arm rest, his feet kicked up on the wood coffee table. He was wearing large, fluffy pink socks. They slouched down over his ankles.

Misha's feet were bare, possibly why they were tucked up under his thighs. Liam grabbed one of the half-dozen fuzzy blankets strewn around the room and draped it over Misha's lap.

"Thank you, Mr. Liam," Misha said, smiling brilliantly up at him before tugging the blanket up to his face to rub the soft fabric against his cheek.

Liam cleared his throat and moved to the armchair, grabbing the remote off the end table. "So, what do we want to watch? I've got everything from the classics to *Jurassic Park*."

"Oh, *Sailor Moon*!" Asher blurted, then turned beat red. "Which I have…definitely *never* watched."

"It's a cartoon! Can we watch it? Please?" Misha turned puppy-dog eyes on Liam.

Before Liam could agree, Asher sat forward with a gasp. "It's not a *cartoon*. It's anime, you heathen!" Now Asher turned pleading eyes to Liam. "We have to watch it now. Please?"

How could he say no?

Chapter Twenty-Six

Asher jerked awake with a start. The living room was shrouded in darkness, heavy curtains blocking out any light that might have filtered in from the Austin city streets. Even the television was sleeping, giving off a dim, blue-gray haze.

Asher didn't remember falling asleep, but at some point, he must have. Misha was sprawled out on the other end of the couch, and they were both tucked under a large afghan. It was soft and warm and smelled better than the one Liam had routinely covered them with back in the camper.

Carefully, Asher disentangled his feet from Misha's before sliding off the couch. He retucked the blanket around Misha's legs, then brushed a strand of hair away from where it was stuck to the boy's lips.

He needed to take a leak, so he tiptoed down the hallway to where he vaguely remembered the bathroom was, not turning on the light just in case Liam was still awake.

After washing his hands, he crept back into the hallway. He didn't think he'd be able to go back to sleep now that he was up, but it was far too early to be awake. He planned to retreat to the couch and curl back up against the armrest while he waited for morning.

Instead, he turned the corner and ran headfirst into a solid wall. Well, a heavily muscled chest, but it *felt* like a wall. He hit hard enough that he stumbled back and only Liam's big hands on his shoulders kept him from falling completely.

"Steady there," Liam rumbled, and it sent a shiver along Asher's skin.

"Sorry," Asher instinctively apologized, whether for running into him or waking him up, though, he wasn't sure.

"No need to be. Can't sleep?"

Asher shrugged. "Did a little, but..." He waved at the bathroom behind him, feeling his cheeks heat at the admission. Everybody poops, sure...but that didn't mean he wanted to talk about bathroom stuff.

"Ah. Wash your hands?"

"You're not my Daddy." Asher glared at the older man, but it was half-hearted at best and faltered when Liam laughed. "Shut up."

"I didn't say anything," Liam said, his lips still twitching.

"You don't need to. I see that." Asher reached up and touched the corner of Liam's mouth, his fingers grazing the soft skin before he yanked them away and stepped back. "Sorry."

"Don't be." Liam's smile softened. "You can touch me whenever you want. I don't mind."

"I should have asked," Asher admitted.

"Well, consider this a blanket yes for the future…if you want." Liam's eyes searched his and Asher felt exposed, like he was standing naked, yet not ashamed. And his heart thumped in his chest, but strangely, he wasn't afraid.

"Okay," Asher said, swallowing as he realized that he *did* want. His fingers itched with the urge to run them along Liam's stubbled jaw, down the corded neck. Instead, he shoved them into his pockets.

"*Only* if you want," Liam emphasized.

"Can… Can you just hug me?" Asher asked, embarrassed at the plaintive way the words came out. Except for Misha, no one touched him—not even his brother, except for a few hesitant brushes that could almost have been accidental. Most of the time, he was grateful, but sometimes, like tonight, in the hallway with Liam… Sometimes he just wanted to be treated like he was *normal*—not like he fragile, a vase on the edge of a shelf poised to break.

Then Liam's arms were around him, tugging him into his chest. Liam's palm cradled the back of his head and turned it so his nose no longer dug painfully into Liam's sternum.

He could hear Liam's heartbeat.

It was steady and calm.

Asher wanted to stay there forever, listening to the soothing sound. He wanted to feel this warm and safe and *loved*. Instead, he reluctantly pulled away. "Thank you." He cleared his throat.

"You never have to thank me for giving you what you need." Liam reached out and tugged gently on a piece of Asher's hair, the one that kept falling into his eye until he blew it away. "And if you ever need another haircut, you know where to find me, yeah?"

"Yeah. Okay. Can you do it now?" Asher dropped his eyes. "Or in the morning... I know it's late."

"Now is fine. We're not sleeping anyway, right?" Liam's smile was wry. "I'll grab the scissors. Are you okay going into the main bath? There's more room..."

"That's fine." Asher yanked on the hem of his shirt. "Do you want me to wait for you?"

"If you want to, but there's nothing in this house I'm worried about you seeing. Feel free to head on back without me."

Liam took a few seconds to steady himself before he grabbed his spare grooming kit out of the guest bath. He had no issue using his main kit, but it was in his en suite, and he wanted to give Asher a few moments. And he needed a few as well, if he were honest.

He centered himself before following Asher to the main bathroom.

Asher was sitting on the closed toilet, wringing his hands like a wet towel in his lap. Liam crouched down and took the boy's hands in his. "Hey, we don't have to do this if you don't want."

"I want to," Asher immediately answered, tightening his grip on Liam's fingers.

"Okay." Liam gave Asher's hands a final squeeze before he stood. "Are you comfortable there or should I grab a chair?"

"This is fine. Let me just..." Asher squirmed around until he was straddling the toilet lid backward, facing the tank. "How's that?"

"Good boy," Liam said. "That's perfect." He skimmed his finger along Asher's shirt. "Do you feel comfortable taking this off?"

Asher nodded and tugged off his top, holding it in his lap. Liam almost asked if he wanted him to put it aside, but the way the boy was holding it made him change his mind. If it got too hairy, Liam would just give Asher one of his shirts to wear home instead.

"Ready?" Liam asked. Asher nodded, so Liam got to work, wetting the strands and working through the blond waves with a comb until it was smooth and tangle free. He took his time snipping the ends and shaping it, humming an old tune softly under his breath, the one his mother always used to hum when she trimmed *his* hair. He didn't know the words, just the melody.

Otherwise, he worked in comfortable silence, so he was surprised when Asher spoke abruptly. "Barnes liked to pull my hair."

Liam stalled, lowering the scissors. He was mostly finished anyway, but there was no way he could go on after that—not with the way his fingers clenched on the handle, his knuckles white. He set the shears carefully on the side of the sink.

"Barnes is going to get everything he deserves. Texas is a death penalty state." Liam spritzed some more water on Asher's hair, more for something to do with his hands than any need. Then, he ran his fingers through the strands, gently massaging the boy's scalp.

"He won't get it, though. He'll make a deal." Asher's shoulders slumped. "Barnes has a lot of friends— influential ones with lots of money. They'll get him set up in some cushy prison somewhere and throw away the key."

Liam wanted to take the bastard out into the desert and bury him alive—dig him back up and beat the tar out of him then do it all over again, until the man was carrion food.

"People who abuse children don't do well in prison. He'll get what he deserves, by the hands of the other inmates, if not the law." Liam finally grabbed a towel and started drying Asher's hair with gentle pats.

"As long as I never have to see him again. My therapist says I need to talk about...what he did. That it's an important part of moving forward, and that...that if I want to ask you to join me and Misha in *our* relationship, I have to be able to trust you with our past." Asher sounded out of breath when he finished, his body taut as a bowstring...like he was preparing for rejection.

"She seems like a smart therapist. We can talk here, if you'd like, or we can go somewhere more comfortable."

"Misha's sleeping on the couch, and I don't want to wake him. Can we lie on your bed? Just...I only want to cuddle. I'm not... I don't want to do anything else." Asher twisted on the toilet to look at him, his eyes pleading.

"Of course we can. Just cuddling, I promise. Cross my heart," Liam drew an X in the center of his chest, then held out his hand. "Come on. Let me help you up."

Asher kept his hand as they moved out of the bathroom and into the bedroom. Liam folded back the covers, lifting them for Asher to climb in. Asher rolled onto his side, his back to Liam, who curled up around him like a big spoon.

"I'm here. You can tell me as much or as little as you want. Nothing you say is going to make me think differently of you, I promise."

Asher's words were halting at first, but slowly, he told Liam his story. "So I met this guy online..."

Chapter Twenty-Seven

Ryder bounced into Mason's study shortly after his brother and Misha had left for their date. "Guess what, Daddy? Guess what! We have the house to ourselves. You know what that means, right?"

"That you can finally straighten up the nursery like I asked you to do yesterday? And the day before?" Daddy spun around in his spinny chair and lifted a brow.

Ryder pouted and shook his head. "No, Daddy, my toys are having a big important meeting today. They told me I had to leave them alone until it's over."

"And do you think it will be over anytime soon?"

"Next week, maybe." Ryder waved away the boring talk. "It's a very important meeting. No, what it *means* is that we can have a naked movie night!" Not a movie with naked people—he'd never really cared about adult films that much—but they could watch his favorite movies in the nude.

Daddy gave him a knowing look. "Is that why it got so hot in here that I had to take my sweater off?"

"Yes! I turned the heat up *hours* ago. Aren't I smart, Daddy?" Ryder bounced on his toes. He knew Daddy wouldn't tell him no, since he'd caught Mason looking longingly at their fluffy slippers more than once.

"I suppose you *also* remembered to close all the curtains this time?"

"Oops! Be right back!" Ryder sprinted out of the room and through the house, closing all the blinds and curtains so not even a crack of sunlight spilled through this time. He didn't want any nosey nellies watching his Daddy naked any more than Daddy did. When he was finished, he followed the sound of something clattering in the kitchen, where Daddy was in the process of making him hot chocolate and a yucky green smoothie for himself.

Ryder stuck his tongue out at the blender.

"I'm not making you drink it, so please don't pick on the blender," Daddy said dryly, looking over his shoulder with a knowing look.

Ryder batted his eyes, the picture of innocence. "I'm being a good boy, Daddy."

"Sure." Daddy shook his head but turned around to finish stirring the hot milk on the stove. Ryder stuck his tongue out at the appliance again before Daddy could see him. Stupid, nasty-smelling health drink.

"Why don't you go pick out a movie if you can't behave," Daddy said, proving that he *must* have eyes in the back of his head. Or he just knew Ryder that well, but he didn't find that thought as fun.

"Okay, Daddy." Ryder bounded off to the living room, dropping down onto his stomach in front of the movie shelf. He really wanted to watch something funny, but he also really wanted rewatch *Lord of the Rings*, which wasn't funny but was his go-to comfort movie. It wasn't really a naked movie night kind of film, though. "Ooh, this one!"

He snagged the case off the shelf and crawled over to the Blu-Ray player to slip the disc in. Daddy came in with their drinks just as the opening credits started rolling.

"*Labyrinth*?" Daddy smirked as he set their cups on the table.

"Yep! Time to get naked, Daddy. You go first." Ryder paused the movie and sat criss-cross-applesauce on the carpet, watching Daddy with rapt attention as, even though he rolled his eyes, Mason started undressing. He yanked his socks off without any flair, then shucked his jeans and boxers in one shove. A second later, his shirt joined them, and Daddy was naked.

"Yes, sexy Daddy." Ryder didn't waste time collecting an eyeful. Daddy was still all muscley from his military days, even if those bulging biceps and six-pack abs had a layer of fluff over them now. He was like, the *perfect* pillow, firm at the center and fluffy on top. "Do a little dance for me?"

"I'm not turning my dick into a helicopter, boy."

"Again. You're not turning it into a helicopter *again*," Ryder clarified.

"One time, and you won't let me live it down."

"But, Daddy, why would a helicopter be going into a tunnel? You should have said it was a train, a nice long one, and that I needed to open my mouth so the *train* could go into the tunnel."

"Try to do something nice, and this is what I get." Daddy crossed his arms like he was angry, but his cheeks were pink, and his lips twitched, so Ryder knew better. Daddy dropped onto the couch, his thighs spread to make room for his heavy balls. "Your turn now, baby."

Ryder bounced up and started slowly removing his clothes, making sure to always give Daddy a good view of his best angles. He dropped his clothes on top of Daddy's before kicking the whole pile under the coffee table.

"Such a pretty boy. How'd I get so lucky?" Daddy patted the couch beside him.

"It's that four-leaf clover you found in Scotland, Daddy," Ryder curled up on the cushion where Daddy indicated, dropping his head onto Daddy's thigh. The dark, curly hairs tickled his cheek, just the way Ryder liked.

"My lucky clover." Daddy started running his fingers through Ryder's hair. It was more soothing than sexual. They were both naked, but Ryder was only half-hard. Right now, even if Daddy was hot and his dick was inches from his face, he didn't want sex. He just…wanted closeness.

So they watched *Labyrinth*, cuddled on the couch and drank their drinks. And it was perfect.

Chapter Twenty-Eight

Misha woke up alone. With the curtain pulled, he didn't know what time it was, but it felt late. He yawned and rolled, keeping the blanket draped around him as he stood up. It tangled in his feet as he shuffled through the house, searching out either of the two men who already held pieces of his heart. The kitchen was quiet, except for the steady drip of an auto-brewing coffee machine. The bathroom door was open, the room dark.

Misha hesitated in front of the final room to check.

The bedroom.

Liam's bedroom.

The door was cracked, but the room beyond was dark. Misha snuck a toe out from the thick blanket and nudged the chilly wood. It swung open on silent hinges. Misha worried his lip with his teeth, inching forward. The bed was little more than a silhouette.

He could almost make out two lumps under the covers.

He had a fleeting moment of jealousy that they were cuddling and he was alone, but he pushed it away. He knew that, for a poly relationship to work, it was important that everyone got to build their relationships separately as well. He'd talked it over with his therapist several times. Misha got plenty of time alone with Asher. And, if Mr. Liam *did* agree to be his Daddy someday, he'd get plenty of alone time with Liam.

He backed into the hallway.

He knew what he would do. He'd make breakfast for when they woke up. He'd helped Liam with pancakes, back in the camper. It couldn't be that difficult to make them himself.

* * * *

It was *very* difficult. The pancake batter looked too thin when he followed the directions, so he added more flour, but then it got lumpy. He couldn't break the clumps apart with his fork, and when he tried to use a whisk, the batter spilled onto the counter. He salvaged what he could and ladled them into the big pan he found in the cupboard beside the stove.

It sizzled when it hit the preheated pan, and it smelled good, but when he tried to flip the pancakes, they tore, leaving a layer of crispy skin on the bottom of the pan and only shredded dough on his spatula.

And when he tried to scrape the blackened pancakes off the bottom of the pan, it was too stuck on to work. He carried the pan over to the sink and dropped it in. He'd wash it later.

He grabbed a second, slightly smaller pan out and put it on the burner. Maybe he needed less heat this time? He turned the burner to low before ladling in more batter.

This time, he thought he had it, but when he went to flip it, they were *too* raw, and the pancake batter flopped off the lightly browned bottom in stringy rivulets. Instead of a pancake, he ended up with a panful of pancake crumbs.

He scraped them into the trash and started over again, on medium heat.

Which left him with pancakes that stuck to the pan *again*.

He gave up on pancakes, throwing the second pan in the sink with the first. Then, he opened the fridge and stared at the measly contents. Mr. Liam needed to go grocery shopping.

Maybe he'd make French toast. He'd never made it, but he'd eaten it at Ryder's. It couldn't be that hard.

He took out a few pieces of bread, ripping off the little bits of mold with his fingers, and shoved them in the toaster. When they popped up, they were more black than brown, but...that was probably fine.

Ryder always soaked them in syrup for him, so he grabbed the maple syrup out of the fridge and poured a liberal amount onto the toasted bread. It smeared on the counter in a sticky mess. Misha wiped it off with his hand, then cringed at the feeling and wiped his hand on his shirt. *Gross.*

The toast went into a third pan, and this time, it didn't burn. It didn't look quite right, either, but maybe Ryder used a different type of bread...or a different type of syrup. It smelled...interesting.

He made up two plates, one with more than the other so he and Asher could share, since he couldn't carry three. As he left the kitchen with them, he pretended he was a waiter, navigating restaurant tables to deliver food to the most important person in the place.

He got halfway to the bedroom when he realized he should probably bring drinks, too, and spun around. Unfortunately, the movement knocked off the top few pieces of soggy French toast from the plate and he couldn't juggle them to catch it.

Maybe he should go back for the drinks...

Liam woke to an elbow in his stomach and hissed. "Sorry, Mr. Liam," Misha whispered, snuggling down into the narrow bit of space between him and Asher. "I didn't mean to wake you up. I made breakfast all by myself!"

Misha, to demonstrate, lifted a plate and shoved it under Liam's nose.

Liam didn't know what it was, except blackened toast covered with syrup, but the boy looked so happy that he couldn't bear to disappoint him. "Looks...yummy."

"It's French toast! I think I made it wrong, but it smells good."

Liam took the plate from Misha with a grin just as Asher groaned and yanked at the blanket, nearly unseating Misha, who flew into Liam's chest with an "*oof!*"

"Too early," Asher moaned under the covers.

"I made breakfast, sleepyhead." Misha held another plate in one hand while he shook Asher with the other. "And there's coffee in the kitchen. I couldn't figure out how to carry both."

Asher sat up at the mention of coffee. His hair was beautifully mussed from sleep, red lines crisscrossing his face from where the sheet must have bunched beneath him. His eyes were still slightly puffy from the crying the previous night as he'd told Liam of the suffering he'd gone through at that *bastard's* hand.

Asher took the other plate from Misha with a confused expression. "What...is it?"

"French toast!" Misha bounced on the mattress. "I made it all by myself."

Liam couldn't hold off trying it any longer, because the boy was too excited. He picked up a piece of the soggy, burned toast and took a bite, trying not to wince at the...*interesting* flavor. "Thank you, Misha. It was really nice of you to get up early and cook for us."

"I tried to make pancakes first, but it didn't work. And you don't have *any* groceries, Mr. Liam. You should really take care of that." Misha's smile was brilliant, but the comment made Liam wince. It was true that his cupboards were fairly bare. He hadn't expected to be hosting the boys this soon, so he'd been surviving on takeout and diners.

"I'll get right on that," Liam replied, forcing himself to take another bite. From the expression on Asher's face, Liam guessed he felt the same way about the toast that Liam did and was *also* afraid of disappointing Misha.

Unfortunately, Misha grabbed a piece for himself off Asher's plate before Liam could think of an excuse for him not to, and he took a giant bite.

Which he immediately spit out into his sticky palm. "That is *disgusting*."

The room was filled with shocked silence, before Asher broke it with a giggle that was soon joined by Liam's laugh.

"It's the thought that counts."

"Gah." Misha stared at the partially chewed not-quite-French-toast like it had *personally* offended him. Liam examined the boy closer and had to hold in another laugh at his rather mussed appearance. Syrup stained his shirt and hands, along with a liberal dusting of flour.

"I think someone is ready for a bath," he commented without thinking.

"A bath?" Misha perked up immediately. "I'm ready for a bath. Do you have bubbles? Ryder lets me use his sometimes, and I really like them."

"Why don't we go see? Here... Put that on my plate and I'll take care of it while you clean up." Liam held his plate out. Misha dropped the discarded bite on the edge of it before scrambling off the bed, narrowly missing Liam's testicles with his knee.

"You've really done it now," Asher said with a grin. "He's going to be in there forever."

"Are you going to join him, or would you rather help me in the kitchen?"

"I'll supervise the water monster. You haven't seen the kind of mess he can make when bubbles are involved."

"I stayed with my sister and her son for a few weeks, and I'm sure it can't be that bad."

Liam spoke too soon. When he finished turning off the burner on the stove and cleaning up the kitchen—and the hallway, where somehow a pile of soggy toast had ended up—and went back to the bathroom, it was to utter chaos.

Misha was naked in the tub, which was surprisingly free of bubbles, considering the sheer number of them on literally every surface, from the mirror to the closed toilet to the ceiling. There were even bubbles in Asher's hair, and Asher wasn't even in the bath.

Liam found himself grateful for the all-tiled room, since nothing was likely to be ruined if it got a little wet—not that he would have overly cared. The smile on both boys' faces was well worth a little bit of remodeling.

His soft laughter alerted the boys to his presence, and both went quiet, spinning to face him for a second like they expected a punishment. When he just shook his head, his face split in a wide smile, they both relaxed. "He got a bit carried away," Asher explained, and while his tone was apologetic, the smirk on his face was not.

Misha giggled. "The bubbles smell like strawberries."

"Hopefully you didn't try to eat them," Liam teased. But when Misha blushed and averted his eyes, looking anywhere but him, he huffed out a laugh. "You tried to eat them, didn't you?"

"Only once!" Misha whined. "It was oily and tasted like soap. *Bleh.*" He stuck out his tongue and shook his head.

"To be fair," Asher added, still grinning, "they *do* smell like strawberries, and the bottle says non-toxic."

"Well, at least you'll have a clean mouth now," Liam joked.

"Fuck that!" Misha answered with a big grin. "That sounds boring!"

Liam choked at the unexpected expletive, grinning when Misha blushed fire-engine red. Clearly, he was unused to swearing. "You might be right. Are you almost finished in here or is there more soap to eat?"

Misha pouted. "Do I *have* to get out?"

Asher dangled his arm in the water. "It's ice cold."

"It's not *that* bad," Misha said, just as he shivered.

"Look how wrinkly your fingers are. You look like an old man." Asher took Misha's hand and waved it under his eyes to demonstrate. "They look like little raisins." Asher mimed chewing on one and Misha laughed, pulling his hands away.

"I'm not *food*," Misha squealed.

"Then get out before I'm so hungry, I don't have a choice but to eat you."

"Quick, Mr. Liam! He needs snacks so he doesn't eat me!" Misha stood up, seemingly uncaring about his nudity.

Liam felt himself flush, his eyes following the soapy water as it trailed over the slim chest and narrow hips. He cleared his throat and tore his gaze away from the erection bobbing at the apex of Misha's thighs.

When he finally looked back, Asher had Misha swaddled in one of Liam's large white towels. It hung nearly to Misha's knees.

"I'm going…" Liam cleared his throat again before continuing. "I'm going to go finish up breakfast. Meet me in the kitchen? There are shorts and shirts and stuff in the dresser. Help yourself to whatever."

Thankfully, both boys were fully dressed when they met him in the kitchen, if not in the clothes they'd arrived in. Liam had to admit that seeing the boys in his clothes — even if they were too big on them — did something to him. They tugged at the dusty heartstrings in his chest.

Since Misha was right about the lack of options, he'd settled on omelets made with the last of his eggs and some onions and peppers salvaged out of his leftover stir fry from yesterday's lunch.

It went over well with the boys. Misha went so far as to lick his plate when he was finished.

"Do you boys have plans today?" Liam asked as he carried the plates over to the sink. Half of his pots, charred and blackened, were sitting in one half to soak. He filled the other side with soap and water to start doing the dishes.

"I have the day off," Asher said. "Misha wanted to go to the library. Do you need help with those?" Asher stood and moved over to Liam's side.

"You can dry, if you'd like. There are towels in the drawer there," Liam said, passing over a newly cleaned plate. "I'd be happy to go with you, if you'd like company. Or I can take you home, if you'd rather."

"Company would be nice," Asher said, steadfastly looking at the plates he was drying instead of Liam.

"You can help me pick out some books!" Misha bounded over with their cups, holding them out sweetly, one at a time. "Then maybe you can come back to the house with us for dinner! So I can show you my room in person?"

"I'd like that."

* * * *

They spent over an hour at the library, picking out books for both boys, then grabbed lunch from a fast-food restaurant on the way back to the Lockhart's house. Everything was going fine until Liam was struck by a sudden bout of nerves while coming up the sidewalk to the door.

The two men inside the house were the only family his boys had. He wanted — *needed* — them to like him. He'd talked to Mason Lockhart several times, and despite the threat at the diner a few weeks ago, the man had seemed friendly enough. There was no reason for the burst of nerves.

It was Asher's hand slipping into his and squeezing that got him moving. He took Misha's hand with his other one and the three of them walked inside.

"Hey, man," Mason greeted, peering around from the kitchen at the sound of the front door closing. "Welcome home, Asher, Misha. Ryder's in the living room if you want to go say hi."

"You'll be okay." Asher squeezed Liam's hand again, and while it sounded almost like a question, Liam knew it was a reassurance.

"I'll be fine. Go spend time with your brother," Liam said. Asher smiled, then he and Misha ran off toward the living room. "Walking feet," Liam hollered after them, grinning when they both immediately obeyed.

"Good luck with that," Mason said as Liam went into the kitchen. "Though your boys are better behaved than mine. Want coffee?"

"Sure, I'll get it."

"Sugar in the cabinet, cream in the fridge." Mason grabbed him down a mug and passed it over, killing the last of Liam's nerves. Liam poured his coffee and leaned against the counter.

"Need any help?"

"Sure. Feel like cutting the onions?" Mason pointed at a small pile waiting by the cutting board. "Diced for tacos."

"Sounds good."

Asher found his brother sitting on a bean bag in front of the television. His laptop was open but abandoned on the coffee table in favor of the cartoon.

Asher nudged Misha into the other bean bag then sat on the carpeting between them, leaning against the couch.

Immediately, Ryder shuffled his bean bag closer. It butted right up against Asher's thigh. "I missed you. Did you have fun?"

"Yeah. We painted flowers then went to Liam's and watched a movie." And talked, but Ryder probably didn't want to hear about it.

"Did you talk?" Ryder pressed, and Asher changed his mind. Apparently, he did.

"Yeah. It went...good. Surprisingly good. He listened and let me cuddle in his bed and didn't try anything, but I knew he wouldn't. I *really* like him, Ryder. So does Misha, right?" Asher looked at the boy who held his heart in his hands for reassurance.

Misha nodded, giving a bright smile. "He's *perfect*. He didn't even get mad that I ruined breakfast."

"You didn't ruin it, but it was certainly...unique," Asher said, defensive over Misha, even when it was *Misha* talking bad about himself.

"It was gross, and you know it. But Mr. Liam fixed it." Misha perked up even more. "After dinner, I'm going to show him my room and ask him if he'll be my Daddy. I think I'm ready."

Ryder lunged over to hug Misha, draping himself half over Asher's lap, but Asher didn't care. He was just so happy that his brother and his—boyfriend? Lover? Soulmate?—his *Misha* got along so well. They were both 'littles', which was perfect. He knew Misha would need a friend who understood that part of him better than Asher could.

"I'm so proud of you. That's a scary step," Ryder said into Misha's hair.

"It's not scary when it's Mr. Liam," Misha replied, pulling away with what seemed like reluctance. "He takes care of me and Asher already."

Ryder straightened up, out of Asher's lap, but gripped his shoulder instead. "How do you feel about it, brother?"

"I think…it's perfect. Liam will be a good Daddy, and I know Misha loves me, no matter what. I can share them both…but *only* with each other," Asher clarified.

"Of course," Ryder agreed. "But you're not going to move out right away or anything, right? I don't think I'm ready for that yet." His younger brother's face twisted, and he looked down, wringing his hands like that was something to be ashamed of.

Asher reached over to squeeze his hands in his. "No, of course not. Maybe someday, but I like staying here with you and Mason. You know you're the only family I have. *We* have," Asher corrected, including Misha in it. "We'll probably spend more time staying with Liam, if he'll have us, and Liam might come spend more time here with us, but none of us are ready for that step yet."

"I mean, not yet. But you know when you *are* ready, it'll go okay, right? I mean, you basically already lived together for months, right? In the camper? And you were in *much* closer quarters." Ryder sounded like he was talking himself into it being okay, not Asher.

"Right!" Misha agreed, half of his attention on the cartoon already. "Oh, did you see that? He has blue hair!" Misha spun to face Asher. "Can I have blue hair like that someday?"

"You can have whatever you want," Asher promised.

"Now would be a great time to ask for that hairless cat," Liam spoke up from the doorway behind him and Asher shuddered.

"Except that."

Chapter Twenty-Nine

Dinner went well, and Liam was stuffed when he settled back in his chair, his plate empty. Even Misha and Asher had cleared their plates with only a bit of nudging. "You're in the wrong career, Mason," Liam joked. "Should have been a chef."

"You say that now, but wait until you try his meatloaf," Ryder teased his husband.

"Brat." Mason wadded up a napkin and lobbed it, Ryder laughing as he dodged. "That was one time, and it wouldn't have burned if *someone* hadn't distracted me."

"All I did was load the dishwasher. It was not *my* fault you were staring at my bum."

"Who loads dishes naked?" Mason turned to Liam for backup. "Seems like entrapment to me. Right, Agent?"

"Definitely." Liam grinned. "Sounds like someone needs a spanking."

All three boys gasped. Liam winked at his two—not *his*, he corrected himself—then grabbed their plates. "Why don't you two come help me in the kitchen."

"Can I show you my room when we're done?" Misha asked, bouncing out of his chair immediately to grab their cups. Asher was slightly slower to stand, though not, Liam suspected, because he didn't want to help clean up. He was looking between Mason and Ryder with what looked remarkably like curiosity as he gathered the napkins and cutlery.

"Of course, I'd love to see it."

Dinner clean-up went smoothly. They were used to working around each other in a much smaller space, and it was like they fell right back into that easy familiarity. Far too soon the dishwasher was loaded and the counters wiped down. Asher even changed the trash.

Misha practically vibrated. "Now? We can go see it now?"

"I don't know. Do you think we should sweep and mop first? Be good guests?" Liam teased, unable to resist.

Misha's mouth dropped open in horror. "That'll take forever! I mean—" Misha turned pink and dropped his eyes, politely curling his hands together in front of his chest. "I can do that, if you want me to..."

Liam laughed. "No, Boy. I was just teasing. Show me to your room."

"Great!" Misha perked back up and spun on his heel, sprinting into the hallway. Asher rolled his eyes but grinned, following at a more sedate pace. Liam took the rear.

Misha spent the next half hour showing him absolutely everything in his bedroom, from his soft sheets to the pretty cream lamp to the books on his bookshelf, explaining why he chose each one and how he'd decided where each thing should go.

Liam listened patiently, unable to keep the smile off his face. There was very little he found more adorable than Misha when he was excited. Asher apparently had already heard the explanations, because he dropped onto his stomach on Misha's bed with an easy familiarity and tugged a comic book off the bookshelf, flipping through the glossy pages.

Misha seemed to run out of things to show him about the time Asher finished his third comic book. The boy didn't seem worried, though. He bounced back over to Liam and gave him a smile.

"Do you like my room?"

"It's perfect, just like you," Liam replied, running his fingertips over Misha's lightly stubbled jaw. It was peach fuzz at best, soft and so pale it was barely visible against his light skin. He wondered absently how long it would take the young man to grow a beard, and what it would look like, but then Misha was speaking again.

"I've been talking with Ms. Allard, and I'm finally ready to tell you what I want. You said that you would consider being my Daddy when I could ask you myself. So...Mr. Liam, will you be my Daddy? I'll be a good boy, I promise. I pick up my toys when I'm done with them, and look, I even folded all my new clothes!"

Misha looked like he was going to continue on, listing the many irrelevant ways he could be a good boy for Liam, when he was already the *perfect* boy...one of two. Liam cupped the boy's cheeks. "Misha, you don't need to be a good boy for me to be your Daddy. I want to be your Daddy, even if you are messy and leave your toys out everywhere."

"Really?" Misha's blue eyes were wide and sparkling with hope. "You do?"

"I really do. I was just waiting for you to be ready." Liam leaned down, pressing his forehead against Misha's. Misha gave him a soft sigh, his breath tickling Liam's skin like a caress.

Asher's gasp was so soft that Liam nearly ignored it, but something about the sound had him pulling back and looking over. He knew immediately that the gasp wasn't of pleasure or arousal. It was of heartbreak, like by Liam agreeing to be Misha's Daddy, Asher was in some way being cut out.

Liam squeezed Misha's hand then moved over to the bed, crawling onto the mattress beside the other boy that held his heart, dragging him into his lap. "You know that just because I'm going to be Misha's Daddy doesn't mean I'll leave you out," Liam said, running his finger down Asher's nose to the upturned tip. "I still care just as deeply for you. We'll just do different things."

"But neither of you will need me anymore. Misha will have his Daddy, and you'll have your Boy. And I'll just be…me, boring and useless." Asher turned his face into Liam's chest like he was hiding.

"You are not *useless*," Liam snapped, voice torn out of him. "Just because you aren't a 'little' doesn't make you in any way *less*. Misha needs you *so much* – and so do I."

"Why? I can't… I won't let you feed me, or pick out my clothes, or… Or any of the stuff Daddies like to do. And I don't want to tell Misha what to do all the time, either." Asher started shaking and Liam could feel the tears dampening his shirt.

Misha sat behind Asher, wrapping his arms around the boy's chest, sandwiching Asher between the pair of them.

"You make me feel safe," Misha whispered, just loud enough for them to hear. "I love you, and I don't ever want you to leave me. And I'll never leave you, either."

"Hear that? He doesn't need you to tell him what to do. Misha just needs you to be *you*. And I don't need to hold your fork to feed you, Asher. You let me feed you every time you eat the food I make you. And who cares if you let me pick out your clothes? Every time you allow me to help you with your hair or take you shopping? That gives me the same feeling. Just because I get something different out of my relationship with Misha doesn't mean that the one I have with *you* is any less valid." Liam curled one hand around the back of Asher's head, combing his fingers through the soft strands, and kept the other one tracing circles over Asher's spine.

"Do you mean that?" Asher said several minutes later, when his sobs had dwindled to little sniffs instead.

"I will never lie to you. I meant every word."

"Okay," Asher said, and the acceptance filled Liam's chest with a warm glow.

Chapter Thirty

Misha was getting his hair done.

He'd been waiting all week for both Liam and Asher to have a day off, and *that* day was today. He was a little bit nervous, but mostly he was excited. He didn't want to cut it at all. He liked the way it fell around his shoulders. He could hide behind it when he was nervous, and fiddle with the strands when he was bored. And he *loved* when Asher or Daddy helped him brush it.

The salon was in a two-story pink house with a pointy roof and a pretty white porch. A wood sign hung off the balustrade, reading 'Blood, Sweat and Shears'. Misha loved it, and he hadn't even gone inside yet.

Instead, he stood on the sidewalk, tucked between his two men, listening to Liam give him another gentle reminder that "*We can leave at any time, even if they were only partway done,*" and "*I've made sure to research the owner and stylists,*" and that Ryder's friend Shiloh had promised that "*Joel will be very nice to you.*"

Misha was nearly vibrating with excitement by the time they let him go inside, and he maybe only *possibly* had to be reminded to use his walking feet once...or twice. Definitely *not* more than three times.

He just wanted to get inside quicker. He fast-walked up to the desk to the receptionist. "I'm getting blue hair, too," Misha said before she even had a chance to greet him. "It's really pretty on you!"

"Aw, thanks, dear! You must be Misha? Shiloh told me to expect you. I'm Delia. We have you set up with Joel." Delia closed the book she was reading — a paperback with a pair of half-dressed men on the cover — and set it aside. Her smile was wide and bright.

"Yep!"

"Great. His chair is that one right there, by the rinse station. You can have a seat. He's just finishing up a class upstairs." Delia shifted, planting the heel of her boot on the cushion of her seat. "He's super excited to be the first stylist to touch your hair. He loves virgins."

Misha flinched back into Daddy's chest just as Asher snarled, "That's *so* not appropriate!"

Delia looked between the three of them with a stricken expression. "I...I meant that your *hair* hasn't been professionally dyed before. I'm so sorry for the confusion. Um...I'll go get Joel. I'm really sorry again."

Misha felt guilty watching her half-run through the door behind her and up a flight of stairs, but he moved over to the chair she'd pointed him to. "I think we made her feel bad." He didn't understand why it would matter whether his hair had been dyed before or not. Anyway, Daddy had used that weird-smelling red stuff from the box back at the RV. Even though it had washed out, he was pretty sure it counted as hair dye.

Asher shrugged, his face still mutinous. "People need to be careful with their words. But..." The anger faded and now Asher looked a bit guilty, too. "Maybe I overreacted."

"We can apologize when we leave," Daddy said, even though of all of them, *he* had nothing to apologize for.

It made him feel better anyway, and he dropped down into the salon chair. "Ooh, it has a bar for your feet!" Misha planted his flats on it immediately, then realized if he put one back on the floor instead, he could make the chair go around in circles. Not too fast, because he didn't want to get dizzy, but enough to make him giggle. Even the woman at the next station's glare didn't strip the joy out of it.

He did slow down a little, though.

"You must be Misha," a masculine voice said, and Misha abruptly stopped spinning, a spike of paranoia hitting him in the chest until he talked himself through it.

He turned with a hesitant smile. "Are you Joel?"

The hairdresser was tall and buff, his hair neatly buzzed. His tank top was black with a cartoon character Misha didn't recognize on the front—a guy with blond hair who wore a black headband with a silver plaque on it.

"That's me. Shiloh told me you were coming, and that this was your first time going to a salon. I have to say, I'm surprised. Your hair looks very healthy. You must do a pretty good job of taking care of it yourself."

"Asher helps me. But today I want it to be blue, and he said it was better if we let a professional handle it. Right, Ash?" He spun the chair to face Asher, who just nodded.

"Probably a good idea. I shudder to even *think* of a box dye touching this hair. It's gorgeous."

Misha decided it would be a good idea to keep the red a secret, since he didn't want to see what would happen to the man if he found out his fear had happened already. Still, it was a weird thing to be afraid of. He'd thought the red had turned out pretty nice.

* * * *

Two-and-a-half hours later, Misha bounced out of the salon, hand-in-hand with both Daddy and Asher. He couldn't resist twitching his head back and forth, watching his blue hair sway in and out of his vision. "I love it, I love it, I love it!"

"Me too, pretty boy," Daddy said agreeably, using his free hand to pull lightly on one of the strands. "Want to do a little shopping now? Get some new clothes to match your new hair?"

"Oh, can we?" Misha asked, looking between Daddy and Asher.

"I wouldn't have offered if I minded," Daddy reassured him. "Now, the real question is, where do we want to go? What kind of clothing does my pretty boy want to get?"

"Something sparkly," Misha decided. "And something glittery. And maybe something shiny, too."

Asher snickered but kept whatever comment he was thinking to himself.

Daddy took them to a store that he promised would have anything they could want. It was two stories tall and filled with everything — from clothing and housewares, to towels and toys.

Misha didn't know where to start.

Thankfully, Daddy did, and by the time they left, he had several bags of cute sparkly shirts and skinny jeans, and Daddy had even let him get a few puzzles. Asher didn't get as much, but not for lack of Daddy trying. Asher kept insisting he had everything he needed already and only let the older man talk him into a few new graphic tees.

Then, they headed out to a diner for dinner. It made Misha giggle to see the way Daddy's lips twisted into a distasteful moue when he had to touch the sticky menus. The fancy restaurants were nice, but sometimes reminded him too much of being with Barnes.

He took his seat on one side of the booth by the window, Asher next to him and Daddy across. Everything was going great until he heard the news program playing on the television behind him.

"Senator Scott, thank you for sharing your time with us today. I know you're a busy man! Can you tell us what makes your campaign for governor so special?"

"It's always a pleasure to be on your show, Lori. As you know, I'm a family man, through and through. I think that resonates with the voters..." The senator droned on, but Misha stopped listening once he placed the far-too-familiar voice. He slowly spun in his booth to stare at the television, praying he was wrong.

The white-haired man on the screen—Senator Ryland Emerson Scott II, or so the caption named him—wore a priest's collar with his suit, just like he always had when Misha had seen him.

Misha felt himself shaking, his hand clenching painfully on his fork, but he couldn't tear his gaze away, not even when Daddy asked him what was wrong. Misha reached out to grab Asher's hand, then pointed at the television.

Asher spun to see the program, then his skin paled as well. He turned a dark glare on Liam. "You said they were all in prison. You *promised.*"

Daddy was frowning. "I don't understand."

"You *promised* that Barnes and *all* his associates were in prison. You promised they couldn't hurt us anymore. You said it," Asher rambled, his obvious anger quickly turning to panic.

"They were...are. What are you talking about?" Daddy Liam looked between him and Asher to the television. "Surely you're not implying that Senator Scott was one of..."

"I'm not lying!" Asher blurted, striking the table with his fist. "That *fucker* held me down and... Why is he not in jail? Running for *governor?* Is that all it takes to get out of prison? Money and a fancy suit?"

Liam immediately reached across the table, curling his hand around Asher's wrist until his fingers unclenched enough that he could take his hand instead. "I swear to you that nobody said *anything* about Scott being involved. Almost everyone flipped on someone, but nobody flipped on *him.* I'll get ahold of my old boss as soon as we get home, see if she can start building a case, but, Asher, I promise you that I didn't know he was involved."

Misha believed him. Master always spoke so carefully to the man in the priest's collar, almost like he was afraid of him. Misha didn't quite understand what a senator did, but he knew it was important.

"Can we go home?" Misha blurted, unwilling to sit out in public when he felt this vulnerable — this *exposed,* like all his secrets were written on his skin and he'd been stripped bare for the world to read them.

"Yes, of course, whatever you need." Daddy Liam stood and threw a wad of cash on the table. Asher clutched onto Misha like a lifeline as they all hurried out of the diner to Daddy's car. Lately, Asher had taken to riding up front so he could play with the radio dials but today, he crawled into the back with Misha, sitting pressed up against his side.

"Do you want me to call Ms. Allard?" Daddy asked, glancing back at them in the rearview mirror as he drove.

"Yes, please," Misha answered, once it was clear Asher wasn't going to.

"Okay," Daddy agreed, then he was using some special mode on his car to call their therapist, talking to her over the speaker about everything that had happened and asking her to meet them at Ryder and Mr. Mason's house for an emergency session. Thankfully, she agreed, promising to meet them there within the hour.

Misha barely noticed when Daddy parked in the driveway and ushered them inside, his new clothes and toys forgotten in the trunk to be retrieved later. Instead, he followed mutely along with Asher and Daddy into the house, where Daddy made quick work of shepherding them up to Misha's bed.

He even promised that he'd explain to Mr. Mason and Ryder what was going on, so Misha and Asher didn't have to.

Misha curled up tight around Asher's chilly frame. "Under the covers," Misha murmured, yanking the blanket out from beneath them so he could pull it over them instead. Asher obediently slid underneath, rolling onto his side to face Misha.

"I hate this," Asher finally muttered.

"Me too."

"It's like every time I think I can put it behind me and move on, something happens and I'm right back there in that hellhole," Asher continued, reaching up to scrub his eyes with the side of his hand. "I don't know how you do it, stay so...*optimistic* all the time."

Misha squeezed Asher's hand. "I just keep telling myself that today is better than yesterday, and yesterday was better than the day before, so tomorrow *must* be better, right?"

"I just hate knowing that *fucker* is out there. It's not fair." Asher grabbed Misha's pillow and dragged it down under his head, then yanked Misha even closer so they could share it.

"It's not. But Daddy said he'd tell his boss. They'll make it better," Misha promised.

Asher just stared at him, a sad expression on his face until he spoke. "I love that you believe that. I never want you to change. Okay, Misha?"

Misha didn't understand but he didn't intend on changing either, so he nodded. "I won't."

* * * *

Liam paced back and forth in Mason's study, his cell phone pressed to his ear. "What do you mean, you won't open a file?"

"He's a United States *senator*, Tennyson. Do you know what the fallout would be of me accusing him of *jaywalking* without solid evidence, let alone *this*?" Deputy Director Heather Knowles sounded annoyed. More than that, she sounded *angry*.

"So your future political career is more important to you than putting a rapist in prison." Liam stopped in front of the window, glaring out at the street. "You think a *pedophile* should get to stay on the streets, get to stay as a *senator.* If voters found out about *that,* do you think they'd still vote for you?"

Knowles huffed in his ear. "That's not what I'm saying, Tennyson. I'll look into it, *if* you can get me more evidence. Until then, my hands are tied."

"I don't work for you anymore," Tennyson snarled, hanging up before his anger could lead him to saying something he'd regret and burning any remaining bridges he had left with her.

He planted his hands on the windowsill, glaring — unseeing — outside. He'd never have dreamed of a time he'd bring something like *this* to his supervisors and they'd refuse to look into it. Any illusion he'd had of there being *justice* served in the Justice Department was shattered.

"Fuck!" He straightened abruptly and fisted his hands in his hair.

"They won't look into it, will they?"

Liam jumped at Asher's voice behind him. When he turned, Asher was standing just inside the doorway, arms wrapped around his chest and face resigned.

As much as it killed him to admit, Liam refused to lie. "No, not yet."

Asher's shoulders straightened and he dropped his arms. "Then maybe it's time we handle it ourselves."

"What do you mean?" Liam stepped closer, tugging Asher's lip free from his teeth when he started gnawing on it. "Because as much as I'd *love* to drag him into the desert and turn him into scorpion food, I don't think I'd do well in prison."

Asher didn't smile. "If the police won't arrest him, then maybe we should take him to the court of public opinion instead. If we spoke to a reporter, people would *have* to believe us, right?"

"It would sway *some* people, yes. But there's always someone who won't believe, and you'd be opening yourself up to a lot of push back. I'm willing to do it with you," Liam promised, reaching out to squeeze Asher's hand, "But you should talk to your therapist first, and make sure you have the resources in place to handle the stress after. And you should probably talk to Misha as well."

"I know." He dropped his eyes, lips turned down in a frown. "If he wants to do it with me, you'll help?"

"I promise I'll help you with *whatever* you decide to do – *even* if that ends me up in prison."

Asher shivered and stepped forward, dropping his forehead against Liam's chest. "No." His voice was rough. "I don't want that. It... It's *nice* to think about him being punished, but not at your expense. We need you too much."

Liam held the back of his boy's head in a gentle embrace. "I need you, too...both of you, and I only want what's best for you. I don't know if this is it, but I'll be along for the ride with whatever you choose. All I ask is that you speak to Ms. Allard first and let me reach out to some of my contacts."

Asher pulled back slightly. "I can do that." He looked up at Liam with his lovely blue eyes. "Liam?"

"Yeah?"

"Can I kiss you right now?"

Asher didn't know where the urge came from. It certainly wasn't the *circumstances* he'd imagined his first kiss with Liam under, but it felt *right*. Maybe it was hearing that Liam would be with him the whole way, maybe it was that Liam was going to support him, even if he didn't agree.

He wasn't sure he *cared* where the feeling came from, as long as Liam said yes. And he did, tipping his head toward Asher, stopping just breaths away from Asher's lips.

Asher closed the gap, pressing his mouth to Liam's. His heart thudded in his chest and neither one of them moved — until Liam groaned and slipped his tongue along the seam of Asher's lips, a silent order Asher was happy to obey.

And when Asher *did,* and Liam began to delve into Asher's mouth, it turned quickly from an exploration to a *conquering,* tearing the breath from his lungs. Asher swayed forward, his knees threatening to buckle, but Liam was there to catch him. He wasn't ready for the kiss to end, rising up on his toes to chase Liam's lips.

"Do I get one too?" Asher didn't realize he'd closed his eyes until Misha's voice made him open them.

Liam held onto him but smiled at Misha. "Of course. Be a good boy and come give Daddy a kiss." He shifted Asher over and tucked him under an arm as Misha bounced over.

The kiss Misha and Liam shared was sweeter, softer — but left Asher wanting to watch them forever. "Stay the night with us?" Asher asked. Pleaded, really, because he was willing to get on his knees and beg.

Fortunately, Liam would never make him. "I'd love to." He pressed a kiss to the top of Asher's head before releasing him. "Asher, why don't you go help Misha get ready and I'll be there in a minute?"

"Oh, can I wear my new pajamas?" Misha asked, spinning on Asher like he thought *he* was the one who was going to give him permission. "The ones with the dinosaurs?"

Asher shrugged. "I can grab them from the car."

"No, don't bother, I'll bring them in," Liam interrupted. "Why don't you both go shower and I'll make sure they are in Misha's room to change into when you're finished."

Asher couldn't find anything to complain about, even if something about it sat wrong in his belly. He wanted Liam to come with him now, to join them in the shower then cuddle up with them in the bed. He didn't want to separate like this—like he and Misha were a partnership and Liam was on the outside.

He gathered up the little bit of courage he'd grown- -like green beans in a tiny plastic pot for a school project—and said, "Ms. Allard says it's important that we communicate our feelings with you, and right now, I feel like you're leaving us."

Liam's face fell and he gripped Asher's hands tight. "I don't want that, not at all. If you'd feel more comfortable helping me with the bags, we can do that instead."

"It's not that. But…" Asher sucked in a breath. "Will you shower with us after?" He dropped his gaze to the carpet. "You don't have to help us wash or anything, if you don't want. But I don't want it to be Misha and me together…and you apart. I want us *all* to be together."

"I want that too. Misha, are you okay with me showering with you?"

"Yes, please!"

* * * *

Liam set the bags down in front of the dresser. He'd go through them later to find Misha his pajamas. Now, his boys were waiting on him. They were sitting together on the end of Misha's bed, their hands intertwined.

"Ready?"

They both nodded but Liam hesitated, worried that they weren't. He never wanted to push them into something they couldn't handle, and they both looked nervous. Before he could ask them if they were certain, Asher stood.

"We'll use Misha's shower," Asher decided. "It's smaller but we don't have to come back through the hallway after. Unless you have a problem with that?" He set his jaw as he met Liam's eyes

God, he hoped Asher never let that stubborn streak die. Misha's sweet obedience was perfect in its own way, but Liam loved Asher's fight.

"You'll never hear me complain about squeezing into tight spaces with you," Liam teased, stripping off his tailored dark chambray shirt and hanging it over the back of the white rocking chair in the corner. He dropped his hands to his belt and popped it open, tugging it through the loops and tossing it aside.

He noticed the way Misha's and Asher's eyes fixed on his hands, watching each movement he made as he stripped down to his skin. If they'd looked scared, he'd have stopped—talked them through their worries and come up with a compromise. Maybe wear his briefs or stand just outside the curtain, like he'd done for so many months.

Instead, the heat in their eyes begged him to continue.

"I'm going to hog the hot water. Feel free to join me." Liam walked into the attached bathroom alone, giving them a moment to work up the nerve or calm their erections. He was happy to go either way with them. Whatever they were comfortable with.

It didn't take them long to decide.

Chapter Thirty-One

Misha couldn't tear his eyes away from the water sliding down Daddy's chest, trailing its way through the curly, black-and-gray chest hairs. It was clearly well kept, trimmed just long enough to be soft. Misha wanted to run his face through it.

"Want Daddy to help you wash your hair?" Liam asked, dragging Misha out of the daze that the sight of his bare chest had pulled him into.

"Yes, please, Daddy...and Asher's." Misha didn't think Asher would ask, but he knew from their midnight talks that Asher needed that closeness.

Daddy kissed his forehead, water dripping off him onto Misha's nose. Then, Daddy shifted them around so he was under the water, budging Asher up beside him. It left Daddy with his back pressed to the frigid tiles, but he didn't complain.

One of Misha's many favorite things about living away from Barnes was the availability of hot water, but now, naked in the shower with Daddy and Asher, he almost wished it were cold. As soon as Daddy squirted shampoo into his palm and started working the lather through his hair, Misha squeaked, dropping his hands to cover the erection growing between his thighs.

"You don't have to hide," Daddy said. "I promise I won't take it as an invitation. The only things we do in here will be what you want, okay?"

Misha nodded, water droplets shaking free from his hair. Daddy helped him tip his head back to rinse out the soap, even shielding his eyes with his hand to keep his eyes clear, which was good, since Misha couldn't bear to close them. He wanted to see everything, from the soft expression on Daddy's face to the way he poked his tongue out between his lips.

"There you go, Misha. Slide over here a little so Asher can stand under the spray a bit, okay?"

"Yes, Daddy."

Asher's heart thudded in his chest as he squeezed by Liam to stand where Misha was. His hands were fisted — from nerves, not anger — and it was all he could do to keep his dick at only half-mast. He knew as soon as Liam touched him, it would be a lost cause.

He was right. Liam started washing his hair and just like Misha, Asher was hard and throbbing. Unlike Misha, Asher wasn't a good boy who'd just stand there and take what Daddy gave him. As soon as his hair was rinsed clear, Asher angled his hips forward, putting the steel rod on display.

"Something else is dirty, too." He smirked up at Liam, daring him to take their play further. It was the closest thing to permission he'd be able to squeeze through his lips right now, and God, he hoped Liam understood.

From the way Liam's lips quirked up and he leaned forward, planting his hand on the tile just over Asher's shoulder and stepping closer, clearly he did. "Well, that's no good. There are only two things to do about that. I can stand right here and watch you clean it." His heated gaze trailed over Asher's chest and lower. "Which *won't* be a hardship at all. Or I can help you, make sure you get all the hard-to-reach places."

"I think you should help me," Asher gasped out, his breath catching in his throat at even the *suggestion* of Liam's hands on him. "Misha, you think Daddy should help make sure we're *super* clean, right?"

Misha nodded, and Asher watched his hand drop to the dip between his hipbones, like he wanted to touch himself but restrained.

The word 'Daddy' felt strange on his lips, heavy and full of promise. A guttural groan burst from Liam's chest, deep enough that even Liam looked startled. His eyes were filled with heat. He leaned in, breathing deep as he slowly lowered himself down Asher's body, dropping carefully to his knees.

"Such a sensitive area," Liam said like he was talking about the weather, only the look on his face betraying his own arousal. "I think it would be best if I clean it with my mouth. Soap could cause so *many* irritations." Liam ran a finger from the root of him to the tip, gathering up a line of pre-cum that was weeping from his slit before sucking his finger into his mouth. "Don't you agree, Asher?"

"I...yes. Too many. Mouth is good. *Please*, Liam." Asher couldn't hold back the tiny thrust of his hips or his full body shiver.

"You can change your mind at any time," Liam reminded him, but Asher had no plans on backing out now. He was ready to beg if Liam needed him to. And seeing Misha's gaze locked on him—watching the man Asher was willing, finally, to admit they both loved on his knees—was like a caress.

Thankfully, Liam took mercy on him, swallowing him down just as Asher thought he was going to die. It was overwhelming, like the most pleasurable riptide pulling him into the ocean. If he died now, it would be worth it.

He clenched his fingers into fists, digging them into the clammy tiles behind him, anything to restrain his urge to curl his fingers through Liam's hair and grip tight.

But Liam seemed to sense the urge building because, with a painfully slow drag of his mouth, he pulled off Asher's cock, running his palms up Asher's thighs. "You can touch me, Asher. I don't mind if you fuck my throat."

Asher whined, just the *image* of confident, *powerful* Liam allowing him to let loose in his mouth enough to have him spilling. "I'm sorry," he cried as he climaxed, his seed painting the side of Liam's cheek and neck before he could twist his hips away.

Liam growled, digging his thumbs into Asher's hipbones as he turned him back, sealing his mouth over the tip of Asher's weeping dick to swallow the last few drops. Only when Asher had wilted did he pull off again, giving him a gentle kiss to the tip. "Don't apologize, darling. It's a compliment." He winked up at Asher. "We'll save that for next time, I guess." Liam shifted his weight and grimaced.

Immediately, Asher flashed back to several of his own experiences in the shower, the way the tiles would pinch and dig into his knees, the bruises that would blossom after, and guilt swam in his chest. He slid around Liam and leaned into Misha, brushing his hair away so he could whisper in his ear, "Daddy's knees are hurting."

Misha glanced at him, and it was clear from his expression that he understood what Asher was hinting at. He gave Liam a sweet smile. "Daddy, I'm getting cold. Will you help me get clean in the bedroom instead?"

Liam looked up at them, a glint in his eyes and a wry grin on his lips. "Daddy isn't as young as you anymore, but he's not deaf yet."

Asher flushed, glancing up at the ceiling tiles in feigned innocence. "I don't know what you're talking about."

Liam laughed and shifted to one knee. He planted a hand on his other thigh for leverage as he stood up with only a little bit of struggle. "I could have helped you. I'm sure we have a cane around here somewhere..." Asher bit back his grin.

"Cheeky brat," Liam said, but he was smiling, and damn, his grin made the air feel ten degrees warmer and growing hotter by the second. "Since I'm so old and slow, why don't you take Misha out to the bedroom and keep him busy for me? I'm sure you know how to put that snarky mouth of yours to better use." He winked and Asher laughed.

"Come on, Misha. I bet I can make you come before your Daddy gets dried off." Asher ushered Misha out, snagging a pair of towels before leaving. He gave his own body a cursory drying but took more time with Misha, teasing him with each brush of the soft, fluffy towel over his skin. When Misha was squirming under his hands and each touch made him whimper, Asher finally draped the towel over Misha's pillow and urged him onto his back.

He knew every inch of Misha's body, could play it like a finely tuned instrument with a single brush of his thumbs along the curve of Misha's ribs, or a dip of his tongue into his belly button. He knew every place that made Misha whimper or cry or scream out in pleasure—or pain, the spots Asher was now careful to avoid.

If he wanted to, he could bring Misha to orgasm a dozen times, have him spilling into his hand or mouth before Liam could stop him. Instead, he brought him to the edge, sucking bruises onto the apex of his thighs and scratching his nails lightly over the soles of his feet and, his personal favorite, pressing kiss after kiss to his gasping lips and swallowing down his moans like candy.

He was so desperate for Misha's taste, his cock perking back up, that he missed Liam coming into the bedroom until he felt the mattress tilt under his weight. Asher sat back with a groan.

"Did Asher take good care of you, Misha baby?" Liam asked, looking on the hazy-eyed boy sprawled on his back with sympathy.

"Uh-huh, Daddy, *so* good," Misha agreed, his voice slurred. His cock jutted angrily up, a red beacon Liam wasted no time in greeting. Asher watched him curl his fingers around the shaft, only the nearly purple head peeking out at the top of his fist. Liam gave him a slow, languid stroke that Asher felt in his own dick.

Misha cried out, his back bowing and hips springing off the bed as he chased the feeling. Asher leaned back on his side, barely swallowing his own moans. He gripped his dick in his fist to stop himself from coming abruptly again.

Liam glanced over at him with a smirk. "Look, Misha. I think Asher likes to watch. Do you like knowing how hot you make him?" Misha nodded but didn't answer, biting into his lip instead, visibly shaking.

"I'm not the only one," Asher pointed out, staring at the large shaft unable to hide below Liam's hips. It was long, with a girth that made Asher's ass clench tight and his body shiver. For the first time in years, he imagined getting fucked, and it wasn't scary but something to desire. He could never fully immerse himself in the fantasies with Misha, since he knew his other lover had no desire to top.

But Liam... He could imagine Liam taking him, claiming him. Holding him down just tight enough and never choking him, never giving him more than he wanted.

Liam leaned down slowly — like he was putting on a show for Asher as much as he was teasing Misha — and followed a stray drop of water over the curve of Misha's hip up to the root of his dick.

If Misha flinched any harder, he'd throw Liam off the bed. Asher shifted onto his belly to watch, rocking his dick into the mattress to alleviate the painful pleasure. His focus kept slipping from the sight of Misha's dick disappearing into Liam's mouth to lower — to where Liam's hard cock dangled inches over the sheets.

Asher could just...

Well, he'd never had great self-control. He crawled over the mattress and rolled onto his back. "Can I suck you, Liam?" he managed to ask, though all he wanted was to swallow the large cock down, feel the weight of it on his tongue.

Erase the memory of all the ones he'd never asked for, so all that remained was him and the men in this room.

Liam groaned around Misha's cock, reaching back to curl his fingers through Asher's locks, pulling off just long enough to say, "Yeah, love, do it."

Asher didn't hesitate, angling his head under Liam's hips, resting it on Misha's knee as he made room for himself between them, sucking on the head like a lollipop, swirling his tongue around the large, seeping helmet. It was soft as silk and tasted vaguely of soap, but underneath was pure *Liam*.

He could feel each bunch of Misha's muscles under his head as he thrust into Liam's mouth and each twitch of Liam's hips that buried him deeper into Asher, an erotic feedback loop that left Asher feeling drunk on pleasure. When Misha's hand fumbled over the mattress to wrap around Asher's shaft, it was over for him and he cried out, the sound muffled by Liam's dick. He twitched uncontrollably with his second orgasm, and it didn't take long before both Misha and Liam were crying out as well.

They collapsed into a boneless tangle of limbs. Asher breathed heavily, his hand dropping onto his chest like limp spaghetti. "I have no bones."

Misha giggled, breath tickling Asher's calf. "Nope, I took care of them for you."

"Silly boys," Liam huffed, out of breath as well. "Give me a second and I'll go get a towel."

Asher wriggled a bit until his other hand could grab the one he'd discarded on the floor. "There. Now no moving. You're comfy." He shifted his head slightly where it was pillowed on Liam's thigh.

"Not the kind of towel I meant, but it'll do." It took a bit of squirming, but Asher ended up curled around Misha while Liam wiped them both dry of cum, then threw the towel onto the floor. He dropped onto the mattress on the other side, his arm thrown over both of them.

"There. I have no more energy left," Liam said, his words trailing off in a yawn.

"It must suck getting old," Asher felt confident enough to tease, grinning over Misha's shoulder. Misha giggled, trying to bury the sound in the pillow without success.

"I prefer to say *finely aged.*"

"Like wine," Asher agreed.

"Or cheese," Misha added with a snicker, and while Asher could see how hard he tried, even Liam couldn't hold back his snort of laughter.

"Go to sleep, brats." Liam reached up to tweak his nose. Asher snickered but snuggled in closer with a happy sigh.

Chapter Thirty-Two

Misha was the first one awake.

He was warm, snuggled in between his two men with a blanket tangled around his feet, and a strand of his hair was glued to his lips, but he didn't want to move. Asher was draped over his back, his morning wood digging into Misha's spine. Liam was lying on his back, softly snoring, one arm curled under the pillow, the other wedged under Misha's side. It wasn't, technically, the most comfortable position Misha could imagine, but it was perfect.

Or would have been. "Daddy," Misha whispered. Behind him, Asher shifted slightly, but neither of the men woke. "Daddy!" Misha said a bit louder, giving him a light shake.

Liam cracked open a sleepy eye. Stubble shadowed his jaw as he yawned. "Hm-m?"

"I have to pee," Misha said reluctantly. It would mean moving.

"Okay," Liam said, but closed his eyes instead of moving.

Squirming to offset the pressure of his bladder, Misha shook Daddy again. "No, Daddy, I have to pee, and I'm trapped. You have to get up!"

"Too early," Liam groaned but stretched, finally sliding off the bed so Misha could wiggle out from Asher's embrace. The other boy just flopped onto his stomach. "Do you want Daddy to help you?" Liam asked, drawing Misha's attention away from Asher.

"No thank you," Misha answered politely. "Will you help me make waffles, though?"

"Yeah, we can make waffles."

"Yes!" Misha spun on his heel and ran into the bathroom to relieve his bladder, then washed his hands carefully at the sink before racing back out to Liam. "I'm ready."

He must have said it a bit too loud in his excitement because Asher tugged one of the pillows over his head like earmuffs. Liam just laughed and shook his head. "Baby, you might want to put some pants on first."

"Oh yeah." Misha was still not used to the concept of nudity as something to be ashamed of after ten years of it being, more often than not, his natural state. He grabbed a pair of silky pajama pants and yanked them up his legs. "There."

Liam pulled on his pants as well, zipping them carefully over his half-hard length. "Okay, let's go make breakfast for the sleepyhead over there."

When they came back a half hour later, Daddy carrying a tray laden with waffles — they'd left half of them in the kitchen for Ryder and Mr. Mason — Asher was in the same position. Misha giggled and bounced up onto the bed beside him, jostling Asher awake with a start. "Get up, sleeping beauty. We made breakfast. And Daddy has to go meet one of his friends when we're done eating, so he said that you and me can have a boys' day with Ryder and Ryder's friend Shiloh and Shiloh's friend Teddy."

Asher didn't look as excited as Misha felt, but Misha blamed that on the fact that they'd clearly worn him out the previous night, since he was currently yawning wide enough Misha could see the strange dangly thing in the back of his throat. Misha leaned forward while Asher was distracted and blew at it, wondering if he could make it wiggle back and forth.

Asher flinched, the look of pure confusion on his face so funny that Misha burst out laughing. "You should see your *face*!"

"You blew into my *mouth*!" Asher yelped.

"Like my *breath* is the worst thing you've had in it." Misha rolled his eyes, shoving Asher's shoulder with a laugh.

"It's certainly the *weirdest*." Asher poked him in the stomach. "You open *your* mouth and let *me* blow in it."

"Okay," Misha agreed and opened his mouth wide.

Asher leaned forward, pursing his lips and blowing out his cheeks like he was preparing. Instead, he moved like a ninja and dug his fingers into Asher's ribs in a vicious tickle assault that had Misha squealing, struggling to escape.

He rolled onto his back but Asher followed, and no matter how much Misha squirmed he couldn't get away. Finally, he cried for help. "Daddy! Please save me!"

Liam laughed and Misha craned his neck to watch him put the tray with waffles down on the nightstand so he could crawl into bed with them. "I don't know. Should I save you? Or should I...join in the tickle assault?" Liam grabbed for one of his feet and started tickling his sole in a move that made Misha scream his laughter.

"Not fair, two against one!" Misha cried, trying to yank his foot free.

"I suppose that's true. Maybe I should get Asher instead." Daddy grinned and let him go, grabbing for Asher. He managed to avoid the first grab but in doing so, finally let Misha go, giving him a second to catch his breath as he watched Daddy and Asher roll around.

"You know," Misha said, the sight making his dick tent his pajama pants, "you never did blow into my mouth." He locked his gaze on Asher, still naked. Asher's cock was hard as well and neglected in favor of the pseudo-wrestling match he was engaged in with Liam.

Asher and Liam both stilled, turning to look at Misha, following his gaze to Asher's hips. "I *did* tell you to open your mouth," Asher finally said as Daddy let him go. He rolled onto his back and fisted his cock for Misha to watch.

Obediently, Misha opened his mouth and lowered himself to his stomach. Asher looked to Liam, as if for permission, then fed his dick into Misha's mouth like a lollipop. Misha gave him a languid suck. He loved the way Asher moaned when he took his time.

Daddy Liam carded his fingers through Misha's hair in encouragement. "What do you think, baby? Should I feed Asher his waffles while he feeds you his dick?"

Misha nodded quickly so Liam would know how much he wanted that. Liam gave him another pet before he reached over them for one of the plates. Misha closed his eyes, just enjoying the weight of Asher on his tongue, the salty sweetness that was so distinctly *him*. Vaguely, he heard Daddy tearing the waffle into pieces, and the way Asher's moans quieted while he chewed and swallowed, but it was a distant awareness, most of him wrapped up in Asher's taste.

It was a perfect way to start his morning.

* * * *

Ryder's friend Shiloh was the first person to show up. Well, technically, the second, if they counted Ryder, since he already lived there, or the fourth if Misha included himself and Asher in the count, but he didn't think that was fair to Shiloh. Misha had met him before, briefly.

The tall, slender dancer had hair the color of Misha's favorite bubblegum and was currently wearing a lime-green crop top and dark skinny jeans that rode low on his hips.

"I love your shoes," Misha blurted, staring at the fuzzy, fur-lined half-boots.

"Thanks. Ryder actually bought them for me for Christmas last year." Shiloh stuck out his ankle and angled it so Misha could see the little charm hanging off the zipper, a pink sparkly ballet shoe.

"So pretty," Misha cooed.

"Aren't they, though?" Shiloh grinned. "Sometimes Ryder has a good sense of style," Shiloh hollered over Misha's shoulder, clearly taunting the other boy.

"Always, you mean!" Misha heard Ryder holler back from upstairs, where he was trying to find the right sweater. Because, as he'd insisted earlier, December was sweater weather, even if it was in the low sixties outside.

Shiloh, still grinning, shook his head. "You didn't see him last Valentine's Day. Poor boy."

Ryder bounded down the stairs, his footsteps like a stampede. "Daddy liked it!"

"That's what happens when you date an old man. They go blind. So sad," Shiloh tsked.

Then he yelped when the older, broad-shouldered man behind him swatted his butt. "Be nice, boy."

Shiloh ducked his head, looking through his lashes over at Ryder. "Sorry. I was just teasing."

"I know," Ryder said, clearly either used to Shiloh's antics…or not offended, anyway.

"I'll let you boys do your thing. Mason in his study?"

Ryder nodded. "Yeah! He and Liam are waiting for you, Gage."

Gage headed upstairs, since he'd visited a few times already and knew where it was. Ryder turned back to Shiloh. "Is Teddy still coming?"

Misha hadn't met Teddy yet, but he knew from Ryder that he was one of Shiloh's other friends, who also had a Daddy. Unlike Ryder and Misha, however, neither Shiloh nor Teddy were 'littles'.

"Yep, he should be here any minute. He had some homework to finish up. Where's Asher?" Shiloh answered, glancing around the living room like he was going to pop out from under a cushion.

"Pouting," Misha exclaimed gleefully. "Come see!"

They made a train up the stairs to Misha's bedroom and into the bathroom, the three of them squeezing together to fit in the doorway to see Asher sitting on the floor, the contents of his makeup case sprawled around him like shrapnel.

"Still can't decide?" Ryder asked sympathetically.

Misha giggled when Asher shook his head and poked one of the lipsticks around with his finger. "No, because *someone* won't tell me what we're doing."

"It's a surprise!" Misha said, stubbornly crossing his arms.

"How am I supposed to know what face to put on if I don't know where we're going?"

"You could go faceless...like Skinny Man."

"Slender Man," Asher corrected, frowning at his eyeliner now. "I still don't think you should be reading those. You'll have nightmares."

"They're funny," Misha insisted.

"You should let Shiloh do your face," Ryder suggested. "He knows where we're going."

"I guess," Asher huffed and shoved his makeup into a pile, crossing his legs and leaning back against the cabinet. "If you don't mind?" He gave Shiloh a pleading look.

"Are you kidding? Favorite part of my day is playing with makeup," Shiloh said agreeably, sinking down to the floor in front of him and pawing through the makeup, making his suggestions.

The doorbell rang and Misha yelled, "I'll get it!"

"Not alone you won't," Asher said without even looking up. "Take Ryder with you."

"Okay," Misha hollered back over his shoulder, already sprinting for the door.

"Walking feet!" Asher called and reluctantly, Misha slowed to a fast walk instead.

Ryder giggled behind him. "So, what's it like having two Daddies?"

"I don't," Misha answered, slowing a bit more to look over his shoulder at Ryder.

"I mean, you don't *call* Asher 'Daddy,' but he Daddy's you anyway."

"He loves me and wants me to be safe and happy," Misha corrected immediately.

Ryder's lips puckered like he was holding in a smile. "What do you think Daddy-ing *is*, Misha?"

"Are you trying to trick me?" Misha frowned, crossing his arms. "Asher said he wouldn't be my Daddy, and I don't want him to be angry."

Ryder sobered and reached out, gripping Misha's shoulder in a gentle squeeze. "No, not trying to trick you. I'm sorry. I shouldn't have said anything. I just thought it was adorable."

Misha perked back up. "That's okay. I forgive you."

Before they could say anything else, the doorbell rang again, reminding Misha that his new, yet-to-be-met friend was waiting. "Coming!" he hollered and went to run for the door again, remembering Asher's warning at the last second and slowing down.

He yanked open the door to see two men on the porch. The closest was his age and pale, with neatly gelled hair and a small scar near his lip. The other stood just behind. He was taller and darker skinned, with close cropped hair and serious eyes.

Misha's excitement paled as nerves sprouted. He reminded himself that these were Ryder's friends, and that meant they were safe, but he couldn't help the instinctive urge to curl in on himself or drop to his knees at the sight of strangers, memories flooding him of all the *other* strangers he'd opened the door to, back with Master.

The ones he had to service and the ones who liked to hit him and the ones, like the man on the TV, who loved to make him cry.

It took every shred of courage to pin on a little smile and whisper, "Hi."

"Are you Misha, or Asher?" The younger man asked, not seeming worried that Misha's greeting was rather small and pitiful. "I'm Teddy."

"Misha," He answered, stepping slightly to the side so they could come in, then closing the door with shaking hands behind them.

"It's nice to meet you. Oh, this is Ian. I made him come in instead of lingering on the porch like a creeper." Teddy grinned and elbowed the other man, who—like Shiloh's boyfriend Gage had earlier—swatted his butt in warning.

"I didn't want to interrupt your boys' day, brat. Liam just wanted to talk to me a bit before we left," Ian said, clearly amused by his boyfriend's antics.

"He's upstairs in the study with Mason and Gage," Misha helpfully said, pointing toward the stairs.

"I'll get out of your hair, then," Ian said, ruffling Teddy's neat coif into an unruly mop with a laugh.

Teddy stuck his tongue out at the larger man's back.

"I saw that," Ian said without turning. "*Someone* will have a nice red bottom when we get home."

"Yes!" Teddy chuckled, then turned back to Misha and Ryder. "Where are the others?"

"Upstairs doing Asher's makeup," Ryder answered.

"Of course," Teddy grinned but shook his head. "I should have known. He does know that the animals won't care if he's *au naturale*, right?"

"Asher doesn't know where we're going," Misha explained, vibrating with excitement. He'd asked Liam this morning if they could do it, and Daddy had said yes. Misha couldn't wait to see Asher's face.

"Someone *also* trying to earn a spanking, I see," Teddy teased.

Misha shook his head. "Asher would never spank me, and besides, Daddy said it was okay."

"Lucky. I asked Ian for one and he told me that we had to wait until we had a bigger place," Teddy said, his shiny lips downturned in a pout.

"Daddy said I can't get one, either," Ryder sighed dramatically.

Misha hesitated, twirling the string of his sweatshirt through his fingers. "Should we do something else? I don't want you to be sad or to rub it in or anything."

"No." Ryder immediately smiled and grabbed his hand. "I'm just being a brat. We'd love to go with you."

"Yeah, ignore us being drama queens," Teddy laughed.

* * * *

Asher stared at the animal shelter, not sure if he should be nervous or excited. He'd always wanted a pet, but his parents had said they were too messy and required too much work, and after that…well, look how that had turned out.

"No snakes, no rats, no mice, no lizards and nothing with more than four legs or less than three. And nothing with pinchers. And nothing that looks at me funny," Asher continued his list as they walked inside.

"Oh, look at the kitty." Misha raced to the counter where a fat calico cat with a bent ear was sleeping on a stack of papers. Asher watched his boyfriend shove his hands in his pocket as he leaned in, like otherwise he'd be snagging the ball of fuzz up and mauling him.

"This is Callie. She's the owner's baby," the perky young man behind the desk said, popping up out of nowhere. Well, likely he was throwing paper in the filing cabinet or something, but Asher still jumped like he'd appeared by magic.

Which was amusing, considering the two crystal balls on his tee, under the words '*Look at my balls*'.

Shiloh had a strange look on his face as he stared at the young man, an expression that looked somewhere between pride and concern, which…didn't make a whole bunch of sense, considering the shirt Shiloh was decked in.

"We're here to adopt a pet!" Misha craned his neck to peer through the doorway they could all hear barking coming from.

"Are you looking for a cat, dog, bird? Something more exotic? We don't get a lot of non-traditional animals in need of homes here, and you'd have to fill out special paperwork to prove you know how to care for them. Oh, I'm Riley, by the way." Riley was no more than eighteen, *maybe*. His floppy hair was pulled back in a bun, several long strands dangling over his neck.

Asher sucked in breath to repeat his list, but Misha interrupted. "Can we see *all* of them?"

As usual, Asher couldn't say no to something that made Misha so happy, so he resolved himself to a long day looking at animals. As long as they only ended up with one at the end, he would be happy.

* * * *

Liam was still waiting for his boys to come out of the animal shelter almost three hours after they'd gone in. It was crowded in Mason's SUV with four men and three pet carriers crammed inside, but none of them had been able to agree on who was going and who was staying home. So, in the end, they'd all gone.

Mason, as owner of the vehicle, had claimed the driver's seat. Liam pulled rank as the oldest—though only by a hair, since Mason was only a few months younger, and took the passenger side, leaving Gage and Ian, Liam's old handler, in the backseat.

Thankfully, they were all adults about it, only elbowing each other a few times out of boredom.

"How long does it take to pick out a pet?" Gage finally groaned. Liam looked back to see him rubbing his lower leg with a grimace. He knew the man had a prosthesis—which allowed him to do his job as a bodyguard for Mason's security company—but sitting cramped in a car probably wasn't doing him much good.

"Want to switch seats?" Liam offered, albeit a bit reluctantly.

Gage shook his head, "Nah, I'm good. My boy won't be when he comes out, though."

Liam wasn't worried. He'd seen the two men together enough to know that Gage, while strict with his oft-bratty boyfriend, would never actually lay a hand on him in anger.

Finally, when they were just about all antsy enough to send in a search party, a herd of giggling boys spilled out of the shelter, with…definitely more than *one* animal in tow. Asher clutched a small black kitten to his chest like a lifeline, while Misha was being dragged along the sidewalk by an over-excited dog more than half his size. It looked like a cross between a German Shepherd and a Labrador, with a little extra something mixed in.

Misha's mouth was open, panting in excitement— and the dog's tongue was, as well. Asher looked like he was giving the mutt suspicious glances, but the canine didn't seem to care about the little fluff ball in the boy's arms. He was rather more excited about the fire hydrant he currently danced around.

Liam laughed. "So much for your plan to surprise your boys with pets of their own!"

Mason and Gage both sighed.

Shiloh held what had to be the ugliest cat Liam had ever seen in his arms. It was miles of matted fur, and little else that Liam could see. From the red stripes down the young dancer's arms, it came fully equipped with claws and apparently didn't hesitate to use them.

And Ryder was holding a pair of puppies of an indeterminate breed.

Only Teddy came out pet-free.

"I should have known better," Gage mused, shaking his head at his boy through the window.

"At least he's only got one," Ian teased. "Mason's going to have twice the poop to scoop."

"And twice the spankings to dole out," Mason laughed. "I wouldn't have let him go if I didn't accept that this was a possibility."

"You still going in to get your boy a baby to coo over?" Liam asked Romero.

"I have to now, don't I? He deserves a reward for following the rules so well. I can't let him be the only one of his friends without a furball."

"It's going to take them a while to get all those animals situated in the car, so I bet you have time to run in, and they won't even notice," Liam suggested.

He was right. When Romero climbed back into the car ten minutes later, a not-quite-grown tabby cradled in his hands, the boys were still struggling to coax Misha's mutt into the backseat. They'd get two legs in before the dog proved he'd been a contortionist in a past life — or was somehow missing a spine — and he'd twisted back out to lick slobbery kisses all over the boys' laughing faces.

Liam was grateful for his fenced-in backyard.
He was going to need it.

* * * *

"Daddy, look!" Misha came barreling out of the
living room while Liam was still hanging his jacket on
the hook by the door. The large beast behind him
tripped over his own paws in his haste to follow, and
Liam laughed.

"Who's this?" He knelt down and let the dog collide
with his chest hard enough to almost knock him over,
giving him a vigorous rub behind his ears and under
his chin. The dog slobbered profusely but Liam
pretended not to care, for Misha's sake. He could
always get his clothes dry cleaned, but a smile like that
was priceless. "Such a good doggy. Look at you," Liam
cooed.

"This is Angel. She's three years old, and her last
family didn't want her anymore because she was too
big and sometimes she pees on carpets—but only when
she's excited—and I can keep her, right?" Misha
rushed, gasping in a breath at the end.

"Like anyone could resist this face." Liam gave the
dog a final pat and stood up, trying to ignore the dog's
silent pleading, wincing when the whipping tail
slapped across his shin. "Of course you can keep him."

"*Her*, Daddy. And good, because Asher got a pet,
too. Wanna see?" Misha's expression was too innocent
to be real, all wide eyes and bright smile—and fiddling
hands.

"Of course, lead the way."

Misha bit his lip and looked over Liam's shoulder at
the closed door. "Are, um... You're alone, right?"

302

Liam barely hid back his smirk, knowing that likely, his boy was worried about getting his friends in trouble with *their* Daddies. "Yep, Ian and Gage had a few errands to run, and Mason decided to stop at the office to finish up some paperwork. Disappointed?"

"No!" Misha's smile blossomed to full wattage again as he ran over and grabbed Liam's hand, tugging him with him down the hallway. Angel danced back and forth between them, tangling her large body between their legs more than once. It slowed their progress, but it was too amusing to worry about.

"She's just excited, Daddy," Misha explained, giving him bigger puppy eyes than the actual dog was. "The shelter promised she'll calm down when she's older."

"Don't you worry." Liam pressed a kiss to the top of Misha's head and pulled him under his arm, "I'm not."

"Good, because we can't take her back. You *promised.*"

"Cheeky boy," Liam teased, brushing his fingers over the pleased smile on Misha's mouth.

"You still love me, though," Misha said, and Liam was grateful it wasn't a question anymore.

"Of course."

They found Asher in his bedroom, lying on his back, propped up by several pillows with a black cat curled on his chest. Seeing it now, up close, Liam realized it was older than he'd thought. It was just so scrawny that he'd thought it a kitten from afar, with the narrow frame and long spine of an adolescent.

Asher lifted his finger to his lips when Misha and Liam stepped into the room. Liam nodded, then nudged Angel out into the hall and closed the door almost all the way. Angel whined in the hallway but quieted down.

Asher didn't speak until the cat shifted, its mouth gaping in a yawn to reveal a broken fang. The boy's expression was plaintive, and he hunched his shoulders, curling his arms protectively around the cat like Liam was going to take it away. "The shelter said no one wanted him because he's black." Asher sounded defensive. "I'll clean his litter box and feed him, and he's so quiet that you won't even know he's there."

"I know you will, sweetheart. What's his name?" It warmed his heart the way Asher spoke, like he needed Liam's permission, even though he lived currently with Mason and his brother — like he knew soon enough that he and Misha would be moving to Liam's.

"Jinx," Asher said, his eyes flashing like he dared Liam to question it.

"Hello, kitty." Liam made sure the cat could see him as he reached out and ruffled its fur. "Are you a boy or a girl?"

"I don't know how he identifies, so I'm calling him a 'he' since he has balls," Asher answered immediately, tongue in cheek and a smirk on his lips. "So far, he doesn't seem offended."

"Well, if he scratches me for it, I guess we'll know." Liam chuckled and pulled his hand back. "How is he doing with Angel?"

"So far he's ignoring her, but he doesn't seem too bothered. I think he's used to dogs from the shelter," Asher explained.

Liam looked to Misha. "And Angel? Not giving him any trouble?"

"She sniffed his butt a few times, but she's more interested in Ryder's new babies."

"Where *are* the other boys, anyway?" Liam asked.

"Ryder is outside with Teddy and the puppies. Shiloh is in Misha's room giving his cat a bath. I was *going* to help," Misha hurried to add, looking up at him with wide, pleading eyes. "I really was, but his cat is really *mean*."

Liam laughed. "Should I go check on them?"

He nodded quickly. "Yes, he definitely needs a Daddy's help right now."

Liam shook his head but smiled, heading across the hallway. He barely opened the door when he already heard the cursing. Stopping for a second, he pulled out his phone and opened the group chat he'd started with the other men earlier.

Liam: *Gage, I owe you ten bucks.*

Gage: *I told you that cat looked mean.*

Liam: *Heading into the scene of the crime. Pray for me.*

He shoved his phone into his pocket and headed toward the bathroom. It was partially flooded with soap and water, and Shiloh was positively drenched, his arms covered in little scratches, some deep enough to bleed. He gripped a squirming cat with one hand and a comb with the other, and he looked like he was about to cry.

"Here... Let me help," Liam offered, kneeling in the puddle to help hold the cat still. "Oh, you poor thing." Getting an up-close look at the creature made Liam want to go kick someone. Clearly, this cat had been neglected and abused for a long time. With the fur drenched, it was clear the cat wasn't fat, just furry. She was little more than skin and bones. And her fur was more matted than not.

The cat gave a pitiful meow as she — definitely a she, since he could feel from where his fingers brushed over her belly that she'd had at least one litter — tried to squirm free.

"I hate to say it," Liam admitted, "but you might be better off to shave her and let it regrow."

Shiloh's shoulders slumped. "Yeah, you're probably right."

Twenty minutes — and several scratches — later, they had a very angry, very bald cat. Liam had kept the clippers as long as he could, but once he'd cut the mats out, there was little he could salvage.

"I'll have to get her a sweater," Shiloh bemoaned as he wrapped the still-pissed cat in a thick towel and carried her across the hall to Asher's room. Liam watched him sit down, holding the cat like a football to keep her from squirming away.

Asher looked over at the cat and shivered. "Yeah, definitely."

Remembering Asher's aversion to all things hairless made Liam laugh as he left the boys to their pets to go get started on dinner.

Chapter Thirty-Three

Asher was able to keep on his happy mask until Misha took Angel outside to play with the others, then he let it slip with a sigh. He loved his new cat already, and he enjoyed spending time with Ryder and his friends, but all day today the Senator had been running through the back of his mind. Or more accurately, several dozen plans on how to *handle* the situation with the senator.

"Everything okay?" Shiloh asked, his newly shorn murder cat finally sleeping.

"Just have a lot on my mind." Asher shrugged, leaning back against his pillows again.

"I'm a pretty good listener, if you want to talk," Shiloh offered.

Asher was halfway through waving him off when he stopped, nodding instead. "Yeah, maybe. Misha and I just found out that one of the men who...one of Mast—Barnes' friends is..." Asher dragged in a shaky breath. "Sorry."

"Don't be. Trust me. I know how hard it is to talk about things like this." Shiloh sounded like he meant it, and when Asher looked over, there was pain clearly written over his face.

"Ryder told you, right? About us? Me and Misha, and...what happened?" Asher clarified. Shiloh nodded, so Asher went on, "Barnes wasn't the only one who...did *things* to us. He would take us to parties and make us service the other guests or put on shows and shit. And he'd have friends over. Men who wanted something from him and would bring him boys to play with, or men who *he* wanted things from, like...like for them to look the other way on a shady business deal or to drop the charges against one of his associates. Things like that. And he would make Misha and me provide *favors* for him, you know?"

Asher looked away, embarrassed to be admitting to all the fucked-up things he'd been forced to do. Ms. Allard kept telling him it wasn't his fault, that the things he'd done, he'd done to survive, and he couldn't hold them against himself, but...it was a slow process.

"He was always talking about wanting looser trade restrictions. I guess he smuggled a lot of drugs in under the guise of importing his company's products from Mexico and South America, so he wanted to pay less tariffs or something. I don't really know exactly. Every time he'd talk about it, he'd invite this man over. A priest... He had the"—Asher fingered his neck—"collar thing that they wear."

"That's fucked up," Shiloh agreed, and when Asher glanced back, his face was dark. He had his knees pulled up, the cat more on his chest now than in his lap. "Sorry... Keep going."

KD Ellis

"You're right, though. It *is* fucked up, especially because I guess he'd been screwing with Misha for as long as he was with Barnes. He was only *ten*," Asher snarled, only the cat on his chest keeping him from getting up and pacing. "But we thought he was arrested, because they *said* they'd gotten all of Barnes' associates. We *believed* them, but...we were out yesterday, and we heard him on TV. He's a fucking *senator*, Shiloh. And when Liam told his old boss at the FBI, she basically said that she didn't believe us and wouldn't do anything about it. So he's just going to...get away with it...all of it."

"No, he's not," Shiloh growled, sitting up fast, ignoring the yowl from the disturbed cat. "We'll make sure of that, won't we?"

"I don't know how, though," Asher admitted. "I told Liam I wanted to talk to the press about it, so maybe *someone* will believe us, but he thinks it's a bad idea. Well, a *good* idea, but he doesn't think it'd be good for *us*."

Shiloh smiled, but it was cold and cruel and, thank God, not directed at *him*. "I think it's a *brilliant* idea. And you know what? It's about time all these powerful, good-for-nothing pieces of *shit* get what's coming to them. You wouldn't know, but my dad's lawyer was fucking with me, too, and when I went to the police, they didn't believe me, either. If you and Misha *and* I all go to a reporter—a *good* one, not a tabloid—we can turn their lives upside down."

* * * *

Asher thought it would take longer.

Instead, two weeks later—just days before Christmas—he stood sweating under the stage lights at a broadcast studio while a makeup artist did last-minute touch-ups.

"Remember... If it gets to be too much, you can ask him to have a second. It's not live, and no one will be angry if you need a break," Liam reminded him again, and even though they'd had this talk several times, Asher was grateful. "Mason and I both did our research, and Noah is one of the top-rated journalists in the country. He isn't going to try to trick you or have any last-minute surprises. He's on your side here."

"I remember," Asher reassured him, oddly relieved that Liam seemed just as—if not more—nervous than they did. Shiloh was laughing with his own makeup artist a few steps away, though his smile was tight, and Misha was already finished and was strangely calm.

Of all of them, Asher had thought Misha would have the hardest time. Lots of people, bright lights and being in a strange place all seemed a recipe for failure, but Misha seemed excited about the prospect of being on TV, even if it was to tell his story. To be fair, Misha didn't have the same problems talking about it that Asher did. If he had to guess, it was because Misha still didn't completely understand exactly how fucked up his life had really been, and Asher couldn't help but hear his mom's voice in his head, calling him a pervert.

At least Liam would be with them the whole time, as would Gage, some lawyer they knew named Beckham and a police officer who had worked on Shiloh's case. Pulling Shiloh into the story was one of the best things they could have done, Asher was quick to realize. Not only did he and his wealthy father have connections all over the country, and not only would his famous name bring in viewers, but it meant that Asher and Misha wouldn't be the center of attention the whole time.

What he'd intended to be a call out on the senator had turned into a whole movement addressing sexual assault and the lack of culpability for society's most influential persons.

And Noah Steele was one of the most beloved, trusted news reporters in the whole country. Even Asher, with his limited knowledge of current events, had heard of him. He'd flown in from New York City just for them. He said they were going to flood the news stations with the broadcast come the new year, when people were coming down from the holiday good spirits, and best of all?

It was an election year.

Senator Ryland Emerson Scott II was going to be *so* fucked. Even if he got reelected, which Asher hated to admit was a good possibility in this country, he'd carry this stain with him like a scarlet letter.

And that thought made this whole production worth it. "Let's do this."

Misha fought the urge to fidget as the reporter, Mr. Steele, spoke to the camera. "Joining us tonight are several brave, young men to share their stories. Due to their nature, the stories will be deeply traumatic, so viewer discretion is advised. Many of you will be familiar with my first guest. No stranger to the tabloids, Shiloh Beckett dances in and out of the media as often as he crosses the boards of the Long Center with the Austin Ballet. Today, he has agreed to share his story."

Shiloh was pale, his shock of pink hair the only color he sported. Today he was dressed down, in simple dark jeans and a plain tee, nothing to distract from his words. His pose was casual, but Misha could see the whiteness of his knuckles where they clenched the armrest of his chair.

Misha shifted in his own chair backstage as he listened. Shiloh's voice was steady, but he could hear the strain as he spoke of his father's lawyer and the abuse he had suffered at his hands. Then, Shiloh spoke of his experience speaking with the police, being told that his history as a party boy meant they wouldn't even open a file.

After Shiloh, Mr. Steele had Shiloh's current boyfriend and former bodyguard speak, as well as one of the officers who had eventually worked on his case when evidence cropped up they couldn't ignore. By the time Mr. Steele thanked Shiloh and he was able to leave the stage, it had been nearly two hours.

Mr. Steele had told them already that it was normal to shoot more than they needed, so they could edit it down later, and that they shouldn't be surprised if it stretched longer than they'd expected.

Watching Mr. Steele with Shiloh helped Misha stress less about his and Asher's own upcoming interview. Mr. Steele seemed kind as he guided Shiloh through his answers when Shiloh stumbled, and if he needed a second, patiently waited.

Misha was grateful that nobody expected him to go out alone. Several stagehands came out and took away the armchair Shiloh had used and replaced it with a long couch instead. Liam claimed the seat on the end closest to Mr. Steele and Asher shoved Misha into the middle so he could take the other side.

"Are you ready?" Mr. Steele asked gently, not gesturing for the cameras to start rolling until all three of them agreed. Misha gathered his nerves and nodded, reminding himself that Asher needed him to do this.

For Asher, Misha could be brave.

Chapter Thirty-Four

With everything going on, Liam had been spending his days—and most of his nights—with Misha and Asher at Mason and Ryder's house. They'd had the lights strung around the roof and front porch since shortly after Thanksgiving, and the Christmas tree up and decorated for two weeks.

Liam's house was looking a little sparse, and he'd been okay with that until he woke up Christmas Eve morning to a text from his sister Lynette that she and the rest of the family were flying in to surprise him and his boys, and their plane would be touching down by dinner time.

He couldn't expect Mason and Ryder to host his whole family, so it left him in a mad dash to the store to do the thing he hated the most—decorate for Christmas the day before. He stripped the remnants of decorations from three separate stores but thankfully, he'd already bought presents for everyone. He'd intended to ship them after the Christmas rush had died down, but now they'd be opened in person, instead.

At least he had plenty of guest rooms.

After he carted the decorations back home, he called Mason's house phone, asking him to see if the boys would like to come over and help him decorate. Mason assured him they'd be over shortly after breakfast.

Liam had barely finished brewing a pot of coffee when he heard his front door open and running feet on the tiles. "Daddy, we're here," Misha called, excitement clear in his voice.

"Walking feet," Liam heard Asher say a second later, and when both boys found him in the kitchen, they were grinning.

"Can I have some?" Asher asked, watching Liam sip his black coffee. It was a taste he'd acquired many years earlier, given the lack of sweeteners in stake-out cars, but not one he expected Asher to follow, so he doctored it up with a dash of cream and sugar before passing it over.

Misha, as usually happened when Liam and Asher shared a cup, poured an orange juice from the fridge into a plastic cup for himself. While Misha loved for Liam to make his plate and cut up his food, he always had a strange fascination with getting his own drinks from the fridge, and Liam tried not to think of the reason why.

It was such a good morning, and he wanted it to only get better.

"So," Liam said as Asher passed him the mug to savor the last swallow, "do we want to start with the Christmas trees or save them for last?"

Misha quivered with excitement, but bit his lip hard, like he had a preference but didn't want to say. Asher chuckled and draped an arm over the boy's shoulder. "He wants to decorate them first."

"Can I put on the star?" Misha blurted, giving him the biggest puppy-dog eyes he could manage. It made Liam think of Angel, who had—rather reluctantly, from what Mason had relayed to Liam on the phone earlier—stayed at home.

"I bought two trees, so there's a star for each of you. How does that sound?" Liam couldn't decide between a fancy white one with fake frost and pinecones and a more traditional fake fir, so he'd bought both.

"Sounds like overkill to me. Where are you planning to put them?" Asher teased.

"One in the living room and I was thinking we could put one at the end of the hall, by the big picture window," Liam explained. "So you can either each decorate one, or we can decorate one first and move to the other together."

"Together," Misha said with a level of conviction neither Asher nor Liam seemed willing to argue—not that Liam would have. He rather liked the thought of the three of them decorating together.

It had always been his favorite part of Christmas—each ornament weighing down the boughs and forming the foundation of a tradition. He and Lynette used to argue quite viciously over where the Santa ornament should hang, and whether Rudolph should be by the sleigh or by the star.

He was looking forward to building similar traditions, though perhaps without the violent near fisticuffs, with his boys.

As he suspected, neither Asher nor Misha had the same competitiveness that Liam had with his sister. They passed every ornament back and forth to each other, muttering quietly, before one of them would decide where to hang it. Even when they disagreed, more often than not Asher let Misha make the final decision with a level of sweetness Liam had never felt and certainly never with his sister, the brat.

And both boys glowed brighter than the star when they placed it, with Liam's help, on top of the tree.

After both trees were finished, they helped him string garland along the stair bannisters and mistletoe over the archway to the living room and stockings off the mantle. The only thing he refused assistance with was stringing lights along the porch, since it required him to climb a ladder, and he refused to watch Asher or Misha do so. Oh, he knew they were capable enough, but the thought of either of them taking a tumble made him cringe.

They had a late lunch at Dai Due.

"What time is your family coming?" Asher asked as they left the restaurant, for some reason looking nervous.

"They should be here in a few hours. They insisted on grabbing some Ubers instead of letting me port them back and forth. Why, darling? What's wrong?" Liam opened the back door of his car for Misha but didn't close it. That way Misha could still hear if he wished.

"Oh, nothing. Just...wanted to know how long we got to spend with you before Mason needs to come pick us up." Asher gave a carelessly nonchalant shrug, but Liam could tell it was forced.

"Oh, honey, no. You don't have to leave. I'm sorry I didn't make that clearer. I want you to meet them, if...if you're okay with that?" Liam had only himself to blame. He should have known to tell them outright, especially given their experiences with their *own* family.

"Oh." Asher flushed and looked away, his cheeks a lovely pink. "I...I'd like that, if you really don't mind." He bit his lip until Liam tugged it free. "They won't care? That you're with both of us? Or should we just say we're your friends? Though they might find it odd, that someone like *you* would be friends with *us*."

"Hey." Liam stepped closer, bracketing Asher against the car with his arms as he leaned in, pressing their foreheads together. "I would be *lucky* to be your friend, both of you. Even if that's all we were to each other, I would consider it a dream come true, okay? I don't want you to talk down about yourself like that. But no, my family won't care. In fact, they already know. That's why they are flying down. They want to meet you."

"You told them about us?" Asher leaned back slightly to meet his eyes with his own surprised gaze.

"Before I even moved back. I had hope that, someday, you—*both* of you—would feel even half as strongly for me as I already did for you." Liam smiled. "I'm glad my hope paid off."

* * * *

Asher tugged on the collar of his shirt. "Should I dress up more? I can ask Ryder to bring me something else?"

"You're perfect, darling," Liam promised, smoothing the fabric over Asher's shoulder in a move that made him shiver.

Asher reached out to trace the stitching of Liam's fancy button-down top. "Are you sure they won't mind?"

"They'll love you. My sister is always telling me I need to stop dressing like a suit salesman at Nordstrom's, as if I've ever *been* in one." Liam rolled his eyes but he grinned when he spoke of his sister. Then, Liam's grin faltered, and he looked self-conscious, an expression that sat oddly on his face. "Do you mind them? The suits?"

"No!" Asher shook his head immediately in denial. "You look *sexy* in them."

Liam relaxed, his smile growing again. "Good, that's…good."

It was strange for Asher to realize that Liam had moments of doubt as well. He always seemed so sure of himself, a paragon of strength and support. It was a relief to realize he was only human as well.

Misha bounded down from upstairs before Asher could think of anything to say. Like Asher, he was dressed casually, though Asher's tee was considerably more plain, just a blue shirt with a V-neck collar. Misha's had a sparkly cat with a pink collar that matched his jeans and fuzzy gray socks.

Asher's own feet were bare, and he had a moment of self-consciousness over the fact. Before he could remedy it, the doorbell rang, and a small herd of people was flooding the house. Immediately, Misha was at his side, tucked under his arm. He restrained himself from putting his back to a corner but only barely, watching what had to be the entirety of Liam's family crowd inside, loud and laughing.

He was never going to remember their names.

He did try, though. Liam's father, Shane Tennyson, was easy to recognize. He looked like a well-aged version of Liam with the same blue eyes and strong jaw. His mother, Linda, Asher would recognize only because she was rarely far from her husband.

And he doubted he'd ever be able to forget Liam's sister, Lynette, since the woman had a devil-may-care smile and teased Liam relentlessly. She was a single mother, and her son, Nolan, was a cherubic little menace with more energy than anyone seemed capable of keeping up with—though Misha spent most of the night trying.

Not even two hours after dinner, Misha was passed out on the rug in the living room, surrounded by Legos, while Nolan laughed maniacally, running his toy cars over Misha's sleeping form like a racetrack.

"He was so good with him," Lynette mused out loud as she flopped down on the couch beside Asher. Most of the rest of the family was still in the dining room, talking boisterously over each other under the guise of an after-dinner drink. Liam had peeked in on them a dozen times, only going back to his family after several reassurances that both of them were *fine,* neither of them cared about minding Nolan and a promise that they'd call for him if they changed their minds.

"I think he wore himself out trying," Asher agreed, smiling at his sleeping boyfriend. Misha rarely snored, but he was making cute little chuffing noises where his nose was pressed into the carpet. "He didn't get to be around a lot of other kids."

Lynette's smile slipped. "No, I imagine he didn't. Well, I promise we will be flying down more."

"Liam would like that. He doesn't talk much about it, but I know he misses his family," Asher said, only afterward wondering if maybe he shouldn't have. It wasn't his place to spill Liam's secrets.

"My brother is too stubborn for his own good, and always thinks he has to do everything alone." Lynette rolled her eyes. "I think you both have been good for him, though. I've not seen him smile this much since we were children."

Asher flushed at the compliment. "I hope so. I just want him to be happy. We both do."

"And I am," Liam interrupted from the door, a fond expression on his face. "Asher, would you help me get Misha up to bed?"

"Yeah, of course," Asher agreed and stood up. Helping mostly meant helping Misha change into pajamas and tucking him in after Liam carried him upstairs to their bedroom, but it was an unspoken agreement that the three of them had. Misha had broken down in sobs the first time he'd woken in a panic to Liam helping him undress, upset more because he feared he'd hurt Liam's feelings than the actual scare of waking up in the first place.

Liam, of course, had been as understanding as usual, and they'd ever since had a compromise that Asher took over undressing duties when Misha wasn't fully awake, more to spare Misha's feelings then Liam's. Asher was convinced that it had been a momentary flashback to living with Barnes that wouldn't happen again, but Liam insisted that there was no need to push Misha about it now.

So, Asher undressed Misha and helped him into pajamas and tucked him into bed, then changed into his own pajamas and brushed his teeth. He hesitated before slipping out into the hallway. Liam promised it was okay to come back downstairs dressed for bed, but Asher couldn't push his nerves away completely. It was something only time would heal—or so his therapist insisted.

"It's a marathon, not a sprint," she kept repeating and he was finally beginning to believe her.

Asher found Liam in the dining room, lounging in his seat near the end of the table, laughing at something his dad was saying. Asher lingered by the doorway until Liam glanced over, his smile somehow growing even wider as he waved him over.

Asher yelped when Liam dragged him into his lap, glancing hesitantly at Liam's father, but the man only smiled. "Asher, my son couldn't have picked a better pair of partners, if I say so myself. Make sure he brings you both with him the next time he ventures up to the city, yeah?"

Asher flushed but nodded. "Yes, sir." He'd never been to New York City, though he'd used to dream of it. It was ironic that he was only going to get to see it now that he lived halfway across the country, after a childhood of being just a few states away.

Thankfully, Liam's family seemed to understand that he wasn't feeling the most social and allowed him to sit quietly, just listening from his spot curled up in Liam's lap.

He didn't remember falling asleep, but the world grew fuzzier, like staring through fog or listening in a tunnel, and the next thing he knew he was being settled into a mattress. He curled up around Misha's back and drifted.

* * * *

Misha wondered how long he had to lie still and quiet. It was Christmas morning—a day that had grown to mean only presents of pain and humiliation at his former Master's hand, but today promised to bring more.

Maybe, if he were careful, he could tiptoe downstairs with no one the wiser. He'd stupidly forgotten to bring his gifts for Asher and Liam with him when they'd left Mr. Mason's house yesterday morning—though to be fair to himself, he'd had no reason to suspect they'd be staying the night.

He'd texted Ryder frantically the night before in between playing blocks, cars and Legos with Liam's nephew, lamenting that he wouldn't have anything here for the men he loved to open.

Thankfully, the house had been so chaotic with dozens of Liam's family members—an aunt and several cousins and parents and a sister—chattering happily, that he didn't think either of his men had noticed him sneaking to the doorway to get the bulging bag of gifts from Mr. Mason. With his defined arms and dark beard, he looked like a sexy Santa. When Misha texted that to Ryder, the other boy had laughed and asked how he guessed their Christmas Eve roleplay so easily.

It wasn't exactly hard, considering the bright red shirt stretched over Mr. Mason's pecs proclaiming him 'Santa Daddy'.

And don't even get him started on the slutty elf costume Ryder was wearing.

The only person who'd caught him hiding the bag in the hallway closet was Liam's sister, who'd promised to keep mum.

Misha wiggled out from under Asher's arm—or attempted to. Instead, he got half free when Asher's grip tightened, dragging him back against his chest. "Where are you going, naughty boy?" Asher teased, blowing a raspberry in Misha's ear and dragging his fingers along Misha's chest to dip under the waistband of his pajama pants.

"To pee?" Misha tried, his voice lifting several octaves.

Asher, who knew him too well, laughed. "I think someone is lying. Were you hoping to sneak a peek downstairs?"

"It's *Christmas*," Misha said plaintively, his hips thrusting when Asher's hand crept lower, brushing across his cock in a light touch.

"Yes, it is," Liam's voice rumbled pleasantly from the other side of the bed. "And what a lovely gift to wake up to." Misha felt the bed shift.

He shivered when Asher blew a stream of cool air into his ear, then down his neck — the gentle not-quite-touch always seemed more erotic than anything, even more erotic than Asher's hand on his dick.

He'd been touched so many times, but no one ever made him feel like Asher did with a simple breath.

"Should we let Daddy watch?" Asher teased, his hand moving glacially slow against Misha's skin. Misha's whole body shuddered as he arched into the touch, trying to get him to move faster or squeeze harder, anything but tease.

"Please," Misha keened, throwing his head back against Asher's shoulder. Asher took that as permission to suck a bruise on his throat, where his neck joined his shoulder.

"You like that, baby? Daddy watching me make you feel good?" Asher gave his dick a squeeze before he pulled away. Misha whimpered at the absence, but before he could miss it too much, Asher had gripped his shoulders and rolled him onto his back.

There was little sexier than watching Asher wiggle out of his pajama bottoms, then straddle Misha's thighs nude. "Hands under the pillow, baby. Let me make you feel good."

Misha shoved his hands under his pillow, his skin heating at the pseudo-bondage. He didn't want to be tied down or cuffed, but he didn't mind being held here like this by only Asher's words and his own obedience. He flushed even harder when Liam rolled onto his side behind him, propping himself up on an elbow and watching with heated eyes.

He'd never liked being watched before, always felt like his performance was being judged — like a mistake would lead to a punishment — but now, with Daddy, it felt different. Maybe it was the lust easily read on his face, maybe it was the little smile of approval on his lips.

Maybe it was just that he wanted Liam to see how good he could be for Asher.

He was going to be the *best* boy.

Asher just stared at him first, not touching except where his ass rested on Misha's thighs. His gaze was so hot that Misha could practically feel it as he looked over Misha's body, sprawled out for his perusal. When Asher finally touched him, it was with a single finger against the hollow of his throat, a finger that then trailed down the center of his chest between his nipples and along the line of his abs.

The well-balanced diet he was allowed — and encouraged — to eat now left him with a thin layer of fat over the previously sculpted muscles. He could still see his six-pack beneath it, but it was softer, less rigidly defined. Now, he knew better than to starve himself to get back the definition. When Asher caught him, he'd been more upset than Misha had seen him since they'd left the estate. And after he'd calmed down, he'd spent hours kissing every inch of Misha's body, physical proof that he loved every inch.

Asher pressed both his palms to Misha's waist, spreading his fingers until they curled around his sides. He slid them up, the deep pressure like an erotic massage. When he reached Misha's chest, Asher slowed, rubbing circles over Misha's sensitive nipples with his thumbs until they hardened almost painfully.

It was all Misha could do to keep his hands under the pillow when his back bowed at the sensation, and he nearly bucked Asher off. "Please, Asher, too good," he begged. If Asher kept touching him like that, he was going to spill, untouched and without permission.

"You can take it. I know you can. Tell Daddy how good it feels," Asher purred, continuing his ministrations, playing Misha like a well-loved instrument. Asher's own cock was hard, the tip dragging over Misha's right hip as he moved, leaving a sticky trail of pre-cum along Misha's skin.

"Daddy, tell him to stop. I can't. It's too good!" Misha turned his head to stare pleadingly at Daddy.

Liam chuckled and leaned forward, pressing a relatively chaste kiss to Misha's lips. "I think you can take it, for Daddy. If you *really* want to stop, take your hands out from under the pillow and everything ends, okay?"

Misha loved that Daddy gave him an out. It was too good, but he didn't want to stop. He wanted to be a good boy.

Asher finally, just when Misha cried out thinking he was going to break, abandoned his nipples, dragging his hands up Misha's chest to curl around his cheeks as

KD Ellis

he leaned down. He captured Misha's lips in a heady kiss, one that stole the breath from Misha's lungs and left him panting.

When Asher pulled back, Misha strained to follow, only barely keeping his hands where he'd been told. Asher's laugh was teasing as he watched. "Needy boy, don't worry. I'll give you what you want."

Then Asher's mouth was sealed over his nipples, first one then the other, flicking and sucking until Misha was sobbing, squirming beneath him, unable to thrust with Asher pinning his hips to the bed, his dick bobbing against only air.

Asher sucked particularly hard, then released him just in time, peering up at him through his dark lashes. "Do you want to come like this, Misha baby? Humping the air and my mouth on your nipples?"

Misha shook his head, knowing exactly what he wanted. "Fuck me, Asher, please? I want to come on your dick."

Beside him, Liam groaned at the dirty words, and Misha flushed with heat. He wanted Liam to watch Asher take him, claim him — mark him inside with his cum. Then he wanted Daddy to fuck it back out of him.

Asher moaned and reached down to grip the base of his own dick like he needed to stop himself from coming. "You'll have to ask Daddy if he has lube."

Misha gave Liam a pleading look, but Asher tsked. "Use your words, baby. Tell Daddy that his dirty boy needs me to fill him up."

Misha burned, the words hitting every one of his triggers, pulling him even closer to spilling. He whimpered, "Daddy, I need Asher to make me not empty. Please let him fuck me, Daddy?"

Daddy leaned between them to reach the nightstand on the other side of the bed, chuckling as he pulled out a bottle of lube. "Is that what you want, baby? Daddy to let Asher fuck you into the mattress? Want him to leave a little present in your ass?"

Misha nodded quickly, needing it now and beyond words. Liam opened the cap and held it out to Asher. "Give me your hand."

Asher held it out, palm up, and allowed Daddy to drizzle the lube over his fingers. Misha held his breath in anticipation as Asher shifted, climbing off Misha's thighs to kneel between them instead. With his unlubed hand, he gripped Misha's knee and used it to lever his legs open. Not that Misha resisted, but he just couldn't hold them back with his hands buried under his pillow.

Asher dipped his other hand below Misha's balls, rubbing gently over his hole until it softened enough for him to slip his fingertip inside and rest it there. Misha instinctively relaxed and Asher pushed in deeper, searching out his prostate with unerring accuracy.

Misha hoped Asher didn't ask him to stay still, because it was an impossible task. He moved his hips to meet Asher's hand, rolling with each brush over his prostate, and when Asher added a second then a third finger, Misha was keening.

Words spilled out of his mouth in a meaningless stream, pleading for Asher to give him more and finally, what felt like years later, Asher slid his fingers out of Misha's ass.

He almost complained, until Asher coated his dick with the last remnants of lube and pressed the tip of it against Misha's winking hole.

He slid in easily and, though he wasn't particularly long or wide, he filled Misha perfectly. When he stilled, his hips pressed to Misha's, settled fully inside him, Misha sighed, content, feeling as close to him as he could get. He curled his legs around Asher's hips, as if to keep him inside forever.

Asher shuddered and leaned down, pressing his face against Misha's neck. He slid his hands over Misha's thighs and up his hips, pulling him that last little bit closer, to where Misha couldn't tell where he started and Asher ended.

"I want to touch you," Misha pleaded, his hands clenched into fists under the pillow to keep himself from moving them out.

"Touch me, baby," Asher panted, finally starting to move, thrusting into Misha with gentle rolls of his hips that left Misha shuddering. He yanked his hands free and wrapped his arms around Asher's back, tracing the smooth lines of his muscles as he tried to grip him closer.

Daddy moaned and Misha heard skin sliding on skin. When he looked over, it was to see Daddy's fist curled around his dick, stroking himself off. "No, Daddy, I want you to fuck me, too," Misha whined.

"God, baby, you're killing me." But Daddy loosened his grip on his cock.

It was Asher who spilled first, his hips stuttering against Misha's, burying his face into Misha's hair as he shook. Misha stroked his back, his own arousal simmering while he helped Asher come down. When Asher finally loosened his grip, he expected Asher to roll off him and make room for Daddy.

Instead, Asher rolled with him, pulling him on top of him to straddle his hips. His cock slipped out and

Misha hissed at the feeling, clenching tight to keep Asher's cum inside where it belonged.

Asher gripped his hips tight as Liam straddled Asher's thighs to hover behind Misha. Then, Daddy tangled his fingers in Misha's hair, using it to angle Misha back against his chest, tipping his head to the side to nip his neck. "Are you okay like this, baby? Wanna sit on Asher's lap while I make you feel good? Let him play with your pretty cock?"

"Please, Daddy, I need you. It's leaking out of me," Misha whimpered.

Daddy used his other hand to angle Misha's hips back, lining his dick against Misha's hole. "Let me in, baby."

Misha tried to relax. Then Asher curled his fingers around Misha's oversensitive cock, and he moaned, dropping his head back against Liam's shoulder. Daddy pushed inside at the same time, and the dual pleasure had Misha shuddering.

"So good, Daddy," Misha moaned. He planted his hands on Asher's thighs, needing something to hold onto. Asher's hands covered his, squeezing for support.

"Yes, you are, baby—such a good boy for Daddy," Liam groaned in his ear. His dick was bigger than Asher's, stretching him wide and making him feel like a virgin again.

Misha loved the burn, the feeling that Liam was carving a place for him inside Misha, where he'd stay forever. Unlike Asher, who fucked him with reckless abandon, like at any moment they could be torn apart, Daddy teased him, each rock of his hips hitting his prostate with surgical precision, drawing him closer and closer to the edge, until he was shaking and gasping.

"Daddy, *please,* I can't stop it. I can't. I need..." Misha rambled, his balls drawing close to his body. He wasn't going to be able to hold off any longer. He felt like he was teetering, on the edge of falling.

"Go ahead, Misha baby. Show Daddy how good he made you feel," Daddy panted. His fingers threatened to leave bruises on Misha's hips, and he loved it, the idea that Daddy was marking him, inside and out. It was enough tip him over and he cried out as he came, pearly seed painting Asher's chest beneath him.

He was still spurting when Daddy growled, and Misha felt the heat of his cum painting his channel. Misha collapsed down onto Asher, breathing heavy.

"Best...Christmas...ever," Misha moaned.

"You never did say if you were trying to sneak a peek," Asher mused.

Daddy chuckled as he slid off the bed, returning a few seconds later with a warm towel and cleaning them up. "Some mysteries aren't meant to be solved."

Chapter Thirty-Five

Liam knew exactly why Misha was trying to sneak downstairs so early this morning and thankfully, it wasn't necessary, though it *was* adorable watching Misha try to stuff a bulging bag of gifts into the hall closet the previous night. He'd waited until both boys were asleep to head downstairs and scatter them carefully under the tree with his own gifts for the boys. Along with several from Santa, of course.

Liam cleaned the last of the lube off Asher before patting his hip. "There you go, all clean. Why don't you and Misha help each other get dressed, and I'll go start breakfast?"

Asher narrowed his eyes, staring at Liam with suspicion. "You just want to peek at the presents."

"I won't pick up, shake, touch or stare at *any* of the gifts. Scout's honor." Liam held up his fingers for emphasis.

"No licking, sniffing or 'accidentally' tearing the wrapping paper, either," Asher added. "Also, I don't believe you were a Boy Scout, so I think you should stay up here where we can watch you."

"Should I be hurt that you don't trust me?" Liam joked as he grabbed a pair of briefs and worked them up his legs.

"Nope." Asher grinned and rolled onto his back, his legs sprawling open. "I trust you enough to let you have my ass after dinner tonight."

"Oh, is that so?" Liam abandoned his hunt for his pants and crawled back on the bed to kneel between Asher's thighs. He palmed them, sliding his hands over the soft skin, watching Asher's face closely for any sign of wariness.

There was none, just a growing heat to match his growing erection, which Liam didn't hesitate to fondle. "You wouldn't let me take just a *little* peek?"

Asher groaned but shook his head. "Nope. And no bribing me with a hand job, either. I want it to be a surprise."

"What about a lick for a lick?" Liam teased, leaning down and swiping his tongue over the pink budded nipples, one at a time. He gave each a little suck, feeling Asher squirm under his hands.

"Uh-uh," Asher panted, holding firm. Liam didn't mind, since he really never had any intentions to peek — again — anyway.

"Well." Liam feigned a huff and slid down Asher's chest to hover over his hips. "If I can't peek at those prezzies, let me play with this one instead?" He blew a cool stream of air over Asher's red, leaking dick.

"I...I suppose. Just the one present wouldn't hurt," Asher decided, his hips twitching. Liam stilled them with his hands then swallowed Asher down with gusto, feeling the tip of his cock hit the back of his throat on the first try. He swallowed around it, grateful he'd never had much of a gag reflex.

Asher might have just spilled inside Misha not that long ago, but he seemed to enjoy Liam's mouth just as much, because it wasn't long before he cried out, barely managing a warning before he came. Not that Liam needed one. He swallowed down every drop, then flicked his tongue a bit sadistically over the sensitive slit for just that last little bit more, until Asher squirmed free, pink-faced and panting.

"Thank you for the treat, darling. You're delicious." Liam winked, watching Asher blush fire-engine red at the compliment. He laughed when Asher swatted at his arm.

Both boys ended up dressed in their Christmas morning PJs — green and patterned with elves for Misha, red with candy canes for Asher. Liam dressed down — for him, anyway — in a pair of slim-cut black trousers and a red cashmere sweater. At Asher's insistence, he abandoned his socks to go barefoot, grateful he'd turned the heat up the day before on account of his mother's aching joints.

How she survived winter in the city, he'd never know, though she'd made some veiled comments about how nice the weather was down here for December. He had a feeling they'd be purchasing a vacation house in Texas sooner rather than later.

It went without saying that Lynette complained more than once about the travesty of not having a white Christmas. If it continued this morning, he fully intended on pouring a bag of flour over her head after breakfast to give her exactly what she was asking for.

In the end, it wasn't a *whole* bag of flour. He made his way downstairs, a rather difficult operation considering Asher insisted on covering his eyes as they passed the living room to go into the kitchen, a feat accompanied by the soundtrack of Misha's giggling behind them, and put on the coffee.

Like any other addict, Lynette arrived moments later, following the scent of roasted beans to pour herself a mug and douse it liberally with cream and Splenda. Liam had confiscated the sugar to prepare enough French toast to feed an army.

So when she glared at the window and sighed, saying, "It's just a tad too green out there, don't you think?" and gave him a little smirk, the battle was on.

Liam pinched up a good palmful of powdered sugar and flicked it at her face, watching it puff around her like a little mushroom cloud.

The kitchen went silent, Misha and Asher both freezing on the stools they'd previously been sitting on while swinging their legs and chattering, and Lynette was a powdered statue.

Then Misha unleashed a little giggle.

It broke the frozen moment like a call to war and Lynette screeched, "You pesky little *asshole!*"

She chucked her half-drank mug into the sink and grabbed the bag of Splenda. She squeezed it at him, and he leaped out of the way. Unfortunately for Liam, Splenda — much like glitter — had a habit of sticking to everything. Despite his fast actions, white speckled his sweater like an uncontrolled case of dandruff.

"That was *cashmere*," Liam cried, but his heartless sister crossed her arms and shrugged.

"You started it."

"You said you wanted a white Christmas! Now you have one!" Liam crossed his arms as well, discreetly eyeballing the other kitchen condiments. There was no way he was allowing her to have the last throw.

A quick flick of his hand and he had the ground coffee dumped over her hair and she screamed, grabbing the gallon jug of milk, already uncapped. Liam lifted his hands and backed away, shaking his head, "Now, that's too far!

"Don't start something you can't finish." Lynette narrowed her eyes. "Admit you've lost, say you're a rotten little boy and I'll let you live."

Liam grabbed the first thing he could get his hands on, a bottle of olive oil, and twisted off the cap, holding it out in threat. "Put it down and we can call it a draw."

Asher and Misha were giggling hysterically by the bar, but Liam didn't have time to scold them for laughing in a serious moment like this, because Lynette moved, the gallon quickly upturned over his shoulder. Cold, white milk streamed out, coating his sweater and plastering it to his chest. Liam gagged at the feeling. He could barely handle drinking the stuff, let alone bathing in it.

He retaliated by squeezing the plastic oil jug, the sticky fluid squirting out of the tip and soaking her blouse, congealing to a clumpy mess with the sugar.

"Oh, *now* you'll get it," Lynette promised, then commenced the Most Epic Food Fight of the Century, or so Liam vowed to recount it later.

It only ended when his mother's voice echoed like a whip through the kitchen. "What on *earth* is going on in here, children?"

Liam slowly lowered the squeeze bottle of ketchup only when Lynette dropped her spatula, both of them turning to stare at the doorway, where their mother was standing, her arms crossed like a prison warden's. Liam gulped. "Sorry, Mother. Did we wake you?"

She shook her head before turning toward Liam's boyfriends, both sitting with their hands smacked over their mouths and eyes crinkled, glimmering with humor. "Come along, boys. Let's leave the children" — she spat the words at Liam and Lynette like an insult, but he could read the amusement in her voice easily — "to clean up their mess. I *do* expect the both of you to work together to prepare breakfast when you've finished."

Both Misha and Asher immediately scrambled off their stools to follow her out of the room. "Traitors!" Liam called, unable to stop grinning.

"Until next time, Li-Li," Lynette said solemnly, like a threatening promise of future retribution.

"This is far from over, Netty-bug."

* * * *

"Do you think Daddy's in trouble?" Misha whispered into Asher's ear as he settled onto the corner of the couch, tucking his feet into the crack between the cushion and the armrest.

Asher dropped down beside him, nudging him closer to his side. "Nah, Mrs. Tennyson didn't look too surprised. I think your Daddy has a naughty streak."

"He always has," Mrs. Tennyson said from behind them, making them both jump. Misha hadn't realized she'd returned to the living room already. She'd left to grab a magazine from upstairs while they'd waited for the Daddy and his sister to finish cleaning up and get breakfast on the table. "I should be grateful he decided at a young age that the only career he wanted was with the Bureau, else I'm certain he'd have ended up seated in the back end of a police car instead. Still, I'm glad he has left it behind. A mother worries, you know?"

Mrs. Tennyson sank into the armchair with a sigh, not even commenting on Misha's slip of the tongue. Apparently, learning that her son was moderately kinky either wasn't a surprise or was old news.

Whichever it was, it made Misha relax, now that he no longer worried that he'd slip up and use the word in front of her and utterly destroy Liam's relationship with his parents.

"Has he told you about the incident in junior high? Well, I suppose there were several, so I should be more clear. Did he tell you about the banana incident?" Mrs. Tennyson leaned forward with a wicked grin.

"Do *not* tell that story, Mother!" Liam hollered from the kitchen, his voice strained.

"A certain boy should be *cleaning* instead of *eavesdropping*," Mrs. Tennyson hollered back, her voice sweet as molasses.

"I swear to God, Mother, if you tell that story, I will—"

"You'll what, William? Put me over your knee? I'm not one of your boys, so you can't scare me with a spanking," Mrs. Tennyson scolded her son at top volume, and Misha choked on a groan, burying his face in Asher's sleeve to hide his flush. "Oh, sorry, dear. I didn't mean to embarrass you. There's absolutely nothing to be ashamed of. Liam's father and I are certainly no prudes in the bedroom. For instance, just last night, we dabbled in a bit of spanking ourselves—"

"Mother!" This time, Lynette and Liam yelled together in stereo.

Mrs. Tennyson rolled her eyes and twittered, "Apparently, my children *are* prudes, silly things.

Anyway, the banana incident. Liam was home all alone, since his father and I were off on a bit of a date night and Lynette had stayed after school for something or other" — she waved her hand — "clearly not important or I'd have remembered, and Liam decided it would be a great time to practice fellatio."

A loud series of bangs sounded from the kitchen, like Liam was opening and slamming cupboards and dropping pots by the handful into the sink. Mrs. Tennyson sighed and twisted in her chair a bit to call over her shoulder toward the kitchen, "Liam dear, you're being a nuisance."

"Don't tell that story, Mother!"

"I spent eighteen hours delivering your little breach butt, so I can tell any story I'd like and you'll say 'thank you, Mother,' afterward! Seriously." Mrs. Tennyson grinned at Misha and Asher. "You'd think he was raised in a barn with those manners."

Misha giggled. "What happened?"

"Oh, he was halfway through deep throating the banana, which he insisted on unpeeling first, when his father and I walked in. Why he thought it was best to practice in the living room, in full view of the entryway, instead of in his bedroom is beyond me. Of course, we'd run into several friends from his father's work while we were out, and they'd come back to the house for a nightcap. So there we were, his father and I, and half-a-dozen partners from the firm and *their* families, watching twelve-year-old Liam choking on a banana."

A groan sounded from the kitchen, but Mrs. Tennyson chose to ignore it, just raising her voice slightly. "Of course, we all thought he'd just forgotten how to chew, the poor boy, and... Oh what was his name, dear? Mr. Battley's boy?"

"Nathan," Liam called back, clearly resigned.

"Ah yes, Nathan. Nice boy... He was a year or two older than Liam. Well, he rushed in to give him the Heimlich, only to find poor Liam wasn't just shirtless — hard to tell with the couch in the way, you know, so we *all* assumed he was wearing trousers — but completely nude, with several rather sticky sports magazines spread across the couch cushions." Mrs. Tennyson shook her head. "It was perhaps a good thing he'd already come out to us, or we'd certainly have figured it out then."

Liam darkened the doorway, leaning against the frame. He was bare chested, clearly having stripped out of his messy sweater at some point during the cleaning, and his skin was red from forehead to nipples. "I'll have you know that I still can't look Nathan in the eye."

"Well, since Nathan is currently living in Guatemala with his husband and stepson, I don't imagine it would be an easy feat anyway, since you've *clearly* forgot how to use a video call." Mrs. Tennyson's lip wobbled in clearly feigned tears. "Heartless boy, won't even call his mother on Christmas for a quick 'hello'."

"You're being dramatic again, Mother. I'd hardly call you from across the living room."

"Why not? Your sister at least sent me a text this morning."

"It was probably one of those auto-scheduled texts she sets up a year in advance and forgets about." Liam rolled his eyes, then smirked over at Asher and Misha. "Never play board games with her. She's a cheater pumpkin eater."

"I'm not the one who hid cards in my lap during Go Fish!" Lynette called.

"I was six!" Liam hollered back, winking at Misha, who giggled. He'd never imagined a family like this. It was a far cry of what he remembered of his own. His father had been the stern, overworked patriarch, his mother the loving but overworked homemaker. Neither of them would have teased each other, or Misha, like Daddy's family did.

"I don't care. You still cheated! Just like you're cheating now, abandoning me to finish cooking while you go ogle your boys."

"I'm not ogling them," Liam yelled back while ogling Misha on the couch.

"I know you are. I'm not an idiot. You've got two adorable boyfriends while *some* of us are sitting out here all alone and loveless!"

"You're aromantic, Netty, or did you forget? You don't *want* a boyfriend!" Liam rolled his eyes and headed back into the kitchen, presumably to help.

"Doesn't mean you can rub yours in when you're supposed to be making French toast. You know I'll burn it if I try."

"I'll make the French toast if you do the eggs."

Misha grinned and settled back against Asher's side, closing his eyes and just listening to the banter. It made him feel happy and safe and, finally, like he belonged somewhere.

* * * *

Asher didn't start getting nervous until after breakfast. Most of Liam's extended family had already flown back to the city, only having come in for a day trip for Christmas Eve—which was apparently something rich people did, who knew?—leaving just Liam's parents, his sister and his nephew. It meant less people making unexpected noises and appearing when he didn't expect it, triggering the not-so-subtle panic attacks that had made him cling to Misha or Liam. It also, however, meant that gift opening was a far more intimate experience than he was prepared for.

What if Liam didn't like his presents? Or what if Liam's parents were upset that Asher and Misha had only gotten them something small? Asher refused to take money from Ryder and Mason, or *especially* from Liam, to pay for the gifts. It was one thing to accept that he needed their help for clothing, but it was another to expect them to pay for their own gifts.

It wouldn't feel like it came from *them* if he did that.

So he'd relied on his still relatively small paycheck from Sephora to fund both his and Misha's Christmas shopping. Everyone had told him — repeatedly — that they didn't need anything from him except a smile, but he would feel guilty opening the gifts he was well aware they'd bought *him* and not having anything to give in return.

It was Misha who quietly told him to remember that it wasn't a competition and that nobody expected him to buy their love, that Christmas was supposed to be about *togetherness* and holiday joy.

In the end, everyone loved their presents. He'd bought Mrs. Tennyson, who he was having a hard time calling 'Mom' as requested, since she was nothing like his own uncaring maternal figure, a soft blue scarf since he'd learned from Liam how much she hated the cold, and he'd bought the elder William Tennyson — who, unlike his son, actually *went* by William — a leather journal that he'd found half-price at Barnes & Noble.

It had been easy to shop for little Nolan — Misha grabbed a fair handful of coloring books and crayons and stickers that Asher suspected he'd have rather kept for himself, but Misha was selfless like that—but harder to buy for Lynette.

Asher hadn't had many female friends growing up, and his extended family was mostly absentee, so the female half of the species he found a rather large mystery. In the end, he'd used his employee discount to buy a neutral eyeshadow palette and an assortment of lip glosses that promised all day, smear-free wear.

She'd seemed to like them.

It was Misha who was the easiest to buy for, and Liam who gave him the most trouble. Misha got an almost-perfect replica of Nolan's gift with the addition of a 3D puzzle he'd stared at and discarded as 'too difficult' for Lynette's son.

Shopping for Liam had caused hours of nervous nail-biting and stress, several dozen "What if...?" questions posed to Misha then discarded and one accidental erection in a hardware store.

In the end, he'd bought Liam a new bottle of the shampoo he liked best—which had an extra number before the decimal that made Asher shudder — *who paid nearly twenty dollars for hair care products?* —a box of fancy chocolates and a secret letter promising a few special kisses later, if Liam wished to redeem the included coupon.

Or *would-have-been-secret* letter, if Liam's sister hadn't leaned over to read it, wagging her eyebrows at Asher afterward with a grin. He'd blushed, of course, but found he didn't mind much. Liam's family was far more open with each other than he'd expected, and neither his parents nor sister seemed unwilling to pry into Liam's sex life with 'helpful' suggestions that in the end, seemed meant more to tease than assist.

Asher himself ended up with a box of glow-in-the-dark condoms he suspected was a gag gift, a fancy wet-to-dry brush from Lynette and bath bubbles from little Nolan. He also received several new tops and jeans Liam's mother promised had been on sale and a sketchbook filled with several colored pictures from Misha.

It was Liam's gift that made him cry, and Liam looked uncertain as he pulled him into his lap, "If you don't like it, I can take it back."

"No! I love it, I just…" Asher cried into Liam's collar.

"I thought you'd like making videos again, even if you only choose to show them to us…" Liam had bought him what amounted to a full video studio, with a camera, tripod and lights included.

When his crying finally stopped, what felt like an eternity later, Asher threw his arms around Liam's neck and squeezed. "Thank you. I love it."

He didn't know if he'd be able to put them online again, not after what had happened before, but maybe someday he'd be brave enough to try. He'd forced himself to forget the joy it gave him, shooting makeup tips and tricks and watching people react to them.

Misha didn't cry over any of his gifts, but Asher could tell he itched to play with them. He ended up with enough stuffed animals to fill a small car, a few new video games and from Daddy, an online art course. Liam had listened when Misha, tentatively, had said over dinner one night that he liked coloring a lot, but he wanted to make his own coloring books for children. With Daddy's gift, now he could.

Asher, as grateful as he was to have the house to just the three of them again, since it meant Ryder would be dropping the pets off soon, was sorry when Liam's family finally departed a few hours after lunch. He'd liked them far more than he'd expected and was surprised to be relieved when they promised to return for a visit soon.

Ryder and Mason arrived before dinner with Angel and Jinx, who chased each other rather recklessly around the downstairs, nearly taking out the tree with a poorly executed leap from Jinx. Asher and Misha had both looked to Liam, waiting for a lecture, but Liam had just laughed and shook his head. "Silly rascals."

Asher managed to talk Ryder and his Daddy into staying for dinner.

It wasn't nearly as hard as he'd expected.

"Would you like to stay for – ?" was all he got out, and Ryder was fist-pumping the air and kicking off his shoes.

"Daddy said I couldn't invite myself to stay, even though I *told* him you must surely miss me by now." Ryder grinned, draping his arm over Asher's shoulder and half dragging him into the living room. Asher could tell that the festivities had Ryder trapped somewhere between 'little' and 'big', especially when he shoved Asher onto the couch before sitting cross-legged on the carpet. "Come on. Show me all your prezzies. What'd you get? Daddy got me a train set and some new Legos, but not the little ones that I wanted because he keeps stepping on them. I told him that's okay, though, since I've got a birthday coming up soon and he can get them for me then."

Asher chuckled at his excitable younger brother and slid down onto the carpet behind him to start going through the gifts. It was no surprise that Misha soon joined them, dropping onto his stomach with a coloring book and pack of stickers, a lollipop dangling out of his mouth.

* * * *

Ryder and Mason left a few hours after dinner after Ryder nodded off into his bowl of popcorn. Daddy told them to go put their new toys and gifts away while he cleaned up the kitchen, refusing help, even when Asher volunteered a second time, just to be sure. Asher helped Misha carry his toys and stuffies upstairs before he came back for his own.

He knew where to put everything, except the glow-in-the-dark condoms. They'd chosen together not to use them, since all three of them had received a clean bill of health from their doctors after their rescue. They wanted to be as close to each other as possible.

What was he going to do with these?

He chucked the box on the bed to figure out later and got started putting his new clothes into his drawers, planning what outfits he wanted to pair with them and whistling Christmas music when he heard Misha giggle.

He turned around to see Misha kneeling on the bed, the condom box open and several foil packets spread around the comforter. He had the reading lamp from the nightstand turned on and shining on them.

"What are you doing, baby?" Asher asked, abandoning the last of his clothes to climb on the mattress beside him.

"It says you have to charge them first," Misha giggled, his eyes twinkling as he held up a packet for Asher to read.

Liam heard the boys playing from outside the door. He couldn't tell what they were saying, but from the tone of the voices, they were playacting something. He stopped to listen, grinning when he heard what sounded like a lightsaber.

It did *not* prepare him for what he saw when he opened the door. All the lights were off and the curtains drawn. The only light came from Misha and Asher's... glowing...dicks?

It took him a handful of stunned seconds to realize that obviously, they'd opened the glow-in-the-dark condoms.

Which, apparently, reminded them of one of their favorite movies. Asher smirked at Liam and gripped the base of his glowing dick, waving it like a lightsaber. He deepened his voice. "Misha...he is your father..."

Misha giggled and flopped back on the bed. "Daddy is Darth Vader."

"Daddy can't be Darth Vader without a lightsaber," Liam pointed out. "Unless my little Skywalker is willing to share?"

He expected Misha to hold out another foil packet for him to use and started stripping, leaving his clothes in a pile behind him. When he stood naked, though, Misha didn't hold out a packet. Instead, he angled his hips and gave a sweet smile. "You can borrow mine, Daddy."

Liam groaned and slid onto the mattress beside him. He gave the glowing dick a gentle pump. Misha whimpered, his hips chasing his hand. "Does baby like that?" Liam teased, keeping his hand moving just enough to keep Misha wiggling. "Or should we convince Asher to lend us his lightsaber as well?"

It didn't take much convincing, just a glance and Asher was on the bed, kneeling between Misha's spread legs. Liam nudged him even closer, until his bobbing erection hovered just over Misha's. Liam wrapped his hand around both, stroking them together.

Liam kept stroking as he sat up onto his knees as well, leaning in to press a hot kiss to Asher's mouth. "Tell me what you want, darling. Want me to stroke your lightsaber off onto baby?"

Asher shook his head, reaching down to still Liam's hand with a groan. "No more playing lightsabers," Asher panted. "Want you to fuck me. Want you to fuck me while I'm inside Misha."

It was Liam's turn to groan at the image that brought up in his mind. "What about you, Misha baby? Do you want—?"

"Yes!" Misha spread his legs farther, an open invitation Asher wasted no time in taking. He sucked his finger into his mouth and dipped it below Misha's balls. Liam tried to watch the narrow index circle the tightly furled pucker, but it was too dark to see much.

"Lube," Liam finally groaned and slipped away, only for a second, to grab the bottle from the drawer by the bed. He flipped on the lamp while he was leaning over, then crawled back.

"Give me your hand, Asher," Liam said without thinking, then paused, hoping he hadn't pushed too far by making it an order. He was naturally dominant, especially in bed, but that wasn't the arrangement he had with Asher.

Asher, though, moaned and obediently held out his hand for Liam to coat his fingers. Liam closed the lid and dropped the bottle by his thigh, keeping it close for when he needed it. He wanted to watch his boys together first.

Asher took his time prepping Misha, moving his fingers slow and steady as he opened him up, seeming to take just as much pleasure in watching Misha writhe and moan as Liam did.

Misha finally reached down between his legs to grab Asher's wrist and still his hand. "Please, Asher, I need you. Please don't tease me. I can't wait anymore."

Liam watched Asher lean over Misha, their bodies pressing together. Asher's lips claimed Misha's in a passionate kiss, and it was more dominant than Liam expected from Asher and yet, somehow perfect. Sweat left a shimmer on their skin. Liam wanted to lick every inch of their bodies. Wanted to suck marks of ownership over each span of flesh.

He settled for fisting his dick to stave off ownership as he watched Asher slide into Misha's body. "Stay still," Liam groaned and slid behind Asher. Liam didn't delve between his cheeks immediately. In this instance, the journey was just as pleasurable as the destination.

He started at Asher's neck, leaning forward to suck a pink spot where it joined the shoulder until Asher cried out and cast his head back. The movement fitted him deeper inside Misha, who whimpered as well, his knees clamping tighter on Asher's hips. Liam slid his hands up Misha's calves then farther, onto Asher's sides.

He waited until Asher was begging, trailing open-mouthed kisses along the boy's spine and massaging the tense muscles of his back, even going so far as to dip his hands around to the front and trace the lines of his abs, before he finally removed one hand to fumble for the lube.

He coated the index and middle finger of his right hand. "Ready, darling?"

Asher shook, bobbing his head rapidly. "So fucking ready, Liam. I need you." He demanded with more than just his words, tipping his hips back as he leaned over Misha, a move that made Misha whimper as well.

"Me too, Daddy. I can't wait any longer!" Misha moaned, scrabbling his fingers over Asher's back, leaving red marks behind.

How could he deny his boys?

He began working Asher open, first with a careful pressure against Asher's hole, then gentle twists of his fingers once they pierced the tight heat. Every gasp and cry Asher made, Misha echoed, since they more often than not accompanied a twitch of his hips.

When Asher finally took three fingers, Liam paused to admire the sight, the pink glistening ring stretched around his thick digits, muscles in Asher's ass clenching visibly, his hole tightening with each movement.

Liam wanted to slide in a fourth, hear Asher moan at the intrusion, but Asher cursed, twisting around to glare over his shoulder. "Are you going to fuck me or do I need to commandeer one of your toys?"

Liam chuckled and finally removed his fingers, lining his aching dick up with Asher's winking hole. "Greedy boy. Patience is a virtue, you know," He teased, giving him just the tip.

Asher hissed, then shifted backward to impale himself fully with a groan. "So is chastity, and I have no intention of practicing *that*."

It drew out a full-blown laugh from Liam and he finally started moving, thrusting into Asher, and by extension, Misha. Hearing them both moan with each movement fueled his dominant streak. It was like he was claiming them both at the same time. Fucking Asher and using his boy's dick like a dildo to draw Misha closer to climax as well.

But it was more than just fucking, even if it was rough and sweaty. It was lovemaking. Every brush of his lips against Asher's shoulder, every trail of fingers over Misha's calves, every thrust of his hips was like taking loose threads and twining them together into rope — a rope which coiled around each of them and drew them together tighter.

Invisible bonds connecting each of their souls.

Misha cried out first, shaking beneath them as he came. Liam dipped his hand between the two boys' chests to gather the sticky cum, lifting his fingers up to Misha's mouth. Misha licked him clean with a blissful smile on his cherubic face, going boneless on the mattress.

The sight of his tongue curling around Liam's fingers was apparently all it took to tip Asher over, that or the way Misha's orgasm had him clenching around Asher's dick. Asher cried out seconds later, grabbing Misha's hand as he shook.

Liam wasn't far behind. The three of them landed together in a tangle of limbs and cooling cum. Somebody's foot dug into his thigh and an elbow pressed painfully into his ribs, but he wouldn't change it for anything. They couldn't stay stuck together long, though.

Carefully, he rolled to the side, freeing the boys from his weight. They snuggled up to his sides instead, Misha's fingers petting through Liam's chest hair, in much the same way he stroked over his stuffies, an absent-minded comfort.

"Perfect," Liam whispered, burying his face in Misha's hair, one hand on his hip while the other sought out Asher's.

"Great, kid. Don't get cocky," Asher mumbled, opening one eye to smirk as he quoted Liam's favorite Star Wars character but dropped his hand down to rest atop Liam's.

"Brat," Liam teased, but closed his eyes. He'd get up shortly to hunt down a wet towel, but for now, he was content to cuddle in the wet spot.

Chapter Thirty-Six

As February faded into March, Liam finally got the call he'd been waiting for. Noah Steele called to give him and the boys a warning that they'd wrapped up the final loose ends on the broadcast and it would be playing the following Friday. They'd timed it to follow one of the senator's campaign speeches.

Neither Asher nor Misha felt like watching the broadcast when it aired, but Liam recorded it, streaming it himself later that evening, after both boys were in bed. It still twisted him up to hear them share their stories, but he needed to be sure that the reporter, honest though he'd seemed, hadn't taken the opportunity to shove himself into the spotlight by painting either of his boys in a bad light.

Steele hadn't. Instead, Liam was left angry at the police system in the country. Steele had somehow managed to take their stories and turn them from a singular accusation against one man and into a critique of the entire justice system, addressing police brutality, race relations and the unfair treatment of sexual assault victims at every level of the process of reporting.

Liam reminded himself to send a thank-you basket before he'd returned to bed to cuddle up with his boys.

It only took him two days to realize that the broadcast had catapulted him, Misha and Asher into a nationwide spotlight. Other reporters—those who believed them and wanted comments on the senator's statement in response, and those who didn't and hoped to make them look bad—had managed to discover Asher and Misha's address. They camped out on the front lawn of Mason's house, blocking the driveway and shoving camera lenses into cracks of windows, until Mason had gotten fed up.

Mason had smuggled the boys out in the back of his SUV and dropped them, after taking an extremely circuitous route, at Liam's. He'd returned with almost his entire staff of personal protection officers, fully armed, to help escort the reporters off the grass.

Since Texas was a stand-your-ground state, the reporters wisely decided the sidewalk was a good enough vantage point for their purposes.

Of course, Mason's fit of pique did draw even more attention as reporters sought to discover why two previously unheard-of boys warranted an entire militia stationed in their front yard.

Then it was Mason and his company, Eagle Security, in the limelight. Mason had laughed on the phone with him this morning, saying the free press had drawn him in half-a-dozen new clients and the few he'd lost, he hadn't really liked anyway.

It took almost a month before another scandal pushed the story out of the limelight and the reporters decamped for fresher pastures. Not that Liam thought they'd be gone forever, and he fully expected the story to flare back up in the fall, as they got closer to the election. Even though the senator was dropping in the polls, it wasn't fast or far enough for Tennyson's liking. The bastard might end up reelected.

But at least the lack of reporters meant he could relax a bit now and take Asher and Misha on dates without worrying about eating a microphone in place of his fork.

Oh, how the newspapers had a field day about their three-person relationship, and about the age difference and the inherent power difference considering his former career and the role he'd played in their rescue.

It was enough to — *almost* — make him second-guess things. Only Asher and Misha's constant reassurances kept him from feeling like an old pervert.

Not that he didn't still feel old sometimes, especially on days like this. His knees just weren't in the same league as his younger boyfriends'. They had started making these little crackling noises when he stood too fast or squatted too long, and he'd taken to popping anti-inflammatories like candy. He thought joint pain was something that came in your fifties, not months shy of your fortieth birthday.

Surprise!

At least neither of his boyfriends complained.

Liam left them in bed to traipse stiffly to the toilet. At least, despite his joint issues, both boys claimed to no longer have bones at all. It was a rather successful midday tryst, if he said so himself.

He returned to the bed to gently wipe them down with a towel before retreating to the shower himself, since Asher was already making moon eyes at him again. He honestly wasn't sure he'd survive another go, so fleeing it was.

Of course, he'd barely spun the water on, steam billowing in the large glass enclosure, when Asher followed him in. "Want me to wash your back?"

Liam supposed another round wouldn't kill him. He handed over the soap.

Misha stayed in bed while Asher went to join Daddy in the shower. He was too content to move, swaddled up in the comforter with Liam's pillow squashed under his cheek.

He should get up and do something productive. He had his GED to study for, and toys in the playroom he needed to clean up. He felt like there was something else lurking on the tip of his tongue that he was forgetting as well, but all he wanted to do was cuddle up with the smell of Liam.

Closing his eyes, he smiled as he heard Asher cry out in the shower. It wasn't pained, it was pure pleasure, and he visualized what they were doing. Was Daddy keeping Asher's cock warm in his hand, or sucking him like a candy cane? Was Asher standing or kneeling?

He was half-hard, enjoying the loose pleasure coiling through his body without need to stoke it further, when he heard the shower shut off, then laughter. Misha gave himself a languid stroke under the covers.

"You should have joined us." Asher's voice was closer than Misha expected.

He opened his eyes, smiling up at him but not making to move anything but his slowly shifting hand. "The bed is warm."

"So was the shower," Asher said. He was naked, his skin flushed. He planted a knee on the mattress and crawled up, wiggling under the cover to press his bare skin against Misha's.

"You can't still be horny," Misha protested as Asher curled around him, his hips flush to his ass, moaning when Asher's dick slipped between his cheeks and prodded his hole.

There was enough lube remaining from earlier that Misha wasn't scared.

"What can I say," Asher purred in his ear, giving him a little love bite that made Misha cry out. "I've got two sexy men to play with all day."

Liam laughed from the bathroom doorway, rubbing a towel over his damp hair. "Are you pestering the baby now, Asher?"

"Do you want me to stop?" Asher shifted, and Misha glanced back to see Asher staring at Daddy with a naughty smirk.

It didn't need saying, but neither of them did.

* * * *

Asher flopped onto his back, truly worn out after he spilled his load in Misha's ass, then dragged him up onto his chest to cuddle. "You're all sweaty," Misha said, rubbing his face over Asher's damp skin.

"You love it," Asher said, and Misha nodded his agreement.

"So do I, but our water bill won't," Liam teased from the other side, where he'd laid to watch them play. He hadn't joined in except for a few hot kisses and a helpful lending of his hand to Misha, claiming that as hot as they were together his dick was officially on strike for the evening.

It was, Liam had said dryly, the perils of dating an older man.

Asher had felt compelled to point out that the only peril he'd stumbled on so far was Liam's ginormous shoe collection, which he tripped on bi-weekly while poking through the closet for a change of clothing.

It had earned him a playful swat to the hip that stirred up the ghost of an erection — not, thankfully, strong enough that he felt compelled to bring it back to life. He had to admit that Misha might be correct in worrying about chafing. Too many more rounds and he'd be concerned his dick would spontaneously combust — and not in the pleasurable way.

Asher let go of Misha for a second to fumble his hand around behind him, until it landed on Liam's wrist. He dragged the stolen appendage over his chest and demanded, "Cuddle me."

Liam mercifully obliged, at least until they heard Jinx yowling for his dinner outside the bedroom door. Asher's furbaby wasn't shy in demanding his God-given right to a can of Friskies or a cuddle. Asher knew better than to deny him, as soon enough he'd start using the doorframe as a scratching post, and Liam hated the sound. He likened it to nails on a chalkboard.

So, reluctantly, Asher abandoned his men to feed his little mischief maker.

* * * *

Riley left the animal shelter with a heavy heart. He hated days like this — when they'd done everything they could and an animal still couldn't be saved. In the six months he'd been volunteering at the shelter, he'd come to love Old Leroy like his own, even if he had been stinky and had a habit of snapping at fingers that drew too near his back leg.

Unfortunately, no amount of antibiotics and pain meds could make the lump by his eye any smaller and today, the vet had come to give them bad news. It was definitely cancer and, while he might have a few months left, there was nothing they could do but make him comfortable.

The owners of the shelter, unfortunately, took that to mean that it was time to put him down. They needed every available cage for the many homeless animals brought in every day. They were always quick to come in and slow to adopt out, always more demand than they could accommodate, and giving a precious crate to a dying animal 'would only hurt the other animals in need.'

Knowing they were right didn't make it any easier for Riley to accept. Not long ago, *he'd* been the homeless one, sick and hungry on the streets, desperate for a bed to call his own. Like Old Leroy, he'd found a shelter to take him in, thanks to an unexpected Good Samaritan who'd left him twenty bucks and an address on a napkin that had changed his life.

Riley regretted that he hadn't taken the opportunity to thank the pink-haired man when he'd had the chance—not then, when he'd still carried the teenage stubbornness forged into iron obstinance by rough living and not when they'd come face to face a few months ago. He'd opened his mouth to, while the man's friends were chatting excitedly, but he'd frozen.

Maybe the man hadn't recognized him? It would be embarrassing. More than that, though, he'd kept his mouth shut and a smile plastered to his face because admitting to the person he'd been then left him feeling hollow inside. He didn't talk about that person, the broken, lonely boy with an attitude and a problem with authority.

The Rainbow Center had *literally* saved his life.

It was a pity the animal shelter couldn't save Leroy's. Having to watch an animal get put down always sent Riley into a *mood*. He couldn't help the fear that if *he* got sick, it would be him put down next. Strapped to a cold metal table and injected with medicine to put him to sleep, never to wake up again.

Even a sniffle would put him in full-blown panic mode. Which, considering it was going into spring and his allergies had started kicking up, only depressed him further. It left him wrong-footed and twitchy.

He wanted a few fingers of whiskey or a shot of vodka, though he'd settle for a yard or two of beer on tap. Unfortunately, at not-quite-nineteen, he couldn't just strut into a bar.

Fortunately, he knew where to go.

He hopped on the bus to Twelfth and Chicon and walked the few streets over to the twenty-four-seven liquor store with the burned-out sign. He'd been a frequent flyer here during his years on the street, until he'd gone to the Rainbow House and they cleaned him up, rather forcibly. He didn't know where he would go when they kicked him back to the streets.

He found himself hoping Mike still worked there, since otherwise he'd dropped a dollar and change on a trip out for nothing. He pushed open the foggy glass door and a bell dinged to announce him. A glance toward the register showed a familiar silhouette, short and wide. It gave Riley the reassurance he needed to grab a liter of Kentucky Gentleman and carry it to the counter. Behind the glass, a newscast played on low volume, captions several seconds behind. He gave it a cursory glance out of curiosity — some in-depth look at police misconduct and sexual assault or something — before he was distracted.

"ID?" Mike asked with barely a glance up from the lottery ticket he was scratching.

"I left it in the bathroom." Riley spoke the familiar words. They left a stain on his tongue the bourbon would do a decent job of erasing later.

Mike dropped the lotto ticket on the counter and gave him a good once-over, recognition flaring in his dirt-brown eyes. "Long time, no see, Riley boy. Here I was thinking you'd forgot about Old Mike."

"Course not." Riley forced a smile. "I've been practicing sobriety, that's all. It wasn't very much fun."

"Course it's not," Mike scoffed and heaved himself off his stool, plodding over to the door to flip the 'Open' sign to 'On break.' Riley would have fifteen minutes, no more, to convince Mike to ignore the date of birth on his ID and scan his own license for the purchase instead.

Riley shoved down the little voice in the back of his head that warned him of falling back into old habits, already imagining the taste of the astringent liquor on his tongue.

He dropped to his knees on the restroom tiles.

Twelve minutes later, he rinsed his mouth out of the bathroom tap, regretting that he no longer carried mouthwash in his back pocket, and headed back to the counter. Mike had his liquor rung up and waiting for him.

He was passing over the cash when a tinny voice on the old television caught his ear and tugged. He looked up and froze. "Can you turn that up?" Riley asked, unable to tear his gaze away.

A reporter Riley vaguely recognized, Noah something, was speaking from the corner of the screen, while the larger section showed a cutaway to one of the last campaign speeches.

Mike said something as he thumbed up the volume, but Riley didn't hear him over the voice ringing in his ears.

"*Senator Scott, currently campaigning for governor, has been accused of participating in a child sex trafficking ring that was recently brought down, thanks to a massive inter-agency sting. Dozens of high-profile businessmen, including the Vice President of Lidman Oil and Gas Company, Henry Barnes, were rounded up during the investigation. While some are currently awaiting sentencing, many others have turned state's evidence in exchange for plea deals and lesser sentences. It begs the question of why, considering the presence of multiple victims willing to speak out, Senator Scott is not even being questioned in connection.*"

The reporter glanced down at a paper in front of him. "*Of course, representatives from the senator's office have denied any wrongdoing on the part of Senator Scott, insisting that these allegations are a vicious and underhanded attempt by the opposing party to smear the senator's good name. It was said, and I quote, 'Senator Scott is a well-loved man who has, consistently and without question, upheld his vows to his family, constituents and the church. He donates to many children's charities and has a voting record that proves his allegiance to the Rule of Law.'*"

Riley snorted, though he found no humor in the situation.

"*One has to wonder,*" the reporter continued, and when he looked up it was as if he was staring straight into Riley's heart through the screen, "*if the senator is indeed as devoted of a family man as he claims, why he's not been seen in the presence of both of his children in the past five years. While he is quite often spotted lunching with his wife and daughter, the twenty-seven-year-old CEO of the dating app COZI, his youngest son Ryland hasn't been seen in public, with or without his family, since he was allegedly enrolled in a private religious school at the age of thirteen.*"

Riley wasn't surprised to hear that Senator Scott was being accused of assault. After all, his father had always been an abusive asshole.

He was, however, caught off guard to hear that, finally, someone was wondering where he'd disappeared to. Why it couldn't have been five years ago, when he'd actually wanted someone to poke their nose into his life, was what really pissed him off. He was only *just* starting to get his life in order. A visit from his dad — or more likely, his dad's cronies — was the last thing he needed.

"Such a shame, what they're doing to that poor man," Mike said, shaking his head at the television. "I voted for him before, and I'll do it again. Fake news, am I right? They've been playing this bull for two weeks."

Riley held back his automatic retort about idiots in a desert who'd drown themselves if led to water and just grabbed his bourbon, suddenly wishing he'd gone for a bigger bottle.

Chapter Thirty-Seven

Asher shouldn't be nervous.

Telling himself that didn't calm the anxiety bouncing like basketballs around his belly. He and Misha basically lived with Liam already, and they spent more nights than not curled together in Liam's big bed. Officially moving, however, felt so much larger.

In the end, it was an easy move. Their bedrooms at Mason and Ryder's were staying as they'd left them, since Asher's brother insisted that no matter what, they had a place with him there, and they didn't need to bring anything except clothes and a few odds and ends. Liam, after all, had everything else they could possibly need.

It was the matter of less than an hour and they were officially moved. Asher shut the last dresser drawer with a sound that rang of finality.

"So, that's the rest of it," Liam said, sitting cross-legged on the floor as he helped Misha fold and tuck away the last of his pajamas.

Asher only hesitated a second before he moved across the bedroom and dropped down into Liam's lap. He rested his head on Liam's shoulder and wrapped his arms around the narrow waist. He felt the need to ask, one final time, "You're sure you want us living with you? We won't be too underfoot?"

"Darling, I've just been waiting on you both to be ready. Be as underfoot as you want. I wouldn't change it for anything." Liam pressed a kiss to Asher's hair before he tipped up his face to deliver one on his lips.

Asher leaned into it, some of his nerves retreating. Liam only pulled back so he could tug Misha in as well, and Asher watched them kiss, affection obvious in every moment, from the way Misha's eyes fluttered shut to the gentle brush of Liam's fingertips along his chin.

It was a tight squeeze with them both sitting in Liam's lap, but Liam didn't complain, and it was Asher who pulled away first. Not because he wanted to but because he doubted the position was comfortable.

Misha clambered off Liam's lap as well and Asher reached out a hand to help their older boyfriend off the floor. He was confident that Liam was capable, but he gave a naughty grin anyway. "Up you get, old man."

Liam lifted a brow as he stood, "Old man? I'll show you an old man!" In a movement too quick for Asher to avoid, Liam scooped him up and tossed him over his shoulder like a sack of flour.

Asher shrieked, wiggling instinctively to try to get down before he froze, not wanting to be dropped. Or, worse, to make Liam throw out his back or anything. He really didn't think Liam was old, though saying that out loud would make people think otherwise, but he wasn't as skinny as he had been when they'd first met.

The extra ten pounds was little in the grand scheme of things, barely enough to move him from scrawny to healthy, but it left him feeling off balance.

He forgot about the momentary worry when Liam tossed him onto the mattress, prowling over his sprawled form with a dirty grin. Thoughts of Liam's age fled in favor of other, more important thoughts. Asher's dick pressed painfully into the zipper of his jeans.

Liam proved he was more than young enough to handle him and Misha both.

* * * *

It was more difficult than Liam expected to lead both of his boys into the backyard without either of them peeking or, worse, tripping. It had been quite a feat to keep them mostly upstairs and away from any windows with a decent view of the backyard, especially since Misha had a habit of drifting toward them like a magnet.

He'd managed it mostly by luck and a dash of advance planning. He was nervous as he uncovered their eyes to let them see the camper he'd bought for them.

It was not, of course, the one they'd lived in during their stint as fugitives from the law. He wouldn't change anything about that time in their lives, since it had brought them to where they were now. For the future, though, he didn't feel the need for them to squeeze into a malodorous tin can with little-to-no elbow room if they didn't have to.

Instead, he'd bought a state-of-the-art RV, complete with a tow package and a rooftop patio for any entertaining they decided to do, if they went away for a weekend trip with family or friends.

The longer Misha and Asher stayed quiet, the more he second-guessed his decision, until Asher turned around with stars in his eyes. "Is this *ours*?"

"Yes. Unless you don't like it? I can get something smaller, if you —" Liam choked on his words as Asher flung himself at him, strangling him in a tight hug.

"Can we go inside?" Misha tugged on Liam's sleeve until Asher let him go and he was able to breathe again.

"Of course," Liam agreed, grabbing each of their hands and leading the way.

Liam stood in the doorway, watching fondly as the two boys examined it from top to bottom, giggling as they scampered up the ladder to the loft bed and back down to start opening all the doors in the top-of-the-line kitchenette.

Only when they'd explored every nook and cranny did they race back to him. "Can we go camping, Daddy?" Misha asked hopefully, Asher echoing him.

"I was hoping you boys would want to go with me this weekend," Liam replied, finally relaxing. A small part of him had been waiting for them to say it was too much and he needed to take it back for something smaller. Or, worse, take it back completely.

Misha was bouncing on his toes, practically quivering with excitement, but Asher's face fell. "Where will Jinx and Angel stay? Ryder and Mason are going out of town."

Liam ran a hand through his hair. "About that... Ryder and Mason are going to come with us. Mason rented a trailer for them, so they had their own space. I was thinking Angel and Jinx could stay in the RV with us. They just said they were going out of town so they didn't spoil the surprise."

Asher perked back up. "You'd let the furbabies come?"

"Of course. They're part of the family. I wouldn't have it any other way."

* * * *

This time around, they chose a luxury RV Park. Well, *Liam* chose a luxury RV park, since Asher had realized quite quickly that he was dating a bit of a snob. Thankfully, Liam could afford to be. Not that Asher would have cared if they were poor, living in a dinky camper that smelled of nicotine and sweat permanently. All he needed was Misha and Liam. He didn't need *things*.

That being said, the luxury RV park was much nicer than the others. Even the dump station was fancy, with expensive soap at the handwash stations and far too many things that shined.

The trailer that his brother and Mason had rented wasn't as fancy as the behemoth Liam had bought but it was still one of the nicer ones at the park, drawing curious gazes from several of their neighbors.

Misha had dragged Ryder through a tour of theirs before allowing Ryder to return the favor, and Asher trailed along, feigning nonchalance like he was above the petty need to inspect every inch of their living space. Secretly, he was just as excited, and he thought, from Liam's smirk, that his boyfriend could tell.

He knew for sure when Liam patted his butt as they crossed from Ryder's trailer back to theirs, grabbing a fistful of his shirt and dragging him into his lap until the other boys went inside without him. "I think my darling deserves a treat for humoring the littles tonight, don't you?" Liam murmured into his ear as he settled him more firmly, pressing his quite obvious erection against Asher's ass.

Asher squirmed, feeling his cheeks heat. They were fully dressed, but anyone could see them, a thought that left him surprisingly hot. "Don't tease me!"

"Who says I'm teasing?" Liam grinned and tipped Asher's face down to steal a kiss. "I was just going to suggest you grab the marshmallows and let me make you a s'more." He gave a dirty wink.

Asher didn't believe him for a heartbeat, especially not when Liam reached across his lap to fix the hem of his rucked-up shirt, skimming the tent in his jeans with his fingers. He barely held back a moan, giving Liam a bit of a glare as he stood and adjusted his dick self-consciously. "That wasn't fair."

Liam's expression was as innocent as a nun costume on Halloween. "I'm certain I don't know what you mean."

"You're *certainly* mean, you mean," Asher corrected as he headed inside after his other boyfriend. He wondered if Misha would spare him a few moments to sneak into the bathroom to help him relieve the tension.

Thankfully, Misha was more than willing to assist.

* * * *

Misha snuggled up to Liam's side on the blanket they had spread over the rooftop patio not long after Ryder and Mason had taken their leave. Asher was curled up on the other side of Liam, all three of them squished close together. Partly out of affection, but mostly because they only had so many pillows and they were currently all laying on them to save their spines from the hard roof floor.

He could faintly hear the sound of fuckery somewhere below them in the camper as Angel and Jynx—or as they'd started calling them, the little wreckers—did whatever things pets did while they were alone. The three of them had wordlessly chosen to ignore it.

"What's that one?" Misha asked, pointing at a particularly twinkly star.

"I think that's a plane," Asher decided when the star moved toward the horizon rather suddenly.

"Oh. That one?" Misha shifted his finger to a different, less twinkly pinpoint.

"Let's see." Liam moved under Misha's head as he pulled his phone out of his pocket and thumbed open an app he'd downloaded just for Misha, the 'stargazer.' It opened his camera app when he pointed it at the sky, then a circle appeared in the centaur of the image, spinning while it thought.

A robotic voice spoke after several seconds. *"Congratulations, Stargazer! You've discovered the Omega Centuari! Did you know that many astronomers believe that this cluster of stars is the remnants of a long-lost galaxy disrupted by our very own Milky Way?"*

Liam closed the app partway through the robot's lecture, laying his phone screen down on his chest. He looked fondly down at Misha. "Is that the one you're picking tonight?"

Misha nodded. "Yep. Tell me a story about the Omega Centauri."

It had become a habit of theirs over the past few months, though normally, they went out to the backyard to stargaze and Asher typically refused to join them, since he said it made him antsy to lie out on the ground where any creepy-crawly could invade their cuddle time.

"Once upon a time, in a far distant galaxy, there lived an Omega Centaur named... Billy?" Liam glanced at Misha for approval. He scrunched his nose and shook his head. "Johnny?"

"If he's a centaur, he needs a fancy name," Misha explained.

"Cyril?" Liam suggested. Misha thought for a few seconds before finally nodding. "Okay. There was an Omega Centaur named Cyril."

Liam's voice was deep and soothing as he launched into Misha's bedtime story about a centaur who'd lost his whole family and went on a quest along the Milky Way to find a new one. Centaur Cyril ended up on a tiny, water-logged planet called Earth.

Of course, Cyril was a bit of an asshole, as centaurs are wont to be, and he found little to like about the tiny, quaint planet. It was too wet for his liking and too cold, and the forests were nothing at all like the ones he was born in. So angry was he about the small details, he turned away several helpful creatures he ran into, including a gryphon, a dragon and a mermaid.

Misha almost cried when Liam got to the part where Cyril, angry over the taste of the grass in the fields, almost ran off his newest friends, a pair of unicorns named Rainbow and Glitter.

He breathed a sigh of relief when Cyril finally realized the error of his ways and joined their herd, living out the rest of his days as a happy centaur.

Asher, of course, didn't get to hear the end of the story. He was snoring well before then, providing a sleepy soundtrack to go along with the story. Not that Misha blamed him, because he was yawning himself by the finale, his eyes drifting shut before he'd jerk awake, unwilling to miss it.

"The end," Daddy whispered, dropping a chaste kiss on the tip of his nose.

Want to see more like this?
Here's a taster for you to enjoy!

It's a Kink Thing: Kinked Up
M.C. Roth

Excerpt

Nav

Nav's apartment key tumbled from his hand as his phone vibrated, rattling his change and his plastic swipe card from work. He fumbled in his pocket, pulling his phone out and groaning at the name on the display.

"This is *not* a good time," he said as he accepted the call, sighing at the laughter that burst against his eardrum. He glanced down, searching for his key that had somehow made it halfway under his apartment door, only the jagged edge visible beneath the crack.

He really needed to get a keychain so the thing didn't disappear on him again. He'd already gone through three keys in the last month, and the hardware store was starting to get suspicious as to why he needed so many spares. There just didn't seem to be much point to getting a sparkly keychain if he wasn't going to keep it for all that long.

"How did it go, Nav?" asked Sasha through the speaker.

No matter how many times Nav lost his things or moved, Sasha always seemed to track him down. He was Nav's self-appointed best friend and number one annoyance.

Nav let out a sigh, leaning his back against the door as he looked down the hall. There were a dozen doors that were identical to his, with grungy numbers barely clinging onto their hastily painted surfaces. At one point, the doors must've been a dreadful forest green, but someone had decided to paint over them with a thin layer of white primer. The results were pale lime rectangles with dark corners where the primer had been rubbed raw. The red apartment numbers completed the nightmarish Christmas look with tacky gusto.

"It went great. Better than great, actually. Everette never wants to see me again, and he got his brother to throw me out of the house." Nav rubbed at his shoulder where he was sure there was a bruise. They'd taken the throwing part a touch too literally, and Nav had found out first-hand how hard concrete sidewalks were.

"Ouch. Not unexpected, though," said Sasha, his laughter booming through the tiny speaker. "Maybe you shouldn't have hit on their dad?"

Nav ran a hand through his hair before he leaned back and let his head rest against the thin door. It sounded hollow to the touch, and it nearly bowed under his weight. "Maybe their dad shouldn't have been so hot. I mean, who the hell walks around in just their boxers then gets offended when they get hit on? I didn't know guys his age could even *have* abs like that. His body was just rocking."

"Gross... I don't need the details," said Sasha, the phone rustling. "How many is that now, though?"

"This year or this month?" asked Nav, sliding down the door until his ass met the thin and filthy carpet. A light flickered overhead, and somewhere a baby screamed. His neighbor down the hall was making their weekly batch of boiled cabbage, if the smell was anything to go by. And who the hell had crushed packets of ketchup at the end of the hall?

"You're such an asshole," said Sasha. "I've never met someone who has as many ex-boyfriends as you have. You must run into one at every bar."

Nav laughed, letting the grief of the situation roll off his shoulders and down the ratty hallway to find a sewer out on the street somewhere. There was hardly any grief there at all, if he were honest with himself. He'd only dated Everette for three weeks, which was two weeks longer than his usual attention span. The guy had been cute, but nothing compared to his dad.

"Most bars are out. Restaurants, too. I ran into Josh the other day, and I swear to God he spit on my salad," said Nav. He'd still eaten the salad, of course. A little spit never turned him off a good meal.

"So, you won't come out for drinks with us tonight?" asked Sasha. "Katie already did her hair up real nice, and I can't wait to fuck it up."

"Your straightness disgusts me," said Nav, letting his eyes drift shut. It had been a long week of too many hours at work and even more wasted on another guy he knew would never work out. His shower was calling to him, and he could definitely hear the cries of his lonely pillow.

"I dunno. I'm really tired, Sash." He leaned his head to the side to cradle his phone against his ear. A noise at the end of the hall made him startle, but he kept his eyes closed. It was probably just one of his asshole neighbors getting home after their day job. They would be able to step by him just fine.

"All the more reason to come out with us. You're in a rut, Nav. You need to relax and stop trying to fuck your way through every gay bedroom in the city. Come out with us tonight for drinks, keep your dick to yourself and I guarantee you'll feel better."

"Drinks do sound good," said Nav, pulling his feet closer when the squeak of shuffling footsteps approached him on the carpet. "Okay, I'll be there tonight. Don't let me fuck up again, okay?"

"Deal." Sasha chuckled. Nav could almost see his best friend's smirk through the phone. "I'll keep you surrounded by women so your dick shrivels up and dies. Then I'll get you so wasted that you forget about Tray."

"Tray was last month, before Scott and Paul, remember? Everette was the guy whose dad I just fucked," said Nav, lowering his voice as the footsteps came closer. He already got enough flack in his life for being gay and he didn't need any more shit from anyone.

"You are fucked up, man. I'll see you tonight. Nine sharp at Pinty's. Bring your long underwear and a chastity belt." Sasha ended the call with a click and Nav sighed, letting his phone slide to the ground with a hollow thump. He could sleep against the door, even with the floor jamming into the bruises on his ass.

Who *actually* threw someone? Concrete was not a fun place for his skinny ass to land. At least they had tossed him his pants.

"You okay?"

Nav's opened his eyes and cursed to himself, scrambling to get up to his feet.

Of course, the person to see him crumpled outside of his door had to be his smoking-hot and totally unreachable neighbor. He was gorgeous, with short blond hair that models would die for, and the softest blue eyes Nav had ever seen. Top that with thick shoulders, strong arms and thighs that could kill and he was everything Nav dreamed of.

The guy was also completely and totally unavailable. His boyfriend was the most average person in the world but had something that Nav couldn't even fathom — commitment. Every time Nav saw his him, the boyfriend was usually close by.

"Sorry... I just lost my key," said Nav as he pushed back against his door, his knees wobbling as his neighbor got closer. His mouth went dry, his throat constricting like nobody's business. His palms went damp as he suddenly began to sweat, his face flushing. Hunger evaporated in his gut like he'd just gotten a whiff of fresh ass, and his priorities had spun one-hundred-and-eighty degrees.

He was also the only one who did *that* to Nav. The beautiful blond specimen transformed him from a bonified slut who was proud of it into a blushing virgin.

Nav had fucked and been fucked by more guys than he could remember, but something about that tall, built frame and those crystal-blue eyes sent him back to his high school days when he'd seen his first cock and decided he was gay for life.

"Oh crap, that sucks," he said, running a hand through his blond locks that were probably softer than actual silk. "Did you call the superintendent?" He shifted a brown paper grocery bag in his hands, reaching into his pocket for something.

Of course he was environmentally aware, too, which made Nav want to drool. There was nothing worse than a hot guy who used plastic bags and drove a car that guzzled more fuel than a loaded transport truck. *Can you be any more perfect?*

Nav shook his head. "N-not yet. I think I probably just dropped it somewhere." Nav wanted to crumple into a ball. His voice was so soft and weak that he probably *sounded* like a virgin, too.

Virgins were the literal enemy. Clingy, flustered and nervous, Nav always steered well clear. He'd been there, done that and returned the T-shirt.

Knowing how thin the walls were in the building, Nav guessed the guy had probably heard his sex adventures from across the hall, which was probably why he was looking at Nav with confusion and concern etched onto his perfectly sculpted face. Statues were probably made of this guy — hopefully the ones with the big dicks and not the little ones.

Nav slid his foot sideways to where he remembered dropping the key, hopefully concealing it. He was such a fucking idiot, but he couldn't even think straight with his neighbor staring at him, his gaze piercing straight through his defenses.

"Did you need a hand? Just let me put my groceries in the fridge and I'll help you look for it." A soft smile settled on his lips as he pulled his own key out before opening his door with one hand.

"No, it's okay," said Nav, his face burning. He slapped his hands to his cheeks as the guy looked away, hoping to draw the heat out with his frigid fingertips. The sight of his wide, strong back had Nav flushing all over again. He looked away and into the apartment instead, his jaw dropping as something caught his eye.

There, on the wall, and hidden in the most unlikely of places, was a painting that he'd never thought he would see again.

"Oh my God, you have one of Brian Maeckery's paintings?" He stumbled across the hall, his key and his bag forgotten as the art drew him through the open door.

Seeing it again was the same as seeing it for the first time. The piece was one that had caught Nav's eye when it had been in the studio. His breath stuck in his throat as his cock swelled against his will, his groin pulling tight.

He couldn't help it. The brushstrokes were perfection, each one laid with such sensual purpose that Nav could almost feel them against his skin. The lovers on the canvas were wrapped around each other in an intimate embrace that made Nav's blood boil. They looked at each other in the peak of their pleasure, love and commitment frozen on their features. It was as unreal as a dream.

But what was his favorite painting of all time doing in a run-down apartment building? Sure, his neighbor had spruced up his place from what Nav could tell, but the painting didn't belong.

"Yeah." He set his grocery bag on the counter, before turning to Nav. "He's actually a friend of mine. He owed me a favor, so he gave this to me as payment. It's a beautiful piece." He shifted, flickering his gaze over Nav once before he turned and started unloading his groceries.

Butterflies erupted in Nav's belly. Brian Maeckery was nearly famous—like a shiny, untouchable doll on television. Nav would have worshiped the ground that he walked on, if only he had been able to find his house.

"I'm so jealous. I'm such a huge fan of his." He let out a sigh, reaching for the muddled color where the lovers' legs met. He hovered a few inches away, his hand trembling. The last price tag he'd seen on it was over one-hundred-thousand dollars. "It must've been one hell of a favor."

It still smelled fresh, the flavors of the paint rolling over his tongue as he inhaled sharply. The wooden frame was pristine, without a hint of dust or fingerprints, but how long would that last? It was something that should have been hanging in a temperature-controlled gallery for the rest of its life behind a pane of thick glass, not in a shitty apartment building soaking up the faint smell of cigarettes and cat piss.

His neighbor paused, a tray of chicken breasts clutched in his fingers. He furrowed his forehead before he let out a small laugh, his eyes lighting up. "Not really, no. My fiancé and I modeled for the painting, so Brian thought it was best if we were the ones to get it."

"Wait…what?" Nav took a step back, his gaze flashing between him and the painting. The faces on the canvas were in shadow, with only their lips visible and a hint of their partially closed eyes. But it *did* look like them, and the hair color was spot-on. And their bodies…*oh God*. Was that really hiding beneath the guy's T-shirt and jeans?

"Shit, I've jerked off to this painting," said Nav, flushing as he smacked his hand to his forehead. "I-I mean, shit. You're Theo?"

His boss had relayed the entire story as they'd hung the painting in the gallery together — how Brian had claimed that Theo was his muse and how he had called to him with each brush stroke. Nav had agreed from the bottom of his balls. That had been the first time the painting made him hard — but not the last.

Nav dropped his gaze, flushing so fiercely that he wasn't sure his cheeks would ever cool again. He couldn't look at him. In fact, it was probably best if he turned around and crawled back to his apartment before begging for forgiveness through the door.

Nav started as his neighbor chuckled. His gaze was dragged back to the gorgeous blond, his heart thudding as he stared at the man with his head tilted back and his lips curled and open as the beautiful sound emerged.

"Theo's my fiancé," he said, wiping the gathering tears from his eyes as he continued to chuckle. "I'm Maverick, but everyone calls me Trick. Thanks for the compliment." He let out another laugh, his body shaking as his chest heaved.

"I'm so sorry. I'm just really tired, and I always say things I'm not supposed to when I'm tired." He bit his tongue as Trick laughed even harder. Trick was stunning when he was silent, but when he laughed, he transformed into an actual Adonis.

Nav looked at the painting again, something new surging from the base of his gut.

As much as he had longed to be the one in the painting in the past, it had always remained an unattainable figment of Brian's imagination. It had been fitting that the only thing that he would ever love was an imaginary scene with a fictional man.

But they were *real*…and the man he'd been fantasizing about was Trick. His heart rate picked up, his chest rising and falling like he'd just run a marathon.

Trick was obviously in love with Theo. He'd smiled, the corners of his eyes crinkling when he'd said Theo's name. And the painting…? Nav hadn't known what true love looked like until he had seen the canvas.

An ugly green monster twisted in his gut, leaving a foul taste in his mouth. It seemed that everyone could fall in love except him, even the not-so-fictional characters in a painting. He was going to be cursed to chase brief hookups for the rest of his life, ditching them before they lost their new boyfriend smell and shine.

"Sorry. I didn't mean to upset you by laughing at you. I was just surprised," said Trick, his humor falling away. "You sure you don't want me to help you find your key? Or I can get you a drink if you want to call the super and wait here."

"No, it's okay. I don't want to intrude," said Nav. He looked back to the painting, but the magic that had enthralled him for months was gone. His stomach lurched as he took a step back.

I'm just overtired. Alcohol required STAT.

"Well, it was nice meeting you..." Trick paused as if he were waiting for something.

"Nav." He shrugged, filling the uncomfortable silence.

"Nav. Just knock if you need something or if you change your mind." He smiled, parting his full lips to reveal white teeth that were perfectly straight. His smile was dazzling, pulling a wave of fresh heat from Nav's core.

"Thanks. Bye." Nav rushed into the hall, shutting the door before Trick could say anything further. His heart was still pounding, and for some strange reason, he felt the first prickling of tears at the corner of his eyes.

He took a deep breath and pinched the base of his nose. He must've been more exhausted than he'd thought if he was already starting to get teary-eyed. He usually didn't hit that level until he'd worked sixty hours in one week. He'd only done fifty-five hours in the last five days, so he should have still been in the glaringly frustrated and angry phase.

He reached for his key, easing it out from where it had squirmed through the crack under the thin door. He grabbed his bag, hauling it over his shoulder and turning the key in the lock before pushing inside.

Unlike Trick, he hadn't spiffed up his floors or counters in his apartment. There really was no point if his stay was going to be brief.

The paint was the original faded ivory with a few cracks around the corners and a smudge of purple along one baseboard. The floors were roll-on linoleum with a few holes in the kitchen where someone had repeatedly dropped a sharp knife. It could have been anyone's apartment.

Except for the art that he'd hung on the walls. The art was all his. Most of the paintings were little pieces he'd picked up in estate and garage sales in the city, with a few originals from up-and-coming artists. His work in the studio gallery put him in reach of a few artists who hadn't hit it big yet and had prices that were within his reach.

He stepped up to one of his favorites. The artist was known simply as *Rachel*, and they had a way with traditional techniques that wasn't too common anymore. A frog on a lily pad would have made most artists scoff, but Rachel had elevated the simple idea and done something beyond anything Nav could have imagined himself. The frog was made of stars, and the lily pad was the cosmos, according to the gods. It always managed to take his breath away.

All the works he had managed to collect were beautiful and unique, but nothing like the scandalous and sensual canvas of Brian's work. It was so far beyond his price range that he didn't *deserve* to be close enough to touch it.

His throat clogged as he thought of the painting in its dismal setting across the hall.

"Christ, I need a drink." He pulled his clothes from his body, letting them trail on the ground on his way to the shower. As the water cascaded over him, he tried to push the painting and Trick from his thoughts.

About the Author

KD Ellis is a professional cat wrangler by day, and an author by night. She moved from a small town to an even smaller village to live with her husband and wife and their two children. She loves reading—anything with men loving men. She writes queer romance in between working her two jobs and cuddling her pets — all six of them, which confuses the turtle.

KD loves to hear from readers. You can find her contact information, website details and author profile page at https://www.pride-publishing.com

PUBLISHING

Sign up for our newsletter and find out about all our romance book releases, eBook sales and promotions, sneak peeks and FREE romance books!